AGE OF VAMPIRES

WRATHFUL
MORTALS

CAROLINE PECKHAM
SUSANNE VALENTI

REALM G

THE
BLOOD BANK

REALM F

REALM E

THE WASTES

REALM H

United States

Realm G

The Blood Ba

New York

Belvedere Castle

Interior Formatting & Design by Wild Elegance Formatting
Map Design by Fred Kroner
Artwork by Stella Colorado

ISBN: 978-1-916926-15-8

Wrathful Mortals/Caroline Peckham & Susanne Valenti – 2nd ed.

This book is dedicated to all those who find themselves fighting a war within their own hearts. Torn in two directions, unsure of where their feet belong. You will find your way between the balance of night and day, moon and sun. Between the shadows and the light is where you belong.

8

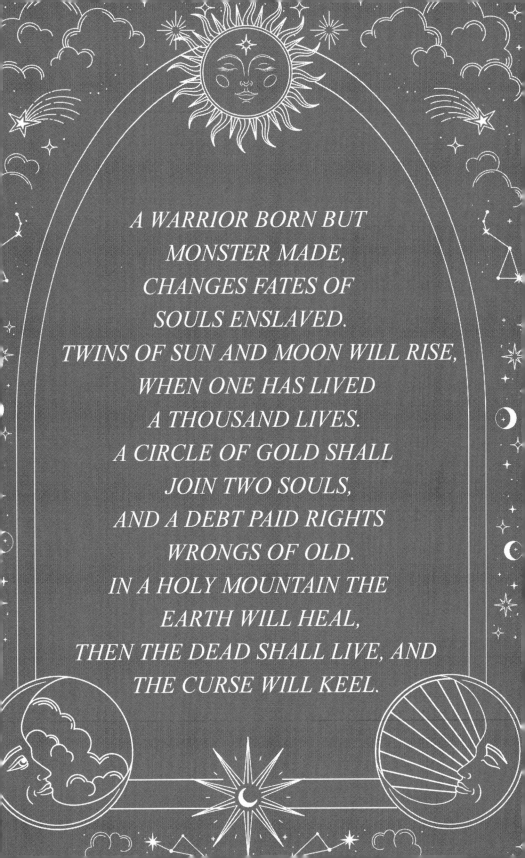

*A WARRIOR BORN BUT
MONSTER MADE,
CHANGES FATES OF
SOULS ENSLAVED.
TWINS OF SUN AND MOON WILL RISE,
WHEN ONE HAS LIVED
A THOUSAND LIVES.
A CIRCLE OF GOLD SHALL
JOIN TWO SOULS,
AND A DEBT PAID RIGHTS
WRONGS OF OLD.
IN A HOLY MOUNTAIN THE
EARTH WILL HEAL,
THEN THE DEAD SHALL LIVE, AND
THE CURSE WILL KEEL.*

ERIK

CHAPTER ONE

1000 YEARS AGO

My family and I made camp in the woods close to the battlegrounds. The lands of Atbringer would be nourished by blood for decades to come. Blood spilled by my hand. My teeth.

Miles sat beside Fabian on a log as they spoke in low murmurs, but I kept away from them, my back to the circle we'd formed under the waning moon.

Clarice moved to my side, taking my hand in hers. "We had to kill them or they would have killed us."

"Every war is the same," I said darkly. "Who is it we're fighting for? I don't see worthy creatures sitting here. I see monsters made by a wrathful god."

"We are your family," she urged, squeezing my fingers. "I love you and our brothers more than anything. We can't let the slayers win."

"Maybe they should win," I muttered. "Did you see what I became today?"

Clarice rested her head on my shoulder and her golden locks

cascaded down my arm, her closeness bringing some measure of peace to my soul. I had gone so long without contact, and her touch was a balm against my skin, even if the two of us were as cold as ice. We were clean at least after we'd washed the blood from our bodies in an icy river. We were immune to the freezing water, and it haunted me that I would never feel the warmth of summer, nor the bite of frost again.

"You're a good man, Erik," Clarice promised, and I released a dry laugh.

"Good? How can you think that? I am a vessel for Andvari to fill with blood."

"If we're his pawns, perhaps it's not our fault," she murmured, a note of hope gilding her voice.

"Many men before us have blamed the gods for their misgivings. That does not make them right. We still have free will." I toyed with the blade in my hand. One strike, deep and true, would end my plague on this world. But the afterlife would bring me no peace. What I had done would leave a permanent stain on my ruinous soul and I would pay for it if I ever stepped beyond death. Remaining here in this body didn't seem like a better alternative though. And at least if I was in the depths of Náströnd being punished for my crimes, I could no longer kill innocent people.

Clarice gripped the hilt of my blade, prising it from my fingers. "Do not do something foolish. I love you, brother. You mustn't give up."

An ache grew in my heart. "I cannot remain like this, Clarice. I thought perhaps changing the slayer warrior into one of us was the answer. But here we are, still in our cursed forms. It has changed nothing, and I have cursed another soul."

"That slayer may have destroyed the last of the clans by now," Fabian called. "It could have changed everything. If the slayers are all dead, there will be no one left to hunt or persecute us."

I didn't turn to him, growing irritated by his lack of guilt.

"Your priorities are all wrong, Fabian," I snarled, gazing at the dirt by my feet.

"My priority is keeping us alive. The slayers were made to kill us. If they are gone, we are free."

I rose sharply, turning to him, and Miles caught Fabian's arm, trying to keep him back as a fierce tension crackled between us.

"And how long do you think the gods will keep things that way? They can make slayers at their whim. If they want us challenged, we *will* be challenged." My shoulders tensed as Fabian bared his fangs.

"Then we will kill them too," Fabian growled, stepping closer.

"Stop fighting," Miles groaned, giving up on holding Fabian back. "I just want to go home."

"To your band of fucking mindless followers?" I spat at him. "You're all giving in to the curse, every one of you." I rounded on Clarice and she gave me a guilty look as I pointed at her. "You draw men to you like moths to a flame, promising them eternity in your arms if only they can entertain you long enough. And Miles, you offer out the curse like it's a gift to be bestowed upon those you deem worthy. You are all building an army of creatures just like us, and for what? For every one of us you make, another slayer will be born. The gods will not let us win. They do not want us to prevail."

"I disagree." Fabian folded his arms, his fury seeming to have dissipated a fraction. "Perhaps this *is* a gift more than a curse. Perhaps they do want us to prosper."

"You were there when they killed our families!" I roared, losing control of my emotions. "You wept at your sisters' deaths. You saw what they did to our mothers and fathers. This was no gift; it is our punishment for their crime. And it is eternal."

Fabian stalked around the edge of the small clearing, infuriated by my tone. "Perhaps the gods have changed their minds. Perhaps they are taking pity on us now. We won that battle. They could have intervened if they didn't want us to succeed."

I thought of Andvari and how he'd given me the strength to win, urging me on with every death I claimed. Fabian was right in one sense; Andvari wasn't done with us yet. But pity? I wasn't enough of a fool to believe that.

"Andvari doesn't want us dead, he wants us tormented," I growled.

"Andvari?" Fabian hissed. "Does the great Andvari speak to you, brother, because he has never once answered me."

Miles's brows rose. "Does he?" he asked me hopefully.

"Yes," I sighed. "He has spoken to me many times."

"And?" Clarice asked, taking my hand again and giving me a desperate look.

"He's lying!" Fabian bellowed, lifting a log from the ground and throwing it into the trees. With a tremendous crash, another tree was uprooted by the collision and smashed to the forest floor.

"I am not lying," I snarled, my muscles flexing.

If Fabian wanted a fight, I'd happily give him one. I had too much energy to expend and I'd revel in taking it out on him.

"You went insane in that cave. I told you not to go." Fabian rounded on me once more, his eyes narrowing sharply. "My brother went in there, but a madman has walked out."

"You're just envious because Andvari chose him and not you," Miles bit at him then turned his gaze to me. "I believe you, Erik. What did Andvari say to you?"

I shook my head, pulling away from Clarice's hold. "Just more riddles and laughter. He wishes to taunt us, that's all."

Silence reigned and Miles fell into a dark reverie, gazing into the trees with total dejection. Fabian stalked around the camp, evidently still hankering for a fight, but if we went there, I would only regret it in the end.

I picked up my blade and headed into the forest, needing to get away. Clarice called after me but I ignored her, moving into the shadows where my soul belonged.

When I'd moved far enough from the others, using my enhanced speed to race away into the heart of the ancient woodland, I took a seat beneath a birch tree and weighed the blade in my palm.

I was no coward, but facing an eternity in Náströnd still frightened me. I'd be torn apart by the beasts that lurked in the underworld, feasting on my flesh for all of time. It was no less than I deserved, and death was so very easy to seize...

I rested the tip of my weapon against my chest, and my heart grew heavy as if it longed for the pierce of the blade to end its suffering. One deep stab and it would be done. Either I would become nothing, or the gods would steal away my soul, weigh it in their palms and decide my fate in the afterlife. Considering what they had offered me in life, I had no doubt I would face far worse in death.

I gazed up at the canopy, glimpsing the canvas of stars above. "I've tried to right your wrongs, Mother...Father. Sometimes I despise you. But most of all I wish to forgive you. To put the pain in my heart to rest for what you have caused." The star-spangled sky seemed to watch with bated breath, whispering about whether I would go through with killing myself.

"I'm done," I whispered. To me. To Andvari. To my family. "I will not be a bane upon this world any longer."

I pushed the blade hard, but no pain came. So I took the hilt in both hands and drove it inward, though still no crack of ribs followed. My skin was iron to most men, but that shouldn't have stopped *me*.

Andvari's chuckling laughter filled the air. "I would never let you take this path, Erik Larsen."

I ground my teeth, fury sprouting in my chest and growing deep roots.

"Let me die," I snarled.

"Death is easy," Andvari purred from between the trees. "I will see you suffer in every way this world has to give. And then perhaps I will let you die and taste the pain of the nether world - if you do not break the curse first, that is."

"Then I shall walk into a camp of slayers and they will end me instead."

Andvari's presence shifted around me, and the leaves stirred at my feet. I could almost sense him kneeling before me, then a warm hand rested on my knee. "I dislike the slayers, Draugr. They are Idun's creation, made to thwart me. I will gift you what you need to fight them."

"Then I am just your puppet," I said, the words more for me than him. I was trapped here living this life until Andvari decided otherwise. And that truth tasted bitter on my tongue.

Dropping the blade into my lap, I rested my head back against the tree. "What do you want from me and my family?"

Andvari seemed to sigh. I could feel it in the way the trees bowed to the wind and the leaves swirled in the gust. "It is time the vampires rose to power. Tell your brothers and sister to sire as many humans as they can. Build an army, Erik. A challenge is coming to you like none you have ever faced before. Your family can only be saved if you rise to meet it."

I felt his presence waning and lurched forward, certain he was about to leave. "They will not believe me. You must speak to them yourself."

Andvari laughed. "I will speak to them in songs and poems and sonnets. I will speak to them in the arc of the rising sun and the shadow of the crescent moon."

"You make no sense," I growled.

"I make perfect sense. The meaning is that I am always here. I am always watching."

"Then speak with them!" I barked.

The air shuddered before my eyes and a small stream bubbled and steamed just a few feet from me. I rose, moving toward it at a cautious pace. The water stilled and I gazed into it as a man seemed to swim up from its shallow depths. Andvari rose from the water like a reflection stepping from polished glass. He was in his own form, just as he'd been the day he'd cursed us. His eyes were as black as tar and his skin near-translucent. His hair was a coarse tangle of brown locks akin to weeds, and his dark robes were perfectly dry, moving about him like the lapping of a wave.

"Lead the way," he whispered with a cruel smile.

Turning my back on him felt dangerous, but I was already snared in his claws. He could end me as easily as he could save me.

I guided him back to my family, finding them all gathered on the fallen log with sullen expressions. Stepping aside, I allowed Andvari to move past me, my skin prickling with tension. His feet were bare and hardly touched the ground as he moved toward them, and even the grass seemed to turn his way, enraptured by his power.

My brothers and sister shrank before him, their strength nothing in comparison to this deity.

When he spoke, his words were fluid and soft. "Sat on by a ruler,

16

polished by a maid. What am I?"

Clarice glanced at Miles, and he tentatively slid an arm around her shoulders.

"A throne?" Fabian guessed, getting to his feet, his eyes wide with awe.

Andvari laughed, opening his arms. "Yes. And it is time you take it, friends."

My hands curled up into fists as my family fell under his spell, nodding their agreement.

"How?" Miles asked, his gaze glittering with hope.

"There is a land far from here, not yet claimed by kings or queens. It is time you go there. Then you must wait until the day of reckoning arrives. And when it does...you may seize power. But do not squander the time you have. Make your monsters. Breathe immortal life into every deserving soul you can find."

"Is that the answer to your prophecy?" I hissed, stepping forward so Andvari had to acknowledge me.

"Do you think it is?" Andvari's pitch black irises dragged over me. I shook my head, having no answer.

"What is it I told you of the sun and moon?" he whispered, drifting closer.

I swallowed the hard lump growing in my throat. I didn't want to voice that answer. I feared how my brothers and sister would take it. But Andvari's smiling face turned into a grimace, and I knew I had no choice. I drew up the memories of my time in the dark cave and repeated what I'd learned.

"We can birth children with humans. Twins perhaps..." I glanced up at the sky and the stars dimmed, like they did not dare to shine too bright in Andvari's presence.

"Is that the answer?" Clarice asked excitedly, her eyes brighter than they had been in years.

Andvari smiled around at us all. "You have much to do. Begin with the nearest town. Sire as many as you can and head to the last of the slayer clans. Finish the battle before Idun can create another army. Buy yourselves times to rise."

Hope reared its head in my chest.

"They're still alive?" Fabian asked and Andvari nodded.

With that, leaves coiled up around the god, swirling in a vortex until he was completely concealed. When the wind died, they fell limp on the ground and Andvari was gone.

Uncertainty burned through me as my family began speaking excitedly. I feared with all my heart what Andvari had said. He had tricked me on the battlefield, and I was sure this was another of his games. The look in my family's eyes told me I'd never convince them of that.

Siring humans was a dangerous thing. I didn't want to bestow this curse on anyone, but perhaps I needed allies beyond my family now. People who could help us figure out this riddle. Men and women with knowledge of the gods. And at least when the curse was broken, they would be free of it too.

There was one thing I'd never do, however. And I made a steely promise to myself that I'd never bear a child with a human. I would not be fooled by Andvari again, but from the way my brothers and sister were speaking excitedly, I sensed they would not be so easily swayed from this path.

MONTANA

CHAPTER TWO

The storm continued to pummel us as we fled from the cathedral, leaving Erik and the other royals far behind along with the shattered pieces of my heart.

Julius took the lead, heading down a darkened alley and hurriedly lifting up a circular manhole cover at the centre of it.

Magnar grabbed Callie's arm. "You go first," he commanded as if he was afraid she might turn back and something about his hard tone set the hairs rising along my arms.

I expected Callie to bite back at him, but she didn't hesitate, quickly descending the ladder into the dark.

My pulse ticked faster as I halted, watching as Magnar followed her, then Julius turned to me expectantly.

I glanced over my shoulder, gazing back at the rain-swept street, shivering as the cold crept into my bones. My wedding dress was heavy, sodden and filthy, a train of white turning black at my feet. Blood tainted its pure colour with a red tinge from those vampires who had not met a permanent end.

The bite marks on my skin were sore, but the venom had been washed out by the rain, leaving a trail of silver marring my flesh. But nothing stung deeper than leaving my prison behind, the shame of that something I could never put words to.

Erik invaded my mind and the cross on my left palm burned with an intensity that begged me to go back to him. To run and never stop running until I was back in his arms.

"Come on," Julius urged, moving toward me with a threat in his stance.

I swallowed the lump in my throat, forcing my legs to move me in the direction of the drain. There was no going back.

"You belong with us," Julius murmured, reaching out to squeeze my hand, his skin burning hot in comparison to mine.

I didn't answer, unsure if that was true. My heart craved Erik in a way that made my body ache. But I'd made my choice. And I'd chosen family. I would always choose family.

With a sharp breath, I lowered myself onto the ladder within the hole and Julius's huge form cast a shadow over me as I descended into the thick darkness.

As I prised my numb fingers from the rungs, Callie's arms wrapped around me. I leaned into her embrace, utterly relieved to be properly reunited at last. With my sister's heart beating solidly in time with mine, I knew I'd made the right decision. She needed me, and I needed her just as much. We weren't meant to walk in this world without one another.

The heavy thunk of the manhole cover sliding into place sounded, then Julius's boots thumped against the ladder.

"Are you okay?" Callie whispered.

"Yes," I replied, even though it wasn't true. "Are you?"

"No," she answered, releasing me.

The bright light on Julius's cellphone suddenly blinded me and I lifted a hand to shield my eyes.

Callie floated toward the ladder, anxious lines forming on her brow. With a burst of energy, she started climbing it, her movements desperate as she raced for the surface.

"What the fuck are you doing?" Julius snatched her waist, ripping her off of it as she tried to claw his fingers from her dress.

"Callie," I reached for her, anxiety tearing through my chest.

"I have to go back," she groaned, then thumped her forehead with the heel of her palm. "No, shit. I don't. *Elder*, help me," she pleaded, reaching for Magnar with a desperate look in her eyes.

"You will follow us," Magnar replied in that forbidding tone again, his eyes as dark as the tunnel surrounding us.

Callie immediately fell still in Julius's arms, nodding firmly, and I frowned, looking between them.

"What's going on? Why did you call him that?" I asked my sister.

"I'll explain everything soon," Callie said, her expression taut. "We just need to get out of here."

I nodded, but my own feet started guiding me back to the ladder and as I gazed down at the cross on my palm, I was sure it was my bond to Erik driving my movements. I forcibly shook off the feeling and rejoined my sister, taking her hand and eyeing the X on her palm.

"It's this. This is what's trying to drive you back to Fabian," I said darkly.

This strange bond must have been the reason she'd thrown herself in front of the royal brother to save him from death too.

Her eyes shimmered as she nodded. "Is this how Erik's been controlling you?" she asked in horror.

A lump lodged in my throat and Julius raised an eyebrow at me, their scrutiny making my chest tighten.

I hesitated, not wanting to lie but not wanting to admit the truth either. Because the truth was a terrible thing.

"It's making you want to go back to him, isn't it?" Callie asked.

"Yeah...it is," I admitted, staying within the lines of the truth. *But that's not the only thing making me want to go back.*

"I hate them even more now for this. They're in our heads," Callie growled and rage glowed in her eyes.

I dropped my gaze, knowing I couldn't be honest because it might just cost me everything with Callie. She despised the vampires, and she had every right to. Hell, I despised most of them too. But not all of them. And I was surrounded by the last people in the world who could ever be swayed to see any good in them.

Part of me wanted it all to have been some twisted manipulation, some spell Erik had cast on me, because then I knew I'd have a hope of being free of it in time. But a deeper part of me didn't want that at all, because it meant that all those secret moments Erik and I had shared, the ones which had lit a fire in me and made me feel things I'd never thought possible, were lies made to shatter.

"Yeah," I muttered, hating myself for keeping the truth from my twin, but how could I explain to Callie that this mark only solidified my love for Erik? That I'd cared for him long before the wedding, that I liked the wildness that came out in me around him.

Callie sighed, seeming to take comfort in our shared predicament. "Once we're far away from them, we'll figure out how to break these bonds. Then we'll never have to think of them again until we're driving a blade into their hearts."

I nodded vaguely. *I'm so fucked.*

Julius strode after Magnar down the tunnel and I followed along with Callie, grappling with the conflict inside me.

"How did you get to the city?" I asked, wanting to distract myself from my thoughts. We had so much to say to each other, but I couldn't bring myself to mention dad just yet. The moment I did, my heart was going to fracture and the pain would spill out until it was all I could feel.

Callie started recounting her story from the moment she'd left the Realm to when she'd taken the train to New York City and poisoned the blood supply, enrapturing me with every piece of the journey.

When she told me about taking the slayers' vow, my heart thundered violently in my chest. She was bound by Magnar's commands. But worse than that, she had sworn to kill the Belvederes. To kill Erik.

When Callie asked about my time in the city, I tried to keep it brief. I didn't mention half of what I should have about my time with the royals. I just couldn't bear to see her expression when I told her how I really felt. That I didn't want them dead like I used to. That some of them weren't all bad. She would think I was brainwashed, or worse, lose her faith in me entirely. And she was all I had. I couldn't risk losing her after everything we'd been through to reunite.

We walked on until the subject of Dad hung too heavily between us to avoid. I took Callie's hand and a ripple of energy flowed between us.

"You were with him...when he died," I whispered, pain lacing my tone. I didn't need to mention who I was talking about. She knew.

"Yes," she said on a ragged breath. "And I know it sounds insane, but like I said, I can Dream Walk. I did it with him just before..."

I nodded, my eyes prickling as I waited for her to continue.

"I saw Mom too. They looked happy. I think maybe it was real in some way. I think they're out there somewhere, together."

A solid lump formed in my throat, but I took an inch of comfort from her words. Perhaps Mom and Dad were together in an afterlife, waiting for us to join them someday. "I really hope so."

Julius led us to the ruins and I was relieved to leave the dank tunnels behind as we resurfaced above ground. It was the thick of night, the moon peering through the clouds above like a watchful creature lurking in the sky.

We came up near a crumbled old playground where a child's swing was moving back and forth in the breeze. I shuddered at the eerie sight, following Julius's broad form as he drew Menace from its sheath.

"Everyone use your blades to feel for Familiars," he commanded as Magnar released one of the large swords from his back.

I raised Nightmare, trying to do as he said and Callie eyed it with longing. The blade remained quiet, and I hoped that meant we were safe.

"Here." Magnar turned to Callie, passing her his other glittering sword. He'd taken it back after their conflict over Fabian, and I'd wondered if he didn't trust her after what she'd done.

"Stay close," he murmured to her, a pit of longing in his gaze. I glanced between the two of them, sensing something much stronger between them than just friendship. Their eyes were constantly drawn to one another, gazes lingering too long, and unspoken words thickening the air in the space that parted them.

As Magnar walked on with Julius, I raised an eyebrow at Callie.

She rolled her eyes, knowing exactly what I was suggesting. We'd always been able to communicate through looks alone. Clearly she and Magnar were a thing. And that made her situation a whole lot worse depending on how important that thing was to her. She was tied to Fabian; a vampire who I had no trust for whatsoever. Anyone would have been better than him.

Raindrops speckled my cheeks as we walked, but the raging storm had died down enough that it didn't obscure our view anymore.

Julius waved us into an alley between two crumbling rows of buildings and we had to jog to keep up with his ferocious pace.

He didn't slow for a few hours, and I was sure we'd long-since passed our old hideout at the bell tower.

When he finally dropped his speed a little, I hurried up to him, running my thumb over Nightmare's hilt. I wondered how long we'd be safe for. Erik may have let me go, but surely the other royals would send Familiars after us soon.

"Where are we going?" I asked.

"As far as possible," Julius said. "I'm not taking any chances. The rain will keep our scent dampened, so we'll use it to our advantage while we can."

Magnar glanced back at Callie and I followed his gaze. She looked so small all of a sudden, like something had broken the strength which I'd seen in her just hours ago. She hugged her arms around herself, her golden hair dulled by the rain and some of the coal-black makeup around her eyes smudged down her cheeks.

Our dresses were sodden and it was taking everything we had to keep the cold out. Walking at this pace was the only thing stopping me from succumbing to it. I wondered if she felt the same because she didn't seem to be shivering as badly as I was.

I turned to join her but Magnar beat me to it, dropping his voice as he spoke to her.

Her eyes warmed as she looked up at him and I left them to it, sensing they wanted a moment alone. Though perhaps it hurt just a little that she had looked to him instead of me.

Julius threw me a dark smile. "So, that mark on your palm must be causing you a lot of trouble."

I scowled at his jibing. "Yep."

"I will cut out Erik Belvedere's heart so you can be rid of this cruel bond then." Julius's eyes glittered with mirth.

I frowned darkly and whispered, "Don't say anything to Callie."

"On your head be it," he murmured then picked up his pace again. "I do not want to be around when the truth comes out."

I hurried to keep pace. "It won't."

"Sure," he said airily, halting at an intersection before taking a left turn.

I gritted my teeth as Nightmare poured heat into my veins. "Don't be an asshole."

"Don't go asking the impossible of me," he warned and I blew out a breath of amusement.

"Seriously Julius. What I said to you about the vampires, let's keep it between us okay?"

"I'm not one to stir the pot. And I'm definitely not one to stir that particular pot. Your sister won't forgive you for your newfound sympathy with the bloodsuckers, as I would not forgive Magnar. But I am still banking on me un-brainwashing you before it even comes close to coming out anyway. So don't worry, damsel, I'll save you once again."

"I'm not brainwashed, Julius. Trust me, I wish I was," I said heavily.

"A brainwashed person wouldn't know they were brainwashed," he pointed out and I scowled up at him. "Fine," he conceded. "Say I believe you, then you really are in deeper shit than I thought."

"Thanks for the pep talk," I muttered.

He frowned, his arm brushing mine as he moved closer, and the heat radiating from his skin made me want to wrap the whole thing around me like a damn scarf. "I will protect you in any way you need protecting. It's what we do for our kind."

"I don't need protecting," I insisted.

"I know you can look after yourself, I simply mean I will also watch over you. I have your back – so long as you don't betray us like a skeevy little storm witch."

I smiled at that assessment. "I'm fully anti-storm witch and will gladly help you turn her to dust."

"Good." He shot me a grin.

I sighed, glancing back at the others to make sure they still weren't listening. "We need to talk about the prophecy-"

He held up a hand to halt me then waved his arm in a sharp signal to Magnar. Taking my wrist, he dragged me into the nearest dilapidated building.

"Don't you listen to your blade?" Julius hissed as Magnar and Callie sped into the ruined building opposite us.

I glanced down at Nightmare, realising it was humming frantically against my palm.

Julius pressed his finger to his lips, forcing me against a damp wall. The rush of large wings sounded overhead, followed by a soft cry, setting my heart pounding.

Familiar, Nightmare whispered.

Julius took his bow from his shoulder, edging beneath a hole in the half-collapsed ceiling. He placed an arrow against the string, gazing up at it intently and releasing a measured breath. He let the arrow fly, the deadly weapon shooting skyward at a ferocious speed and I caught sight of the eagle just before it burst into dust.

I let out a breath as Nightmare fell quiet again, and Julius gave me an intense look. "When Nightmare connects with you, it is trying to tell you something. Pay attention."

I bit into my lip, feeling berated. "Okay," I muttered.

My shoulders started shuddering from the cold. Since we'd stopped moving, the tiny piece of warmth I'd held onto from walking had abandoned me.

Julius strode toward me with a frown, shrugging out of his dark jacket and handing it to me. "Take it, no questions. I don't feel the cold like you do."

I pulled it on and the heated sleeves were a blessing against my frozen skin. "That's the second time you've given me your clothes," I said, recalling the cloak he'd given me once.

His mouth pulled up at the corner. "Yes, if I continue to do so, perhaps you'll have me naked one day."

"*Julius*," Magnar growled as he ducked his head through the doorway. "Stop flirting and start walking."

I shot Julius a taunting smile at being told off before stepping out onto the quiet street. Callie eyed my jacket with a glimmer of interest and my gaze fell to her bare shoulders. No goosebumps lined her skin. It hit me that she was a slayer now and the cold obviously didn't bother her in the way it did me.

As I walked among the group, I felt suddenly adrift, like I no longer really fit in. They were united by their vow, their blood, their cause. And I held a secret in my heart which went against all of that. One which I would more-than-likely have to take to the grave. Assuming Julius didn't spill it first.

Three more hours passed and I could sense dawn was close by the paling of the sky. My feet ached as Julius finally guided us toward a tall building with a balcony jutting from the side of it. One half of the structure had fallen down, but the rest seemed fairly intact, and it would certainly give us some shelter.

"We'll stop here. It's the highest building around, so we'll be able to keep a lookout," Julius announced.

My hair was plastered to my cheeks, and I was exhausted right through to my bones. None of the others looked as bedraggled as I felt, and I guessed that was another slayer gift. I was so tired, I almost wanted to take my vow just so that I could feel a little less like the walking dead.

We moved inside and I took in the frosty but fairly dry space before us. A cold wind drilled through a hole in one wall and Julius moved past it, heading up a stone stairway.

We followed, rising four levels and finding ourselves in a much more appealing room with floorboards and even some old furniture dotted around the space. Magnar strode to the opposite wall, pushing a door open and revealing the balcony beyond it. "Good. This will do. Two of us can keep watch and two of us can fetch supplies."

I didn't like the idea of remaining here in the cold. The sooner I found some dry clothes, the better. Julius seemed to be on the same line of thought as he scrutinised me. "Me and Montana will go. She needs to get out of those clothes. And I'm very experienced in helping women out of their attire."

"However would I cope without you, Julius?" I asked dryly.

"You wouldn't, damsel." He smirked.

"I'm pretty sure you promised to stop calling me that," I accused.

"Pretty sure I don't recall that." He shrugged and the asshole won a smile out of me. Damn him.

Magnar pursed his lips, looking to Callie who had stepped out onto the balcony, not seeming bothered by the gust that whipped her dress around her legs. He nodded to us, grabbing a wooden chair and breaking it as he started to build a fire. His expression was achingly sad, and I wondered if this burden on Callie weighed heavily on him too.

"I'll be back soon," I called to her. "I'll bring you some warm clothes."

She didn't seem to hear, lost to her own thoughts as she stared out across the ruins. My heart broke for her as I followed Julius back into the stairway, fearing how deeply this bond with Fabian was affecting her. It felt like things had changed between us in ways I couldn't even fathom too. We'd both gone on our own journeys and now we were standing on opposite sides of a rift that I didn't know how to cross. But I was determined to find a way to do so.

We'll be alright, Callie. We'll figure out a way to fix everything. Then it will be us against the world again.

CALLIE

CHAPTER THREE

The remains of the crumbling, concrete balcony jutted out before me. Its left side had been blasted away in the Final War, but the right side remained intact, though the railing that had once ringed it had broken away almost entirely.

The rain had finally stopped, and a cool breeze blew in with the dawn. The sun was just about to rise and though it hadn't crested the horizon yet, the sky was beginning to lighten to a pale blue in the distance. Above my head, I could still see the last stars glimmering. I wondered if Valentina planned on letting the sun shine over the city today or if she'd draw in the clouds again once it came up.

The mere thought of her sent a spike of furious anger through me. She'd betrayed her people, sold me out to Fabian, and now it seemed as though she'd betrayed the royals too. What was she planning? What was her motivation? Surely it was all driving her towards something, but for the life of me, I couldn't figure out what.

In the distance, beyond the sprawling ruins, I could just make out the river which led on to the sea. My lips parted as yet another of my dad's stories finally came to life before my eyes. I wished he could see me now, looking out at the water he'd always promised to show me. I hoped that wherever he was, he knew that I'd finally begun to see the world, just like he'd wanted me to. Though I doubted this tangled mess I found myself in was the dream he'd had in mind.

I lowered myself to sit on the cold floor and hung my legs between the last of the rusted railings, looking down at the drop below my high heels. My right shoe was covered in blood and mud, the white lace ruined beyond all chance of recovery. But strangely, my left shoe was still fairly clean. A few spots of blood stood out across the toe, but that was it. It reminded me of one of Dad's stories about the girl who'd lost her shoe and found a prince.

I had a royal looking for me too, promising me the world and happily ever after. Literally. Seeing as he planned on killing me and bringing me back from the dead so I could stay by his side for the rest of time. In reality, it was less of a fairy tale and more of a nightmare.

I touched the crown which still sat upon my head and wondered if Cinderella had ever felt that its weight was too much. I pulled it off and twisted it between my fingers, frowning at the diamonds which shone dimly in the light. What a strange thing to give me. I'd been nothing more than a bug beneath their shoe my whole life, but now they wanted to pretend I was something special. Place a crown on my head and call me a princess just to disguise the ugliness of their true intentions.

I dropped the crown beside me, turning away from it so I didn't have to keep thinking about it.

Leaning forward, I gazed down at the drop below my feet. We were four floors up but I wasn't afraid; my gifts would allow me to survive that fall. It was strange to think that making a single promise had granted me such power. I'd gone from a helpless girl, destined to live my life under the vampires' rule, to a warrior capable of ending them. If only it really were so simple.

The breeze swept around me again, pulling at my hair and raising goosebumps along my bare arms. Despite my gifts helping me resist the cold, the sodden dress and low temperature were beginning to take their toll on me and I shivered a little. The dress was ruined but I had nothing to replace it. It was torn and filthy. A beautiful thing destroyed.

I held my left hand in front of me and traced the star on the back of it with my fingertips. One half of my soul was bound to Magnar. I turned my hand over and traced the cross on my palm. The other half was bound to Fabian. So where did that leave me?

Stuck between two mortal enemies while waiting for them to destroy me.

I was tied to so many rules and commands that I could barely count them anymore. This form of freedom wasn't very liberating and I was starting to think that my escape from the Realm had only locked me in a different kind of cage. Were we destined to dance to the tune of the gods forever? Were our souls ours to own, or our lives ours to live?

I was unable to be with the man I knew I wanted in the depths of my soul, unable to so much as speak his name aloud. And even if we could have been together, he could control me with a single command. I was powerless with him. Ever the underdog in a game which should have been played from equal positions.

My thoughts drifted to Fabian and a surge of longing raced through me which I knew wasn't truly my own. But that didn't stop the ache I felt, the desire which stirred my blood, the memory of his mouth against mine. I gritted my teeth as I rejected it. I hated his dark eyes which were so deep that I could get lost in them... right before I cut them out of his face. The thought of his stupid, perfect smile made me ache for Fury with a desperate need. I had no idea where my blade was now and I missed it like a lost limb, certain it would have helped remind me of my own mind. Without it, I was caught between wanting to kiss Fabian and kill him while unsure if I really wanted either.

This was all Idun's fault. What had I done to deserve such a curse from her?

Malicious bitch.

If there was a way to kill a goddess, then I'd be sorely tempted to find out how.

I wanted to scream my rage at the ruins before me, but as we were on the run and trying to evade the notice of the Familiars that hunted us, I guessed that wasn't the best idea. I settled for grabbing a lump of broken masonry from the wall beside me and hurling it out into the ruins instead. I threw it with all my strength and watched as it soared

35

away from me, much further than I would have been able to send it before taking my vow. It clattered into the rubble and I reached for another, launching it after the first to see if it would go any further.

The third brick I grabbed had a sharp edge which jabbed into my finger. I hissed in pain as blood bloomed and I dropped it beside me, quickly sucking on my finger, scowling at the jagged rock before wondering if it could be exactly what I needed.

I picked it up again and held it above my left palm as I glared at the cross which bound me to Fabian. If I couldn't fight off the desire to be with him while it marked my flesh, then maybe I could cut it clean out of me instead.

I took a deep breath as I touched the sharp edge to my skin and psyched myself up for what I was about to do. It was going to hurt like hell, but if I was lucky, it'd pay off.

I can't do it. I can't do it. Maybe I should just go back and find Fabian? If I hurry I could be kissing him within a matter of - just fucking do it!

I pressed down and pain flared through my palm just as a hand landed over mine, dragging the brick out of my grasp. I blinked up at Magnar in surprise as he sat beside me, turning the piece of jagged masonry over in his hands.

"That won't work," he said quietly, his dark presence settling around me like a wave of shadows had followed him to my side.

I opened my mouth to say something, *anything,* that could make this better but I was at a loss for words. I knew the sacrifices he'd made to end the Belvederes and I'd thrown myself in the way of him fulfilling that destiny, ruining the chance he'd been waiting on for a thousand years. How could he even look at me after that? How could he bear to sit down beside me after I'd sabotaged his shot at vengeance after he'd given so much in pursuit of it?

The inch of space between us was like an uncrossable abyss. It was filled with pain, and loss, and so many unspoken words that I had no idea how to bridge it.

"I'm sorry," I breathed because it was the only thing I could say that was entirely the truth. It was the one thing I could stand behind and know I was feeling for myself without any input from deities, or vows or curses.

"For which part of it?" Magnar rotated his arm back and launched the rock out into the ruins. It landed so much further away than mine had that I could barely even hear the clatter as it hit the ground.

I chanced a look at the strong slope of his brow and the breath-taking ruggedness of his features, now cast in even harsher lines than before, like the world just kept heaping weight upon his shoulders and it was all he could do to carry that burden.

"All of it. Everything that's happened since my dad died. Probably most of what happened before then too. I can't help but feel like all I've done since we met is make your life more difficult," I said, my gut twisting with those words as I thought over all he'd lost and how much of it came back to me.

"That's not true," he replied, his voice laced with grit which chafed against my soul.

I didn't bother to contradict him, but I didn't know what else he wanted me to say. I crossed my ankles, looking down at the drop again as I released a heavy breath.

"I need to understand what they did to you." Magnar reached over and took my hand, turning it so he could inspect the silver cross on my skin. My heart stuttered at the feel of his rough palm against mine, the memory of those hands and what they were capable of silencing any protest I might have had. There was no caress in his touch as he tilted my wrist to see the mark more clearly, so Idun allowed it, but the feeling of his hand on mine still sent shivers racing across my skin, the ache of longing sinking deep inside my chest where I wrapped it up tight and refused to let it go.

"I've never seen this before," he murmured, his hold tight, the anger he felt clear in every piece of his muscular body.

"I told you; it was Idun. She bound me to your enemy because she's cruel and it amused her to do it. She knew you were there, she knew what we…what we might have…" I swallowed thickly and forced myself to go on because we hadn't voiced what we might have been becoming to one another and this didn't feel like the moment to try and define it. "She made me look right at you before I..." The memory of Fabian's lips against mine made me shudder in disgust and ache with desire in equal measures. It wasn't fair. Why plant those feelings into me? It was like she wanted me to go to him now, to abandon Magnar and take up with those he hunted. It didn't make any sense. I'd sworn to help her end the vampires and Magnar was her devoted warrior, so why do this to me? To us?

"So she laid claim to your body in the same way she held me when Valentina betrayed us?" he asked and I could hear the relief in his tone as he made that assessment.

I nodded, wanting to leave it at that. To pretend that she'd taken my limbs hostage and used them without my permission. But it was so much worse than that and he deserved to know.

"At first, that was all it was. But once we were married, once this mark appeared, it was like I..." My bravery stuttered out and I bit my lip, afraid to tell him the whole truth, afraid to admit the whole truth to myself too.

"Like you what?" he prompted, his eyes lifting from my hand to my face, his expression guarded like he could already tell it was worse than he wanted to believe.

I took a deep breath, forcing myself to tell him the whole truth. Or at least as much of it as I understood.

"Like I *want* to be with him. To be in his arms and give every part of myself to him. I want to feel his mouth on mine, I want him to pin me down and-" I slapped a hand over my mouth to stop the foul words from pouring out. "Shit," I cursed, recoiling from those words, and tightening my hold on his hand. I could see him withdrawing, see the walls going up within his dark gaze.

"But I know that I don't really," I added quickly as I felt the tension building in Magnar's posture. I dropped my eyes. I couldn't bear to look at him and see what my confession was doing to him. "All I truly want is to hunt him down and cut his fucking heart out. I want him to burn for all the terrible things he's done...but when I saw you standing over him, about to finish him..." I shook my head, unable to rationalise what I'd done.

"I should have killed him. Perhaps his death is the only way you'll be free of him," Magnar spat.

"Maybe," I agreed, although the idea of a world without Fabian in it still filled me with dread. "But in that moment, I feared for his life like it was worth more than my own. I felt certain that his death would break something in me which I'd never get back."

The silence stretched between us and I finally dared to turn and look at him again.

His brow was furrowed with concern and he seemed lost in thought as he gazed out over the ruins. As the sun continued to rise, the rich bronze colour of his skin appeared to drink in the light, like he was born of it and made for it alone. The sight of him like that made my heart rate finally settle.

With him close to me, I didn't feel like I was second guessing myself anymore. Fabian paled into insignificance. *This* was real. *He* was real.

Butterflies danced in my stomach as I continued to stare at him and his gaze slowly slid to meet mine. An inferno raged in his golden eyes, blazing hungrily as he drank me in just as I did him.

"And did you mean what you said to me before we left?" he asked carefully, like he wasn't really sure if he wanted to hear my response.

"Yes," I breathed. The answer was easy as I looked into his eyes and the fractured parts of my soul knitted themselves together just for the chance to be with him.

The wind blustered around us and my hair swept across my face. Magnar caught it and pushed it behind my ear, his hand cupping my cheek. I leaned into his touch, wishing I could do more as I felt Idun's will urging me to move away.

I fought against her as I looked into his eyes and his thumb brushed across my lips. My skin burned beneath his touch and desire built in me, sweeping from the pit of my stomach right down to the tips of my toes. I wanted him unlike I'd ever wanted anything. He was the most desperate desire of my heart and the greatest longing of my flesh, but it was as though the whole world was working against us.

His arm grew tense as Idun pushed against him too and his hand slid from my face as he was forced to pull away. His fingertips skimmed a pattern down my neck and my throat bobbed as I fought to stay still. He managed to trace a line over my collar bone, finally touching the skin above my pounding heart for half a second before he dropped his hand.

"You're everything I've ever wanted, Callie," he said, his voice rough with longing. "I'll do whatever it takes to free you of this curse and then I'm going to claim you for my own. No vampire bastard will take you from me and no goddess will stand in the way of that."

I opened my left hand in my lap and frowned at the silver mark on my skin. I hated it. It felt like the touch of a monster, branded onto me like I was his belonging. It killed me that Montana had the same bind to Erik Belvedere. That she was as trapped by him as I was by Fabian. What right did those monsters have to try and claim us for their own? Like we were possessions instead of people. As if our own wants and feelings were irrelevant.

My hate for the vampires burned hot in my blood. What was it with immortal beings believing themselves to be so superior? Our lives may have been shorter but they held so much more meaning because of that. Each breath could be our last. Each moment could change our fates. And I'd be damned if I was going to let them take what little time I had on this Earth and mould it to their desires. My life would be my own again, no matter what I had to sacrifice to claim it.

Magnar ran his finger over the cross on my palm and it burned angrily in response. I snatched my hand away, forming a fist as pain flared in my blood. I squeezed so tightly that I could feel my nails cutting into my skin and a trickle of blood dripped onto the white dress.

"I just don't understand why Idun wants to fuck with us like this," I muttered. "Why she's doing this to us...we've devoted our lives to her cause. Why would she be so cruel to those who are trying to help her?"

"I have been asking that question ever since she tied me to Valentina. I don't understand why she chooses to punish her most loyal followers. She claims to be testing my devotion, but I have never wavered from my path. Allowing me some small measure of happiness would not mean that I'd abandon my hunt for the Belvederes. If she can see into my soul as she claims to, then she would know that that is the truth. So I have no answer for you."

I turned over his response in my mind as I looked back towards the horizon and the sun spilled over the edge of the river in the distance. I watched it for several achingly beautiful moments before the clouds began to build in the sky and it was hidden from view.

Valentina. I ground my jaw as I thought of that bitch and all she'd done.

She'd gone beyond turning her back on the slayers and becoming their mortal enemy; she was leading the Biters. At least the Belvederes were making *some* attempt to protect humans from their kind. The Realms might have stolen our freedom so they could take our blood, but at least our lives were fairly safe under that system. If Valentina and her followers got their way, humans would be hunted. Prey to monsters who far outmatched them.

"Would you hate me if I killed your fiancée?" I asked, giving Magnar half a smile.

He laughed as he leaned back, resting his weight onto his elbows. "Are you jealous, Callie?"

I scoffed. "Of that bitch? Though I guess she is very beautiful, if you're into that kind of thing."

"She's a vampire," he replied, his features written with disgust and I couldn't help but smirk at that.

"She was beautiful before she was a vampire," I replied, remembering the girl he'd shown me in his dream and wondering if there had ever been a point when he'd desired his union with her at all. Had they been together? Should their story have ended a thousand years ago with a dozen slayer babies and a happily ever after?

"She pales to insignificance beside you. And in any case, I managed to avoid marrying my betrothed for over a thousand years," he replied. "You married yours within the day. Perhaps I have more reason for concern than you do."

I snorted with amusement. "I had no choice about that. And I did try to fight it until Idun forced my hand. I stabbed him pretty good – fucked up his whole face and ruined his eye. Though I'll admit my attempt to strangle him was a poor choice."

Magnar released a low groan. "You attempted to strangle a creature who is without need to draw breath?"

"Well I had very few weapons available to me so it seemed like a decent enough plan at the time. Suffice to say, it didn't work."

"And yet after trying so hard to do so yourself, you wouldn't let *me* kill your husband." The way he said the final word sent a shiver of fear along my spine. I glanced down at my hand and pulled the wedding ring from my finger, glaring at it as I tried to deny the part of me that wished to keep it on.

"No," I agreed. I wasn't really sure what else I could say to that. I didn't understand it myself, so how could I expect him to?

"Did he hurt you while he held you?" Magnar asked, his voice dropping to a low growl which reminded me just how deadly he could be when he wanted to be.

"No," I replied on a breath. "I probably did more harm to them; they were just trying to convince me to go along with the wedding. They seemed to really believe it could have helped them break their curse. And I can't help but wonder…if they were right about it, shouldn't I be willing to make that sacrifice? For the good of all the humans?" I asked bitterly.

That question had been gnawing at me even though every part of my being rebelled against the thought of it. I hated the idea right down to the marrow of my bones, but wouldn't a better person agree to it? Wouldn't a better person do anything they could to end this and save the rest of my kind?

I held the wedding ring out in front of me, intending to drop it into the ruins but I couldn't force myself to release it, Idun's twisted magic keeping it locked between my fingers.

"I cannot believe the answer to the curse lies in whoring yourself out to a monster and carrying his demon children," Magnar growled.

I turned to look at him again as I returned the ring to my finger.

"Fabian isn't a monster," I snapped before I could slam my mouth shut.

Magnar's gaze dropped to my wedding ring and something dark and terrifying flared in his eyes. He pushed himself to his feet and strode away from me without another word.

"Elder?" I called, my throat thickening as that damn title left my lips instead of his name. I shoved myself to my feet and took a step after him, needing him to help me with this, hating that I couldn't simply switch off this link to Fabian and be done with it.

"Don't follow me," Magnar growled without turning back and his command hit me like a punch to the gut, my feet stumbling to a halt against my wishes.

I tried to fight against the command and managed to take three steps after him, my feet feeling like they were weighed down with lead while I cursed him out for using that bullshit power against me again. I attempted to lift my foot for the fourth time but it was impossible.

My lungs felt like they might burst from the pressure of the force which worked against me. I staggered back and a sob escaped my lips as I dropped down to the floor once more.

Tears fell from my eyes and I hugged my knees to my chest as the cold wind whipped around me. I shivered as it battered against me, easily pushing through the thin material of my dress and chilling me to my core.

The sun climbed higher in the sky beyond the clouds but I was trapped where I was, unable to move back inside while Magnar's command immobilised me. He'd gone in there and I couldn't follow.

Rain began to fall in a persistent drizzle, slowly soaking me and mixing with the tears on my cheeks. I was so fucking stupid. I never should have given myself to the vow, never should have gotten myself mixed up with the deals between gods and mortals. Now I was trapped in the midst of their games, a pawn to be used and manipulated. And there was nothing I could do to escape them.

I grew colder but I still didn't move. I couldn't. And the knowledge that my body had once again been snatched from my control sent an ice-cold fear pounding through me. But there was nothing I could do about it. All I could do was wait.

MAGNAR

CHAPTER FOUR

1000 YEARS AGO

The storm raged on around us and still none of us moved as the goddess's new powers surged through our veins. It was as though every remaining member of the clans was frozen by the grief of my father's death. Each man, woman and child down to the stable boy I'd brought back from my travels were utterly still as we mourned and Idun poured her strength into us.

I could feel everything like it was the first time my body had experienced it.

Every inch of my skin was more sensitive, every sound more defined. Even my eyesight grew sharper.

My gaze fell on Venom which was still grasped in my hand and I noticed my ring finger straightening before my eyes. I'd broken it as a child and it hadn't set right, but now the dull ache I always felt from it in the cold was gone.

Strength surged through my muscles like a tide until I felt certain that I could rip a man in two with my bare hands if the notion took me.

The land grew darker as the storm built and my mother's sobs finally came to an end. It seemed the sky was mourning our father's passage as much as we were and whatever strange gifts we had been given in the face of his death paled at the weight of his loss.

I forced myself to rise as a huge flash of lightning lit up the heavens, strength saturating my limbs like never before.

In the distance, beyond the row of tents across the plain, far further than I should have been able to see, I noticed a figure approaching.

I had never seen the Golden Whore for myself, but I knew her as soon as my gaze landed on her. No beauty such as hers could be natural among the world of mortals. She stole the breath from my lungs at a single glance, her unnervingly bright gaze pinning me in place with the power of her stolen immortality. She was a monster dressed as an enchantress; a trap poised to steal the hearts of all who looked upon her so that she might sink her teeth into them while they still beat with want for her.

Venom hissed her name like a curse in my ear. *Clarice.* I held the blade loosely in my right hand as she advanced across the plain, my blood pumping with a deep and violent hatred which begged to see her end.

Julius stepped to my side, holding his own blade at the ready and I moved to retrieve Tempest from where I'd left it thrust in the ground. Though I had used all of my strength to drive the blade into the dirt only hours before, removing it was as easy as breathing with my newly gifted muscles. The power of the goddess roamed rampantly through my limbs and as I looked at the monster who stole towards us across the open plain, I knew what purpose this power was meant for. Idun had gifted us the strength we needed to match even the worst of their kind in battle. To best them.

I began to move between the tents, making a beeline for the place where I'd spotted the immortal harlot. I'd lost sight of her without the lightning to illuminate the plain but I could feel her moving closer through the shadows, a creature of darkness hunting in her natural habitat.

I swung the two blades in lazy circles as I advanced, getting a feel for the way they moved as I wielded them at once, feeling a rightness in that which sang within my bones. My father's sword would be mine now too and every drop of tainted blood I spilled with it would be in homage to his memory.

"Do you think they've all come?" Julius asked darkly as he moved at my side. I could tell his thirst for vengeance was as powerful as my own and I couldn't help but draw further strength from his company.

"I hope so," I growled, the need for death like an ache in my soul.

The power of the goddess flowed through my veins like lava, heating me to my core despite the fact that I strode shirtless through the pounding rain. Something told me I would never suffer the full bite of winter again.

We made it beyond the tents and stood at the edge of the plain, waiting for the monsters to strike, knowing they skulked out there in the shadows.

"Show yourselves!" I bellowed. "You four beasts of the night who play with lives and souls like they're worthless. Come and let us see your unnatural faces!"

The night grew deeper as I felt the gods pressing close, their eyes glued to our actions as they waited for the battle to commence. We were just pieces on their game boards as always, but this time, I was more than willing to play.

Someone moved behind me and I turned my head as Valentina stepped forward to take a position on my left. As I caught sight of her eyes, I could see the power of the storm swirling within them, lightning flickering in her pupils, a static charge lifting her dark hair. It seemed the gods had included her when they'd bestowed these enhancements to our gifts. The power of the Clan of Storms raged within her unlike ever before, and I could almost taste the oncoming storm as I inhaled.

She raised her arms and electricity hummed in the air as she harnessed the fury of the storm. Lightning flashed blindingly across the clouds and four figures were illuminated on the far side of the plain, their porcelain features etched with uncertainty as they assessed us.

They could see it too, this new power in us, and they hesitated to meet it like the cowards I had long known them to be. They hid from death after all, from the promise of endless days in the halls of Valhalla.

Only a coward would accept such a fate.

My gaze fell on Erik at the left of the group and my lip curled back in a feral snarl, the desire for his death a brutal ache in my chest. I slowly lifted Venom, pointing the blade at his heart and sending him a silent promise. I would be his end. No matter the cost.

"Is this all that remains of the great race of slayers?" Fabian called, his voice laced with amusement as he began to draw closer, his steps full of swagger and dripping bravado.

Our mother moved to stand on Julius's other side, four slayers to face four vampires.

Behind us, those remaining members of the clans gathered too. Even those who had no business fighting stood with us; old warriors whose warring days were long passed waited shoulder to shoulder with children who were barely strong enough to wield a blade. Mothers stood with their babes in one arm and a weapon in the other. Even Elissa and Aelfric joined our ranks, clutching blades they had no idea how to use while glaring at the vampires with all the rage of seasoned warriors.

The total was likely less than two hundred, a fraction of our numbers from just days ago. But the goddess had blessed them all and we stood against our enemies, stronger than ever before. I didn't like their chances at victory.

Beyond the Revenants, I could make out a moving shadow filled with their foul creations. As I'd expected, they'd wasted no time in siring more vampires and I felt a pang of pity for whatever town had fallen prey to their curse.

I turned to meet my brother's gaze and found raw power brimming through him too. The gods had been generous with their gifts, spreading them amongst my people and giving us the chance to meet the vampires on equal footing. I would be certain not to squander them.

"I will follow you to the end, brother," Julius growled, lifting his sword higher in anticipation of my command. These were my people now. My father's death had made me their Earl. And they waited on my command to slay these beasts. The first I would make, but not the last if I had any say in the matter.

"For our father," I said fiercely and Mother's gaze hardened as she nodded. "For Earl Mallion!" I bellowed for all of our people to hear.

A resounding battle cry met my own and I took off across the plain, sprinting faster than I'd ever run before, the power of my muscles a strange and wonderous thing. A gift I would use well.

The storm raged and the rain poured upon us in an unyielding cascade of freezing droplets, but I didn't feel the biting cold the way I should have. My very skin seemed to be alive with energy, creating heat where there should have been none and saving me from suffering beneath the torrent which Valentina encouraged to fall from the skies.

The Revenants knew there was something different about us and all four sets of eyes were drawn to me as I led the line against them.

Fabian was closest to me and he was the first to break ranks and run to oppose us.

I smiled bitterly as I raced to meet him, ducking beneath him as he leapt for my throat, the movement far easier than should have been possible. He spun to stare at me in surprise but I wasted no time and swung Tempest straight for his neck. He twisted away from me but I already had Venom waiting to block his retreat, a feral grin parting my lips as I found myself more than a match for this heathen.

Fabian leapt aside but not before the blade carved a line along his forearm, spilling his bright red blood and staining the dirt between us. He hissed in pain as the wound sizzled from the magic in the sword and the air was tainted by the stench of burning flesh.

I didn't miss the look of horrified wonder that filled his eyes. I guessed no one had gotten that close to killing him in a long time.

I roared as I pushed my advantage and he tried to lunge at me again. He caught my right arm in his iron grip, his inhuman fingers tightening in an attempt to break my bones. Before he could do more than bruise me, I swung my other arm at his face, Venom's hilt still grasped in my fist.

My knuckles connected with his jaw and he was thrown off of me, crashing into the mud six feet away and skidding through it. When he regained his feet, he was covered from head to toe in filth, and bright red blood still dripped steadily from the wound on his arm.

Fabian bared his teeth at me and I bared mine right back as I began to advance.

"What are you?" he hissed as he retreated a step.

"I am your death," I replied.

I leapt forward, swinging both of my blades in a vicious arc designed to cleave his head from his neck.

Fabian threw himself aside, barely a breath parting him from death before he spun away from me and fled back towards his kin.

I bellowed a challenge and took chase. My mother and brother ran behind me, blades ready and warrior cries on their lips as we raced after the monsters who had taken everything from us.

The four Revenants grouped together across the plain, staring at us in confusion and with more than a hint of fear, seeming to accept that we were not what we had been, that we were now more than a match for them.

"Do you feel the thirst driving you on?" Clarice cried, turning her gaze on the newly sired vampires behind them as she hunted for a way to save her own neck. "Go forward and feast!"

The vampires shrieked in excitement and flooded past their creators like a tide of ruination, the thirst turning them into little more than feral beasts blinded by their need for blood. They raced to intercept us and the remaining members of the seven clans thundered to meet them at my back.

"These creatures need reminding that they're already dead!" I yelled and the replying roar of my kin joined with a great crash of thunder as Valentina continued to wield the storm with her newly enhanced gifts.

The Revenants stood behind their army and watched as our forces collided. I did no such thing; no warrior of mine would be asked to sacrifice themselves without me by their side. I led the charge from the front, carving a path through the vampires with Julius and our mother beside me.

We cut down more vampires than I could count and the dust from their demise mixed with the thick mud at our feet, clogging the air with the stench of their deaths.

Again and again, I swung my blades but the fatigue I expected with such use of my energy never came. My muscles thrummed with strength and the promise of death for all those who came against me, the gifts of the goddess pumping through my limbs powerfully.

As the rest of my people battled against the new vampires, my family sliced a path through the mayhem towards the demons who had caused it.

I plunged Tempest into the heart of a beautiful vampire clad in the dress of a noble and as she dissolved before me, the Revenants were revealed beyond her cascading remains.

"This isn't possible," Miles hissed as he glared at my family, trying to deny what we were now. A true match for their monstrosity.

"The gods have levelled the field," Julius growled. "Are you afraid to find out if you can match us now?"

"Why?" Erik breathed and I got the feeling his question was meant for one of the powerful deities who watched our exchange, but I answered all the same.

"For the curse you bestowed on our father. No Earl of the slayers should ever have met the fate you dealt him. I will repay that debt in blood." I advanced on them, my gaze fixed on Erik as his eyes narrowed in confusion.

"Your father was the slayer I turned?" he asked as realisation hit him. "I saved him; I sent him back to you-"

"You sent back a demon wearing the skin of the man I loved!" my mother yelled, her broken heart making her voice crack with emotion, but her axe was steady in her hand.

"You forced me to plunge a blade through my own father's heart," I growled as I took another step. Venom and Tempest hummed in anticipation as I closed in on the monsters who had started it all, their demands for their deaths thick in my mind.

"You killed him?" Erik asked and I didn't miss the horror that flashed through his eyes. Did he dare mourn the loss of the foul creation he had placed in my father's skin?

"*You* killed him," I corrected angrily.

The thunder cracked above our heads again and I ran at him, no longer willing to hear his abhorrent voice. I would take his head from his body and pay the blood debt I was owed.

51

I took three long strides and leapt forward, spinning in the air as I swung both of my blades for his head.

Erik's eyes widened as he saw death coming for him and his sister leapt forward to knock him aside before I could land my blow. Venom sliced across her shoulder and she howled in pain as bright blood spilled from the wound.

Erik snapped out of his momentary inaction and wrapped his arms around Clarice, leaping away from me and hauling her to safety.

Miles and Fabian stepped in front of her too, the three foul brothers protecting their monstrous sister. I almost laughed at the false display of love. A creature sustained by death could never be capable of such an emotion.

Julius yelled as he charged at them and I ran to join him with Venom screaming for vengeance in my palm.

The Revenants bared their teeth like beasts as they sprinted to meet us.

Julius tucked his head low and barrelled towards them like a human battering-ram. His shoulder connected with Miles's chest and a sound like falling rocks filled the air. Miles was thrown backwards, slamming into his sister and sending them both crashing into the mud.

Fabian leapt onto Julius's back, sinking his teeth into his shoulder with a feral viciousness. My mother screamed as she aimed a kick at Fabian, dislodging him before he could drink my brother's blood.

I only had eyes for Erik as I advanced on him steadily, swinging my blades in a clear challenge. Vengeance called my name, drawing me closer.

He leapt at me but before we could meet in battle, lightning struck the ground between us.

The vampire fell back and my heart leapt with surprise.

Again, lightning forked from the sky, slamming into the ground between us and driving the demon back. The third fork arced towards the other Revenants, carving a space between them and my family.

I looked around and found Valentina striding towards us. Wind billowed around her and pulled her usually perfect hair into a maelstrom of her own creation.

The vampires looked between the four of us in undisguised horror, their eyes drifting to the slayers who drew close behind us. As I followed their gaze, I found my kin closing rank at my back, the newly-sired vampires reduced to nothing but piles of clothes and ash on the battlefield.

Only the Revenants remained to face our host of over a hundred slayers gifted with the new strength of the goddess.

"Is that fear I see in your eyes?" I cried.

The slayers at my back yelled their own challenges, the air rumbling with our combined rage.

The Revenants moved towards each other, taking a step back, then another.

"Stand and face us, cowards!" I roared as I saw the urge to flee in their expression.

"This fight will keep, slayer," Fabian spat as his hand closed on Clarice's wrist and he pulled her further back.

The four of them exchanged a brief glance which held the weight of destiny in it, then they turned and fled.

I released a battle cry as I took chase, my people joining me as we raced to hunt down the monsters, refusing to let them flee this fate.

But despite the new power in my muscles, their pace outmatched my own and they began to increase the distance between us in their desperate bid for freedom.

I didn't relent, my feet tearing a path across the sodden ground as I began to put distance between myself and my people. Only Julius kept pace with me, his hatred and thirst for revenge matching my own, but despite our efforts, we couldn't keep up.

The sea loomed ahead, and we skidded to a halt as we found ourselves on the top of a cliff which looked down onto the roiling waves.

I cursed as I realised what they had done. The vampires had taken refuge beneath the water where they knew we couldn't follow. Fucking cowards.

"We are the sons of Mallion Elioson!" I roared into the night, knowing they would hear me where they hid like rats in a hole. "Your deaths await you at our hands! We will have vengeance for our father and we will hunt you to the ends of the Earth!"

"You may run but we will find you!" Julius bellowed in agreement. "You are only delaying your fate!"

MONTANA

CHAPTER FIVE

Julius and I headed deeper into the ruined city, passing rows of old stores with faded names above the doorways. A hardware store, a gas station, even an old bridal shop which I scurried past at a ferocious pace. I had no intention of exchanging my current wedding dress for another one. If I never saw one of those flouncy white gowns again, I'd die goddamn happy.

A large building loomed up ahead with a shattered glass doorway. Several of the letters on the wall above it had fallen away, leaving B-y Plaz- Mall.

I vaguely recalled the term mall from my dad's recounts of the past and started sprinting toward it with hope lifting my heart.

"Hey- wait up!" Julius called, dragging his attention away from a lingerie store window and chasing after me.

I slowed as I stepped through the broken doorway, my dress trailing over the shards of glass, making a plinking sound as they shifted. Inside, was an impossibly pristine corridor lined with rows upon rows of clothes stores. Relief ebbed through me at escaping the pouring rain. And now I finally had a chance to get out of this damn dress which was so wet, it weighed a tonne, and the skirt was coated in grime.

"Julius -*look*," I gasped as he joined me.

His mouth parted, his eyes trailing from store to store. "By the gods, what is this place?"

"It's a mall, a place people used to shop for stuff." I jogged towards the nearest store with Nightmare tight in my grip, wrenching the door open and finding an expanse of untouched clothes hanging on rails all over the place.

My heart lifted as I took it all in, the cold so deep in my veins that I practically groaned at the sight of endless sweaters and cosy leggings.

"Shit," Julius cursed. "I've never seen a market with so many fine things."

He raced past me into the menswear, tugging off his shirt and tossing it to the floor before unbuckling his pants. He was down to his underwear in no time, revealing his deep bronze skin and the thick muscles that clad his body like armour. Then he dropped his boxers, and I turned away fast before I got an unwanted eyeful of his cock, his gleeful laughter reaching me as I started searching through the women's clothes.

Several of the items were thin and sparkly, and there were a bunch of dresses that I swept right past. They wouldn't be any use against the cold so I forged a path to the back of the room where the sweaters were waiting for me along with a whole range of more practical items. I grabbed a dark, long-sleeved shirt off a hanger and smiled at it in relief, certain it would keep me warm.

I placed it down along with Nightmare then reached behind my back to undo my dress, desperate to get out of this thing and abandon it forever. My fingers fumbled against the tiny buttons, failing to free myself and causing my heart to riot in frustration. There were so many of them. How the hell was I supposed to get out of it?

Your husband was supposed to get you out of it, Montana.

My teeth clenched as that thought passed through my head and the mark on my palm suddenly blazed with energy, making me yearn for Erik so much it left me breathless. I shut my eyes, working to force away the sensation.

"Need a hand?" Julius's voice made me jump, and I opened my

eyes, finding him striding toward me in a pair of jeans with a navy t-shirt gripped in his hand. My gaze shifted to his huge chest and the packed muscles of his torso, heat crawling into my cheeks.

"No," I blurted, and he cocked his head in amusement.

"How are you going to escape from your final cage then, damsel?"

"I'm not a damsel," I growled, sick of him calling me that.

"It's not a weakness to ask for help when you need it, you know," he said.

I chewed the inside of my cheek and Julius went to turn away, but I swallowed my pride and called, "Wait."

He glanced back at me, tucking the t-shirt into his waistband as if he had no intention of putting it on anytime soon. Though I wished he would because his abs were a distraction I didn't need right now.

He sauntered over to me, all cockiness and I pursed my lips at him before he moved behind me and started on the buttons. "Come on you little bastards," he hissed, failing to get purchase on them.

"What's the problem? Your big man hands?" I taunted.

"They've never been a problem for anything before now," he said with a smirk in his voice.

"Were you born this arrogant or is it another curse of the gods?"

He laughed. "Fuck it." He gripped the dress and ripped it clean down the back, sending buttons scattering everywhere.

I could breathe again as the tight bodice finally released me and I was so relieved that as I stepped out of the rumpled material and turned to face Julius, I completely forgot that I wasn't wearing a bra and I had a see-through pair of lace panties on.

His gaze dropped to take in my nipples which were pointing right at him thanks to the cold. His throat bobbed and I snatched a sweater off the nearest hanger, clutching it against my body.

"Turn away," I snapped.

But instead of doing as I asked, he frowned, reaching out to touch a bite mark above my left breast, scoring his thumb around it before his hand trailed to more bite marks along my neck. "The rain has washed a fair bit of the venom out, but we need to make sure it's all gone or they won't heal."

The heat of his fingers against my ice-cold skin made me pull away, my heart thundering as my mind turned to Erik.

"I'll go find some water," he said, then turned, the broad muscles of his back flexing as he headed out of the store.

I picked up Nightmare and moved to the underwear section where I pulled on a pair of black panties with a sports bra. I tugged on a pair of warm leggings too, along with socks and some new, thick boots as I waited for Julius to get back.

It wasn't long before he returned with a few bottles of water, walking over to me and gesturing for me to lie down on a bench in the shoe area. I did so and he knelt beside me, twisting off the cap of the water bottle and shifting my hair away before tipping it over the bite marks. The pain was sharp, but it eased dramatically as the last of the venom was washed out and I released a breath of relief, only now realising how much the bites had been stinging.

He grabbed the shirt out of his waistband, using it to dab at the bites and dry them, and I looked up at his dark eyes, his brow drawn low as he concentrated.

"Why are you taking care of me?" I asked. "We barely know each other."

He knelt back, pushing a hand through his damp hair and mussing it up as he did so. "I'm nothing like the parasite company you've been keeping lately. I look after my own." He stood up, moving to fetch himself another shirt and pulling it on at last.

"They're really not that bad," I muttered, not intending for him to hear, but he immediately responded.

"Yes they are."

"Not all of them."

"Wrong," he growled, fixing me in his gaze as he walked back to me. "They are all undead, blood-thirsty creeps. And if you think Erik Belvedere wouldn't suck you dry the second he got the chance then-"

"Stop it," I snarled, grabbing the long-sleeve black shirt, and pulling it on. Anger flowed through me and the X on my palm prickled. "He would never hurt me."

"He wants to though. He had to fight the urge to bite you every moment he was around you. How could you stand it?"

I glared at him, striding closer. "Just drop it, okay? I know Erik. He's not like those twisted biters who attacked us. Who left these marks on me."

He pushed a hand into his damp locks again as they fell into his eyes. "Look, I'm not trying to upset you, Montana. I care about you."

I frowned as he reached out and brushed his fingers over my arm. "It's a slayer thing, I suppose. I'm lost without my kind. So I feel protective over you. It's hard for me to accept that one of my own actually feels something for one of *them*. Especially Erik Belvedere."

"Maybe all of this is to do with the prophecy," I suggested with a heavy breath, my heart beating harder as I looked at the silver X on my palm.

"Did you speak to Andvari?" Julius asked, his tone darkening.

I nodded, a shudder running through me at the memory. "He said I'm part of the prophecy. Half of it. So I guess Callie has to be the other half."

"What else did he say?" he asked, a hunger growing in his gaze for my answers.

"Nothing." I dropped my eyes as the dark memory swallowed me up. "After he tortured me and Erik for a while, he just left."

"Did the god hurt you, Montana?" he growled.

"Not really...it's hard to explain." I wrapped my arms around myself and Julius tugged me into a hug, resting his chin on my head. He was right, I had to admit it, even if only to myself. Us together felt right. Like we were both part of something bigger and we were bound to it together. It shouldn't have felt so natural to seek comfort in the arms of a man who was still practically a stranger to me, but it did. And after all I'd been through, I couldn't help but steal a moment in the warm comfort of his arms.

"We'll work it out," he muttered.

I knew it must have been hard for Julius to understand my feelings for a vampire. Erik had killed his father, and hell if I didn't know the pain of such a loss. But if Julius's vow urged him to end the curse, maybe that would be enough for him to put his revenge aside one day.

"Thank you for keeping your word not to hurt Erik back at the cathedral." I pulled out of his arms and he gave me a slanted grin.

"I am nothing if not a man of my word. But don't ever ask that of me again."

I frowned at his words, but there was nothing I could do to make him hate Erik less than he did.

I picked up Nightmare from where I'd left it on the bench, the warm metal humming in greeting. But that soft hum turned to an abrupt buzz, almost like a warning blazing through my flesh. Julius's head lifted just before a bang sounded behind us and I swung around in alarm, raising my blade defensively.

A haggard vampire stood beyond the window with his forehead pressed to the pane. He wore a fine suit, even though the rest of him looked filthy. My gut clenched as he opened his mouth and drool slid down the glass as he mouthed a word that looked like 'blood'.

"Rotter," I hissed.

Julius pulled Menace from its sheath which he'd strapped to his hip, his eyes narrowing.

"Stay here," he breathed, and I frowned, my pulse thumping beneath my skin.

The moment Julius reached the door, the vampire darted toward him, his eyes wild with hunger.

"Blood – thweet nectar – the godth have ansthered my prayers!" he cried with a pronounced lisp to his tone.

Julius shoved him back and he hit the floor, skidding out across the corridor from the force the slayer had used.

The vampire scrambled up and I hurried toward Julius, eying the vampire's open mouth in surprise. He had no fangs, his gums swollen and bloody where they'd once been as if his body couldn't heal the wounds.

The rotter's eyes turned between us, desperate and starving, looking so despairing that I almost felt sorry for him. But then he rolled to his knees and sped toward us like an animal, his tongue lolling as he closed in. Julius kicked him squarely in the face, but the vampire hung on through sheer desperation, sucking on the toe of his boot and clinging

62

to his leg.

I grimaced, backing up as Julius shook him off and pointed Menace at his heart.

The vampire lifted his head, drool sliding down his chin as a bitter acceptance filled him. "End it then. Kill me. Thith life ith not worth living without blood." He broke a sob, pressing his chest to the sword.

Pity sped through me, but Julius stabbed his sword forward and cleaved the vampire apart, sending dust pluming out around his feet.

"Julius," I gasped. "What the hell happened to him?"

"Banishment," he said darkly, his upper lip curling back. "I've seen it once before. It seems vampires who break certain laws are de-fanged and cast out of the city."

I took a shaky breath. This was what Fabian had wanted for Wolfe. This would be his punishment. And in a way, it seemed almost worse than death. With no blood to feed on out in the ruins, he would surely starve into insanity.

Nightmare cooled in my palm, seeming content after the vampire's demise, but I felt unsettled more than anything.

"Come, let's gather supplies and head back to the others. It's fucking freezing and I want to be sleeping by a warm fire before midday." Julius's tone was light as if he hadn't just cut a man in two.

Vampire, I corrected internally. Shit, I was in trouble if I started pitying them. But he'd been so hopeless, so emaciated.

I battled away the thoughts, focusing on the task at hand. The vampire had no doubt deserved his fate, his past almost certainly dirtied with the blood of humans just as all of their kind were. I needed to get supplies and head back to my sister with an offering of warm clothes and as much food as I could carry. One dead vampire was *not* going to distract me from that. Callie was relying on me, and as I remembered how lost she'd looked when I'd left, my heart hardened. Survival was what mattered now.

CALLIE

CHAPTER SIX

The sun rose higher in the sky behind the clouds but it did nothing to raise the temperature. I clutched my arms around my knees and tried to stop my teeth from chattering as yet another freezing wind threw ice-cold sleet over me. I huddled on the balcony, against the wall with my head down as I shivered, the anger I felt fading into a dark and furious thing which grew more solid within my chest with every passing moment.

I was no stranger to the cold. Back in the Realm, the winters had always been harsh and we'd never been able to warm the entire apartment. We'd spent more nights than I could count huddled together in the front room before the meagre heater, using our combined body heat to ease our suffering. Dad had always taken the spot furthest from the warmth while Montana and I rotated between spending the night closest to the heater or sandwiched in the centre. I'd always preferred being squashed in the middle, though it had often led to waking with a crick in my neck. It meant I got to spend the night curled between the two people I loved most in the world. What I wouldn't have given to feel my dad's arms wrapping around me now.

Though I'd spent my fair share of time combating the harsh winters in the Realm, I knew I'd never experienced anything like this. If it wasn't for my slayer gifts lending me strength and some resistance to the elements, I was fairly certain I would have succumbed to them already.

"Callie?" Montana's voice sounded as if it were far away, and I blinked the freezing water from my lashes as I looked towards the door which led into the building.

"Monty?" I called in return but the wind stole my voice, faint as it was while weakness clung to my limbs.

My teeth clashed together uncontrollably and I spotted her stepping through the doorway, her eyes widening in shock as she noticed me huddled by the railings.

"What the hell are you doing out here?" she gasped as she ran towards me, raising an arm to shield her face from the hammering rain. She caught my hand and dragged me to my feet though I stumbled a little with the numbness in my limbs. "Come inside!"

Her wedding dress was gone and she'd replaced it with warm, practical clothes which made my heart ache with longing, though some part of me doubted anything would ever be able to heal me of this bone-deep feeling of cold.

"I c-can't," I stuttered.

I couldn't feel my feet and I swayed unsteadily in the three inch heels. I wanted to rip them off but I equally needed the small measure of protection they offered my feet from the rain.

"What are you talking about? Come inside before you catch your damn death out here." Montana frowned at me and yanked on my arm, trying to get me moving but my heels dug in despite how much I wanted to go with her, the bond of Magnar's words leashing me in place despite every effort I'd made to refuse them.

Montana's dark hair was quickly becoming drenched and her fresh clothes were saturated with raindrops already.

"M-Magnar made me st-stay here." I shivered harder as her face scrunched in confusion. I could tell she had no idea what I was trying to say and I didn't know how I was supposed to put it into words when my lips were numb and I could barely form a coherent sentence. "I c-can't follow h-him and he went in-inside."

Her features transformed from confused to furious in half a second as she suddenly realised what I was telling her. I'd explained his hold over me when I'd told her about taking the vow but this was the first time she was seeing how far that power extended, and I could see comprehension building in her gaze.

"I'll kill him," she growled. "Come on, there has to be a way around this. You must be able to move if that's what it takes to save your damn life."

I shook my head hopelessly, my own anger a quiet thing in the face of the unending cold. "He has t-to release me."

"He's not here," Montana ground out, her chestnut eyes bright with fury while she tried to figure out what to do. The rain was soaking her through and I could tell she was fighting the urge to start shivering herself. "He went to scout for Familiars."

My heart sank as I realised I wasn't going to be released from his command any time soon. My fingertips were already blue and I was so cold that it was painful. I doubted I could withstand this cold for much longer, but Magnar could easily be gone for hours.

Montana looked around helplessly as though she thought she might be able to find something to shelter me on the exposed balcony but it was no good. There was nothing around us except cold concrete and stacked rubble.

"G-go back inside," I urged.

There was no point in both of us being stuck out here and she didn't have any gifts to help her resist the elements. I might not have been able to do anything to help myself, but I wasn't going to watch her suffer for my choices too. I was the one who had made the damn vow. It was my own pig-headed fault that I was in this mess. Not hers.

"I'm not leaving you." She frowned as if she was concentrating on something then her eyes lit with an idea. "He said not to follow him, right? Well maybe you can follow *me* instead?"

I opened my mouth to protest but something told me she might actually be on to something. She smiled encouragingly and started tugging me back towards the door. I took a step after her and nothing stopped me, the power of the gods releasing me as if it had never been there at all. Relief flooded me as I stumbled after her through the door and finally escaped the unending downpour.

As soon as I was out of the pounding rain, I released a shuddering breath. Montana kept going, leading me through the rotting building until we made it to the fire Magnar had lit.

I groaned as I held my hands above it and the heat of the flames washed over me. The cold had sunk all the way down to my core and I was shivering so violently that I couldn't do anything more than stand there and relish the burn of the flames.

"I'm so sorry, Callie." Montana chewed her lip and concern filled her eyes. "Magnar found us a while ago and said he was going to scout for Familiars, he seemed like he was angry about something. I guessed maybe you'd had a row and that was why you weren't with him. If I'd known that he'd done that to you-"

"It's alright, Monty. H-how could you have known?" I managed to kick the shoes off of my feet but I still couldn't feel my toes. I'd gone beyond being angry at the situation and had fallen into a desperate kind of acceptance, my hurt and rage over what Magnar had done to me sinking down into a knot which tightened itself around my heart and took root there.

"Come on, there's no way you'll warm up with that dress on." Montana moved behind me and started unfastening the saturated gown. Her anger permeated the air around us but she was holding it in check in favour of helping me.

I tried to stop my fingers from trembling as I held them as close to the flames as I could manage without actually touching the fire.

"Julius hasn't brought the rest of the supplies up yet but I'll go and find him, get you something warm to put on-"

My heart lurched at the idea of that, the possibility that Magnar might return here before her and I would be forced to face him alone. Normally I'd want the opportunity to rip into him for myself, hell I'd even be aching to do so but something about what he'd just done to me had ripped the fire clean out of my gut. It wasn't the argument or the way he had looked at me that had sucker punched me – it was the humiliation of being bound like a dog to his will. Of being left out there to freeze like I meant nothing at all to him and my wellbeing was of no concern to him at all.

"No," I said quickly, swallowing at the flash of surprise and then pity which danced through my sister's eyes. "Could you just stay with me... for a bit, please?" Now that I was out of the rain, I would dry out soon enough with or without fresh clothes and despite how tempting the thought of wearing something warm was, I just needed the comfort provided by her company. We'd been apart for far too long already.

The wedding dress fell to my feet with a wet splat and I shuffled away from it before sinking down next to the fire. Montana scooped it back up and wrung the excess water out of it before draping it over a battered desk close to the heat. The underwear I was left in was wet too but I kept it on, not needing to add my nudity to the list of things which were utterly mortifying about this entire situation.

Montana tossed a wooden chair onto the fire to stoke the flames then lowered herself down beside me, taking my hand between hers and trying to rub some warmth back into it.

"When you told me he could control you, I had no idea it would be so... literal," she said in a low voice, her anger like cold steel. "What the hell was he thinking leaving you out there like that? Even if we ignore the storm; there could be Familiars hunting us. You could have been seen. Why would he think-"

"Do you mind if we don't talk about it?" I asked quietly.

"I didn't mean to go on about it. It's just so fucked up."

"I just feel so..." I shrugged, unable to come up with the right word. Helpless? Powerless? Used? "I'm worried that with so many things controlling me, I'm going to end up losing who I am," I breathed.

I drew my knees up to my chest and placed my chin on top of them. I hated to admit how close I felt to breaking, but I was really beginning to wonder how much more I could take. Ever since Dad had died, I felt like I'd slowly been losing control over my own fate. It was like the closer I got to freedom, the more of my own will I had to sacrifice.

Montana opened her mouth to respond but her attention was snagged by Julius and Magnar returning instead.

I kept my eyes low, staring at the flames so I didn't have to look at him. A sharp pain tugged at my chest which had nothing to do with the cold, and though my usual reaction would have been to rage and scream and probably try to punch his fucking arrogant face, I just…didn't have it in me.

How could he have done that to me? Was I fool to believe he cared about me at all? How could I tally up his supposed feelings for me with someone who could be so fucking cruel?

"Did I miss the invite to go dancing in the rain or something?" Julius asked with a laugh as he moved closer to me and noticed my missing dress and dripping hair.

I tightened my grip on my knees; the scraps of material Clarice Belvedere had forced me to wear beneath my wedding dress were transparent and I was already humiliated enough without needing to add exposing any more of my body to the mix.

Montana got to her feet and rounded on Magnar. "What the fuck is wrong with you?" she yelled. "It's freezing out there! She could have died!"

I glanced up as his gaze slid to me, but I dropped my eyes again as tears prickled the backs of them. I scrunched my toes up and wished the ground would swallow me so the two of them would stop staring. Shame and hurt warred within me and I couldn't help but feel utterly pathetic. I should have been the one yelling at him, but where vicious words would normally have come so easily to my tongue, all I could taste in their place was shame.

Julius tilted his head in confusion and stepped between Montana and his brother before she could punch him.

"What are you talking about, damsel?" he asked.

"Ask *him*," she spat, pointing over Julius's shoulder at Magnar whose eyes still hadn't left me. "He made her stay out on that balcony in the rain. I only just found her; she'll be lucky to keep all of her fingers!"

I clenched my hands into fists, relieved that they did as commanded so I could be sure she was wrong about the chances of me losing any of them.

"What?" Magnar's brow furrowed with confusion and he tried to move towards me but Montana stepped into his path, practically spitting venom.

"You stay the hell away from her," she growled and despite her being a fraction of his size, she seemed utterly formidable in that moment. I doubted even the great Magnar Elioson could have forced his way past her.

Julius caught my sister's arm to try and restrain her, but her glare swung onto him, and his brows rose in surprise at her fury. I could still feel Magnar's eyes on me, but I kept my head low, not wanting him to see the pain he'd caused and feeling like a coward for hiding from his gaze. I'd never backed down from him before but I felt like a whipped creature, afraid to risk testing him again.

"I still don't understand what's supposed to have happened," Julius said, looking between everyone as he hunted for his answer.

"*He* left Callie out on that balcony and told her not to follow him when he went inside. She's been out there for hours," Montana hissed.

Magnar sucked in a breath and Julius cursed as the reality of what had happened dawned on them.

"I didn't mean..." Magnar tried to move closer to me again, and I huddled in on myself, wishing he wouldn't.

I'd opened up to him about everything that had happened to me, I'd laid it all on the line in an attempt to show him everything so he would know how much he meant to me. And in return, he'd bound me to his will and punished me for something I had no control over.

"Callie?" he asked.

There was raw emotion in his voice, but I didn't raise my head. I just wanted him to go away.

"You bloody fool." Julius released my sister and caught Magnar's arm instead, forcing him back a step. "I need to have a word with you, brother. *Now.*"

I peeked between my lashes and watched as Julius shoved Magnar towards a door on the other side of the room. Magnar hesitated, seeming torn between following his brother's instructions and continuing his advance on me.

Julius kept shoving and Magnar finally gave in, stomping away from us and heading through the door.

I let out a breath of relief and Montana turned to face me with pity in her eyes which honestly only made me feel more pathetic.

"Here," Julius said, turning back to us instead of following his brother. He dropped a heavy pack from his shoulder and pulled it open, taking out a thick blanket and draping it around me.

"Thank you," I breathed as I drew the blanket tighter against my skin. I was still shivering. It felt like the cold had made roots in my bones and would never leave.

"It's nothing." He shrugged as if my gratitude made him uncomfortable. "There's clean clothes and food in the pack too."

Montana pursed her lips as he passed her by and I could tell she wasn't impressed by his attempt to make peace.

"He'd better be grovelling by the time he comes back in here," she growled, and Julius gave her a nod before disappearing after Magnar into the other room.

As soon as he was gone, she moved to the pack and started rummaging through the things they'd found.

"You'll feel better once you've eaten," she said and I wasn't sure which one of us she was trying to convince.

I started chewing on my thumbnail as I waited for her to finish her investigation of the pack. It was a habit I'd given up as a child, but I always found myself doing it when I felt helpless.

Montana pulled out a fresh black shirt, some thick socks, new underwear and a pair of grey sweatpants then passed them to me. I quickly stripped out of the ridiculous underwear and tossed it onto the fire, feeling a surge of satisfaction that it had never served its purpose. Then I pulled the new clothes on and felt a little better as the cold finally began to leave my bones. It was immeasurably good to have dry fabric against my skin.

I pulled my hair over my shoulder and wrang the water from it before twisting it into a braid. Magnar liked me wearing it loose, but I didn't feel at all inclined to satisfy his desires.

Montana started making us something to eat and I watched her, my mind falling blank.

I'd never been one for talking it out when I fell into a sullen mood so she stayed silent while she worked. I hoped she knew I treasured her companionship while I attempted to figure out my roiling emotions. Montana knew me better than anyone in this world, and we'd survived rougher days than this together. If there was anyone who knew what I needed right now, it was her.

The wind found its way into the building for a moment and the door which Julius and Magnar had headed through blew open a crack. With the aid of my gifts, their voices floated to me and I sat up a little straighter as I heard my name.

"Callie knows I would never hurt her-" Magnar rumbled angrily.

"No. She doesn't," Julius snapped in response. "Can't you remember how it felt when Father bound you to his will during your training? I recall you plotting to slip rotten mushrooms into his meal so that he might spend a few nights puking and give you some respite. At least until you realised he'd just force you to clean his vomit."

"Yes, I hated having my will stolen from me. And because of that I managed to break his control over me in less than a year!" Magnar retorted.

"You can't just presume everyone is like *you*," Julius replied in exasperation. "You've been telling me how much she means to you and yet your actions tell a different story. You could have killed her today, Magnar. Do you get that? And all because you're angry with her for something she can't control!"

"Fabian Belvedere still draws breath because of that mark on her hand. I allowed him to *live* for her sake. I couldn't give her greater proof of my devotion-"

"And yet when she tried to explain the reason why she had to ask that of you, you abused the trust she put in you when you became her mentor," Julius countered.

"You know I never meant for her to stay out in that storm," Magnar snarled. "Don't you think I feel bad enough for that mistake?"

"That's the problem; you shouldn't have made a mistake like that. You never should have been her mentor. Your feelings for her make it too complicated. Do you ever remember Father putting you in danger with one of his commands? Or Mother endangering me? You've only been bonded to her for a matter of days and you've managed to do it *twice*."

"I know, but…" Magnar's voice dipped, and I missed what he said next.

"Well if that's the case, then you need to fix this. She needs you now and I honestly don't know how you're going to unravel this mess."

Silence descended and I glanced at Montana, wondering if she'd heard them too. She'd filled a metal cooking pot with something and was busy stirring it, showing no sign of having overheard the brothers.

"Am I going to regret letting you cook for me?" I teased as she noticed my attention.

Her attempts at cooking for us in the Realm had often ended up with something tasting a little too much like charcoal. Dad used to say she could have burnt water given half a chance.

"You know that's not fair," she protested, pointing a sticky spoon at me. "It was just that one casserole and the omelette-"

"And the soup *and* the pasta. And I'm pretty sure you gave me an apple once which tasted decidedly smoky-"

"Shut up!" She flicked the spoon at me, and I laughed as some of her culinary creation splattered my sleeve. I scooped it onto my finger and licked it off.

"Hmmm," I said, considering the flavour of the glob of oatmeal. "Tastes... sooty."

"It does *not*." She laughed again as she started spooning the oatmeal into bowls and I couldn't help but grin at her.

"I missed this," I said as she passed me an overflowing bowl with a spoon sticking out of the top of it. "I mean, I missed the little stuff like this. Who'd have thought I'd crave sleeping on the floor, or pretending I couldn't hear Dad waking us in the mornings...or badly cooked meals."

I released a heavy sigh as the loss of our father pressed close again, but I gave her a playful smile as I lifted a spoonful to my mouth. The darkness couldn't have us right now; I just wanted to bathe in the joy of having her back, not wallow in the sadness of our grief.

I had to resist the urge to moan in pleasure as the oatmeal slid down to my stomach. I'd refused the food the Belvederes had offered during my stay with them and I hadn't eaten in nearly two days.

"I miss him too," Montana said quietly. "I still can't believe... I mean, I saw it, but it just doesn't feel real. How can he just be gone?"

I swallowed a thick lump in my throat and reached out to take her hand as the tears I'd been fighting for days overflowed. She shuffled closer to me and pulled me into her arms as her grief met with mine and we cried for the man who'd raised us.

I didn't want to let go of her ever again.

All of it, from the moment she'd been taken from me, every single thing I'd done right down to the vow I'd made had been for this. And here she was, back with me where she belonged. I didn't know how we would move on from here, where we would go or what it would take for us to build a new life, but I did know that I was never going to let us be parted again.

Julius cleared his throat loudly as he and Magnar returned to the room. I pulled away from Montana, hastily wiping the tears from my cheeks.

I glanced at Magnar for half a heartbeat as he hesitated by the door then dropped my eyes to my meal and focused my attention on that.

"I think these two need to clear the air, damsel," Julius said gently and Montana bristled beside me.

"I'm not going anywhere," she said, all mama bear for her shipwreck of a sister.

"It's fine, Monty," I breathed before she could object any further.

Our situation was what it was – I was bound to Magnar, at least for the foreseeable future. And as much as I didn't want to face him, I knew we had to move on from this. We were stuck out here, hiding from the Belvederes without a plan for moving forward. We had to be able to work together at the very least, and that didn't seem likely to happen all the time I couldn't even bring myself to look at him.

"Are you sure?" she asked, her gaze filled with concern.

I nodded, wishing I didn't feel like I was lying about that.

Montana narrowed her eyes as she got to her feet, passing a bowl of oatmeal to Julius and keeping the last one for herself.

"Oh, I forgot to dish out a bowl for you. But maybe you can command my sister to do it for you if you're hungry," she said bitterly, scowling at Magnar as she walked past him.

Julius chuckled as he lifted a heaped spoonful to his mouth and followed her from the room. Magnar watched them leave and waited several long seconds before he approached me.

I kept my eyes on my food as I felt his gaze boring into me, but I still couldn't bring myself to look at him.

"I'm sorry, Callie," he said eventually, lowering himself down to sit beside me. He didn't sit as close as usual and the space between us opened up endlessly.

I lifted a shoulder in response to his apology. It didn't really make any difference to what he'd done to me or how it had made me feel.

"I only wanted some time to clear my head," he went on. "I never intended for you to be stuck out there-"

"It's fine," I replied, even though it was obvious that it wasn't.

He reached out to me and for the first time since Idun had forbidden us from touching, I was glad of her rules. I shifted away from him as he fought against her control and his hand fell to the floor between us helplessly.

"Please let me make this right," he breathed.

"I said it's fine. It's like you told me before; this is all my fault anyway. I did it to myself."

"I shouldn't have said that to you," he rumbled, but he had said it and he'd meant it too.

I shrugged again.

"I should be used to people stealing my will from me by now anyway. If it's not you, it's Idun... or Fabian. Between the lot of you, I'll lose who I am entirely at this rate," I murmured.

"Don't compare me to them," he replied, his tone rough with accusation. "I'd never force you to be anyone but yourself. I'd never intentionally make you do anything that would harm you-"

"So long as it's unintentional, that's alright then," I muttered.

"I didn't say it was alright."

I nodded vaguely, staring into the depths of my oatmeal which had lost its appeal despite my growling stomach.

"Please will you look at me, Callie?" he begged.

I pursed my lips and dropped the spoon into my bowl before forcing myself to turn towards him. It took another wrench of effort to raise my gaze to meet his and his eyes swam with discomfort as he stared back at me.

"Why are you looking at me like you're afraid of me?" he asked and I could see the pain it caused him.

I wanted to dismiss his question but he caught me in his gaze and I took a deep breath as I forced myself to be honest with him.

"Because I am," I admitted, though it galled me to say it but I was helpless in this bond with him. He had all the power, all of the advantage and I simply had to trust him with it. But he'd just proven that I couldn't do that. "You can hurt me so easily. And you don't even notice you're doing it. You said it yourself – it was a mistake. So maybe you didn't want to leave me out there in the rain, but the fact remains that you did. And that you could order me back out there right now and I'd be powerless to resist. This bond, whether you wanted it or not, has given you complete control over me. You've stolen my freedom whether you asked to take possession of it or not."

Pain filled his expression as my words hit him and he tried to reach for me again. "I would never want to hurt you."

"Just because you don't want to, doesn't mean you don't do it." I eyed his hand as it hung in the space between us and shifted back slightly.

His face crumpled as he dropped his arm again, pulling it back to lay in his lap. My heart throbbed as I could see what my words were doing to him, but I couldn't keep feeling this way and he had to know it.

"I don't know how to do this," he said quietly. "I've never... I was betrothed to Valentina when I was sixteen. I've bedded other women but she always saw them off before I got any chance to have anything else with them. And I've never cared about any of them like I care about you. Please don't tell me I've ruined us before we even got started."

I swallowed thickly at those words and gazed into his eyes. I wanted to fall into their golden depths. To drink in the strength and power I saw there. But it wasn't my own. My heart and soul felt shredded between the different vows which bound me. I was a slayer and a vampire's wife. And somewhere in the middle of that, I was starting to lose who *I* really was.

"I just need some space," I breathed. "I need to figure out what's happening to me. And I can't do that with so many rules and commands screwing with my head. How am I supposed to keep hold of who I am when you can force me to do anything you want just because you feel like it or lose your temper? Or when thoughts of my enemy keep pushing through my mind as if he's something else entirely?"

Magnar's jaw pulsed at the reminder of what I was being forced to feel for Fabian now too, but he bit back the words which had come to his tongue.

"If that's what you need, I'll give it to you," he replied carefully like he was afraid saying the wrong thing might break whatever was left between us. The problem was, I didn't know if there was anything now. "I only want to help you."

"I need to deal with this on my own." I looked down at the wedding ring on my finger and took a deep breath as I slid it off. Placing it on the floor, I gritted my teeth against the aching loss I felt and forced myself to withdraw my hand, leaving it there.

Magnar watched me in silence as I stared at the silver wedding band, fighting against the desire to put it back on. The harder I pushed against the feelings that I knew weren't my own, the easier it became, until eventually, I dragged my eyes away from the ring altogether.

It wasn't going to be simple but I was determined to find a way to regain control of my own fate. And if Idun didn't like it, then she would find out what it was like to be my enemy.

ERIK

CHAPTER SEVEN

1000 YEARS AGO

We swam for miles until the sea stretched in every direction toward a dark, boundless horizon. We never grew tired, never faltered, never stopped

"Andvari spoke of another land," Miles called above the lapping waves, his golden head bobbing close by.

"Do you think he'll guide us?" Clarice asked, but none of us answered.

I didn't like the idea of fulfilling Andvari's plans for us. I suspected there was more to his promises than he let on. But the others drank in the idea of us taking power somewhere else in the world as if we were no longer cursed, but blessed.

Leaving my homeland behind pained me, but the gods had strengthened the slayers beyond our wildest imaginings. They matched us now, and they had come close to killing more than one of us. My fear had been stoked and protectiveness had taken over. I would not see my family murdered, so running from them was our only choice. And every mile we put between us and them brought a calmness to my soul that I hoped meant we had made the right choice.

Would they follow us now? Even if they did, they would surely never find us. We had decided to swim as far as we could, making our way into an ocean that led to the unknown.

As days merged to weeks, time became as eternal as the maddening years I'd spent in solitude. When the sun blazed, we were forced to shelter beneath the waves, to swim deep in the infinite blue. It was a cold, barren place where little life stirred around us, the creatures of the deep keeping away as if they sensed a plague passing through their waters. Within the quiet, suffocating silence of the ocean, my mind almost cracked time and again.

Sometimes, I saw Andvari watching us beneath the waves. Other times, he whispered his encouragement or pointed out the way by creating a glowing path through the sea, urging us on when we were at our most desperate.

One day, impossibly, land grew visible in the distance, and hope found me once more, just when I'd thought all was lost. We must have been at sea for months and despite my immortal body never failing me, I still grew anxious to have my feet on dry land. My hunger was keen, but I had endured two hundred years without blood and nothing compared to the pain of that. The rest of my family would be on the verge of losing themselves to the thirst.

We doubled our efforts as a shore came into view and Clarice cried out her joy as we finally made it to a sandy beach. Dragging our drenched bodies from the sea, we strode onto our new land. I drank in the sight of the trees stretching away into the distance, and the twitter of birds sounded as dawn painted the cloudy sky in pastel pinks and copper tones. The sun crept above the horizon at our backs, promising to weaken us further as its rays slipped into the sky.

Fabian rubbed his throat, looking haggard, his hair a mess of clumping strands and his clothes half torn from his body by the harshest of waves we'd met out in the ocean. "What if there're no humans here? How are we going to eat?"

I perched on a piece of driftwood in nothing but a sodden pair of trousers, wondering if he was right and we'd just isolated ourselves from blood for the foreseeable future. It would be ironic for me to end up starving again after I'd decided to try and make this hellish life work.

"There will be humans," Miles sighed, running a hand into his wet hair.

We'd had this argument before, out in the water when our hope had been waning, and we had decided to keep going anyway. Andvari hadn't answered our questions, only urging us onward. If he wanted us here, I was sure it was for a reason more than starvation.

A gull hopped closer to us on the shore, tilting its head as it observed us.

"Just what we need," Fabian growled, stalking toward it and slashing his nails across his wrist. In a flash of movement, he caught the bird by the neck, prising its beak open and allowing the blood to flow inside.

The gull squawked as Fabian snapped its neck, but as he released it, the animal stretched its wings and rose into its undead life.

Fabian pointed to the sky. "Find humans. Summon me when you've located them."

The bird took flight and I angled my head toward the brightening sky, my body beginning to weaken as the sunlight licked my skin. Andvari had sometimes given us a reprieve from the sun during our journey, drawing the clouds thick and low for us, so we hadn't always had to swim under the waves during the daytime. But I wondered how far his kindness would extend now that we'd arrived.

We moved between a line of palm trees, sitting in the shade on the beach side by side, waiting in silence for the gull to bring news to Fabian of the humans. After I'd killed so many slayers in that monstrous battle, I knew there was little point in trying to avoid blood from now on. But I had come to a new decision along our journey here. I wouldn't kill again unless I had to. If there was any chance my soul could still be saved, I had to try and live a better life. One with as little death in it as I could manage.

Fabian stood abruptly, his laughter filling the air as he saw something through the eyes of his newly-made Familiar. "A village is close! Come, let us go to them and sate our thirst."

"Fabian," I growled, rising too. "I will not attend another slaughter."

"We don't have to," Clarice said keenly, pushing her damp locks from her neck and smiling at me. "We can pretend we are gods, have them worship us. They will give us blood willingly."

"It always worked for me," Miles said in agreement.

I didn't like the idea of giving in to the ways of my brothers and sister, but I didn't have much of a choice now. And anything was better than mercilessly killing the innocent. So all-powerful gods, we would be.

MONTANA

CHAPTER EIGHT

Julius and I stood in the dark room downstairs and goosebumps rose on my skin as the icy wind blew in through a hole in the wall. I might have been freezing my tits off, but Callie needed time to figure things out with Magnar and I had to respect that. Even if I was still pissed at him for what he'd done to her. *Maybe* he hadn't meant to. And if she could find a way to forgive him, then I guessed I'd have to as well. But if he pulled one more move like that on her, I wouldn't be letting it lie.

"So *Monty*," Julius said with a wide, mocking grin, spooning oatmeal into his mouth.

I scowled. "I already dislike one of you slayers, let's not make it two."

"But Callie calls you Monty."

"She's allowed to," I said, folding my arms. "Only her."

He smiled even bigger as he continued to eat, and I knew all too well that Julius wasn't going to forget that name anytime soon.

Moon Child, a whisper filled my ear and set my pulse racing. But it wasn't Nightmare, it was something...else.

An energy thrummed through the room, filling the air with an electric charge. The hairs on my arms rose to attention and a sliver of ice drove itself into my chest.

Julius stopped eating, his face growing hard as he surveyed the room.

"Show yourself," he hissed.

"Who's here?" I whispered, stepping closer to him and touching Nightmare's hilt where it was strapped to my hip.

Julius didn't answer but drew Menace and adjusted his stance.

This way, Moon Child.

"Do you hear that?" I asked and Julius nodded in confirmation.

An icy stream slid into my veins, dripping through my muscles and taking control of my movements. I gasped, fear resounding through me as my legs walked me through a doorway to my left.

"Julius," I gasped, unable to turn back, or to unsheathe Nightmare, or do anything at all to stop this.

The room I arrived in was exposed to the elements, the walls crumbled low on two sides and debris scattered around the place. One of the walls that remained held an oval mirror, the ornate frame embellished with silver flowers, looking out of place in this desolate house.

My breathing slowed as the presence continued to control me, drawing me toward the mirror as if I was one end of a magnet and it was the other.

Only half of the roof was still intact here, a hole in the floorboards above me letting rain gush over it like a waterfall. As I stepped through the run-off toward the mirror, sounds beyond the rain became suddenly muffled.

I heard Julius calling my name, but it was so far away, like a distant echo from a whole other world. I couldn't turn to look for him as I closed in on the mirror where my reflection gazed back at me. Except it wasn't me.

I wore a silver crown on my head and a blood-red gown flowed around my body like liquid. My skin was deathly pale, my eyes wide and alluring and my lips deepest crimson. I blinked, but the reflection didn't. She smiled like she knew me, tilting her head to one side and beckoning me closer. When she spoke, she did so in my voice and yet it wasn't mine too. It was lilting and sweet, as if it was designed to keep me hanging on every word.

"Is this what you wanted to know?"

I parted my mouth to speak, but no words came out. I wasn't sure if it was fear or some other force stopping me from answering, only that my tongue wouldn't wrap around a response.

My reflection lifted a hand, running a finger across her lips, revealing the reason they were so red. Blood.

My stomach coiled into a tight knot of horror.

As she laughed, the blood poured from her mouth, revealing glinting fangs within her mouth. *My* mouth. I shook my head in terror, stumbling back and suddenly a weight crashed into me from behind.

"Montana!" Julius yelled, dragging me from my trance. My heart stuttered back to life as I absorbed his anxious expression, and I realised I could control myself again.

"Slayer," hissed a vile, acidic voice, cutting through the air like a knife. *Andvari.*

I grabbed Julius's shirt, meaning to push him back the way he'd come, fearing what the god might do to him. But he remained sturdily in front of me, refusing to budge as he turned to face the mirror.

Our true reflection was cast back at us. Julius and I looked somehow similar, as if we were cut from the same cloth. Though our appearances were nothing alike, it was the way we stood, the way our eyes flashed. Something about us simply screamed slayer, and more than that…it looked right. Arm in arm, warrior beside warrior. We had been made to stand like this together.

Andvari's true form appeared behind us in the reflection and I inhaled in shock as he pushed between us, feeling cold hands on my skin.

I whirled, turning to find him there, his eyes two white discs and his too-perfect face a thing of pure sin. Julius raised Menace with a snarl but Andvari wafted a hand, knocking him back into the wall and pinning him in place. The sword trembled violently in Julius's grip as if it was furious to see Andvari, and his lips sealed shut, keeping him subdued despite how hard he fought to get free.

"It looks like you might enjoy blood upon your lips, little mortal." Andvari rounded on me with a wicked smile, his eyes growing darker until two earthy pupils grew within them.

My breath stalled as I gazed up at him, sure he was more forbidding now than the last time I'd encountered him. Like this creature fed on chaos, growing stronger in the thick of it, and we were all feeding it to him in large doses.

"*Never*," I hissed, finally finding my voice and it struck at him like a whip.

He tapped me under the chin and his touch sent flames burrowing into my core. I stood my ground, trying not to show weakness even though I was sure this god could destroy me with a single thought if he decided to.

"Erik Larsen would be so very pleased," he purred, and my throat thickened at Erik's name. "But however will you say goodbye to your sweet sister?"

"I wouldn't," I snarled, despising the mere suggestion of it.

Andvari's eyes wheeled to Julius and he clawed his hand through the air. Julius bit down on a cry as his shirt was torn to ribbons, deep nail marks slashing down his chest. "She is a slayer...like this one." Andvari spat the word, clearly despising their kind.

"And what's wrong with that?" I demanded.

"What is right with them?" he asked casually, his vicious demeanour abruptly abandoned. He stalked toward me and I backed up to the mirror, finding myself trapped by a wrathful god.

As he walked, his form changed, morphing entirely until it was Erik who stood before me. My heart cracked at the sight of his angular face and deep eyes, the all-too-familiar tug in my heart urging me towards him.

My thoughts seemed to speed away as fast as I could hold onto them. One moment I knew what was happening, the next I was lost in nothing but a dream world where only me and Erik existed.

"My love," Erik whispered, reaching out to hold my waist, pulling me closer.

A meadow sprawled out around us and the darkness vanished entirely, leaving me in a daze with the man I had been craving since the moment we'd parted. *No, not a man...*

"Erik?" Something was screaming on the verge of my senses, but I couldn't focus long enough to figure out what it was.

"Yes, it's me. Come closer, Montana." He dipped his head low and the sun shone off of his pale skin. Birdsong filled the air and the scent of a thousand flowers sailed under my nose, so sweet, so heady.

I blinked heavily.

This wasn't right.

The sun...how is Erik in the sun?

He leaned in to kiss me and my thoughts sharply realigned, reality crashing back in on me. I shoved him hard, forcing him away and the ruins flooded back into view, the shadows sweeping aside any lingering lie of the sun.

Andvari stood before me again, cackling a laugh. "You must forgive an ancient being for having his fun."

"What do you want?" I snarled, retreating so my spine pressed against the icy pane of the mirror.

I looked to Julius as he struggled against the control Andvari held over him, considering calling out to Magnar and Callie. But even if Andvari allowed them near us, it would only have put them in danger too. The god was in control here, and there was little I could do until he decided he was done with his game.

"I want a slayer's head." Andvari's smile stretched into something sinister, his gaze turning sharply toward Julius as he raised his hand.

I screamed in fright, diving on his arm, trying to wrench it away from Julius and protect him from the god's cruelty.

"No!" I begged, but if Andvari noticed me at all, he didn't show it. He was immovable, his body like stone given life, and my mortal strength could do nothing against it.

Julius gasped, then a line of blood formed on his neck circling around it in a neat slit.

Panic seized me, my mind latching onto the only thing that might help. I grabbed Nightmare from my hip and drove it towards Andvari's heart with all my might. But the god batted a hand and I was thrown away, slamming into the wall and smashing the mirror. I hit the floor in a shower of glass and pain lanced through my back.

Take heart, Moon Child, Nightmare urged, the warm hilt offering me courage.

I groaned as the cuts on my exposed skin flared and a shudder ran through me.

How was I going to save Julius when I couldn't do anything to stop Andvari?

Julius spat curses as the god approached him, the cut on his neck deepening with every stride Andvari took.

"Stop!" I cried. "What do you want? What will it take?!"

The blood abruptly stopped growing on Julius's neck and slowly receded altogether. Relief tangled with my veins as Julius sucked in a deep breath.

"Spiteful bitch," Andvari spat, but I didn't know who he was talking to.

The air shuddered and heat stretched over my skin like warm water, the sense of some new power crackling in the atmosphere. The world rippled before me and the running water on the roof turned to a thick, milky flow.

I gathered myself up from the floor, running to Julius's side, terrified of what was happening.

"Idun," Andvari snarled as the strange water parted and an ethereal woman appeared from within it. She ignored Andvari, moving toward Julius and placing a kiss on his cheek.

He released a noise somewhere between a whimper and a moan. "Idun?" he breathed.

"Yes, dear slayer. Here I am," she purred, her eyes flicking to me. She was too beautiful for words. Her hair was a golden sheet that seemed to move in an invisible wind around her lithe body, and she was clad in nothing but vines that coiled over her naked skin and somehow maintained her modesty.

Her bright eyes slid to Andvari. "You do not touch one of mine."

Andvari rolled back his upper lip, revealing serrated teeth that set my heart thumping. "The time is coming for penance. And the royals are not the only ones I seek it from."

"Do you mean *me*, Andvari?" Idun tittered, placing a long golden nail against her chest. "You wouldn't pick a fight with me on equal ground. Must we always play this game? I countered your vampires with slayers...but you have written a dark little secret into your prophecy haven't you? Another dagger in my side." She reached for me, taking my arm and moving me in front of her. Her touch was liquid heat, sending calm inching into every space in my body, quieting the rioting of my pulse. The feeling silenced any more words on my lips, and the urge to lean into her crept into every pore of my skin. This goddess was connected to me in a way I couldn't explain, her power written into the fibres of my flesh. And it seemed she might have come to save us.

She scraped my hair from my neck, pulling it over my shoulders as she presented me to Andvari.

"Warrior born and monster made," she snarled. "You would have one of my slayer-born turn into one of your monsters. I won't see it happen."

Andvari laughed darkly. "Then we shall spend the next thousand years at a stalemate. And the next, and the next. If you wish to see my curse unravelled, you will have to allow it."

My thoughts jarred with that knowledge, the truth painted so brutally upon his lips. And I saw everything starkly, knowing why he had shown me that mirage of myself. He was guiding me to that fate. A slayer turned vampire. The thought of it was so terrifying, so awful, I could hardly stand it.

Idun caressed my cheek with a long finger, and my fears shattered once more as her calm essence floated over me.

"Let's not pretend you haven't had a hand in messing up my prophecy just yesterday, Idun," Andvari accused, lifting a gnarled finger to point at her. "The mark of partnership was meant for Erik and *this* girl to ensure she was turned. That he would do as she asked when she knew the truth about the prophecy. But you made your own mark, didn't you? You bound her sister to another of mine. What strange game are you playing, Idun? Is it just for your amusement, or is it to taunt me?"

Idun moved around me like a summer breeze and I regained control of myself, stumbling back against Julius. He fought to free himself from the wall, but Andvari's power still held him in place.

"A little of both," Idun mused. "Love is the most powerful emotion in the world, Andvari. How many times will you forget that?" Her tinkling laughter crackled in my ears like rustling leaves. "Your bond between the vampire and this girl gave me an idea. I needed to keep my new slayer girl from loving someone who owes me a debt. And your little trick with these two made me realise I could have some fun whilst doing it."

"Well how foolish of you because your game resulted in Fabian's life being saved," Andvari taunted her.

Idun's face grew cold. "Clearly I underestimated the strength of Magnar's feelings for the girl. The fact that he would stay his hand against one of your monsters only proves how much harder I must work to keep him away from her. He will continue his chosen path and end the Revenants like he promised or I shall never give him the only thing he truly wants - love."

The cruelty of her words spiked rage in me. She was keeping my sister and Magnar apart for the sake of her vendetta against the vampires.

"Well I wish for blood to sate my rage, Idun. Step aside," Andvari demanded, pointing at Julius.

Fear sped through me, Idun's influence dropping away once more.

"He is not yours to kill. You stole what is mine so perhaps I shall steal from you in kind," Idun said, her ire making the earth rumble.

Andvari raised a hand as if to strike her, but a vine from Idun's dress whipped out and caught me by the waist, yanking me between them.

"I will rip her heart out and you shall never have your debt paid," Idun snarled, and terror snaked into my chest.

"Enough," Andvari hissed. "Have it your way for now, but if your games continue for too long I will strike against you personally."

Idun's laughter filled the air and thunder rumbled above us. "I would gladly accept that challenge."

Andvari shrugged his shoulders. "Then perhaps when we meet again, it shall be on a battleground."

In an instant, the two of them vanished and Julius stumbled forward, sword raised and muscles tensed.

He staggered to a halt where Idun had been standing, releasing a breath of frustration. Thankfully, his injuries were gone too, and I sagged against him, the weight of my reality sinking in.

"Do you think what Andvari said is true?" I whispered, fear pounding through me. Even if I had accepted that some of the vampires weren't evil, that didn't mean I ever wanted to become one of them. "If I become a vampire, will it really unravel the curse?"

I shuddered, burying my face in Julius's chest at the horrifying thought. I couldn't.

"I cannot be sure. We must never trust the gods," Julius growled, and a flame of hope flickered inside me as I peeked up at him, my fingers biting into the muscles of his arms.

"Should we tell the others what they said?" I breathed.

Julius's eyes darkened, his throat bobbing as he considered it.

"I fear they would not react well. They already know of Idun's wrath against them. And I think it would be best to hide the possibility that the prophecy intends for you to be one of those monsters. At least until we can figure out how to avoid it."

I nodded, biting back the lump of emotion in my throat. "I'm afraid, Julius…"

He drew me into his arms, gripping me tight. "I won't let you be made into a beast."

I nodded against his chest, breathing in the small moment of comfort. But I was sure the second I stepped away, fear would find me again and I'd be devoured by its sharp teeth.

CALLiE

CHAPTER NINE

I reached out and my hand swept over silky sheets, the material slipping through my fingers like a spill of oil. I frowned as I pushed myself upright, knowing this wasn't where I had fallen asleep.

I squinted around in confusion at the room I found myself in which was lit with a deep red light. I was sitting on a black four poster bed and all sorts of strange things were hanging from the walls. There were shackles and whips, gags and ropes.

What the fuck is this?

I glanced down at myself and found my clothes replaced with some kind of weird leather underwear complete with elbow-length gloves.

I was still wondering whose dream I was in as footsteps sounded beyond the door, making my pulse spike in alarm.

I gritted my teeth and used my power over the dream to replace my clothes with black leggings and a blue sweater, covering every inch of exposed flesh.

The door opened before I could think about getting out of the bed and Fabian stepped in. Horror clutched at me as I realised whose fantasy I'd stumbled into, the emotion quickly replaced by anger.

Fabian was wearing a pair of blue jeans slung low on his hips, but his chest was bare, his sculpted muscles drawing my attention for a moment before I forced myself to stop looking at them. His eyes lit with surprise and his mouth fell open as he drank in the sight of me, but he didn't say a word.

My mind spun as I tried to figure out how I'd done this. The only other people I'd dream walked with before had been right beside me in the real world. Had he found us in the ruins? But then how could he have been sleeping? No, he wasn't near my physical body yet I'd still managed to dream walk across the city and slip into the machinations of his mind.

"Callie. You look...different," Fabian said slowly, taking a step towards me.

I pushed myself out of the bed, feeling vulnerable in this strange place conjured by his mind. He closed in on me, and though I was fairly certain that nothing that happened to me in a dream could affect my real body, if there was a creature on this earth which might be able to bend the rules of that logic, then it would be a Belvedere.

I wished I had my blade. As soon as the thought crossed my mind, Fury materialised in my palm. The illusion didn't give off any of the energy the true blade had held though and the sight of it only made me miss it more.

"I shouldn't be here," I said as I tried to ignore the urge to stay. Those weren't my feelings. I knew it. And yet, as I looked at the monster before me, I couldn't completely stifle the desire to move closer instead of backing away.

I glanced around as if I might find a door or something which could lead me back out of his dream, but there was nothing. I had no idea how to control this new power and no way to get myself out. Not that I was entirely convinced I would have left even if I knew how to.

Fabian tilted his head and his eyes rounded in realisation.

"Valentina told me that some of your kind could walk between dreams. Is that what this is? Have you come to seek me out?" he asked, his eyes brightening with hope.

He began to close the distance between us and I backed up, holding Fury out to ward him off. But my traitorous heart was pounding to a rhythm that had nothing to do with fear and my gaze fell to his bare chest again for a moment before I snapped it back to his face.

"Not intentionally," I growled. "I don't know how to control all of my gifts yet."

"So your heart brought you here?" he asked, cocking his head as he inspected me.

He ignored the blade I held between us and moved so close that it was pressed to his throat.

I glared at him, or at least I thought I did but my mouth seemed to be hooking up at the corners as if we were playing some game.

"Not my heart. Just this curse that links me to you," I replied firmly.

Fabian caught my hand in his and pulled Fury from my grasp. I wanted to resist but I couldn't bring myself to. We both knew I wasn't going to hurt him anyway, and the thought made a part of me sick while another part sang with joy.

My breaths came quickly as he moved my hand so my palm was pressed against his chest.

"My heart has been trying to lead me back to you," he said, his voice rough with desire.

My gaze slid over his broad chest and I had to force myself not to move any closer to him.

"I can almost feel it stirring when I think of you. Like it wants to beat once more," Fabian went on.

His words were a sharp reminder of what he was and I gritted my teeth as I threw my strength into my arm, shoving him away from me.

"Stop it," I growled. "You have to know this isn't real. Whatever it is you think you feel for me wasn't there before the wedding. It's some trick Idun is playing on us."

"Why would my love for you be a trick? She has given me back something I thought I lost over a thousand years ago. I haven't known love like this before, but it fills every empty corner of my haunted soul. I didn't even realise how alone I had been until this gift was bestowed upon us. I know we're meant to be together-"

Heat rose in my blood at his words and I was struck with the strongest desire to press him back onto the bed and-

"Shut up! You don't even know me. How could you love me?" I moved to the wall and grabbed a black leather whip with long tassels hanging from it, brandishing it at him with a sneer on my face as I fought against the unwelcome feelings which had invaded my body.

"This isn't love, it's lust. And I have no interest in your perverted dreams." I slashed the whip across his chest then tossed it at his feet.

A frown gripped Fabian's features as red lines appeared on his skin before slowly fading away.

"You're right," he muttered, and I took a steadying breath as he finally seemed to accept what I was saying. "I wouldn't want to bring you here. You mean so much more to me than this."

"What?"

The red-lit room began to dissolve around us, the bed and assortment of sex toys disappearing as a faint breeze picked up.

I looked around, curious despite myself as a burbling stream appeared beside me. Tall trees sprouted from the ground, growing higher and higher until they towered overhead. In the distance, I could see a village, though the buildings were all wooden instead of the concrete jungle I was used to.

There was something utterly foreign about the landscape and I frowned as birdsong erupted around us and a cool wind tugged at my hair.

"Where are we?" I asked.

"This was my homeland. Across the great ocean. I lived here before I was cursed," he explained, his voice rough with emotion.

I turned to look at Fabian again and my breath caught in my throat. His appearance wasn't that of a monster anymore; his skin was flush with life and coloured by the sun. His beauty was diminished, but if anything, he seemed more attractive with his features more rugged and a faint scar lining his jaw. He wore fighting leathers similar to those Julius and Magnar favoured and a long sword was belted at his hip.

"You look like... like one of us. Like a slayer." I couldn't stop staring at him, at this version of him who was yet to be cursed. It was harder to think of him as a monster when he stood before me as a man, and that was dangerous in its own right.

Fabian gave me a faint smile. "No. Not a slayer. But we were all Vikings once."

I stepped towards him, utterly thrown off by seeing him this way. His hair was shaved on one side of his scalp and a tattoo swirled over the exposed skin there. He noticed my gaze on it and raised a hand to it with a smirk.

"Your kind always were fond of tattoos. My immortal form pushes the ink from my skin now, so I no longer have any..."

"Magnar's tattoos are a mark of his gifts, not a fashion choice," I replied lightly.

Fabian released a growl at the sound of his name. "I'd prefer it if you didn't mention him here."

I considered conjuring an image of the warrior to spite him, but I couldn't bring myself to do it. I felt like Fabian bringing me to this place was about so much more than reminding me he'd been human once. It was the most personal piece of him. Something that he could only visit in his dreams. There was no way he could have shown it to anyone else before me and despite how deluded he might have been when it came to me, him and this curse Idun had given us, I couldn't deny the honesty of this moment. He was offering the truth of himself up to me and despite all the animosity I felt for him, I couldn't ignore this nor spit on it with petty defiance.

"You just don't want me mentioning him because you know I'm with him," I said, trying to keep hold of my own feelings of hatred while my heart was tempted to soften. My eyes were drawn to the village in the distance again and I found it easier to remember myself when I wasn't caught in his gaze.

"You're only with him because you're afraid of what we are," Fabian hissed.

"I'm with him because I belong with him," I replied defiantly. "And because I love-"

"Don't," Fabian interrupted, silencing me. "I can't hear you say that."

I turned back to look at him and found him right beside me. Haunting pain flashed in his eyes and guilt stirred in my gut. I didn't want to hurt him. But I didn't want to lie either. Not to him. And not to myself. I had to keep the truth present in my mind or I knew I could so easily be lost to my false feelings for him.

I wanted to step back but the strangest sound caught my ear and my eyes widened as I realised what it was. I reached into the space between us, my hand trembling uncertainly as I laid my palm above Fabian's heart.

I inhaled sharply as I felt it thundering against my skin. I knew it wasn't real, but the intensity in his gaze made me feel like it was. Like if we'd met a thousand years ago he would have fought wars to claim me as his own and his heart would have beat only for me.

"Did it hurt?" I asked softly. "When it stopped beating?"

A dark shadow crossed behind his eyes and for a moment we weren't standing by the river anymore. We were in the centre of the village and everything ran red with blood. He was covered from head to toe in gore, and dead bodies lay all around. The other Belvederes stood beside us, their faces written with the horror of what they'd done while Andvari's laughter filled the air.

"More than you could ever know," Fabian breathed.

I stared around in disgust at what the god had forced him to do, but the scene before my eyes slipped away as if Fabian could hardly bear to look at it.

When it settled again, we were standing at the top of a tall cliff, looking out over a stormy sea. The sun slowly broke through the clouds and Fabian stilled as if he were afraid of it. But when it finally fell on his skin, he didn't recoil, and the golden rays lit a warmth in his eyes which I'd never seen before.

"I never chose to be what I am," he said slowly.

I felt my hatred towards him melting a little as pity pulled at me.

"This isn't fair," I breathed as I looked up at him. "You know I don't want this."

"You wouldn't be here if that was true."

I opened my mouth to object, but the look in his eyes made me pause. He seemed so different from the monster I'd built up in my head. There was something desperately vulnerable about him and he looked at me *as if I could be the answer to all of his fears.*

He seemed to take my silence as agreement and caught my hand in his, pressing our marks together. I gasped as the power which bound us to each other flared intensely, every piece of my flesh coming alive with the ferocity of it.

Fabian moved towards me before I could react, his mouth pressing down on mine as he tried to force me to admit to feelings I refused to have.

Desire pooled in my flesh, the power of the mark immobilising me as it screamed for me to accept this while another part of me rioted for release. I almost gave in, almost let him call me to ruin and have whatever pieces of me he needed so very badly, but I managed to pull back instead.

"Stop," I begged him, my breathing ragged as my hand on his chest pushed him away, forcing an inch of space between us. "I didn't ask for this, I didn't want it."

"Neither did I," he replied, his hands on my waist, refusing to let go as his brown eyes shone with need. "But I should have. We're fated, Callie. It's written in the very fabric of the stars. The gods chose us for each other-"

But he'd definitely chosen the wrong argument there, my hatred for the gods and their flippant use of their power over us a potent thing which made it all the easier for me to remember myself.

I forced my way out of his arms and stepped back, shaking my head.

"I don't care," I growled, hunting deep in my heart for the part of me which I knew was my own.

I'd grown up smothered by the rule of his kind. I hated him and everything he represented. I could never love him. And dressing himself up as a human didn't make him a man. He was still the monster I'd always feared. Still the enemy I'd sworn to destroy. Still the demon who'd hunted me and forced me into marriage. Nothing he could ever say would change that.

"Whatever the gods might have planned doesn't interest me. My life is my own. And I refuse to bow to the pressure of some long-forgotten deity. Idun may want us to be together but I don't, and nothing you can

say or do will ever change that. I am your enemy. And you shouldn't forget it." I backed away from him as my words hit home.

His expression shifted, hardening with every cruel word I tossed his way.

"What can I do to make you see that I'm not the monster you think I am?" he demanded, the authority in his tone only making it easier to remember what he was.

I let out a humourless laugh. "Go back in time and don't take my mother to the blood bank because she was ill. Don't let that murderer Wolfe come for my father. Or your twisted brother kidnap my sister. Or go further back than that and don't imprison every human who managed to survive the Final War. Don't treat us like animals only valued for our blood," I spat. "The list is endless Prince Fabian. You placed a crown upon your head and your foot upon our backs, leaving an imprint upon every single one of my kind. How could you ever think I could love you?"

He tried to follow me as I continued to back away from him and I swiped my hand at the ground savagely. The earth rumbled as a huge split formed in the dirt, carving the soil apart until a giant fissure separated us.

"I can fix it," Fabian pleaded. "Let me show you how much I love you. I can prove it to you, just let me prove it!"

"How? How could you ever make all of that right?" I scoffed, growing a cage of steel around my heart and refusing to let him breach it again.

I would close myself off to him no matter how much it took from me to do so. Idun would not make this choice for me. I would never bow to her will in this. And I would break through every piece of her power over me even if it cost me my life.

"I'll fix it. I'll improve the Realms, I can provide schools and hospitals and...and nicer food...anything. I'll give them anything you want. Everything you want-"

"Freedom?" I asked, arching an eyebrow in disbelief.

"I... If I could, I would. But without a constant supply of blood, the vampires can't control themselves. It wouldn't help the humans, it *would only make them targets. When we feed from the vein, accidents happen. Especially if we are particularly thirsty-"*

"So you claim to love me. But the truth is you love my blood more." I sneered at him and his face fell.

"I wouldn't bite you. I would never bite you. I swear it-"

"I don't believe you," I hissed, and the flinch which passed across his features told me he didn't believe it either because he knew just as well as I did that he was a monster first and foremost. No promises, pretty declarations or even good intentions, let alone his supposed love for me would ever be enough to change the truth of that.

I walked towards him, crossing the air above the fissure I'd created as if it were solid ground. My clothes shifted around me and my wedding dress returned.

Fabian's eyes widened hopefully as I moved to stand before him. I snapped my fingers and his human body transformed so he was a vampire again, wearing the charcoal suit he'd married me in.

I pushed my will against his, convincing him he hadn't tasted blood in a hundred years, my power of this place and everything in it utterly complete.

Fabian clutched at his throat, his eyes widening in horror as I pulled my hair behind my shoulder and tilted my chin so he could see my pulse pounding in my neck.

I held his eye, waiting as he tried to fight the demon within him which craved my blood above all else.

His upper lip pulled back, revealing his fangs and he moved towards me. He snarled as he fought against the need which drove him forward and his hand moved to fist in my hair.

His eyes bored into mine and I felt like I could see his heart breaking as the thirst began to win. That shouldn't have hurt, but it did, the fracturing of this thing he wanted so desperately spearing through me despite my resolve not to feel it.

But none of that was real. This was.

An endless second hung between us painted with the truth of what we were, even though he fought it with all he had.

Fabian yanked on my hair and his fangs slid into my flesh as the beast within him won the battle just as I had always known it would. He clutched me against him and groaned desperately as my blood flowed over his lips and pain flared through my skin.

I gripped his biceps, pushing with what strength I had, but it was nothing compared to the might of his savagery.

Fabian drank and drank, utterly lost to his need for my blood and my knees buckled so the only thing holding me upright was him.

He groaned, a pained and desperate sound escaping him, but didn't stop. He didn't stop until there was nothing left to drink and I sagged in his arms. The truth of that death wrapped around us both because I had no doubt that it was the future that would await us. It was what would become of us were we to ever pretend to be what he wanted.

Fabian's arms shook as he held me, murmured apologies and denials racing from his lips, but none of them mattered because this was what we were and there was nothing that could change that. I would die before becoming a vampire, and he seemed to understand that truth in me if nothing else.

"See?" I breathed, my eyes meeting his for an endless moment, and I fought against the pain which drove into me at the look of pure anguish in his eyes.

I yanked my consciousness away from him with a wrench of effort and everything around me disappeared. Fabian Belvedere was left alone in his dreams, with nothing but the knowledge of our impossibility to soothe the ragged pain in his immortal soul.

I sat bolt upright, panting in the darkness as I touched a hand to my neck where the memory of Fabian's bite still haunted my flesh.

"Callie? What is it?" Montana asked sleepily beside me.

I glanced at Magnar but he still slept soundly. Julius was on watch outside somewhere and I resisted the urge to dismiss what had just happened as insanity, needing to tell her the truth.

I took a deep breath as my heart rate slowed and the dream faded away. It had been so real, every thought, feeling and sensation had seemed just like this, yet none of it had actually happened.

"Just the answer to a question that never needed asking," I said.

"What do you mean?" Montana pushed herself upright and scooted closer to me, reminding me of the many times we'd climbed into each other's beds after a nightmare back in the Realm.

"I visited Fabian's dream," I admitted uncomfortably, glancing at Magnar again to make sure he was still sleeping. After joining him in his dream in the past and what we'd done while I was there, I was sure he wouldn't be happy to know I'd ended up with Fabian instead of him tonight.

"Oh... I'm guessing that wasn't intentional?" she asked gently.

"No." I rubbed a hand over my face. "I don't know how to control my power and this stupid mark obviously led me to him."

I lay down again and Montana followed suit so we could whisper to each other from beneath our blankets like we used to.

"And what kind of dream was he having exactly?" she asked innocently, but I knew what she was driving at.

My mind fell on the bed and whips that I'd first found when I arrived and warmth filled my cheeks. "Well…"

"Oh shit," she exclaimed, correctly interpreting my awkward pause. "So did you-"

"Fuck no. I put a stop to it as soon as I arrived. He had some whole weird sex dungeon dreamed up but I dissolved that shit and covered my body from neck to ankle before he could even catch a glimpse of me."

She laughed and I couldn't help but join in. It hadn't seemed that funny at the time, but in hindsight, it was kind of hilarious.

"Okay so what did you do then?" Montana asked.

"He showed me some other parts of himself," I admitted slowly, not liking the way my opinion had been altered by what I'd just seen. It was far easier to think of them as nothing but my enemies when I wasn't forced to see them as anything else. "I saw him before he was turned-"

"He showed you himself as a human?" Montana asked in surprise. "Why?"

"I think he wanted me to remember that he hasn't always been a monster." I shrugged, wanting to dismiss everything I'd seen, refusing to face the seed of pity he'd sown in my heart.

"Really?" she asked. "And did it change anything for you? Do you see them any differently?"

I shifted uncomfortably, not wanting to consider that as a possibility and certainly not wanting to admit it to her after she'd just spent weeks as their captive, subject to countless horrors and manipulations at their hands. It wasn't fair to think of them as anything other than the beasts I knew them to be. They were the reason our parents were dead, the reason we had grown up without freedom. One brief look at the man Fabian Belvedere had been a thousand years ago shouldn't have changed anything about that.

I shook my head, not wanting to let the dream affect the way I viewed the vampires but despite myself, unwanted thoughts were creeping in. "I guess…I felt bad for them in a way. I saw what Andvari forced them to do to their families, their entire village. I saw the horror they felt at killing everyone they'd ever loved. But it doesn't excuse what they've done since, does it? It doesn't mean it's okay for them to have created thousands of their kind. Or to have set themselves up as monarchs above all of us and ruin the lives of every human unlucky enough to have survived the Final War."

"No, I guess not," Montana replied, and it almost sounded like she was disappointed.

We fell into silence and my mind wandered as she slowly fell asleep once more.

I rolled over and my gaze drifted to Magnar. I wondered what he was dreaming about and whether he wanted me to visit him or not, whether it would be easier to face him there where I wasn't restricted by the vow I'd made and wasn't bound to his word.

I found myself not wanting to visit him though; it was bad enough that my own thoughts and feelings were a whirlpool of confusion without dragging him into them too. And my anger hadn't faded, the sense of injustice and helplessness clinging to me like oil which wouldn't wash off of my soul.

I realised that I was staring at him while sorting through the chaotic mess of my own feelings and closed my eyes abruptly, feigning sleep.

I doubted I'd be drifting off again though. I'd had enough of other people's dreams for one night.

MAGNAR

CHAPTER TEN

1000 YEARS AGO

Three years was a hell of a long time to wait for revenge.

I sat on top of the cliff and looked down at the fleet of ships we had built. Enough for an army. An army created to slay the undead.

I twisted a knife in my palm impatiently as I waited for the news which would finally set us on our course. We were so close to being ready to sail and I knew it would be any day now, but the wait was excruciating. It was as though the closer we got to it, the slower time seemed to pass.

"Elder?"

I glanced over my shoulder at Elissa as she approached. In the years I'd spent training her, she'd become a strong warrior. The goddess had been generous when she'd created the new race of slayers. She'd named us the Blessed Crusaders and we were far stronger than any other mortal. But Elissa's lack of training in her youth had left her at a disadvantage to the rest of us. I'd felt responsible for bringing her to join a dying race, so I'd taken on her training myself. Much to the disgust of my betrothed.

"Speak," I replied, turning my attention back to the fleet. I doubted she carried the news I was waiting on.

"Aelfric asked me to remind you of your promise to him."

"Did he now? And what promise would that be?" I asked, feigning memory loss.

It had turned out that the stable boy I'd rescued from the abusive barkeep had been older than he seemed. Aelfric was born under the same moon as me, but years of neglect and sparse meals had kept him small. His time with the slayers had transformed him into a man to be reckoned with. And his gift with horses had been blessed by the goddess when he'd joined us on the battlefield against the Revenants. It practically seemed he could converse with the animals these days. Thanks to him, we had the finest band of warhorses who had ever lived.

Baltian was the only horse who wasn't entirely entranced by him. And though my stallion allowed Aelfric to handle him, that was the most he would permit.

"You promised him a wife of his choosing if he could ride Baltian," she prompted, and I could hear the desperation in her voice despite the way she tried to hide it.

I hid my smile as I continued to stare out over the sea. The two of them had been slipping into each other's tents for months, but they believed no one had noticed. I was fairly sure half the camp knew, especially as she wasn't very quiet in expressing her pleasure in his company. They seemed to believe that I wouldn't grant them permission to wed for some reason and watching them squirm as they'd tried to figure out a way to convince me had become highly amusing.

When Aelfric had suggested this elaborate way to win a chance at her hand, I'd agreed to it instantly. Why not let him prove his devotion to her whilst providing me with endless entertainment as my bad-tempered steed continuously threw him to the dirt?

"That sounds vaguely familiar," I agreed as Elissa shifted uncomfortably behind me.

"And you'll stick to your word on that? No matter who he chooses? Even though he isn't truly a slayer?" she pressed.

"I am a man of my word, Ocean Stirrer. You know you don't need to confirm that. Anyway, what does my promise to him have to do with you?" I turned to her and raised an eyebrow, hiding my amusement as she flushed red.

"Nothing, Elder," she replied nervously. "It's just...he's done it."

"Really?" My interest piqued at the idea of him finally conquering the brute.

"Yes, he asked if you might come and see?"

"Let's go then." I got to my feet and Elissa started to head back down the cliff. "Take the short route," I commanded casually, pointing at the drop beside me.

Her eyes widened as her feet forced her towards the edge.

"Elder, please!" She shook her head as she tried to fight off my hold over her and her fear of heights shone in her eyes.

I folded my arms as I waited for her to buckle. "The water is deep, you'll be fine."

She dug her heels in and turned her eyes down to the sea. At least she wouldn't have to fear the landing; her gifts gave her command of the ocean and she had become adept in wielding its waters.

The seconds dragged and pride stirred in my chest as she managed to fight my control. It wouldn't be long before she threw off my power over her entirely and became a warrior in her own right.

Water droplets hit my skin and I turned my eyes towards the sky, but no clouds hung above us. As the tang of salt brushed across my lips, I moved towards the edge.

Elissa smiled at me as she stepped from the cliff onto a platform of sea water. I laughed as she turned to face me triumphantly. She had been finding ways around my commands more and more often. I'd done much the same thing before managing to break my father's hold on me.

"Are you coming?" she asked, her eyes like two deep whirlpools as her power simmered beneath her skin.

I stepped towards her and looked over the cliff at the tower of water she'd raised to carry her down. She offered me her hand and I took it so that she could use her power to transport us both to the bottom.

I stepped onto the platform and the water writhed beneath my boots as if it knew it should not be doing such a thing.

We descended slowly and I marvelled at her power. My own gifts allowed me to fight and heal in a way which no one from the other clans could match, but gifts like hers defied nature.

We made it to the bottom of the cliff and I eyed the beach where most of the clansmen were working on preparing the ships.

"I hope you like swimming," Elissa murmured, and my heart leapt as she dropped me into the sea.

I plunged beneath the waves and powered my way back to the surface, laughing as my head broke free of the surf. Elissa was grinning at me from her perch above the ocean, still completely dry as she kept the sea from touching her anywhere but the soles of her boots.

I swept my arm across the water, throwing a wave in her direction and she batted it aside with a flick of her wrist, sending it flooding back over me instead. I laughed again as I dropped beneath the waves for a moment then kicked back to the surface.

"Come, witch, let's see what Aelfric has to show us," I teased as I started swimming for shore.

Elissa walked beside me and rode a wave right up to the beach. I strode from the water to join her, shaking my hair like a dog so she was splattered with salty droplets.

"You were asking for it," she said.

"I was," I agreed.

She led the way between the slayers who were working on the ships until we left the beach behind and crossed the dunes. My mouth pulled into a smile as I spotted Aelfric riding Baltian in neat circles within the paddock beyond the beach. The chestnut horse seemed less than pleased with the arrangement, but he was tolerating it despite the wild look in his eyes.

I whistled to Baltian and he turned his head sharply, setting a fierce trot towards us, no doubt hoping I might save him from this situation.

"Magnar!" Aelfric called excitedly.

I would never have recognised him as the small boy who'd chosen to follow us all those moons ago. His pale complexion never seemed to darken no matter how much the sun beat down on him, but that was the only thing about him which hadn't been altered by his time with the clans. Muscles bulged beneath his fighting leathers and he held his chin high, no longer afraid of any man.

"I had to see it for myself," I said as I looked up at him.

Baltian snorted in protest and I reached up to tussle his mane affectionately.

Elissa took a step back; she knew well how my horse enjoyed to bite anyone unwitting enough to stand too close to me.

"And you remember the deal we struck?" Aelfric asked, his eyes slipping to Elissa for a moment before flicking back to me.

"I do. But I cannot permit a human to marry a slayer," I said seriously.

His face fell and Elissa sucked in a sharp breath beside me.

"Leave that poor horse be and come with me. I'll give you your reward." I turned away before he could voice his objections and headed towards the tents which lay further from the shore.

I set a quick pace, but I could hear the two of them following me, their whispered objections finding my ears as they balked at the injustice of their situation. No doubt they were trying to come up with some way to convince me, but I was well known to be a stubborn bastard so I doubted they had much hope.

I kept moving, a smile pulling at my lips as I headed for Humbar's tent. Pushing the flap open, I strode inside without bothering to call out a warning. I was Earl; no one could refuse my entrance anyway.

"Wake up, you old bastard!" I called.

It was almost midday, but I knew he wouldn't have risen yet. Humbar rose late each day and drank himself stupid until the early hours - but if he could be caught between those two points in time then he was the best man for the job I required.

"What do you want?" he grumbled as he hoisted himself out of bed and stared up at me, not bothering to hide his nudity.

"Your skills are needed. Now. Get dressed and bring what you require to the fire pit." I turned and headed back out of his tent, leaving no room for objections.

Elissa and Aelfric were waiting for me outside and they began to voice their complaints, but I waved them off as I headed for the fire pit.

They followed me and I could feel their disappointment and fury as we took seats around the fire, but they held their tongues at a stern glare from me.

It wasn't long before Humbar arrived and set himself up before us, laying out his tools and muttering curses about the early hour.

"I appreciate the gesture, Magnar," Aelfric began, but I waved him off again.

"I gave you my word that you could have your pick of a bride if you managed to ride my horse," I said and he managed to hold his tongue as he listened to me. "But as Earl, I cannot allow Elissa to marry a man who has not taken his vow now that she has taken hers."

The two of them glanced at each other, clearly shocked that I knew it was her hand he wanted and I allowed myself a smile.

"But I am not slayer born," Aelfric protested. "You know I would take my vow if I could. But I have no mark, no way to channel your gifts-"

"Then we shall have to fix that." I grabbed his right arm and held it out towards Humbar. "Give him a mark; make him one of us."

Aelfric's eyes widened with astonishment as he realised what I was offering. Elissa gasped before flinging her arms around me and I laughed as I held her close for a moment.

Humbar began to tattoo a mark onto Aelfric's skin, and I sat back to watch. It wouldn't grant him the gifts or power of our race, but I was Earl; if I said he was one of us then no one would question it. Aelfric was one of the best men I knew and a fierce warrior, he deserved to have a true place among us.

"I welcome you into my clan, Aelfric of the Clan of War," I said, clapping a hand on his back.

His eyes shone with deep emotion and he gripped my arm with his free hand as Humbar continued to work.

"This means more to me than you can imagine, Earl Magnar," Aelfric said. "My blade is yours, my life is yours. You will not regret bestowing this gift on me."

"I know I won't. You can take your vow at sundown," I said. "I'm sure Julius will be happy to train you. Then tomorrow you can be wed."

Elissa burst into tears and the smile on Aelfric's face was enough to light a fire in my soul. I grinned at both of them, delighted I could grant them this gift. They deserved to be happy together.

I only wished my own betrothed was someone I could feel an ounce of their love for.

I awoke with a pounding in my head. The wedding celebrations had gone on long into the night and I'd consumed more than my fair share of ale.

I squinted around at my tent as I blinked away the effects of the alcohol and tried to remember what had woken me.

"If you won't answer me then I'll just let myself in!" Valentina called angrily.

My mood soured at the sound of her voice. She was less than pleased that I'd performed a wedding which wasn't ours, and that I'd spent the better part of yesterday avoiding her throughout the celebrations.

She ripped open the tent flap and stalked across the space towards me. The look in her eyes made me wonder if I should locate my swords to defend myself and I arched a brow at her curiously.

Valentina's gaze fell on the two naked women in my bed as they stirred, and her eyes turned to stone. A strong wind battered the tent and thunder rumbled overhead.

"Get out," she hissed.

They looked to me as if I might shield them from her wrath, but I only shrugged. I couldn't remember their names, so I certainly wasn't going to waste my time offering them any protection from my betrothed. She'd soon forget about them once they were out of sight anyway.

"Good morning, Valentina," I sighed. "Or is it afternoon?"

The pair scrambled for their clothes and scurried out of the tent as she seethed. Rain slammed against the canvas above me and I was sure they were getting drenched as Valentina's anger filled the skies.

"Really, husband? It's not humiliating enough that you perform yet another wedding before our own, but you have to bring two whores to your bed as well?" she spat.

"I'm not your husband yet," I reminded her for the millionth time. "And they weren't whores. They were from the Clan of Prophecies and they foresaw our night together. I couldn't very well go against the will of the gods now, could I?"

She scowled at me and I could see her fighting the urge to call me out on that lie.

"You know, if you took me to your bed, you'd never want any other woman again," she said, lowering her voice seductively and changing tact.

"Perhaps that's why I don't dare attempt it," I replied dryly. "Did you want something other than to chase away my company?"

She pursed her lips then finally let the subject drop. Perhaps the repetition of this scene was wearing thin for her too, though I somehow doubted it. "Yes. I came with good news; we're ready to sail."

I beamed at her as I got to my feet. "Truly?"

"Truly." Her gaze slid over my body, and she made no secret of what she wanted.

My pleasure at the news almost tempted me to make use of the desire I could see growing in her eyes. But I knew if I crossed that line with her, I'd never be able to turn back.

I pulled my trousers on before approaching her. "Then this really is the greatest day. And once I have exacted revenge upon the Revenants, you may get your wish. A husband to marry." I didn't mention the fact that I hoped it would never be me. If I could rid the world of the Revenants, then Idun had promised to rid me of Valentina. Once the goddess had broken our betrothal then I was sure Valentina would find herself another man to call husband – one who might actually be capable of making her happy.

"You mean you'll set a date?" she asked hopefully.

"I imagine I'll have no choice," I replied.

Her face lit with hope, and I pressed a brief kiss to her lips to appease her. The rain stopped hammering the tent as her mood shifted and I sighed, so tired of playing this game.

She tried to snare me in her arms, but I pushed her back.

"No consummating before the wedding," I reminded her, guiding her towards the exit.

She blew out a breath in defeat and stepped outside at my insistence. Honestly, I couldn't see what possible reason she had to want this union so badly after enduring years of my debauchery and clear lack of interest, but she was like a dog with a bone, refusing to relinquish it.

I dropped the tent flap and shook my head as I gathered the rest of my clothes and weapons. That woman was more persistent than a wolf with the scent of blood. She had waited six years for me to wed her and she still wouldn't take the hint.

Once I could be sure she was gone, I headed outside in search of Julius and nodded to the unsworn boy who rushed to start dismantling my tent. If we were to sail today, then everything would have to be loaded aboard the ships and the camp was already alive with movement as our people rushed to get us ready to leave. Many supplies were already on board but it would take several hours to load the rest.

Idun had provided us with all the knowledge we needed to track down the monsters who had murdered my father and we were finally ready to cross the great sea and claim their heads. Today was a good day indeed.

I strode through the camp and headed straight for the biggest ship in our fleet, climbing aboard and making my way to the prow so I could look out at the horizon.

Somewhere out there lay my destiny and my freedom.

I'm coming for you Erik Larsen. You will never escape me now.

MONTANA

CHAPTER ELEVEN

I sat with my legs folded on the make-shift bed I'd slept in last night, watching Julius pace around the room. He'd attached his cellphone to his arm with a strange black strap that glowed blue as he moved.

"What are you doing?" I asked.

"Charging my cellphone," he said. "Kinetic energy makes it work. When I awoke in this new era, Idun led me to a place of long-dead warriors. A base of sorts, full of strange weaponry and technology beyond my comprehension. She gifted me enough knowledge to stifle my fears and help me make use of some of it."

"Right. So what does 'charging' mean?" I frowned, not really understanding as he continued to circle around us.

"Well there are two definitions. The old one I knew better than this." Julius went charging across the room with a battle cry and Callie jolted from sleep beside me, looking a little pale as she sat upright.

"Are you alright?" I murmured.

"More bad dreams," she whispered.

Magnar eyed her from the moth-eaten chair he was sitting in. "The kind with Fabian Belvedere in them?" he growled, but Callie didn't answer, getting to her feet and taking a bowl of oatmeal which I'd warmed on the fire.

Magnar stroked the hilt of one of his blades, eyeing Julius's cellphone with unease. "I don't like these devices. What if a vampire can use its mystical ways to find us?"

"Not a problem," Julius said lightly. "I have the phone cloaked so neither the GPS, internet, or radio signal is traceable."

"I do not understand," Magnar grumbled, seeming irritated, and I had to agree with him on that.

"Leave it to me, brother." Julius continued his pacing and Magnar finally rose to his feet.

"Enough. You're driving me insane. If you wish to expend energy then spar with me. The gods know I could use a distraction."

"We all could," Callie agreed, dropping down beside me with her breakfast as if readying for the show. She waved her hand at them. "Go on. Let's see which brother is the strongest."

"It's no competition," Julius said cockily, rolling his shoulders. "I shall prove to you that I am the finest, most skilled-" Magnar's fist slammed into his jaw and Julius almost hit the floor, catching himself on the edge of a broken table. He released a dark laugh. "Oh, is that how you're going to fight today, asshole? You've got the fires of Muspelheim in you this morning."

Julius swung out a leg, catching Magnar by the backs of his knees and knocking his next punch off balance.

I watched in awe as the brothers set into a furious fist fight, parrying every blow, their technique and ferocity a true gift of the gods. Magnar suddenly fell back and started circling his brother like a predator hunting its prey.

Julius drew his sword from his hip. "Let us do this properly or not at all."

"Prepare to lose then," Magnar warned, his eyes lighter than they'd ever been since I'd met him as he picked up one of his swords.

"Prepare to be shamed!" Julius leapt at him, bringing Menace down at a terrifying speed.

Magnar lifted his blade, easily knocking the blow aside, and the clash of metal rang in my ears as they slashed at each other again. My heart rate picked up, the thrill of this fight setting my blood ablaze.

"Who do you think will win?" I asked Callie and she threw me a grin.

"Magnar, but I'd like to see him get knocked on his ass first."

Magnar glanced over at her, hearing the comment and Julius pressed his advantage, knocking him right onto his ass just like Callie had hoped.

My sister laughed, and Julius beamed in victory. "Someone's getting in your head, brother. Whoever could it be?"

Magnar growled his fury, lunging forward and toppling Julius as he snatched his legs from under him. He straddled his brother, throwing punches into his gut with wild abandon. I gasped at the sight, wondering how far this would go.

Julius spluttered, slamming his knuckles into his brother's chest and Magnar reared back, but as Julius tried to rise, Magnar took hold of his throat and forced him down onto the floorboards again.

"Yield," he snarled.

"Ne-ver," Julius coughed.

Magnar's grip only tightened, and Julius started turning blue, his legs kicking as he tried to unseat his brother, but it was no good. The seconds ticked into a minute, and I rose to my feet in alarm.

"Magnar, let him go!" I yelled, concern warring in my chest.

"Yield!" Magnar bellowed.

"*Fine*," Julius wheezed and Magnar released him, pulling him up by one hand.

I gazed at the two of them, shaking my head as they embraced each other, their bond only growing keener from the violence.

"You're both crazy," I half laughed.

Julius rubbed his throat. "It's just a bit of fun. Do you want a round, damsel?" He moved toward me, playfully jabbing my arm.

I rubbed the spot with a frown. "No thanks."

"I will." Callie sprang to her feet, gazing straight at Magnar. "You game?"

His mouth curved up into a hungry smile. "Always, drakaina hjarta."

"At least wear this." Julius took the phone from his bicep, holding it toward Magnar. He recoiled like it might burn him and Callie took it instead, strapping it to her arm.

"Um...Callie? Are you sure about this?" I asked.

Magnar was twice the size of her and he'd nearly strangled his own brother five seconds ago. That was two major reasons for her not to get into a brawl with the beastly dude, but I could definitely come up with more.

"I've never been as sure of anything in my life," Callie snarled, a wildness entering her tone.

My heart lifted at the life in her eyes. This might have been insanity by definition, but she seemed more herself today. And if she was certain she could handle this fight, then who was I to stop her?

"No blades, but you can fight as dirty as you like," Magnar announced, taking his leathers off and leaving them on the chair with his swords.

Callie grinned. "Even better."

"I'm not going to go easy on you," Magnar said, flexing his arms above his head.

Callie aimed a straight kick at his exposed stomach, and he lurched backwards.

"I didn't say begin!" Magnar barked as she collided with him, locking an arm around his neck.

"It was implied," Callie laughed, taking hold of her hand as she choked him like a hellion.

"Go on, Callie!" I urged excitedly.

Magnar grabbed her waist, throwing her away from him and she rolled with impossible grace across the floor, gaining her feet in an instant.

My mouth parted in awe. She was incredible, fierce and clearly able to take on a warrior like Magnar. I could hardly believe how much strength the slayer's vow had given her.

She charged at Magnar and he prepared for her attack. Instead of delivering it, she ducked past him, grabbed a chair and smashed it over his back.

I gasped but he barely reacted to the blow, spinning and catching her arm, then tugging her forward to meet his other fist. She cried out as his knuckles slammed into her abdomen, once, twice, three times. My gut dropped and my excitement was lost in an instant, horror taking its place.

"Stop it!" I cried, running toward them.

Magnar's elbow shot backwards for another punch, catching me right in the chin and knocking me from my feet.

I tasted blood as Julius rushed to me, pulling me upright. "Magnar, watch it."

Magnar glanced my way, his brows dropping as he noticed the welt on my lip. "Shit, sorry."

"I'm fine. Just don't punch my damn sister," I growled, dabbing at my lip with my sleeve. Shit, between these three, I felt like the only breakable person in the room.

Callie leapt onto Magnar's back, wrapping her hands around his neck with a viciousness that said she was making a bid for revenge in my honour. He released a rumbling laugh, reaching above his head and pulling her over his shoulder with ease. She fought frantically, but he clamped an arm across her back, forcing her to remain there. But a second later she landed a solid punch right to his cock.

Magnar stilled, groaning under his breath as his whole body went rigid. He released Callie so she slid down to the floor and gazed up at him with a grin.

I bit my lip, but my laughter burst out anyway as Magnar turned sheet-white.

"Yield?" Callie asked, throwing her head back as she laughed too.

Magnar nodded stiffly, shuffling his way over to a chair and sitting down, dropping his head into his hands.

"Dick punch. Harsh," Julius commented, chuckling to himself. "Though I'm not complaining because that was fucking hilarious." He moved to Callie's side, unstrapping the phone from her arm. "And we are charged!"

A jingle sounded through the room as he turned the cellphone on and my thoughts wheeled to Erik. I could contact him with that. And that was a very tempting idea. The cross on my palm prickled with yearning and I released a breath as I willed my thoughts to turn elsewhere, but they wouldn't shift.

Callie floated toward Magnar, and he lifted his head. "You okay?" she asked with a teasing smile.

"I will be in a minute," he said through his teeth. "I hope that was practice for if you ever see Fabian again."

"Sure," she said airily.

I stepped toward Julius, glancing over his shoulder at the phone. "So...you can still see the cameras in the castle from this, right?"

"Yes, we can keep an eye on the bloodsuckers," Julius said, bringing up the live feeds.

My pulse ticked faster as I immediately tried to located Erik on one of them. He suddenly felt so close, like the cellphone was a portal to him, offering me the chance of seeing him again. Even if just for a moment.

Julius tapped on one of the boxes so it filled the screen and my stomach knotted as I spotted Erik and Clarice talking together in a grand hallway. My heart crashed violently against my ribcage as I drank in the sight of him, his dark hair pushed back and the chiselled lines of his face set into a cold, distant kind of expression that made me ache to know what troubled him.

Julius increased the volume and their voices filled the room.

"-he doing?" Erik asked.

He looked tired somehow, his face paler than usual and the spark in his eyes was diminished. The mark on my palm heated and a longing to go back to him nearly overwhelmed me. But I'd made my choice. And it could never have been him.

"Better. The wound is healing, but it will take a little longer because of the damage the slayer blade caused. I think it's Fabian's pride which is hurt the most though," Clarice said with a frown.

Callie stiffened, immediately moving to my side as she watched the feed, but Magnar remained in his chair, his expression sour.

"He keeps ordering people to do insane things," Clarice said.

"Like?" Erik asked in concern.

"He has his people fixing up the Realms. All of them. He's hardly got any Elite left in the city."

"Well I've been telling him to do that, perhaps he's listening to me at last," Erik mused.

"I don't think it's that. He keeps talking about Callie. He asks everyone who attends him how he might appease her. And everything they suggest, he does." Clarice twirled a finger around a lock of her golden hair, looking worried. "I think it's the mark of partnership. Is it affecting you too?" She took Erik's hand, turning it over to reveal the shimmering cross there and my throat tightened.

Erik curled his fingers into a fist. "Montana has always affected me, this mark is just a testament to that." I glanced at Callie, and she gave me an intense look, but didn't comment on what he'd said.

"Oh Erik," Clarice cooed, bobbing up and down on her heels. "How wonderful."

"Quite," Erik bit out, not sounding so pleased.

My heart broke and rebuilt itself all over again. Or maybe it was the other way round, because right now, all I felt was the loss of him and the weight of my choice to leave him behind forever.

"We'll get her back," Clarice promised. "Once Fabian is well enough, he'll create more Familiars. Most of them have been lost to the slayers' blades, but there are still more out there looking. We could make our own, but his are more powerful and will probably find them quicker. Either way, we'll find Montana and her sister soon enough, especially if you send your forces after them."

Erik's eyes darkened. "I am not sending any Elite, Clarice. I told you. Montana chose to leave, and I promised not to seek her out."

"We both know you're going to break," Clarice said in a low voice. "You want her more than I have ever seen you want anything. But Erik…" She stepped closer. "There is only one thing you desire deeper than blood, and that's breaking the curse. She can be yours; we can have it all. But this noble act will only keep us in chains longer. Don't you want to be free?"

Erik's lips pressed into a thin line and my breaths came quicker as I awaited his answer.

"My decision remains. And you won't find them if they don't wish to be found. They could be well beyond the borders of the city by now. They could have boarded a supply train back to the west coast, or maybe they've headed south toward the desert. If they make it there, they shall be lost forever." His hand fisted at his side like the thought of that pained him.

Clarice pressed a hand to his arm. "You're a hunter, Erik. Eventually you *will* hunt her. Better now than before she reaches a sun-drenched desert, because I have the feeling you will find yourself walking the sand, seeking what you lost, knowing that if you let her slip away now, you will regret it for all eternity."

His expression darkened to something purely villainous. "You think I don't know that? You think I am not in agony grappling with the beast in me who demands I go after her? You think I am not suffering with the knowledge that I will likely fail to hold out against my demons?"

My heart knotted at his words, the admission making my breathing ragged.

"We'll never let that happen," Julius muttered to me, his muscles tensing.

Clarice stepped closer to Erik, sadness pooling in her bright green eyes. "Maybe you should let that desire win out. Maybe it's meant to."

Erik said nothing, and I wondered whether he was considering her words. The darkest pieces of me wanted him to, but a greater part of me didn't. Because there was no future that existed for us, no matter how painful that was to accept, even if my heart shattered further with every moment we spent apart.

"We need to focus on catching Valentina," Clarice changed lanes. "My Elite are searching for her in the east of the city where most of the rebels are known to reside. But a few of them have been killed in the process. And Erik..." She bit her lip. "Some of my sirelings have gone to join them. Miles has told me the same thing. Our people are abandoning us."

"Not the ones who count," Erik snarled. "I will kill Valentina myself when we have her location."

"You know I'll be by your side," Clarice said. "We'll take her down together. She's the biggest threat to our empire since we took control.

But I know we can handle her, so long as we remain as a unit. We can't show weakness now."

"Of course," Erik sighed. "I do have one idea. But it may be a bad one."

"What is it?" she asked.

Erik ran a thumb over his lip as he prepared to air his thoughts. "Wolfe is a biter. He may have some information that could help us locate her, though I doubt he will tell us willingly. However, he is due to be banished tomorrow. Perhaps we could allow some news to reach his ears that Valentina has gone into hiding. Then once he is banished, we could follow him to see where he goes. He could lead us right to her."

"Erik, that's genius." Clarice nodded quickly. "I'll have a guard leak the information to him. We'll stage it so it seems he is told by accident."

"Thank you." Erik nodded. "If it came from my men, he would suspect my hand in it. Wolfe must not be underestimated."

The two of them parted, heading separate ways and my soul ached as Julius pocketed the phone. I missed Erik more than anything. I was suffocated by his absence, like a vital piece of myself was gone, and I was never going to get it back.

"He's going to free Wolfe," Callie snarled.

"Not free. Banish," I pressed. "And if they hunt down Valentina that way, maybe it's worth it."

"Montana is right," Magnar said from across the room, surprising me. "I despise the Belvederes, but if they cut off Valentina's head, I will be more than happy. It will save me the task of doing it anyway."

"At least we know they're not looking for us too hard right now," I said. "It sounds like Fabian is still bedridden from his injuries."

Callie nodded, looking sad. "I hope he feels better soon." Her nose wrinkled in disgust at what she'd said. "Ergh. Good enough for me to stab him again, I mean."

I squeezed her arm and she gave me a forlorn look.

"It's alright," Julius spoke to her. "We know you really want him dead. Just like Montana wants Erik dead." He glanced at me with amusement in his eyes and I fought the urge to punch him.

"Exactly," I forced out, and Callie's shoulders dropped a little, leaving that lie burning on my tongue.

"I think we should use this window of opportunity to move to a more secure place," Julius said thoughtfully. "Once Fabian is on his feet again, he'll send a host of Familiars to find us and I doubt we will be able to outwit them for long."

"Where will we go?" I asked.

"I know a place. But we will need to travel under the cover of darkness," he said. "We'll be in plain view on the river otherwise."

"The river, Julius?" Magnar questioned.

"Yes, there's an island between Manhattan and New Jersey. A place no one goes anymore. I holed up there for a while when I arrived at the city. There's an old statue there of a huge green woman in a dress. And there's a room inside her head."

"That sounds like a fairy tale," Magnar rumbled, his brows drawn low.

"You'll see," Julius said with a devilish glow in his gaze. "Her head is even bigger than yours, brother."

ERIK

CHAPTER TWELVE

1000 YEARS AGO

Life was easy at last. The village we had discovered was filled with simple farming folk. They were adept at craftsmanship. Their houses were stone and square, interspersed with crops, the dwelling sitting right at the base of a large cliff, surrounded by a lush forest and sheltered from the world. It was a haven and it wasn't long before we'd gained the people's respect.

We kept them safe from enemy tribes, and any predators who crept up on their children soon regretted it. After a few months, they had built us a temple of stone, large enough to shade us even in the midday sun. Andvari had long stopped assisting us with the gifts of clouds, so our lives were lived in the moonlight.

I sat on a throne of gold, shifting a beautiful obsidian blade between my hands, gifted to me by the village people.

Before me was a steep set of steps leading down to the exit where a trail led into the village. Every side of the temple contained a room like mine. One for each of us. The four gods. Or so we called ourselves now.

My gaze lifted as a young woman in a thin white dress hurried up the steps with her head bowed low. They sent the most beautiful women in their tribe as if they thought they would appease us most. Blood was blood, to me. I didn't care whose vein it came from.

The woman knelt at my feet, laying a wreath of white flowers there before placing her wrists on my knees in offering.

I took her left hand, eyeing her bronzed skin with a hint of desire lighting the darkest corners of my mind. It had been so long since I'd allowed myself to indulge in a woman. Unlike Fabian who often cavorted with members of the tribe. Or Clarice who was growing a sizable harem of men. Miles would even sleep down in the village at times with his favoured men, but I was the one they feared most. The god who never spoke to them. The one who never walked among their people. The beast who stalked under the moonlight in quiet contemplation.

This human was beautiful. Young, but not too young. She was past the age of womanhood. I'd fed from her since she was eighteen. But today, I could see she was in her twenties.

"What's your name?" I never asked them that. But today, I made an exception. Because today felt different to most. My monotonous existence broken by a singular curiosity. One which would likely pass me by as quickly as it had come. Though I might as well indulge it while it remained.

She glanced up at me in surprise then quickly bowed her head. They rarely looked at me. Sometimes that infuriated me. Other times it suited me well. But I didn't want her at my feet today. It seemed wrong to make the humans bow, though my siblings didn't share my sentiment in that.

"Name?" I growled in her tongue. We'd quickly learned their language since our arrival. Another gift of our immortality. Something we could do without much thought. Within days, we had been able to speak with them as easily as if we had spoken their tongue our entire lives.

"Kuwanlelenta," she whispered.

"Kuwan- forgive me, what?" I balked.

She laughed softly and it was the sweetest sound I'd heard in a very long time.

"You may call me Kuwana, if it is easier?" she offered, her eyes still downcast.

"Kuwana," I tried out the name, liking the feel of it in my mouth. "Stand, Kuwana."

She did, but kept her head dipped low.

"I have noticed the women in your clan do not bow to men, so why is it you bow to me?" I asked.

"You are a god, it is a sign of respect," she said.

I leaned forward, taking her chin and forcing her to meet my eyes. A feather hung in her dark locks and a line of white paint was marked across her cheeks.

"Beautiful," I breathed, drinking in the sight of her warm, golden flesh. How I wished I could still feel what she could: The beat of a heart within my chest, the rush of heat within my veins, the blaze of the sun upon my skin. She was an enviable creature, just as they all were. But this one, I desired a deeper bite of.

"You are too kind," she said, her lips trembling and revealing her fear.

A coldness washed through me as I remembered what she saw when she looked at me. A god she believed me to be, but one of wrath and blood. Her terror was well placed.

I released her, sitting back. "You don't like coming here," I stated.

"Of course I do," she said quickly, holding up her wrists to me again. "I wish to make you happy more than anything else, oh great one."

I snorted a laugh and she looked at me with fear sparking in her gaze like she thought she had said the wrong thing.

"I am not great," I muttered, though I knew I was breaking my siblings' rules. We had to uphold the idea that we were deities. But I craved some normality. My life was lonely and too quiet. I wanted to run into battle again, I wanted to chase after women, attend feasts and drink ale. I wanted to enjoy myself for once.

She bit her lip, seeming unsure of how to answer.

"Are you married?" I asked.

She nodded meekly. "Yes, to an old warrior. He is quite the bore."

"Is he now? Tell me about him," I urged, and slowly she started opening up to me about the oaf who had claimed her as his bride. I knew the man, he had come to me many times praising my name and asking me to bestow gifts on the town. Begging for rain for his crops, for his animals to grow fat, for the enemy tribes to stay away. The few times the village had been attacked, the four of us had seen them off anyway. It was easy. We were their protectors and so they worshipped us. But I was growing very tired of being worshipped.

"Sit." I patted my lap and Kuwana shook her head in alarm. In truth, I only wanted to feel the warmth of her skin again. I wanted to take a bite out of life. And the only way I could was by getting as close to it as possible. "But only if you wish to," I added and she hesitated a moment before dropping onto my knees.

I pulled her to me, tracing the line of her collar bone with my finger and breathing in her earthy scent. She was a tantalising piece of humanity, coiled in my arms. She shivered as I inspected her, taking in the hue of sunlight in her flesh, the scent of life upon her. I wanted more. I wanted her heart to beat life through my own veins, to offer me just one more moment in humanity.

"God, you are great and kind, but I am afraid of you too," she said, her warm breath floating over my neck and intoxicating me.

"Don't be afraid. I would never hurt you." I lied. One she bought easily into thanks to my seductive aura that always worked to lure in my prey.

I shut my eyes, leaning closer to listen to her beating heart. My mouth grew dry as the bloodlust rose in me, my hands tightening on her, her life caged in my arms. I could take it from her so simply. A crack of her neck, a bite that drove too deep.

She began to caress me, her hands sliding tentatively into my hair and our eyes met, lust making her lips part with want. But I wasn't sure what I craved anymore. Her life, her body, or her blood. My lust for her was already fading though, and the thirst was rising above it all. The momentary desire for her faded and boredom set in once again. No one ever drew my gaze for long.

"Excuse me, brother," Fabian's voice pulled me from my trance. He walked out from a door to the right of my throne, shirtless, his hair long and loose and red markings were painted on his chest. He loved to take part in the village ways, his role here suiting him perfectly. I couldn't say I felt the same.

Kuwana sprang from my lap, dropping to her knees and flattening herself to the floor. Fabian stepped past her, acting as if she wasn't there at all.

"We have a problem," Fabian growled and I sensed a tension in his posture that concerned me.

I snapped my fingers at Kuwana. "Go," I commanded and she scampered away, darting down the golden steps out into the growing light of dawn.

"What's wrong?" I asked, rising from my throne.

Fabian took a measured breath, his brown eyes struck with woe. "The slayers are coming."

A beat of silence. Two.

I came undone, grabbing Fabian by the shoulders as the world tipped upon its axis. "How do you know this?"

"Some of the villagers have been fishing at sea the past three days. They returned just moments ago and speak of a great fleet heading our way. They say a fierce tribe of warriors ride in it. They fear for their own lives, but it is ours I am more concerned about."

"How could they find us?" I demanded, anxiety scraping my insides.

"The goddess, of course. No doubt Idun has led them right to us." Fabian rested a hand on my shoulder, giving me an intense look. "We will face them together, brother."

"And we will lose," I snarled. "Unless Andvari helps us, we cannot beat them now that they are gifted with Idun's power."

"Then you must speak with Andvari," Fabian begged. "You are the only one he listens to."

I nodded, floored by his words. I wondered how long we had until the accursed barbarians arrived. No doubt Magnar Elioson and his brother would be among them. They hungered for my death like madmen. If only they could see the control Idun had over them. That they were a slave to her like we were to Andvari.

"Let's go to the holy Kiva, the Shaman has a pane of polished glass.

We can use it to speak with Andvari."

Fabian nodded then suddenly wrapped his arms around me, taking me by surprise. I patted his back as he clapped mine. "We will always protect each other, won't we?"

"Of course," I swore. Despite our differences, our bond had never faltered in all our three hundred years of friendship. "No time exists where we shall not stand together as brothers."

CHAPTER THIRTEEN

I rolled my shoulders back and tried to shake off the ache I felt across my spine. With little to do while we waited for dark, I'd spent most of the day sparring with Magnar and Julius, and I was beginning to suffer the consequences of letting them use me as a punching bag.

The fire was dying out but there was no point in us building it up again; the sun was almost set and we were getting ready to head off. We had a long way to go, passing by the city filled with vampires before finally making it to the statue Julius had spoken of. I hoped he was right about it being a good place for us to lie low because heading closer to those creatures didn't feel like the safest option. From there, perhaps we could head south by water and keep sailing until we found a place to call home.

I'd be closer to Fabian soon, and the knowledge made doubt build in my chest. I was managing to keep a lid on most of the urges I felt toward him, but I was worried that closing the distance between us would make it harder to resist the temptation to go to him.

I wondered if Montana was struggling with her bond to Erik too. She'd barely mentioned his name since we'd been reunited, and I was starting to worry that he'd done something to her which she didn't want to recount. If moving nearer caused the bond to draw her towards him again, would she be able to cope with it? It had been hard enough for me to spend a single day as the Belvederes' prisoner. How had she managed to survive so long?

I glanced across the fire at her, but she'd fallen into an anxious mood as the sun had started its descent, and I wanted her to have a bit of peace before we had to leave.

I flexed my fingers, inspecting my reddened knuckles which had split in places. My opponents had hard faces rough with stubble and I was quickly finding out what that meant for my fists.

The air stirred as the door opened and closed again downstairs and embers twirled above the fire like a thousand of my tangled thoughts racing away to freedom. I watched their path towards the roof and tried to let my mind empty out as they retreated, but it was no good.

Magnar appeared at the top of the stairs; he'd been out scouting for Familiars in preparation of our departure and he offered a faint shake of his head, letting me know he hadn't found any. I couldn't decide if that was a good thing or not. It might mean that they were looking in the wrong place or perhaps had even given up. Then again, it might mean that they were lurking in every direction, waiting for us to make a move so they could report our positions back to their masters.

There was no sign of Julius, so I guessed he was still working on getting us a boat.

I tapped my fingers against my knee to try and expel some of the anxious energy which was building in my limbs.

Magnar moved to sit beside me and took my hand in his, making my heart jerk violently and my eyes snap to his face. I furrowed my brow at him in surprise, making to pull my hand back again but he ignored me, rubbing some green mush over my split knuckles. The cuts tingled as the concoction worked its way into them and I stopped trying to withdraw my hand, letting him rub it into my skin.

"What's that?" I asked as he released my right hand and took my left, his eyes on his task and not meeting mine.

"Just some mixed herbs to help you heal faster," he murmured. "You aren't Clan of War like us; we have an unfair advantage when it comes to healing."

"Oh yeah, I was thinking that must be the advantage you have over me. The fact that you're three times my size is irrelevant," I muttered.

A smile pulled at the corner of Magnar's mouth, and he looked up at me, my hand still in his.

My heart thundered wildly as I caught his gaze, the intensity of his golden irises burning a path right through me as though he could see straight to the heart of every concern, every fear and feeling of inadequacy I possessed. He saw it all and yet he didn't look at me like my roiling emotions equalled some failing. He looked at me like every one of them was utterly captivating to him and he wanted nothing more than for me to whisper the truths of my heart to him alone.

I bit my lip as I tried to remember why the hell I'd asked him to give me space. Yes, the bullshit with the rain had left me feeling infuriated and helpless, but my anger with him was really more aimed at the gods who had bound us in this way. I knew he hadn't wanted to hurt me with his command, and he had kept any such orders from his lips since then.

Magnar's fingertips shifted across my skin, his gaze never leaving mine as the feather-light touch had me swallowing against a lump in my throat. I turned my hand in his, offering him more access to my flesh. He dragged his fingers over my wrist, his thumb scoring a line against my palm before it brushed against the mark which had been branded there.

I sucked in a sharp breath as heated agony flared through me, the intensity of my bond to Fabian rising, filling my mind with thoughts of him and the vows I'd made to be his. Before I knew what I was doing, I snatched my hand out of Magnar's grasp and slapped him hard enough to make his head wheel sideways.

"I'm sorry," I gasped as I sprung to my feet, cradling my traitorous hand to my chest and backing up. That hadn't been me, it hadn't been what I'd wanted to do. "I didn't mean to-"

"It's fine, Callie. You were hitting me a lot harder than that this afternoon." Magnar held my gaze for a moment, reading the truth of what had just happened as easily as if I was pouring my entire heart out to him, then he pushed himself to his feet.

"It's not fine," I breathed miserably. Because I didn't even know myself anymore. I couldn't even feel my own emotions without others pressing their way into my mind, my body. The gods had infected me with this bond, from the thoughts in my heads to the actions of my flesh.

Montana had sat up straighter but she didn't interrupt as she watched us, her eyes moving from me to Magnar and back again, her posture telling me that she was ready to step in if she had to.

Magnar moved closer to me so I had to tilt my head back to look up at him. He didn't try to touch me again though and my heart ached, wishing he would and praying he wouldn't in equal measures.

"You'll figure this out," he said quietly. "I'm not going anywhere."

"You shouldn't have to...deal with this," I replied in a low voice.

Why should he have to stand for me playing hot and cold with him? Why should he have to endure the knowledge that every time I looked at him, a part of me pined for his enemy? It was fucked up. I was being unfair to him simply by standing before him, but I was utterly helpless to stop it too.

"I'm fairly sure you're worth it." He looked at me intently for a moment and heat built in my veins at the promise in his eyes.

He should have been telling me that he couldn't do this, should have been putting some distance between us, but he wasn't. He was looking at me in that way which made the blood in my veins burn, refusing to balk at the weight of the curse I now carried.

Magnar finally released me from his golden gaze and handed me the remaining green mixture rolled in a leaf.

"For your sister's bites," he murmured before walking away to begin preparing our meal.

I let out a shaky breath, wondering how I was supposed to figure out my own feelings while vows and bonds and dreams kept mixing them up and spitting them out inside my own head. I turned and discovered Montana staring at me with a raised eyebrow.

I moved around the fire to take a seat beside her and rolled my eyes as she continued to give me that probing look. As I passed her the herbs, she began rubbing them onto the bite marks on her neck with a mutter of thanks.

"So when are you going to tell me about the two of you?" she whispered expectantly.

Magnar was on the far side of the room, filling a pot as he made our meal but it was nowhere near far enough away for me to start talking about him.

"He can hear you," I breathed.

She frowned over at him, looking like she didn't believe me. "How could he possibly-"

"I can," Magnar confirmed without turning back to look at us.

Her mouth fell open and a line formed above her brow as if she were annoyed. "You know, living with you guys is a lot like living with Erik. He could hear every little-"

"What do you mean *living* with Erik?" I asked, catching her arm. "You never... I mean when you were being held there, did he force you to..." My eyes dropped to her stomach instead of saying the words out loud. I knew the Belvederes had said they had a rule about waiting until after the wedding to consummate it, but she'd been there a lot longer than me. And after what that monster had done to Magnar's people, I couldn't help but wonder if he wouldn't have just taken what he wanted from her whenever it suited him. If there was any chance she could be pregnant already, then I didn't know what we would do to save her.

Montana stared at me in confusion for several seconds then seemed to grasp what I was implying.

"*No*," she replied suddenly. "Of course not. He'd never do anything like that to me; he's not a monster."

I opened my mouth to argue against her, wondering why the hell she'd defend him but then Fabian entered my mind. I remembered how broken he'd looked when he'd shown me what he'd done to the people of his village...

"It's okay, Monty. I get it." I reached for her hand and turned it over so the silver cross was illuminated in the firelight. "This makes it hard to remember what they are."

She started shaking her head, her eyes glimmering with some deep emotion, and I wondered how much harder this had to be for her. I had my feelings for Magnar to counter the false emotions for Fabian. When

I was caught up in the idea of the Belvedere brother, I could search my heart for the place the warrior had taken hostage and find myself again. She was caught adrift in the swirling emotions Idun had forced upon her. How could I expect her to fight them off when I was having so much trouble doing the exact same thing?

I curled her fingers shut, hiding the mark and wrapping my own hands over her fist.

"We'll find a way to break free of this curse," I promised.

"But it's not like that for me," she replied earnestly. "Erik is-" Her gaze slid across the room to Magnar whose shoulders were tense with anger, and I could tell he didn't want to hear anything more in defence of the creature who had killed his father.

"What is it?" I pressed, sensing she was holding back on something.

She took a deep breath and shook her head, retrieving her hand from mine. "Nothing. It's just that so much has happened, the wedding and the mark. It's a lot. But I'm okay. I promise."

I opened my mouth to protest, knowing she was still concealing something but she got to her feet before I could convince her to confide in me.

"I need to pee," she announced.

I watched her as she walked away from me and an ache built in my chest. She was hiding things. I knew it. And it carved a hole in my heart. We'd always shared everything with each other. I couldn't remember once keeping a secret from her, but now she was running from me instead of admitting to whatever truth burdened her.

I frowned at the mark on my palm and my rage against Idun built once more. Now her vile magic was driving a wedge between me and my sister too. That goddess had a hell of a lot to answer for.

I stared into the fire, losing myself to my thoughts as Magnar cooked our meal.

My mind kept catching on the look in Fabian's eyes right before he'd bitten me in our dream. I knew I'd done the right thing in forcing him to see why we could never be together, in making him see the truth of us. He had to realise that Idun was just playing with us, toying with our emotions for her own vile amusement. He was a creature of the night. My sworn enemy. My predator... So why did I feel so guilty?

He's a monster. He doesn't have feelings, so you didn't do anything wrong.

But why did that feel like a lie?

I lost myself to the endless cycle of my thoughts once more while Magnar continued cooking in silence.

Eventually, he handed me a bowl of food and I fell on it like a ravenous beast without bothering to look at it. He moved to sit across the fire, and I couldn't even blame him for the distance between us as disappointment built in my chest. Why would he want to be close to me when all I did was push him away? I was a fucking mess and I wasn't sure how the hell I was going to fix it. Or if I even could.

Julius reappeared with Montana in tow, and I frowned as I realised she'd been missing for far longer than it took to pee. Now I was being a shit sister too. She looked calmer though, and the weight I'd seen pressing down on her had lifted from her gaze a little. Julius had an amused look on his face and I got the feeling he was the reason for her improved mood. I wondered vaguely if their relationship might be turning into something more than friendship, but I hadn't seen any real signs to suggest it. It might be what she needed though – a distraction from the bond to Erik Belvedere.

"I'm sorry if I upset you," I said as Montana moved to sit beside me, accepting her meal from Magnar with a word of thanks.

"It's not that," she replied, her eyes on her food.

Silence stretched between us and I shifted uncomfortably.

"You know you can always tell me anything," I urged gently.

She glanced up at me, her dark hair framing her face. "It's just hard to explain everything that's happened properly. I promise I'll try, but there's just so much going on at the moment and-"

"And we need to go." Julius finished for her. "I know you two need time for a whole heart to heart. Probably while braiding each other's hair...and bathing together...while I may or may not be watching-"

Magnar tossed his bowl at the back of Julius's head and it connected with a dull thunk before clattering to the floor.

"You're sick," I accused, but I couldn't help but laugh as Julius gave us a wolfish grin.

"Well that last bit may just be a suggestion. But I'm game if you are. And either way, we need to get moving." He shovelled the last of his meal into his mouth and moved away to finish packing our supplies into the bags.

Montana breathed a laugh, exchanging an amused look with me as she hurried to finish her food too, and I grinned. Julius was right though, whatever was bothering her would have to wait for now. We needed to get the hell away from this place before the bloodsuckers caught up with us.

Magnar walked towards me and handed me Tempest. I offered him a small smile as I accepted the heavy weapon once more. I missed Fury though. That blade had become a part of me somehow and no matter how many times I wielded Tempest, it would always be loyal to Magnar.

Greetings, Dream Walker, Tempest purred through my mind and I smiled as it made an effort with me. I guessed it was weird that I wanted to bond with Magnar's blades but I had the strangest feeling that he'd care about their opinion of me.

Julius led the way out of the building we'd been using for shelter and I fell into step with Montana as Magnar took up the rear.

We crossed over the protection runes on the threshold and Magnar struck them out, using Venom to carve a line through the stone. I felt the safety they'd been offering fade from my skin and goosebumps rose along my flesh as the cool night air claimed me.

Julius started running and we hurried to keep up as he weaved a path through the ruins towards the river. The sound of the water called us on, making sure we couldn't lose our way and moonlight glimmered overhead.

I kept my senses tuned in to Tempest's presence, but I couldn't detect anything drawing close. It seemed we were alone for now.

We turned a corner and suddenly the river was before us. I stilled, my mouth dropping open as I spied the huge span of water. I'd never seen such a thing before, the rush of the current making my heart somersault inside my chest. Surely Julius didn't mean for us to try and cross that.

I looked to him for an answer to the roiling terror which was building inside my ribcage, but Julius kept moving towards the waterfront. He looked around cautiously then pulled a thick tarp from a wooden rowing boat which was concealed on the shore.

"No," I breathed, my voice coming out so faint that none of the others heard me, but I dug my heels in all the same.

Julius shoved the tiny boat towards the river and Magnar tossed his pack into it before helping him.

The boat perched on the water, bobbing up and down precariously in the current as Julius held it in place.

"Are you sure this is a good idea?" I asked as Magnar helped Montana to climb in. "That boat is really small and there's a hell of a lot of water here. What if we fall in?"

I had thought I'd done a fairly good job of concealing my panic as I spoke but one look from Magnar told me he saw right through me.

"Get in the boat," Magnar commanded, and I was struck with the power which bent me to his will.

If some part of me had thought that he would no longer use that power after the rain bullshit, any such daydreams were shattered as his will wrapped around me and I found myself at the mercy of his words once again.

Anger flashed through me and I glared at him as my body began to move without my consent.

I took a step forward then jammed my heel into the riverbank as I forced myself to stop. Julius's mouth twitched in a smile as he watched me, and sweat began to bead on my forehead as I focused all of my energy on holding my position, refusing to give in.

The furious words I wanted to spit at Magnar burned my tongue as the seconds ticked by, my limbs trembling with the effort of remaining rooted to the spot.

Magnar's eyes glittered with fire, and I ground my teeth furiously as my traitorous body took a second step. My fingers grasped the edge of the boat against my will, but I refused to move another inch.

The compulsion pushed at me more forcefully, my body shaking and inching forwards in jerky movements until I finally caved to his hold over me and jumped into the boat.

Montana's eyes were wide as she watched me and she took my hand as I sat beside her, silently asking me if I was alright.

"Good," Magnar said, and I couldn't help the flush of pride at how much I'd managed to fight his command. Though I still threw him a heavy glare as I settled myself in to the seriously unsafe-looking vessel.

I blew out a breath and tried to go over what I'd just managed in my head, fixating on precisely what I'd done when I was resisting him and making sure I remembered it for the next time. I was so over my fate being outside of my control and I was determined to break the ties which held me.

Magnar and Julius pushed the boat out into the water before leaping in beside us, splashing cold droplets over us as they did so and making the boat rock wildly.

"I've never seen a novice fight the compulsion like that so soon after taking their vow," Julius said as he lifted an oar and began rowing. "You must *really* want to get into my brother's britches."

Montana laughed and I muttered irritable refusals of his assessment, despite the heat which crawled over my flesh as Magnar's penetrating gaze drank me in. I fixed my eyes out over the water instead and refused to look at either of them as we steadily made our way across the river.

Nerves pulled at me as we made it to the centre of the river and the current began to pull us along. I was trying very hard not to focus on the violent bobbing of the boat or the endless expanse of water which spread away beneath me. A cold wind followed us, and I tugged my coat closer around my neck as an icy chill settled into me veins.

Between the current and Magnar and Julius rowing, we made quick progress along the river despite my concerns. Soon, we were leaving the ruins behind and crossing the boundary to the city. My skin prickled uncomfortably as we passed so close to the vampires' homes. There were plenty of windows overlooking the water, some illuminated, suggesting the residents were home.

I felt exposed despite our quiet passage through the dark. It would only take one set of inquiring eyes to spot us, and if they did, the Belvederes would be quick to respond.

"That's our destination," Julius murmured as he pointed up ahead.

I followed the line of his arm and spotted an enormous green statue of a woman holding up a torch in the distance, highlighted by the moon. I hadn't expected it to be so big and I couldn't even begin to imagine how such a thing had been created.

A sense of unease twisted my gut and I tightened my grip on Tempest. It was almost as if something was drawing closer, but every time I felt near to telling what it was, the knowledge slipped away from me.

"Elder," I said quietly, unable to ignore the prickling in my gut any longer. "Something feels...wrong."

Magnar stilled and pulled the oar across his lap before reaching over his shoulder to grasp Venom. His brow furrowed with confusion and suddenly his head snapped up to scour the sky.

"Shit," Julius cursed as he drew his bow and aimed at something above our heads.

I held my breath as a huge shadow swept across the stars and Julius loosed his arrow. The owl shrieked, shifting to try and avoid the blow but it exploded into dust as the arrow hit its heart.

A dark shape tumbled towards us, and I shoved Montana aside at the last moment just before a black stone slammed into the wooden seat where she'd been sitting.

I picked it up and the urge to vomit washed over me as I felt a dark power writhing within it, quickly passing it to Magnar.

"That's pretty fucking clever, I've never seen someone cloak a Familiar with one of these before," Julius cursed as he frowned at the rune stone. "And it damn well worked too. Whoever was linked to that bird knows exactly where we are now."

"Do you think it was Fabian?" Montana asked with concern, her eyes roaming over the riverbank.

I ignored the thrill I felt at the sound of his name and stared out across the water intently.

"There's no sign of anyone coming for us," I said slowly.

"Then we should get out of here before they do." Magnar dipped his oar back into the water and hurried on through the night.

Tempest was growing warmer in my palm and I looked around, my gaze flicking from place to place, trying to figure out if it was just the city full of vampires which angered the blade, or some closer threat.

The water stirred unnaturally around us and a prickling sensation crawled up my spine. I listened hard for any sounds of approach, but the world was achingly quiet. Even the wind had fallen still.

Something thumped against the base of the boat and my heart lurched into my throat.

I grabbed the wooden seat to steady myself and looked to the others in alarm.

Magnar and Julius stopped rowing, drawing their blades as they searched for the threat too.

My pulse thundered as I gazed into the black water, hoping I was imagining the dark shape moving beneath the surface.

I pointed towards it, a tremor of fear bleeding through me though I didn't dare to speak. There was something moving in the river.

Montana leaned closer to me as she looked out into the rippling depths, her face pale in the moonlight, her hand gripping my forearm.

I released a shaky breath which spiralled from my lips in a cloud of vapour as the eerie silence pressed closer.

A heavy bang juddered through the boat as something collided with the base of it again. My heart jackhammered in fright as the entire boat rocked so violently that we were nearly thrown from it. I grabbed Montana's hand and reached for my gifts because I sure as shit couldn't swim without the aid of my ancestors.

The boat rocked wildly and Tempest burned hot in my palm, the blade screaming at me to ready myself, warning of the attack which I still didn't understand. I gripped the edge of the boat as something collided with it again, my entire focus honed on the effort it took to remain upright in the tiny vessel.

Adrenaline coursed through my limbs as I fought to keep my balance and Montana's breaths came quicker, her eyes meeting mine.

"Shit," Magnar cursed.

"Hold on tight," Julius directed.

The boat shuddered violently again. I looked to Magnar and Julius as my heart thundered in my ears, but I found no answers in their steely gazes, only a terrifying reality.

"What should we-"

A scream ripped from my throat as something collided with the boat so hard that we were launched into the air.

I tumbled backwards, falling from the vessel with panic consuming me as I clung to Montana. We hit the icy water and the breath was knocked from my lungs in a torrent of bubbles as I sank beneath it.

I flailed desperately, drawing on my ancestors' knowledge of swimming until I managed to start kicking for the surface, dragging Montana and Tempest with me.

My head breached the water and I sucked down a lungful of air as I pulled Montana up beside me. She started coughing and I stared about wildly while Tempest burned in my hand, urging me to fight. Vampires were drawing closer, but I couldn't see them anywhere-

A cold hand clamped around my ankle and dragged me back beneath the surface. Terror raced through my bones as fingernails bit into my skin. I released my grip on Montana as I was submerged once more, the darkness beneath the water so complete that I lost all sense of where I was.

I couldn't see anything in the pressing darkness, and I was dragged further and further away from the promise of oxygen. Panic gripped me as I tried to kick my attacker off, my boot colliding with an arm and a body, but not hard enough to dislodge the beast who had hold of me.

The vampire's grip moved up my leg and its teeth sank into my thigh so suddenly that my senses were overloaded by the agony for several terrifying heartbeats. I screamed in pain and fury, my thoughts snapping back together as I focused, refusing to allow myself to fall prey to this monster after all I'd survived to get here.

Tightening my grip on Magnar's blade, I stabbed Tempest through the water, letting it guide my hand as it carved a path towards my attacker.

The blade must have found the vampire's heart as the bloodsucker's grip on me vanished while Tempest growled its appreciation over the meal.

I kicked for the surface, desperate to satisfy the aching need in my lungs and find Montana again.

I had to battle the current as I swam but the silvery light of the stars egged me on. I was so close but still painfully far away, my limbs sluggish beneath the water even with the knowledge of my ancestors to help me navigate it.

I ground my teeth in determination and finally made it back to the surface, gasping down air as I whipped around, trying to see over the bobbing water, hunting for the others.

Dark water surrounded me in every direction and I spun around, searching for any sign of my sister.

"Montana!" I bellowed, not caring if every vampire in the vicinity heard me. She couldn't swim and she had no gifts to help her fight off the freezing touch of the water either.

"Callie!"

I turned at the sound of Julius's voice and found him swimming towards me.

"Are you alright? Where's Montana?" I asked desperately.

"Magnar has her. We have to get to shore; the water is full of-" He disappeared beneath the surface, and I yelled in alarm as I started swimming after him.

I dove beneath the water, straining my eyes to try and see anything in the murky depths. Tempest urged me forward and I swam towards a glimmer of metal as fast as I could.

Strike true, the blade commanded and I swept it forward as a body lunged for me. I made out swathes of black hair just before Tempest met with the vampire's heart, destroying it.

A hand clamped around my elbow and I yelled in fright, releasing a stream of bubbles before realising it was just Julius.

He guided me back to the surface and I followed him quickly, adrenaline saturating my veins.

"Come on!" he yelled as we met with the cold air again. My heart pounded violently at the fear of more vampires lurking beneath us and I clung to the heavy slayer's blade with all I had.

Julius began swimming away from me and I had no choice but to follow him and hope that Magnar and Montana had already made it to land.

Tempest growled warnings to me as I swam on and more vampires followed beneath my legs. My heart pounded with fear, and I threw all of my effort into powering through the water to escape them. This wasn't a battlefield I wanted to fight on and certainly not one where I wanted to face the beasts who hunted us.

My knees finally collided with the riverbank and I scrambled upright, taking Julius's hand as he hauled me away from the water.

I panted heavily, my boots slipping on the stones as I scrambled away from the water's edge then spun around, searching for any sign of Magnar and my sister.

"Where are they?" I demanded as Julius raised his blade and the first of the vampires rose from the river.

I held Tempest before me as they came at us and a sound carried to me on the wind, spearing panic right through my heart. Montana was screaming and I had no idea where she was.

MONTANA

CHAPTER FOURTEEN

I flailed in the water, trying to remember anything Miles had taught me in the swimming pool. But this wasn't like that. It was freezing, dark and vampires were attempting to pull me under.

Fear coursed down my spine as I thrashed and kicked at the hands trying to seize me, to drown me in this hellish river.

I stayed afloat for two more seconds before cold fingers took hold of my ankle and I was dragged beneath the surface. I sank towards its endless depths, taken from my sister, from the slayers, from any chance of ever seeing Erik again. Nails raked across my back and panic tore at my insides.

I will not die.

I frantically treaded water, trying to release Nightmare from my hip, kicking and fighting to get free. As I snatched the blade and swept my arm out in desperation, I knew I was done for. No matter how much it guided my movements, I couldn't hit my target.

I won't give up.

A glittering sword plunged through the water and the vampire met a brutal end. Arms seized me, strong powerful arms that could only belong to a slayer. I crashed through the surface, colliding with a solid chest as I drew in deep, ragged breath of sweet, sweet air.

Magnar held me, his eyes fierce as he stabbed his sword into the gloomy water around us.

"I've got you, hold on," he said, and I looped my arms around his neck.

"Thank you," I whispered, clinging to him and knowing he was my only chance of escaping this dreaded river.

The moon watched our predicament from above, but clouds drew over its eye and a thick darkness stole my vision. I sucked in freezing breaths of air as Magnar pulled me along, the splash of his sword hitting the water seeming like the only noise in the world.

I looked left and right, hunting for Callie across the murky river, but it was too dark. The city lights were all I could see as Magnar hauled me towards them. I let him assist me, trying to move my numb limbs to help. We finally clawed our way up the riverbank and I coughed up water which had found its way to my lungs.

"Callie," I croaked, turning back to the river in desperation.

A vampire surged from the water, lunging for my ankles with a feral hunger. Her hair was lank and dripping as she grabbed me, her fangs bared. A scream tore from my throat as I kicked out at her, but Magnar's blade found her first and she disintegrated into dust.

I scrambled to my feet, trembling as I searched for Julius and Callie, fearing for their lives. I went to call out, but Magnar clamped a hand over my mouth, tugging me away from the water's edge with such strength that I could do nothing to stop him.

"Quiet, we're too close to the city." He gazed over his shoulder at the closest skyscraper which loomed above us. Lights flickered on in some of the windows as Magnar led me back to the high wall which separated the bank from the city. I leaned against it, squinting into the darkness, desperate to see a glimmer of blonde hair out in the water.

My pulse thundered in my ears. "What if they're hurt? Or- or-"

Magnar shook his head, eyeing a star-shaped mark on the back of his hand. "Callie is alive, the mark of the vow would have faded otherwise. And I have no fear for my brother's life when dealing with lesser vampires like these. They must have washed up elsewhere."

My shoulders dropped with relief, but it didn't last long as more vampires poured from the water. Magnar moved to intercept them and I raised Nightmare, my resilience renewed.

None of us are going to die today.

Magnar kicked a male in the chest, bringing him to the ground before driving his sword into his heart. A female raced toward me, a cruel smile on her lips and I raised Nightmare, terror pounding through me as Magnar was attacked by two more of them, stopping him from helping me.

"Valentina awaits your head," the vampire purred before leaping at me.

As she collided with me, I brought Nightmare up with all my might, a growl of determination ripping through my throat. I stumbled to the ground as her weight slammed into me, but the blade sank deep into her flesh and ashes cascaded around me.

Bruised and frozen, I staggered upright. These were *biters*. And Valentina must have been using them to hunt us down.

I ground my teeth, anger flowing freely in my blood. I'd kill her. She was vile. Worse than any vampire I'd ever met.

Magnar dispatched three more vampires before the onslaught stopped, and I eyed the river with a shudder fleeing across my skin. Who knew how many more biters lurked in its depths.

Magnar glanced over his shoulder toward the city. "We'll have to head toward the statue on foot."

"But what about the others?" I gasped, anxiety burrowing through my chest.

"They know where to go. We'll meet them there."

I nodded, accepting it was our only option, but I hated the idea of parting from my sister again.

Magnar gave me an intense look. "They're slayers. They'll be fine."

I sighed, figuring he was right. I'd seen what Callie was capable of; she was a force to be reckoned with. "Alright. Let's go."

We sped up the beach, hugging the wall at its summit and remaining in its thick shadow as we sprinted alongside the river. I could just see the statue far out in the water ahead of us, but how on earth were we going to get to it without a boat?

The beach soon tapered to a thin point, leaving us stranded at the water's edge with no obvious passage onward.

My heart stumbled as Magnar took a sharp right and we arrived in a damp stairway which led up to the city roads.

He paused on the steps and I could barely make out his features as he turned to me. "We have to get as close to the statue as possible before we swim again. The biters could be anywhere along this stretch of water."

"Swim?" I squeaked.

"You can hold onto me again, I won't let any harm come to you," he rumbled and I sighed, nodding firmly. Magnar had saved my life. And whatever anger I'd felt toward him before was melting, its place taken by a growing trust.

He gripped my shoulder. "We stick to the shadows. Any vampire who sees us dies, understand?"

I gritted my teeth as I shivered in the icy air. "Let's try not to be seen."

"Agreed." He turned and I followed him up the steps, praying Callie and Julius could find safe passage to the statue.

I started to doubt if leaving the ruins had been a good idea. But we didn't have any choice now. We had to continue and hope we made it to our destination unscathed.

We emerged on the road which was lit with the orange glow of street lights. It was late, but the vampires thrived in the night, and we were now on the outskirts of their hive.

This area of the city seemed quiet though. Traffic rumbled close by but there were no cars here. Not yet anyway.

Magnar took a left and we started jogging down the road, two of my paces needed to match one of his. I eyed the windows above us as we moved past tower blocks, hoping no one was looking out.

The cross on my palm began to throb and a need grew in me that took over everything else. I slowed to a halt, thinking of Erik. If I was seen, someone would take me back to him...

"Montana," Magnar growled and I shook my head hard, forcing the urge away.

I hurried to his side, murmuring an apology as I kept pace with him again.

"It's that mark," he muttered as we moved.

"Yes, but I can handle it," I promised, curling my left hand into a tight fist. Idun wouldn't get the better of me.

My fingers were numb, but the faster we ran, the more my blood heated and battled out the cold.

The road soon opened up and a dock came into view ahead, crowded with boats. Huge, white vessels sat on the water, bobbing gently on the waves. They were luxurious things with large sails, too big for us to even consider taking one.

Laughter reached my ears from the streets behind us and we quickened our pace, darting onto the closest jetty and ducking down in the shadow of a large boat.

Magnar took a slow breath, eyeing the water at the end of the pier. The boats around us were quiet and no lights shone from within them. I hoped that meant we were alone.

I ran my thumb over Nightmare's hilt, but it gave no further clue of our safety; it had been humming with energy ever since we'd entered the city's streets.

"Okay, let's move." Magnar nodded toward the river and I followed him, creeping along in the dark.

Nightmare vibrated a little harder and Magnar stilled. I nearly bumped into him, bracing myself on his back.

"What is it?" I breathed as fear tip-toed down my spine.

"Stay back," Magnar commanded as a splash sounded ahead of us. He pushed me against the closest boat, shielding me with his body.

A rough laugh sounded from up ahead. "You're coming with us, slayer. Give us the girl and we'll make her death quick."

I sucked in a breath, peering around Magnar's huge form and spotting the imposing male vampire at the end of the pier, dripping wet and holding a large chain in his hand.

Magnar lifted his sword with a feral snarl. "The only thing I'll be giving you is a ride on the wind when I turn you to dust." He stepped forward to meet his opponent and suddenly something clicked together inside my head.

He'd said *we'll* make her death quick.

A hand burst through the boards at my feet, grabbing my ankle and yanking so hard the pier broke beneath me.

I cried out and my heart soared as I slashed Nightmare down to defend myself. But I plunged into the freezing water and darkness stole my vision, kicking wildly as arms surrounded me, hauling me along beneath the waves. Salt water seared my nostrils as I swiped Nightmare along my attacker's arms, but they didn't let go.

Panic sped beneath my skin as my head broke the surface and I gulped down air, blinking to try and regain my senses.

I was deposited on a small, sloping beach beneath the line of piers and terror consumed me as I took in the group of vampires standing there. They were all dripping wet and deathly pale, their fangs bared as they stared down at me with a desperate hunger in their eyes. It took me a beat longer to realise why they hadn't attacked me yet.

Valentina stepped forward from the group, her full lips pulling up in a dark smile.

"Use her as bait for Magnar," she commanded the biters. "Then you can all have the blood you're owed."

A heavy scuffle sounded on the pier above us and I was sure that more than one vampire was taking on Magnar now. His roars of defiance swiftly ended in the screams of dying biters and my heart swelled at the noise.

I gritted my teeth as I pinned my gaze on Valentina, hatred coursing through me. I rose to my feet, lifting Nightmare and baring my teeth right back at the group despite the fear snaking through my body. "Monster," I hissed at her.

Valentina released a tittering laugh, stepping forward and reaching for Nightmare. I swiped my blade through the air in a vicious arc, but she snatched my wrist, squeezing tightly until pain lanced through the bone and I yelped as I was forced to drop it. She bent down, taking it into her grip and I lurched forward to try and grab it from her. Strong hands caught me from behind, holding me back and immobilising me.

"How are we going to bring the slayer down here, Basil?" Valentina asked the vampire holding me.

"We make the human scream," he suggested, and his icy breath floated over my neck.

My heart thrashed as I tried to jerk free, but Valentina gave him a signal and he tilted my head sharply sideways, his fangs brushing my throat.

"No!" I threw an elbow back in alarm, somehow managing to keep my blood away from this beast a second longer.

Valentina slapped me hard across the face and a tremor rocked my body. I turned to look at her again as her palm print left a heated mark on my cheek. She caught me by the throat, dragging me out of Basil's arms and into hers.

She bared her fangs with a furious glint in her eye. "You took everything from me when Erik chose you. Do you know how many years I have waited to be crowned at Erik's side? How close I was to taking my rightful place in the New Empire?"

My mind tangled with her words, that she believed Erik would have offered her that position. That he must have promised it to her, even if only as a lie.

"You're nothing to him," I hissed and her eyes flared in fury at those words.

Her nails pinched my skin, and I hissed between my teeth as she drew blood. Her followers started shifting from foot to foot, salivating as the scent of my blood filled the air.

"Stupid girl. You think you meant something to a Belvedere prince?" she scoffed. "You were just a distraction, some pretty legs to spread for a while to entertain him, but you could never offer him the pleasure I could."

"I wasn't his entertainment," I snarled, the words tearing from my lips.

She grinned keenly, her malicious gaze tracing my expression. "Wait...Erik didn't even bother to fuck you, did he?" She threw her head back, laughing hard and the biters joined in like the mindless creeps they were.

Anger seeped through my bones and I brought up a fist, slamming it into her smug face. She blinked in surprise, then a battle cry filled the air and the pier broke apart above us. Magnar came falling from the sky, crashing down on top of Valentina and crushing her to the ground with his weight. I was thrown onto the rocks as she shrieked in alarm, trying to roll beneath him and Nightmare slipped from her hand.

"Grab him! I want him alive!" she cried at the others and the vampires swarmed forward to take hold of Magnar.

I stooped low, snatching Nightmare, letting it guide my hand. *Turn them to ashes*, it purred.

I lifted my arm and drove the dagger forcefully into a male's chest with a cry of effort.

He exploded around me and a female screamed at the sight, making a direct line for me. I steadied myself, digging my feet into the sand, fuelled by rage alone. She swiped for my head, snatching hold of my hair and pain flared across my scalp. She yanked me closer, trying to sink her teeth into my arm, but Nightmare guided my hand and I planted my blade in her heart before her teeth broke the skin.

Spinning around, I spotted Magnar being dragged off of Valentina by the remaining three lessers. The slayer snatched one by the waist, cleaving the female apart with his sword before turning on the final two. They shared a look of fear then fled into the ocean.

Valentina sucked in a breath of shock, glancing between us then racing up the beach toward the road.

"Stop!" Magnar boomed. "Do you still ache for a wedding, Valentina? Let me marry your heart to the end of my sword." The slayer stormed up the steep beach, taking chase as she made it onto the road above.

Valentina's feet hit the concrete just as Magnar reached for her. Lightning tore the ground apart between them, throwing him back into the sand with a heavy thud. She fled into the city and anger rattled my bones.

I ran to Magnar's side and he cursed, rubbing soot from his face with his hands which were badly blistered.

"That woman is a bane that never ends," he snarled.

"Are you alright?" I asked, fear punching a hole in my chest.

Magnar sat upright and I took in the extent of his injuries. His shirt was burned away and angry welts lined his skin.

He gritted his teeth. "I'll heal. I just need some time."

I sat beside him and rested a hand on his back, patting him vaguely then wondering if that was a weird thing to do.

He raised an eyebrow as he turned to me. "You're done hating me then?"

"I never hated you," I said with a small smile, dropping my hand to my side. "I just don't like you bossing my sister around."

"I only do it to protect her," he swore and I nodded.

"I know that now. You're like your brother. He tied me up once to 'protect me.'"

Magnar released a low laugh. "I don't doubt that. Julius has his eye on you, you realise?"

My cheeks heated and I dipped my head, looking directly at the silver cross on my left palm. "Well he's going to be disappointed."

"He's quite determined when he sets his sights on a woman." He chuckled. "You would make a fine pairing. My brother has a good heart and a strong spirit. Like you."

I smiled vaguely, not wanting to offend him. Julius was a good man, but my heart belonged to someone else. The vampire he and Magnar despised more than any of them.

I noticed some of the burns on Magnar's body had already become less red and the blisters were slowly fading away.

I frowned deeply. "Valentina said she wanted to take you."

"Yes," he grunted. "My betrothed still seems to have some intention toward me. But if she thinks I'd ever look at her with affection, she is deluded. Even before she was a monster, I held no love in my heart for her. I have never felt that way for anyone until..." He cleared his throat.

"Callie," I finished for him with a smile lifting my lips.

"Yes," he said and his eyes glittered with longing as he ran his thumb over the star-shaped mark on his hand. As his skin slowly knitted over, it seemed to stand out even more starkly than before.

The water lapped calmly against the shore and Nightmare's aura became more peaceful. The biters were long gone, but I didn't think Valentina would give up so easily. I thought over what she'd said about Erik and a knife dug into my heart. How could he have been with someone like her? Had he really promised her a position at his side?

"Come, let's move. We must leave this place before Valentina returns with more of her vile followers. As much as I'd like to finish her now, our fight would draw the attention of the vampires in the city and I cannot face them all at once." Magnar rose to his feet, sheathing his sword on his back. "Hold onto my neck," he instructed and I did so, wrapping my arms around him and gripping him tight.

"Ready?" he asked.

"Yes," I said, and he lifted me onto his back before striding into the water.

I held my breath as we lowered into its icy embrace and I gripped on fiercely as Magnar cut a path through the waves, reaching one arm over the other in powerful strokes.

We made our way out of the harbour and the cold slid deeper into my body. I was looking forward to a fire and some hot food, but most of all I was looking forward to reuniting with my sister.

The statue was a hulking figure under the dark clouds, guiding us toward it. Magnar's strength never faltered as he carried me and my heart bloomed with a newfound trust. He may have been an asshole at times, but he sure was a reliable asshole. And if Callie had feelings for him, I had to let go of the mistake he'd made in hurting her. I could see in their eyes how much they meant to each other. I would never stand in the way of that. I just wondered if Callie could ever feel the same way about me and Erik.

CALLiE

CHAPTER FIFTEEN

My heart throbbed as Julius grabbed my hand and yanked me further up the beach, away from the river and my sister. The hoard of vampires seemed to never stop racing out of the water despite the fact that we must have killed ten of them already. But as even more of them clambered from the water, their ravenous gazes fixed on the two of us, I was sure there were far too many for us to fight off at once.

I had no choice but to let Julius drag me away, to break into a sprint and hope to all the gods in the sky that Magnar had gotten her to safety.

"Run faster," Julius growled.

"What about Montana and Magnar?" I asked desperately. We couldn't just leave them behind.

"You still have your novice mark. If Magnar was dead it would be gone. And he'd give his life to protect Montana so we can assume they're both okay. *We* won't be if we don't move though," Julius urged.

Relief spilled through me as I glanced at the mark on my hand and I upped my speed, giving all of my attention to our escape.

Vampires continued to swarm from the water and I focused fully on our retreat in the hopes of leading them after us, knowing we needed to fight them on our own terms.

"Here," Julius commanded, pointing to a narrow set of steps carved into a high wall which surrounded the river. "Choke point. Let's finish these assholes."

I set my feet as I took up position beside him and raised Tempest before me. We barely had a moment before the vampires were upon us. Fifteen of them raced our way, baying for our blood like a pack of bloodthirsty dogs.

I ground my teeth at the sight of these monsters who thirsted for my life force. There was no way in hell they'd be getting a drop of it.

Julius miraculously still had his bow as well as his pack and he fired arrow after arrow at the approaching demons, sending six of them spiralling to dust before they could reach us.

I leapt forward to meet the first one who made it close enough and carved a path straight through his chest with the heavy blade. Tempest thrummed excitedly as it bathed in his blood and I fell into the rhythm of the fight.

I ducked low as the next vampire lunged for me, driving the sword straight up through his groin while he screamed in pain. Carnage descended as Julius unleashed Menace and he stabbed it through the vampire's heart to finish him off for me.

He carved through two more of the monsters before I made it upright, and I spun away from him, swinging Tempest wildly and taking the head from a male.

"Is that the slayer Valentina wants?" one of them hissed as he eyed Julius.

"No. This one's fair game," a female replied as she leapt towards him.

Julius kicked the female in the chest and she fell onto my blade where I held it ready. My mind reeled. Why were they hunting Magnar? But the ferocity of our fight drove it from my mind as I was forced to focus on killing them.

The remaining three vampires rushed Julius at once and I took four running steps towards him. He noticed my approach and reached back for me, catching my hand in his and swinging me forwards as I leapt to

170

meet the last of our foes. I collided with them, sending them crashing to the ground and I drove my blade through the one in the centre.

Julius wheeled Menace over my head in a wide arc that slashed through the final pair, and I closed my eyes as their remains cascaded over me, the ash clinging to my drenched clothes.

Everything fell deathly quiet and Julius offered me his hand. Our adrenaline peaked at our victory as he pulled me upright and we grinned at each other.

"Not bad, novice," he said, slapping my upper arm and causing my saturated coat to spray water over both of us.

"That was fun," I admitted. "Did you hear what that male said though? About wanting to catch a slayer for Valentina?"

"I don't tend to pay much attention to the ramblings of my victims. Lessers such as these would have no chance of capturing my brother anyway," he replied dismissively, though that did little to ease the worry twisting my insides. "And it's no surprise to learn that Valentina is searching for him. Her obsession with Magnar is well established."

"And that doesn't concern you?" I asked uneasily.

"No. And it shouldn't concern you either. If Magnar had ever wanted Valentina then he would have had her. I've never seen him look at any other woman the way he looks at you."

I flushed, shaking my head and refusing to dissect that little nugget of information. "I'm not worried because I'm jealous. I'm worried because she's a psycho with a band of bloodthirsty followers and control over the elements."

Julius chuckled like I was joking, stooping to pick up the pack he'd dropped while taking on the vampires.

"You can finish the last one," he offered, pointing at the vampire I'd decapitated.

I nudged its head with the toe of my boot and looked down into the male's glassy eyes.

"Could he really heal from that?" I asked curiously.

"I'll show you," Julius said with a grin. "Hold your blade ready to finish him."

"Okay," I said slowly, resting Tempest against the vampire's chest above his heart.

Julius picked up the head by its hair and clasped its chin between his fingers. "Hi, I'm Headward," he said in a stupid voice as he forced the mouth to open and shut like it was talking.

I snorted a laugh. "You're twisted."

"You have no idea," he replied suggestively before placing the head back onto the vampire's neck.

My mouth fell open as the skin slowly began to knit back together and the vampire's eyelids fluttered.

"Holy shit," I breathed in fascination.

"Fucked up, right?"

The vampire's eyes snapped open and I flinched before driving the blade down and turning him to dust.

"Come on then, we need to beat Magnar and Montana to that statue." Julius turned away and started jogging up the steps.

"Beat them? I didn't know we were racing."

"Of course we're racing! Everything's a game if you make it into one. And we're gonna win!"

My coat was totally saturated and the thick material was weighing me down so I reluctantly shrugged it off and left it on the steps. I squeezed the worst of the moisture from my hair as I ran to catch up with Julius, frustrated that every time I found myself a nice, warm coat, it always ended up leaving me.

As I emerged at the top of the steps, Julius held out an arm to halt me. I concentrated on Tempest's energy but there were so many vampires nearby that it was impossible to lock on to any one threat.

"It's clear," Julius whispered and I followed him across a dark street into a side alley. "Let's take the rooftops from here."

"What?" I asked with a frown.

"It's the best way to get around the city without being noticed," he assured me.

I still didn't know what he meant, but I trusted his judgment as he'd spent weeks in the city before we'd arrived and he hadn't been caught.

Julius leapt towards a window several feet above his head and caught it easily, hoisting himself higher before clambering up the wall to the next floor. I watched him for several seconds as he climbed away from me, taking note of his movements and preparing myself to mimic them. With a deep breath, I shook off my doubts and ran at the wall too.

My fingers found a space between the bricks and I dragged myself higher. I grabbed a window ledge next and began to pick up speed as I got the feel for it. When I made it to the top of the building, Julius caught my hand and helped me onto the roof.

I glanced back at the drop below me and let out a shaky breath. We were sixteen floors up and the concrete far below beckoned me, promising to splatter my body if I fell.

"There she is," Julius breathed, pointing along the river to the huge statue which was bathed in moonlight.

"Not too far to go," I replied. "But how does being up here help us?"

"You know, your sister didn't love this idea either. But I won her 'round in the end." Julius smirked at me then took off across the rooftop.

I sucked in a breath as he reached the edge and dove off of it like a fearless madman. He landed neatly on the next building and turned back to me expectantly.

I stared at him for several long seconds, wondering if I was really crazy enough to follow him. A tingling started up in my muscles and adrenaline flooded through me as I considered it. With a surge of bravery or, more likely stupidity, I took off.

I raced across the rooftop and before I knew it, my boot landed on the edge and I launched myself into the sky. My gut plummeted, my heart leapt, and the air bit at my cheeks, but then it was done. My feet hit the next roof and I skidded to a halt as a laugh bubbled from my lips.

"That's more like it," Julius said with a wild look about him. "You've been way too serious the last few days. You need to remember why being one of us is so great."

Before I could respond, he was running again and a savage smile pulled at my lips as I sprinted after him. My legs pounded with energy and I chased him from roof to roof, keeping the huge statue in sight as a lightness filled my chest. He was right; being a slayer kicked ass. I could do without being bound to so many rules by a petty goddess, but when I let my gifts have free rein, I was fucking unstoppable. And it felt seriously *good.*

Julius leapt to a roof on our left and I smirked as I raced towards one on our right. I charged across it, pulling my gifts to me in a flood as I launched myself over the next ledge. The statue was getting ever closer and he had said he wanted a race.

A street divided our routes and I could see him tearing along in the corner of my eye, keeping pace with me as I threw all of my effort into beating him.

I landed on a gravel rooftop and my boots skidded awkwardly, my heart lurching as I caught my balance. The street ahead was a dead end and there was a single building which stood at the closest point to the statue before we'd have to descend again.

I hurled myself toward the next roof, catching the edge of it before heaving myself up, the thrill making my head spin. I started running again instantly, the final building looming with promise right in front of me. Just one more jump-

I rolled as I hit the roof and sprang back to my feet just in time to see Julius launching himself over from the building opposite. A smile lit my features as he jogged to a halt before me and folded his arms over his broad chest.

"You cheated," he announced.

"How?" I asked, arching an eyebrow at him.

"Your route was easier."

"Sure. If you say so." I rolled my eyes at him and moved towards the far side of the building, gazing out to where the statue stood on an island in the river.

With a violence that set my pulse thrashing, a fork of lightning shot from the sky and hit the ground on the far side of the river. I held my breath as I stared at the spot, wondering if it could have been Valentina, if she was close.

The mark binding me to Magnar remained firmly on my skin though, so I forced away my concerns for him and my sister. The sooner we were reunited at the statue, the better. Until then there was no point in wasting effort worrying.

Julius peered down at the street below and I followed his gaze.

There were several bars open with colourful lights illuminating the sidewalk as vampires came and went. The street was busy, and it was going to be damn difficult to cross it.

Julius pressed a finger to his lips and led me over the roof to a metal fire escape. We descended silently and dropped down into a dark alleyway, my senses sharpening at every noise.

We crept towards the street and Julius glanced around the corner, but he lurched back suddenly and hoisted me into his arms, pressing his body to mine and pushing me up against the wall. I gasped in surprise as he placed his hand against the bricks beside me, pinning me in place and concealing our faces as he leaned closer.

"Try to pretend you're enjoying yourself, sweetheart - sometimes it's easier to hide in plain sight," he breathed as he dipped his face towards mine.

I held Tempest out of view and hooked my other arm around his neck as I caught on to what he was doing, making it look like the two of us were simply enjoying each other's company in the questionable privacy of the alleyway.

A group of vampires passed our hiding place and a few of the females giggled as they noticed us locked in our compromising position. They hurried on by without looking any closer, and I grinned at Julius as he released me.

"You're pretty good at this sneaking about stuff," I said lightly.

"I'm pretty good at everything," he replied, winking at me with such casual confidence that I had to roll my eyes at him. "So when you're ready to switch your attention to the better looking brother just let me know."

"There's a better looking brother? I didn't know there were three of you."

"Harsh. So harsh." He grabbed my hand and pulled me out onto the street.

We slipped across it quickly and jogged down another dark alley between the low buildings which lined the river, moving ever closer to our destination.

We kept running all the way to the water's edge and I eyed it nervously.

"Do you think there could still be biters in there?" I asked.

"Nah. Why would they hang about at the bottom of the Hudson? That was purely for our benefit before. They're either dead at our hands or they fled now they've lost us."

I nodded, clinging onto his certainty as I prepared to swim for the island.

"Well if you wanna beat Magnar and Montana, you might want to hurry up." I took a running jump and dived straight in, the freezing water swallowing me whole as I let my ancestors guide me once more.

I breached the surface and started swimming for the statue as fast as I could, but Julius kept pace beside me, his powerful arms carving through the water with ease.

I tried not to think about grasping hands reaching for me from the murky depths and before long we were striding out of the water beneath the giant statue.

"Oh fuck no!" Julius took off and I started laughing as I spotted Magnar racing towards the statue on the far side of the island. He'd lost his shirt somehow on his way here and I bit my lip as I eyed his muscular body appreciatively.

I jogged over to meet Montana and pulled her into my arms, relieved to be reunited. Fate was *never* going to tear us apart again.

"Are you okay?" I asked as we turned towards the statue.

"Thanks to Magnar. But we ran into Valentina on our way here," she replied gravely.

"Really?" I gasped. "Where is she now? Did Magnar kill her?" I asked hopefully.

"Sadly not. She ran away, but before she did, her followers tried to catch Magnar. I don't know why, but she definitely wants him for something."

I looked over at Magnar with concern. He'd fallen into a scuffle with Julius and their laughter carried to us, making my heart lift with joy. He'd been so endlessly alone and filled with grief when I'd first met him, but now that he had his brother back, I could see that pain lifting from him more and more.

"Let's hope the Belvederes manage to track her down and kill her before she comes for him again," I growled, somewhat thankful for the knowledge that Valentina was being hunted just as surely as we were.

Montana nodded in agreement and we started walking towards the slayers. "Are you alright?" she asked.

"Still in one piece," I confirmed as we closed in on a door at the foot of the towering statue.

Magnar and Julius were shoving each other and bickering in low voices as they waited for us, the two of them seeming much younger in their rivalry, the seriousness stripped from them for a moment.

"Tell this cheat who won," Magnar demanded as we reached them.

"I, err, wasn't looking." I shrugged at him unhelpfully and they both turned to Montana instead.

"Won what?" she asked.

They stared at us in disgust and stomped away into the building whilst continuing their argument.

I looked at Montana with an eyebrow raised and she pursed her lips, hiding an amused smile before we followed them inside.

MAGNAR

CHAPTER SIXTEEN

1000 YEARS AGO

The ship swayed gently as we gained some respite from the journey and both Elissa and Valentina got some rest. We had members of the Clan of Storms and Clan of Oceans on each of the ships in our fleet but as the strongest of their kinds, the two of them travelled with me. When they wielded their powers, the vessel moved so quickly that it had been enough to turn many warriors' stomachs, and more than one had given their meals up to the sea.

Their skills had made for a quick and safe crossing as Elissa gave us a strong current beneath the keel and Valentina drew the wind to our sails.

Idun had lit a glimmering golden star in the sky at the edge of the horizon so we could keep our aim true night after night. I eyed it with my arms folded as I lost myself in memories of my father. Sometimes it seemed that the closer I got to paying the debt for his life, the further I felt from him.

I was losing the shape of him in my mind. Had we stood eye to eye or was I taller than him in the end? Had his laugh been as deep as I thought I recalled, or was it softer than that? Were his eyes the colour of his blade or the same shade as the depths of a fire?

No matter what happened, when we finally tracked down the Revenants, I would never get that back. They had stolen him from me, from all of my family. And there was no amount of blood that could pay for his return.

"What are you thinking about?" my mother asked softly, placing a hand on my arm and pulling me back to the here and now.

"Just that in the end, all men die. All are lost and forgotten to time... or at least they should be." My frown deepened at the thought of our immortal enemies, and I scowled at the calm water surrounding us.

"We may forget some of the details," she replied. "But those we love will always live on in our hearts."

"But what about once we are gone too? Who will remember him when no one remembers us?" I asked, allowing myself that vulnerability with her because she of all people must have understood what I felt too.

"It is enough to know that we loved him. His life was full and happy because of us. And we will be reunited with him in Valhalla."

I nodded vaguely. The hall of the gods didn't hold as much desire for me as it once had. Idun was cruel and cunning despite claiming to love us as her people. And what of Andvari? He had created the creatures responsible for my father's demise. Would the afterlife truly be great if I had their company to look forward to?

"Land!" Aelfric cried from his position up on the mast. "Land, Earl Magnar! We've made it!"

I squinted at the horizon as my blood hummed with anticipation.

"Wake Elissa so that she can hasten us to shore," I said and my mother squeezed my arm before hurrying below deck to locate the Ocean Stirrer.

I moved to grip the railing as I peered towards the horizon and a dark smudge came into focus. He was right; we'd damn well made it.

I strode away from the glorious sight of land and headed to my quarters to collect my swords and fighting leathers. If luck stayed with me, I'd be bathing my blades in Revenant blood within the day.

I hurried into my room and quickly changed. As I pulled Venom

180

into my grasp, it sang with knowledge of my enemies. I hadn't felt the presence of the parasites through my blades in three long years and the weapons were hungry for blood.

The ship suddenly shot forward as Elissa commanded the waves to propel us onward, and I almost tumbled onto my bed, catching myself at the last moment with a bark of laughter.

I strapped my scabbards across my back and placed my blades into them before hurrying back up to the deck.

The sun had begun its ascent into the sky and I smiled as the view ahead of us was revealed more clearly.

The smudge on the horizon had grown into a sprawling landscape thick with tall trees and a pristine sandy beach which called us towards it.

"By the gods, I am looking forward to setting my feet on dry land again," Julius exclaimed as he moved to my side.

"And eating a meal made with fresh ingredients," I replied.

The stores we'd brought with us were growing stale and though we hadn't gone hungry, my stomach ached for some fresh fruit and vegetables.

"We'll take this land for our own once we've destroyed our enemies," Valentina said as she joined us too. Wind filled the sails and our speed increased further as she raised a hand to direct it. "Our children will grow up enjoying the wealth of this country."

I grunted in a non-committal way and Julius smirked at me. She always knew how to sour the best of days.

"Perhaps you should focus your mind on the wind instead of eyeing up my brother's potential parenting skills. Though if his horse is anything to go by, then he may bring his children up to be a bunch of savages, so you might be better not to marry him at all," Julius said.

He always tried to give Valentina reasons to doubt my suitability as a husband, but she never took any notice of him. I appreciated his continued efforts all the same.

"I can be pretty savage myself when I have to be," she replied dismissively.

The boat sped towards the coast and the wind Valentina had conjured picked up as if she were proving a point.

My blades grew warmer on my back as we closed in on the Revenants. I was sure they were more than just *somewhere* on this land; they were within close range.

I walked away from Valentina and climbed up onto the rigging as we drew close to the shore. The sun rose higher as our destination became clearer and I drank in the sight hungrily.

When we finally made it as close to land as the ship could manage, Elissa used her power over the waves to bring us to a halt and the wind blustered away as if it had never been.

Cries went up as the anchor was dropped and everyone prepared to disembark.

I gazed down into the crystal blue sea and leaned forward to watch as a giant turtle swam alongside our ship before diving beneath it. The rising sun shone down on us and I could already feel its warmth reaching out to me, like it too was glad to have us here, an enemy of our enemies.

This land seemed like it had been made for the people of the sun and I found myself glad to be here. My vow had driven me to cross the sea and I'd never really considered whether I could be happy leaving my homeland behind, but something about this place seemed right. Like I was destined to be here.

I glanced back over my shoulder and noticed Valentina weaving her way towards me once more. My lightened mood was a fragile thing and I wished to hold onto it for as long as possible.

"Mother?" I called, spotting her directing the clansmen at the front of the ship.

She turned to me with a faint smile and I couldn't help but be reminded of the radiance which had been absent since Father's passing. She'd lost something of herself when he'd been taken from us, and it saddened me to know she'd never smile like she used to.

"Running off again?" she guessed, and I couldn't help but smirk. She was so much better at the day to day running of the Clans than I was anyway. I was built to lead our people into battle, not organise the layout of our tents.

"Scouting the area," I explained, though we both knew it was a job

I could have easily designated to someone else.

"We'll look forward to your return around nightfall no doubt," she replied teasingly.

"No doubt," I agreed before diving off of the boat into the pristine water.

The tang of salt met my lips and I opened my eyes to gaze at the shimmering light beneath the waves. Schools of small fish darted around me, drawn close by the glimmer of my blades then frightened off again by my movements.

I powered through the water towards the beach and walked up the golden sand, feeling the solid ground beneath my feet with glee.

I quickly crossed the beach and pulled my swords from my back as I entered the swaying palm trees. Everything was a much more vivid green than I was used to from my homeland, and the smell of the flora was sharper too.

I drank in all the details with joy as I began to discover this new place and its secrets.

Blood thieves are close, Tempest growled through my mind, and I stilled.

Murderers near, Venom agreed.

The Revenants were closer than I'd dared to hope.

My blades urged me on and I chanced a look over my shoulder towards our fleet. It would have been sensible to head back and gather my people before hunting them down. But if they caught on to us approaching, they might just run again. And a single man would be much harder to detect. Besides, I'd never been one for sensible.

A fierce smile captured my features as I pressed on into the jungle. Perhaps this was the day that I paid the debt I owed my father and ended them for good. The Revenants were about to find out just how far my wrath would take me.

MONTANA

CHAPTER SEVENTEEN

We headed through a dusty old museum inside the statue and Magnar started breaking up wooden display cases for a fire.

I was shivering more violently now that the adrenaline had worn off and Callie kept giving me concerned looks. The slayers were much less affected by the biting cold. Even in their damp attire, they barely seemed bothered. I, however, was freezing my ass off.

"You need to get out of those clothes," Julius commented, helping Magnar to build the fire a few meters from a broken window.

"Y-you'd l-like that, w-wouldn't you?" I teased, but my joking tone was lost to my chattering teeth.

Julius snorted a laugh. "I can always warm you up once you're naked?" he offered, and Magnar thumped him on the arm.

"Do something useful or shut the fuck up," he joked.

We soon had a fire going and I sat before it in my underwear, having had no real choice but to strip off. Thankfully, the others did the same so I didn't feel alone in my nudity. We'd hung our clothes and the contents of our packs up to dry on a few glass cabinets and they fluttered in the breeze that sailed through the window.

Julius took his phone from the strap on his arm, his face lighting up as he pressed something on the screen.

"Full charge," he announced.

My eyes dropped briefly to his golden chest as it glimmered under the firelight. He and his brother were so muscular, it was impossible not to stare. I noticed Callie's gaze drifting to Magnar more than once too.

Julius caught my gaze, his eyebrows rising curiously, falling to my bare skin in kind, and suddenly I looked away, thinking of someone I shouldn't have been thinking of. Julius was kind and warm and good, exactly the sort of man I should have been looking at. But the thought of letting him closer brought a solid wall up in my chest, and all I could see in my head were the intense, steely eyes of a man my heart should never have beat for. But one who was so deep in my blood, I didn't know how I would ever forget him.

"Maybe you should check on the royals? They could have found Valentina if she ran into the city," I suggested, hoping the real reason I wanted to do that wasn't written all over my face.

I shifted toward Julius as he pressed something on the screen, feeling Callie's eyes on me, her scrutiny making heat crawl up the back of my neck. She knew. She had to know. Because my twin knew the essence of my soul, and right now, it was tethered to a vampire. One I couldn't stop thinking about, no matter how hard I tried.

"Yeah, good idea," she said a second later and I was relieved as she dropped down on Julius's other side, saying nothing yet again but feeling the weight of my secret sitting between us. Every time I tried to broach the subject, I choked, knowing that no explanation in the world was going to convince Callie that Erik was anything more than a heartless monster.

Magnar grunted but made no further comment. His clear mistrust of technology didn't seem to be waning and I wondered what it must have been like for him to try and adjust to so many things changing since he'd woken. Idun had given Julius the knowledge he needed, but Magnar still eyed the cellphone like it was some kind of dark magic.

"Party boy is having fun," Julius said, enlarging the box so that the dining room in the castle came into view. The place was thronging with people and I spotted Miles at the heart of them, grinding up against

Warren as they danced together, their smiles brightening their eyes.

"He doesn't slack off even when his whole empire is going to ruin," Julius muttered. "He celebrates his misdeeds, the blood he's drank this day. Look at them all dancing like they have no other cares in this world, they make me sick."

"Yeah all those hot women must really be turning your stomach," I jibed, taking in the party and smiling at Miles and Warren as they danced to the quickening beat.

"*Vampires*," he corrected me sharply and the bottom dropped out of my stomach.

"Monty! How can you even joke about that? They're disgusting," Callie agreed, and my lips pursed, a flash of frustration passing through me.

"They're just people," the words slipped out before I could stop them, and Callie's mouth fell open.

"What did you say?" she hissed, her eyes narrowing.

I'd rarely been on the receiving end of Callie's anger. We'd always been on the same side growing up, and I'd been more than grateful for that. She'd once reduced Jeremy Harper to tears after he'd pushed me in the mud. But now she was staring at *me* with the full force of that fiery rage and it made me achingly sad. Everything that had happened to us had driven a wedge between us, and I couldn't carve out the parts of me that had been altered by what I knew now.

"I just..." I sighed. I didn't want to lie anymore. And I was done pretending that I hadn't been changed by my time with the vampires. Telling her about my feelings for one of them was probably too much of a headfuck right now, but maybe I could explain myself a little.

"I just don't think they're *all* bad," I said, my heart thumping in my ears as I stood up for the vampires to a bunch of their sworn enemies. It wasn't like I was sticking up for the biters. They were true monsters. But Erik and some of the others weren't like that. They lived in shades of grey.

Callie gaped at me, then her eyes softened. "It's the mark," she said knowingly, reaching for my hand.

I inched it away from her, the sting of her dismissing my words too hurtful to ignore. Like I was just some brainwashed idiot who didn't know her own mind.

"What's going on?" she asked, frowning as she sensed my pain.

"Nothing." I shook my head as Julius glanced between us, looking awkward.

There was no point trying to explain, that was clear enough. Callie was set against the vampires, just as Magnar and Julius were. Just as I had been not so long ago. But there were clearly no words that could change their minds on that, or even open up to the possibility that maybe the vampires weren't simply soulless creatures with no desires beyond blood. Yes, they did bad things. Fucked up, twisted things. And I wasn't excusing that. But I'd witnessed moments of purity in them too. Of love, of devotion, of suffering.

I thought of Erik and that yearning I'd witnessed in him from time to time, that persistent desire to be more than what he had been cursed to be. From what the slayers had said, Idun had been a trickster just as Andvari had been. So weren't the slayers and vampires just different sides of the same coin? Wasn't the true fight between the gods, not us?

I dropped my gaze to the cellphone, grinding my teeth as I felt everyone's eyes on me, their accusations, their concerns, I felt it all like a weight upon my back. Slowly, Julius and Callie returned their attention to the security feed, but I didn't feel any less judged. I should have been comfortable sitting here among my kind, at home. But instead, I felt like I was sitting in a place that didn't fit me quite right, yet everyone kept telling me it was where I belonged.

Heat crawled up and down my spine, and the guilt of what I'd become washed through me. I was a traitor to everyone in this room. My heart was crying out for someone I couldn't have. Someone they thought was an abomination. And I would have agreed with that not so long ago, but I couldn't undo what I'd learned. And I wanted to stand up for Erik now. I wanted to scream my lungs out until they believed me. But they never would.

"Here's Prince Charming himself." Julius nudged me and my eyes whipped to Erik as he strode through the castle with Fabian at his side. Erik looked miserable, his brows drawn low, his white shirt crumpled and his eyes void of light. His brother looked pale and moved with a disjointedness that said he was in pain, his hand moving to clutch his stomach.

"Thank fuck he's alright," Callie sighed, then clapped a hand to her mouth in horror.

Magnar grumbled something from across the fire, but she didn't look at him, clearly pained by what she'd said. I hated that she'd been bonded to the wicked prince who ran the Realms, and honestly, could I really blame her for thinking that my feelings for Erik were driven by that same bond?

"Turn the volume up," I encouraged, and Julius complied, filling the room with their voices.

"You don't have to come with me, you know?" Erik said to Fabian.

"I want to be there," he growled. "I want to rip out his fangs and see him bleed for what he did to Callie's father."

Erik gave him a sweeping glance. "Firstly, *I* will be the one to de-fang Wolfe. And secondly, you are acting like a madman since the gods bound you to Montana's sister, so please keep it together in front of the cameras. We need to set an example to the people."

Fabian turned suddenly, grabbing Erik's arm and staring intently into his eyes. "I love her. I didn't get it before when you said you had feelings for a human. But I know now. And you understand this pain, don't you brother? You know how this feels." Fabian pressed a hand to his heart as if it hurt.

Erik hesitated then nodded, and a darkness entered his eyes that reached right into my soul. "Yes, but we can still act like rational people, Fabian. You are behaving like a love-sick puppy. For example, did I hear correctly that you're having a statue built of Callie Ford in Realm G?"

Fabian grinned widely. "Not just Realm G, Erik. All of the Realms! The whole of the human race will praise her name."

"Fucking hell," Callie muttered.

Erik's eyes narrowed dangerously. "You are losing your mind. Don't you think that money would be better spent improving the Realms?"

"Er- yeah. I'm dealing with that too. Plus your men are already there taking care of that. No harm in a little side project."

Erik scowled. "If you're going to insist on coming with me to banish Wolfe, you must keep it together. I don't want you causing any... embarrassment."

My heart clenched at his words, a mixture of passionate feelings passing through me over my desire to see Wolfe killed and my desire to see him lead Erik to Valentina. Regardless, Wolfe was going to be banished. *Tonight.*

Erik went on, "And don't mention a fucking thing about the slayers showing up at the wedding. Or the fact that Montana and Callie left with them. We don't need the headache that will cause." I spied him rubbing the cross on his left palm and the bond flared, my palm igniting and sending a bolt of need through me. I clenched my fist, the desire to get up and go to him burning a passage through my chest, but I fought it away, refuting it.

"I've got your back." Fabian nodded firmly, and Erik's expression softened.

"Well, that's the only good thing that's come from all this. I think you're acting more like your old self."

Fabian's eyes filled with light. "I have been a royal ass for more than a century."

"More like five centuries," Erik muttered as they headed out of sight and their voices faded away.

"They're leaving the castle," Julius announced. "But it sounds like they're going to broadcast the banishing, so we can tune in."

"I can't believe Fabian's building a statue of me," Callie breathed, her eyes flaring with emotion.

"Not just one," I pointed out and Callie threw me a grin, suddenly bursting into laughter. I couldn't help but join in and Magnar glared at us with daggers in his eyes.

Callie reined in her amusement, immediately looking regretful. "It's a little funny in a completely fucked up way."

"It is," Julius agreed. "Especially because if Fabian comes hounding after you with that doe-eyed expression, I'll use you as a distraction to take his head off."

Callie punched him so hard, his head wheeled sideways.

"Sorry!" she gasped immediately.

Julius rubbed his cheek, frowning deeply. "On second thought, I'm growing tired of that mark binding you to a parasite, Callie. At least Montana means it when she says she has feelings for a vamp-" he stalled, and my heart free-fell in my chest.

Asshole!

"What?" Callie gasped, glaring at him as if she couldn't accept what he'd just implied.

My eyes burned, my throat closed up.

Callie's gaze turned on me. "Say it's not true. You don't mean it. You're bonded to Erik like I am to Fabian. It's nothing more than that."

I opened my mouth, but nothing came out. I didn't want to lie to her anymore. I didn't want to deny something that was so deep in my soul that it was driving me to insanity.

"I care about him," I whispered, my voice cracking. "Erik isn't good for me, I know that. But he isn't some evil creature with no heart. I saw something in him worth saving. I care for him, Callie, and maybe it's more than that. Maybe I'm so goddamn scared of how much more than that it really is."

I got to my feet as Callie remained in shell-shocked silence.

"The mark-" she started again and I shook my head to stop her, snatching my shirt and trousers from the closest cabinet and tugging them on.

"Everything I feel for him was built long before the wedding," I revealed.

"No." Callie got to her feet, denial flaring in her features.

Magnar drifted toward her like a dark shadow, and the two of them stared at me while Julius gave me an apologetic frown.

"Look, it's not all bad-" Julius started.

"Not all bad?" Callie snapped at him. "What do you mean it's not all bad? She has feelings for a *vampire*. A Belvedere! A *rapist*!"

"Erik is not a rapist," I snarled, anger burning a pit into my chest. "He's flawed, I know that. Shit, I know he's far from perfect. But he's-"

"He's a parasite," Magnar spat, and I backed up, their combined fury suddenly frightening me. I'd been a part of their group just seconds ago, but now I felt like an outsider, unable to claim a home with the slayers *or* the vampires.

"You're confused," Callie begged, seeming desperate for that to be true, taking a step towards me as if trying to bridge this gap between us.

A tear slid down my cheek, burning a trail all the way to my chin. "I'm not. You don't know him, Callie. You don't know any of them. They're not all like the biters. Erik and I found something between us that defies logic and I'm still struggling with what it all means, but I do know that I want him. And I'm afraid, so fucking afraid that you'll hate me for it, but I can't stop myself. I can't sit here and let you all call him a monster anymore, because he isn't."

Silence stretched on, the void between me and my twin growing deeper by the second.

Julius took a step toward me, but I lifted a hand to warn him off. The disgust in Magnar's eyes and the pity in Callie's was too much to bear.

I turned and ran away, moving at a fierce pace through the museum and darting into a dark stairwell. I started climbing, running faster until I was panting. The stairs seemed endless, circling higher and higher and higher until finally, I stepped into a circular room. My breaths came in ragged pants as I moved into the space.

A crescent of windows looked out at the water ahead and to the right, New York City glittered like starlight.

I moved toward the view, momentarily distracted by the impossibly beautiful sight. I must have been in the crown of the statue, so far up it was dizzying.

I pressed my palm to the cool pane, surprised it was still intact. How many years had this statue stood here? What had it meant to the people who had stood in awe of its magnitude?

I thought of Erik out in the city somewhere, on his way to banish Wolfe. I wished I could be there. Stand by his side and punish the man who'd hurt me and my family so deeply, but I had faith he'd make it as torturous for him as possible. If it led to Valentina being caught and executed, it would be worthwhile keeping him alive a while longer. But if I ever got the chance to kill him again, I'd damn-well take it.

I took a deep breath as my heart rate finally settled, sadness filling me over the rift that had grown between Callie and me.

I was caught between two powerful enemies in an ancient war. And I loved people on both sides.

Shit... Love? Did I really love him? That word was weighted with too many ruinous thoughts to count.

And what did it matter anyway? I'd already chosen my sister over Erik, but the idea of living like this with Callie glaring at me every time Erik's name was mentioned was unthinkable. I didn't want to have to choose. But it was an impossible dream to think they could ever get along. Even tolerate one another. No... my fate was set. A broken heart and the memories of a twisted desire were all I'd have left of my time with Erik soon. I couldn't go back. But I didn't know what lay in front of me anymore.

Time ticked by and I wondered how soon I'd have to shamefully return downstairs and accept the berating I was going to get. I just wanted to hide from the world for a while. Drink in the silence and the beating of my own heart which told me that I shouldn't doubt myself, even if everyone else did.

"Montana?" Callie said gently from behind me, not using my nickname for once. Which meant things really weren't good between us.

I didn't turn to face her as more tears tracked down my cheeks. "I just need some time alone, Callie. I know you can't ever understand this."

Silence fell, but I sensed she was moving closer even though her footfalls were entirely quiet.

"I just...I don't understand," she whispered. "We hate the vampires. They've controlled us our whole lives. Are you sure it's not-"

"It's not the mark," I spoke over her, my voice firm.

"Okay," she breathed and a trickle of pain ran through my veins. I couldn't stand the idea that things were somehow broken between us. We were two halves of one whole. I wasn't ready to lose that. "Can you try to explain?" she asked.

She moved to my side and I forced myself to look at her, finding her dressed in her almost-dry clothes. Her eyes were filled with longing, not the anger I'd expected. And my shoulders sagged as I gazed down at the moonlit river stretching away ahead of us.

"I don't think anything I ever do will convince you. But Erik didn't even know the conditions we lived in-"

"And you believed that?" she balked, and my heart jerked once more.

"Yes," I said. "And I'm not saying that makes it okay. All I know is that the vampires are people. They have hearts. And some of them *care*. Some of them even regret."

I could see Callie shaking her head in the corner of my eye, and I resigned myself to the fact that this was pointless.

She placed a warm hand on my arm. "It doesn't change what they've done. They locked humans up, they sent old people to the blood bank, they sent Mom-"

"I know," I choked, shutting my eyes as I tried to will away the ache in my soul over all that knowledge. "I know, Callie. But Erik didn't realise what it was like in the Realms. And I know he should have done more to make sure things were better. But he made mistakes. And he's trying to make up for some of his wrong-doings now."

"He'll never do enough," she snarled, and I pulled my arm away from her, feeling a chasm opening up between us again.

I was falling, drowning, losing everyone I loved all at once. And I didn't know how to fix it.

"But..." Callie whispered and hope speared a path through my body. I turned to her with desperation in my gaze, and she took a deep breath before she went on. "I know you. And if you say you haven't been brainwashed and these feelings are real, then of course I'll trust you on that." She seemed to struggle to say the words. "And if you think Erik is trying to change..." She hung her head, the battle inside her evident on her face. "Then I don't know, maybe he is."

It was something. Not much, but at least she was accepting the possibility that Erik was more than just a bloodsucker. Or she was saying it to appease me.

"But he killed Magnar and Julius's father," Callie hissed, her upper lip curling back. "He has done so many unspeakable things, he's never going to do enough to make up for that."

"I know." I nodded, a frown creasing my brow. "I know that."

I didn't have much else I could say. Erik had told me that things hadn't happened quite how Julius has explained, but I didn't know what his story was. Or if it even mattered. If the Eliosons' father had died because of Erik, what could really make that right? I certainly wouldn't forgive Wolfe for taking our dad from us. So I could never expect them to forgive Erik.

Emotions warred inside me. I didn't have a good enough explanation for loving Erik, and I wasn't going to ignore all he had done. But these feelings were confounding, inexplicable. They just *were*. And I didn't know if I could shake myself of them.

"The thing is, Callie, I don't know who Erik was a thousand years ago. Hell, I don't know who he was one year ago. But I know that he loves his family more than anything, he'd do whatever he could to keep them safe. Just like we would. And he cares for me in a way that makes me feel alive. I never thought I'd feel something like that. I didn't think love was ever going to be a part of my future. And one month ago, I would have died before I let myself feel that way for a vampire. Something in him answers a question in me I never even realised I'd been asking my whole life." I turned to her, finding her mouth parted as if she understood entirely what I was saying. "I never realised before that you don't get to choose who your heart gives itself to."

"The choice is made for you," she whispered, quickly wiping her eyes with the back of her hand.

"Magnar?" I asked gently, and she nodded.

"You're so strong." I took her hand. "You'll break this bond to Fabian. You'll overcome that slayer mark, too. I know you will. Then you can be together."

She nodded again but seemed unsure. "Eventually I'll break out of these binds, then we'll see."

I glanced out at the city with an unyielding weight pressing down on me. "Eventually having the one you love is better than never having them. I won't return to Erik. I know he's bad for me, that what we had was twisted, toxic, even if it did bring me moments of joy. My heart might want him, but I'm the one who gets to choose what's right for me in the end. But it's fucking destroying me to let him go."

"Oh Monty." Her arms encircled me and she squeezed me tight.

I clutched her, relief filling me that she wasn't mad. That in some way, she understood. Even if she couldn't ever accept it. And maybe there was hope for us yet to cross this void between us, if only she could accept the honesty of my soul.

"We'll figure it out," she said, and I smiled at her words. Dad had often said them to us when we were feeling at our lowest. *We'll figure it out, girls. Whatever it takes.*

Someone cleared their throat and we parted, finding Julius standing in the doorway dressed in nothing but his jeans.

"The banishing ceremony is about to begin." He waved his phone at us. "But if you want to finish up your bonding session with a pillow fight first... I'll wait."

"How about you and Magnar have a pillow fight and we'll watch instead?" I tossed back at him.

"That's fucked up," he balked at the idea and I cocked an eyebrow until comprehension filled his gaze. "Ohhh, *I'm* fucked up."

"Yup," Callie said.

"Noted. Incest jokes are off the table." His light tone made me smile and I felt the weight lifting from me a fraction. At least two out of the three slayers were willing to overlook my attachment to one of their enemies. But I didn't think the third was going to be so forgiving.

"Instead of pillow fights, how about I have a fist fight with a big ugly slayer instead?" Callie offered with a dark smile.

"Ugly? Okay, I'll go fetch Magnar," Julius said as he turned back into the stairwell, and we hurried to follow him downstairs, sharing an amused look.

We soon arrived back in the museum and closed in on the fire where Magnar was dishing out pasta for us in bowls. He was dressed again, his damp hair hanging around his broad shoulders.

He passed a bowl to Callie and Julius, then held one out for me. I took hold of the edge of it, but he didn't let go.

His dark gaze scorched right through to my bones. "A word of advice, Montana. You will be a lot less upset when I kill Erik Belvedere if you try to get over him now. Let your heart shatter so that it can be rebuilt anew, and when his head falls, you may yet celebrate his demise."

I glowered at him as heat raced under my skin and I released the bowl.

"Keep it. I'm not hungry anyway." I turned my back on him, dropping down beside Julius.

Regret filled me as my stomach growled unhappily, but I was too stubborn to eat now.

Callie gave Magnar a look as if to say, *what are you playing at?* and Magnar promptly moved to my side, placing the bowl at my feet. Still, I didn't reach for it.

Magnar sighed and I felt he was sharing another look with Callie. He crouched down beside me, awkwardly patting my arm. "It's best to move on."

I glared at him, so angry that he was still pushing the issue. "Would you kill Callie if she was turned? Would you stop wanting her just because she was a vampire?"

Magnar's mouth parted and he glanced at Callie who turned scarlet at my words. "That would never happen."

"But if it did," I pushed, and his jaw ticked with his discomfort at the question. "Would you hurt her?

"Of course he would," Callie stepped in. "Because if I was one of *them,* I'd tell him to end my pointless existence anyway."

I ground my teeth, but suddenly Magnar didn't look so sure. He cleared his throat, moving to sit beside her with a bleak expression.

"It's starting," Julius said, seeming happy to interrupt the tense conversation. He planted himself between the four of us, holding the phone out so we could see the broadcast.

My throat thickened as I recognised the same courtyard I'd been presented in on my first day in New York. The camera was angled down over the sloped seating area which was filled with vampires. On the other side of the courtyard was the podium where two thrones sat side by side. Erik and Fabian were sitting on them in regal black suits, facing the crowd.

Erik's voice suddenly boomed through the speaker. "Ladies and gentleman of the New Empire, we come together today for two reasons. The first is to mourn the loss of so many after the events which took place at our wedding. The second is to send a reminder to the people of our city. Especially to those who rose against us. Who stood at the side of the traitor, Valentina Torbrook, and killed the wife of our brother, Miles. He is too upset today to attend this ceremony, but he sends his love to all of you and hopes you can give him the time he needs to mourn his bride. Countess Clarice is currently doing everything in her power to hunt down the biters. To make our homes safe once more."

Applause rang out and people started calling Erik's name. Even though Magnar wasn't close to me, I could almost feel him bristling, but I was too caught up in the reminder of Paige's loss for me to care. She hadn't deserved that fate. She had been a good person, and Valentina would answer for her death.

As the crowd quietened, Erik continued, "Today, I bring before you a man who was my own sireling. A man who I believed was loyal to me, to our empire. But he betrayed you all when he viciously murdered my wife's father with his teeth and now I renounce him as mine."

A collective gasp sounded from the crowd, and my heart stuttered at his words.

Erik waved his hand and the doors in the courtyard were flung open. Wolfe was escorted by two large guards who dragged him to the centre of the space. He was dressed in a suit and looked freshly-washed. Anger spilled through me as he turned his ice-blue gaze to the crowd. "We have the right to bite!" he cried and boos sounded in response.

Wolfe snarled, his eyes whipping across those seated in the front row. "You all want it. You all crave human blood from the vein. Surely you remember the delight of succumbing to your true nature?" He turned his eyes to Erik, raising a finger to point at him. "You have abandoned me. I served you loyally for hundreds of years and this is how you repay me? You know as well as I do that humans are nothing. They're insignificant beings who should be hunted like the animals they are. The true queen will lead us to that path!"

Erik rose from his throne, his upper lip peeled back, and Fabian moved to stand beside him, pushing up his sleeves as if he was preparing for a fight.

A trickle of adrenaline slid into my veins as Erik leapt from the podium, landing before Wolfe and stalking toward him. The general slashed a hand at him, but Erik caught him by the throat and forced him to his knees.

"You dare try to strike me?" he snarled.

Wolfe thrashed in his hold, but Erik was too strong, forcing him into submission.

"I will not bow to you any longer!" Wolfe shouted.

Erik raised a hand in a signal and Fabian jumped down beside them, taking something from inside his robes. A flash of silver caught my eye as Erik took the object from his brother.

Fabian grabbed hold of Wolfe, wheeling him around to face the crowd and pulling his mouth wide with his fingers. Wolfe struck out with both arms, but a sharp kick from Erik snapped one at the elbow and my pulse picked up at the sight. Erik took hold of his other arm and broke it with a vicious twist, so Wolfe wailed his pain to the sky and his agony sparked a hungry energy in me.

I took in a slow breath, excited and terrified of what was about to happen. Wolfe was a monster. Less than dirt. He'd murdered our father in cold blood and now he was paying the price.

The crowd cheered as Erik lifted the object in his hand and I realised he held a pair of pliers.

Callie leant forward with tears of anger in her eyes. "Give him hell," she whispered.

"For dad," I breathed and she nodded, taking my hand as she reached across Julius's lap.

Erik tightened the pliers over Wolfe's left fang.

A hushed silence hit my ears then he wrenched his arm backwards and blood poured. Wolfe screamed, trying to rear away from Erik as he lifted the pliers again.

"St-stop!" Wolfe begged through a mouthful of blood, but Fabian prised his mouth wide once more.

Erik angled the pliers toward his teeth, taking hold of his right fang. "You are cast out of this city. You are no longer a citizen of the New Empire." He ripped the fang from his mouth and held it aloft for the crowd to see.

Fabian shoved Wolfe to the ground, placing his boot on his chest. "No one will give this man sanctuary! If he is seen within the borders of our city, you have the right to kill him."

A cheer rang in my ears as Fabian and Erik hauled Wolfe to his feet and threw him toward the door across the courtyard. As they followed him through it, Erik planted a punch in Wolfe's gut. I suspected he was going to get a hell of a lot more than that before they let him go. And I thirsted for every ounce of justice they dealt him.

CALLiE

CHAPTER EIGHTEEN

Julius switched the cellphone off and silence fell among us.

"See?" Montana said in a hard voice, turning her eyes on me. "He's trying to fix this. They've banished Wolfe; ripped out his fangs and told every vampire in the New Empire that they can't bite humans."

I shifted back as I tried to hear what she was saying. I could see how desperately she wanted to believe that Erik Belvedere had some good in him, but banishing Wolfe wouldn't bring our father back. The fact that he still drew breath only told me that the vampires valued the lives of their own so much more than ours.

"They left him alive," I replied eventually. "That monster tortured Dad for days-" My voice cracked but I forced myself to go on. "He was *covered* in bites. You know how painful their venom is. And he was beaten too, chained from the ceiling and starved."

Montana's eyes filled with tears and she squeezed my hand tightly as if she expected me to pull away from her.

"Erik didn't know," she whispered. "He sent Wolfe to bring Dad here. He was meant to be setting him free-"

"Free?" I stared at her in disbelief. How could she have possibly thought that Erik had ever had any intention of freeing him? "If Erik Belvedere cared about you so much that he was willing to set Dad free, then why was he still happy to keep *you* captive? Surely he'd have given you freedom too if he loved you?"

She shook her head like she wanted to deny what I was saying, but I knew she could feel the truth in my words. He'd kept her caged, and in the end, she'd had to run from him because of it.

Magnar and Julius stood and moved away from us, clearly deciding this was something we had to discuss alone. They headed outside and the silence thickened.

"He did let me go," Montana breathed, her voice barely audible. "In the end. He let me run with you."

I chewed on my thumbnail as I tried to contain the outburst which was desperate to part from my lips. When I was sure I could contain my anger, I closed my hand into a fist and dropped it into my lap.

"The only reason the Belvederes are still standing is because of this mark on my hand," I said evenly. "Magnar had Fabian defeated, and if I'd been able to fight alongside them properly then we would have destroyed the others too. Erik didn't have a choice in letting you go. If he'd tried to keep you, he knew we would have finished the lot of them."

Montana shook her head again, her gaze cracking as she ached for me to understand what she was feeling, but it was so difficult for me to attempt it. The vampires had caused us so much pain and heartache - how could I just turn a blind eye to that because they claimed ignorance or regret?

I felt like the two of us had landed on differing sides of some great fissure and I had no idea how we could bridge it. This war had been raging for a thousand years and somehow we'd found ourselves on opposite sides of it. Erik had managed to convince her so thoroughly that I could see I wouldn't be able to change her mind back. But asking me to alter my opinion too felt like asking me to change the tide. I'd felt our father's blood pouring from his body. I'd been with him in his dream when he'd had to say goodbye. And the creature responsible for it still walked the Earth.

"I don't understand how you can be so loyal to him when you just watched him set Wolfe free. So he lost a few teeth? They'll probably grow back. He won't even suffer from those injuries for any real amount of time... I can't- I just don't get it." I gazed at her imploringly, begging her to help me understand because if she couldn't then I didn't know how we would move past this. It felt like she was saying that what they'd done to Dad was okay, and I knew that couldn't be how she felt. But making excuses for them didn't change the facts.

"I know," she said, and a tear slid down her cheek. "Erik was going to kill Wolfe. He was going to let me do it; I was standing over him with Nightmare in my hand-"

"So why didn't you kill him?" I demanded, and she flinched away from my anger.

"I would have! I tried - but before I could land the blow, Fabian stopped it. He said it went against their laws. That's why they had to go through with the banishing instead. They said killing him would incite the rebels and-"

"And our father's death was less important to them than their shiny castle," I growled.

"I don't know what to say. I want him dead just as much as you do. But so much else happened between me and Erik. It's hard for me to explain. You said that Fabian showed you himself as a human though? Didn't that make you question anything? They never asked for this."

My heart thumped against my ribs painfully as I was reminded of the Belvedere brother who'd claimed a portion of my soul. I'd never wanted the bond between us, but I couldn't deny what she was saying. Seeing him in his mortal form had stirred doubts in my heart and though I'd refused to face them all day, I forced myself to do it now. Not for him. And not out of any desire to see him as anything other than a monster. But for my sister. Because she was looking at me like every word I uttered was breaking her in two and I had to find some way to fix it.

"He showed me what happened when they were first cursed," I said slowly. "They were driven mad with the thirst for blood. The four of them killed their entire village. Every man, woman and child. Even the animals. They drank the blood of their own family members."

Montana pressed a hand to her mouth as the abhorrence of what had happened to Erik and his immortal siblings washed over her.

"You saw it?" she asked in horrified fascination.

"Briefly." I nodded, though the imprint of that image was seared into my brain.

I'd felt the mountain of guilt which filled Fabian's soul when he'd come to his senses again. I knew how he'd wished for death himself. I even knew that he'd tried to do just that several times in the years that followed; hurling himself from a cliff and cutting his own throat before he found out that their kind could only die one way. Only his love for his siblings had stopped him from plunging a blade into his own heart in the end.

"I know how much it cost them," I admitted.

I swallowed against a lump in my throat, not wanting to say more. If I let myself see the vampires as anything other than monsters, then what did that make me? What did it make Magnar and Julius? They'd killed countless numbers of their kind.

"All Erik wants is to break the curse," Montana said quietly, seeing the crack in my resolve. "He doesn't want to be the creature we grew up hating."

"But he is," I said, unable to break through that final barrier and see them as she was clearly starting to. "Even if I allow for the fact that they never asked to become what they are. Even if I understand the loss and the pain they've endured, they still chose to create more of their kind. They still caged us and drained us and treated us as if our lives meant nothing at all until it suited them to see us differently."

"I don't think Erik expected to see me differently," she said in a dark tone. "But since he has, he's been listening. He's been trying to change things for the better-"

"And what if we hadn't escaped the wedding? What do you think would have happened to me if Fabian had kept hold of me? Would Erik have stopped him?"

"He had a plan to get you out of there. I got Magnar and Julius involved to rescue you, but if they failed, Erik's people were planning to get you away too-"

"And what? Set me free?" I raised an eyebrow doubtfully and I could see in her eyes that she knew that wouldn't have been the case. "What if both plans had failed and Fabian still had me? Would Erik have fought against his own brother to save me from his marriage bed?"

"He never would have let Fabian hurt you."

"Are you sure about that? Because Miles and Clarice were definitely okay with it. I mean they spouted some shit about me being strong enough to survive giving birth to his demon children - in the undead sense of the word - but they were definitely up for giving me to Fabian and letting him do whatever the hell he wanted with me."

"I know. But it's just because they think that's how they'll break the curse. I'm not saying it makes it okay, but Erik doesn't believe any of that, he's never taken wives or had children. He thinks *we're* the answer. You and me."

"How?" I demanded.

"I don't know. But Julius agrees that it could be possible. There's a prophecy and some of it sounds like it could apply to us."

I sighed, rubbing a hand over my face. I didn't know what to think of all of it. My beliefs were being challenged and I wasn't sure I could just flip the switch on them. My hatred for the vampires was ingrained in my bones. How was I supposed to try and rewrite an entire lifetime of seeing them as my enemy?

"I can't think straight," I said. "My brain is so full of everything... I just need to sleep. But I promise I'm trying, Monty. Maybe, I dunno, give me a bit of time?"

She nodded and I pushed myself to my feet. I folded a blanket to lie on even though it was still a little damp then settled down beside the fire with my arm beneath my head.

Montana glanced over at me then slowly reached for the phone Julius had left lying on the floor. She tapped the screen a few times and I wondered if she was looking for Erik on the CCTV. Did she miss him that much? She noticed me looking and quickly placed the phone back where she'd found it again before laying down to sleep too.

I closed my eyes and thought about what she'd said. If she really believed there was something good in the Belvederes then maybe I owed her a chance to find out if she was telling the truth.

I wasn't entirely sure how I'd ended up inside people's dreams before but as I concentrated on the idea of what I wanted to do, I felt it. It was like there were hundreds of little pinpricks of light in the distance, each of them a sleeping soul waiting for me to join them. One of the lights shone brighter than the others and as I focused on it, I recognised it as Fabian.

I felt for the souls sleeping around him and brushed up against another one I recognised. I didn't understand how I knew it, but I could tell it was Clarice. The other Belvederes didn't appear to be sleeping and I was glad; I had thought to confront Erik myself but I wasn't sure I was brave enough to face him yet.

I turned my attention back to Fabian instead. His newfound affection for me would probably make him the easiest monster to question anyway.

My heart fluttered excitedly as I moved towards his dream and I ground my teeth in defiance of it. I wasn't visiting him for any reason other than to try and understand what my sister saw in these creatures, and I refused to recognise any other emotions which tried to present themselves to me.

Slipping into his dream felt like diving into an icy pool. My skin tingled all over as the light grew brighter and brighter.

I was standing in a wooden room with a wide bed taking up almost all of the space before me. As I'd chosen to come here myself this time, I was dressed the way I wanted to be in a simple black outfit with Fury at my hip.

Sunlight shone in through an open window and the view outside was of a sprawling mountain range tipped with snow.

Two figures moved beneath the sheets, moaning in pleasure at each other's efforts. I presumed one of them must have been Fabian and heat crawled up the back of my neck as I realised what kind of dream he was having.

I was half tempted to leave again before he noticed I was here, but I'd come for a reason and I wanted answers.

Steeling myself to front out the situation, I folded my arms and cleared my throat loudly.

Fabian threw the covers off of him and looked up at me with wide eyes. He was in his human form and was totally naked. I set my face to a scowl as I refused to let my eyes dip below his waist. I glanced at the girl beneath him and a mixture of embarrassment, horror and mortification washed over me as I realised she was me.

"What the fuck is this?!" I exclaimed as the false me stared at Fabian like he was some kind of god. She was butt naked too and her hands were reaching out for him like she desperately desired his attention again.

"You're back?" Fabian asked in astonishment before sheepishly glancing at his fantasy version of me. She vanished and some pants appeared to cover him up.

"No shit," I replied, hoping my bravado was veiling my embarrassment and forcing myself to hold his eye.

"Did you want to take her place?" he asked hopefully.

"No thanks," I replied lightly. "It sounded like she was faking it to me."

"I assure you she wasn't." He prowled towards me and my gut tightened at the look in his eyes.

I pushed aside the unwelcome desires and held my ground as I concentrated on our surroundings. The room faded away and houses sprung up around us. People started screaming and the streets ran red with blood. There was so much that I could smell the iron tang of it in the air. The other Belvederes leapt between the fleeing townsfolk, ripping out throats and feasting on the fallen.

"Stop it," Fabian gasped.

I could feel him trying to reclaim control of his dream, but I had it in my grasp. I batted aside his attempts with as much ease as if he were a fly buzzing around my head. His own body was coated in blood and I pushed against his resistance until he started chasing after the townsfolk too.

I could feel his panic as I wrangled the nightmare around him and guilt stirred in my gut, making me hesitate short of letting him rip one of the fleeing humans apart.

I snapped my fingers and it all disappeared. I gave Fabian control of the dream again and he stared at me as though he saw the truth of this part of me and understood it at last. And if I wasn't mistaken, he was afraid.

It took him a moment before he managed to think of anything to add to the darkness which now surrounded us but I waited as he reclaimed control over the space.

Slowly, a table appeared between us and I lowered myself into a comfortable chair opposite him. A faceless vampire laid two glasses on the table and placed a bottle of amber liquid beside them before disappearing again. We were inside but there were no other details to the room apart from the table and the two chairs.

Fabian didn't move to pour the drinks so I did it for him. I slid a full glass across the table to him and some of the contents sloshed over the edge.

"That's seventy year old scotch," he said quietly. "You don't drink a full glass of it."

"It's dreamed up bullshit," I replied evenly. "So I can bathe in it if the notion takes me."

He nodded slowly and lifted the glass to his lips before draining the full contents. The haunted look in his eyes was beginning to fade and I bit my tongue to stop myself from apologising.

I took a sip from my own glass then spat it out. "That tastes like crap," I said in disgust as my throat burned.

Fabian chuckled. "It can be an acquired taste."

"Well I won't be acquiring it any time soon." I blinked at the glass and replaced the drink inside it with a clear liquid.

"Gin?" he asked, eyeing it.

"Water," I replied with a frown. "What's gin?"

"Oh, I forgot you don't drink alcohol in the Realms."

"Water is the only drink in the Realms," I replied. "But no doubt *you have many more options than we do. We're only the food supply after all."*

"You know you're much more to me than that," he breathed.

I decided to ignore that comment. "I'm surprised you aren't having blood anyway. I didn't know you could drink other things."

"Yes, we can enjoy other drinks but we need blood to sustain us. Are you going to tell me why you came or was it just to terrorise me?" His eyes were filled with betrayal, but I refused to blanch.

"I wasn't terrorising you," I replied. "I was... trying to figure you out I suppose. I wanted to see what you'd been through again. I wanted to be sure I hadn't imagined the regret you felt for it the last time you showed it to me."

"Why not just ask me then instead of forcing it from me?" he growled.

"I could say the same to you about our wedding," I hissed.

"Well the difference is that I wouldn't have said no." He leaned forward and reached for me. His fingertips brushed against the back of my hand and a thrill raced along my skin despite my best intentions. I slid his fingers between mine for a moment and my heart leapt with excitement, the bond between us throbbing.

I gritted my teeth as I tried to remember why I'd come here and managed to pull my hand back.

"Why do you fight it?" Fabian whispered. "I want you more than I've ever wanted anything in my life. Come back to me. Be mine. I will give you the world. I can change everything to suit your desires. I've already divorced my other wives and I've sent all of my sirelings out to improve the Realms-"

"I hear you're putting up statues too," I said, rolling my eyes.

"I only want everyone to worship you as I do. What can I say to make you return to me?" He reached for me again and the table disappeared. His hands were upon me before I could react to the change in scenery. "I can make you feel things no other man can..." He dipped his mouth towards mine, but my mind was filled with thoughts of Magnar.

I forced the dream to bend to my will again and Fabian found himself clutching nothing as I reappeared standing beside him.

"No," I growled. "I came here to ask about you and your siblings,

not to bow to your sordid desires."

"Okay. Whatever you want," Fabian said as he seemed to realise I was considering leaving. "Ask me anything you want..."

"I want to know why my sister thinks you're not all evil. Why she thinks Erik isn't evil."

"Erik? He loves her as I love you. The four of us can all be together here if only you'd come and-"

I imagined the sun into existence above us and forced its burning rays to slam down on him as I returned him to his vampire form.

"Answer my question," I growled, not wanting to hear any more of his damn declarations.

He collapsed to his hands and knees while the sun continued to blaze, and I slowly withdrew it, hiding it behind a cloud of my own design.

"Okay," Fabian panted. "I'm sorry. Erik is...the best of us I suppose. He has always fought the hardest against the thirst."

"He murdered hundreds of slayers," I spat, not wanting to hear any lies.

"Slayers aren't normal mortals," Fabian replied. "Your kind hunted us for hundreds of years. Of course we fought back. Of course we defended ourselves. But Erik never even did that willingly. He starved himself of blood for two hundred years to try and break our curse."

"Why would he think that would break it?" I asked in confusion.

"'A debt paid rights wrongs of old.' It's a line from the prophecy. He thought he could pay the debt in suffering. The gods clearly didn't agree." Fabian shrugged like he wasn't sure what else he could say on the subject.

My mind spun. If what he was saying was true, then Erik really had tried to fight against his nature. And he truly intended to break the curse. But if that was the case then shouldn't we have been helping him instead of trying to kill him? Our vow was taken to end the reign of the vampires, but that could be achieved by solving the prophecy just as easily as it could be by ridding the world of each individual vampire.

My head swam with the implications of what he was saying, and I started to back away. It was too much. I didn't know what to think or what to do with the information he'd given me.

"Callie, wait. Please don't leave me again!" Fabian called. "I can't bear being away from you. It's carving me in two!"

"I'm not meant to be with you," I replied and the truth of my words drove out the false feelings for him as my heart pounded only for Magnar.

"You are!" Fabian cried but he was already fading away as I pulled out of his dream.

I slipped back into my own body and I could still feel my heart thrumming with longing for Magnar. I needed him like a drowning woman needed oxygen. I wanted to throw myself into his arms and beg him to take me despite my broken pieces because with him, somehow, I knew I could hold them together.

I shouldn't have been driving him away from me so I could deal with this. I should have been drawing him closer. And as I fell into my own dreams, they were all filled with him.

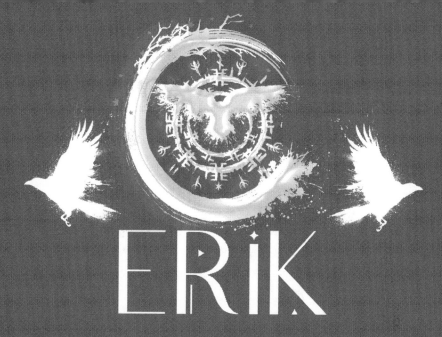

ERIK

CHAPTER NINETEEN

1000 YEARS AGO

The sun was unrelenting today. The gods were against us. I'd tried to contact Andvari with the Shaman's mirror, but he hadn't responded. Did he want us dead? Was this our fucking fate? To cross an entire ocean only to be caught in daylight when the slayers reached us?

We didn't have much time, each passing moment turning to dust before our eyes. I stood under the sun in the centre of the village, shaded by nothing but a wooden awning, thinking on what was to be done. The stone houses stretched up the hill before us and the people had gathered at its base, anxious as they gazed at our weakened forms. Every time we set foot in the sun, black veins encircled our eyes and our energy rapidly depleted.

The leader of the village, Takoda, stepped toward us: a slim man with a shaven head and red stripes painted across his bare chest. "We will fight with you to the end, dear gods."

I glanced at the others. Fabian looked willing to fight, but Miles and Clarice seemed unsure. I was torn apart inside, uncertain of what to do.

I didn't want the villagers getting caught up in this. They'd be cut down by the slayers' immense power. And after all they had done for us, it wouldn't be right to lead them to their deaths.

"We could turn them?" Fabian suggested in a low tone, so only the four of us could hear.

"No," I snarled. "We cannot do that to them."

"But we need an army, Erik," Fabian urged, and Miles nodded, warming to the idea.

I caught my sister's eye, my last hope. She wore a dress of blue silk and her golden hair was braided with flowers. "No, Erik's right. We should leave, get as far away as possible to protect them."

Relief unfurled in my chest.

"Curse those slayers, I do not want to give up this place," Fabian snarled.

"Me neither," Miles agreed. "This is our home now."

A pit of despair grew in me, surprising me at the attachment I had found to this village. Boredom trailed me everywhere in this world, but at least here there was the beauty of the forest and the winding trails along the peaceful river. There was no need for carnage, no deaths without cause. There was balance between us and the humans, their blood in exchange for our protection. It was as close to harmony as we had ever found.

So no, I didn't want to leave, but what choice did we have? We had sworn to safeguard these people and guiding the slayers away from them was the only way we could do that.

"Your enemies are our enemies!" Takoda called, lifting the sharp spear in his hand. "We will protect you as you have protected us!"

A cry of assent went up from the villagers, and I spied children watching us from the doorways of their homes, seeming excited by the spectacle.

I sighed, my body riddled with concern. We could not do this to them.

I eyed the forest beyond the village, expecting the slayers to descend upon us at any moment. Their blades would guide them here. They were coming, it was just a matter of time. And I wanted a decision made before that happened.

"We could head into the forest to meet them and fight under the cover of the canopy." I turned to my siblings. "We can fight on our own terms. And the villagers will not be involved."

Fabian looked ready to disagree, but Clarice stepped in first. "Yes, we'll take weapons and hide in the trees. Perhaps we could win with the element of surprise on our side."

"How will we surprise them? They will sense our presence," Miles hissed, running his hand into his hair. It was getting long, curling around the nape of his neck like a waterfall of gold.

"Draugr," Andvari's voice rolled through the air and power rippled across the land, setting my skin prickling.

The villagers looked around in alarm and my soul shuddered as he appeared among them. The god walked toward us in his brown robes, his grisly hair floating about him and a sense of utter power slipping from him into the atmosphere.

The villagers raised their weapons but I lifted a palm, warning them off.

"Leave him," I commanded, and they slowly parted, letting him move through the crowd toward us, muttering their fear.

Andvari observed us beneath the awning, coming to a halt just before the four of us where the shade met the sun.

"You need my help," he purred, seeming to revel in our predicament.

"Yes. What can you do?" I asked, wary of more tricks, more lies, more curses.

Andvari stooped low, picking up four black rocks from the dusty ground. He cast his hand over them and they smoothed out, rounding into shining spheres. A rune appeared upon them that resembled a trident, glittering silver in the light. "The rune of Algiz has altered these stones. They will stop their blades from detecting you. Carry them always. They will help you evade the slayers." He stepped into the shadow of the awning, passing us one each.

I took the final glossy stone, running my thumb over it, sensing power emanating from the rune of protection that was etched into it.

"A thank you would be polite," Andvari growled, and the others quickly bowed their heads in subservience, offering their thanks.

Andvari's eyes slid to me when I remained quiet, unmoving. "Shall I pull it from your ungrateful tongue, Erik Larsen?"

I warred with the defiant streak in me but felt the pleading stares of my siblings around me.

"Thank you," I bit out, dipping my head.

"A gift will suffice." Andvari turned toward the villagers, lifting a finger and pointing at a child hugging her mother's legs. "A gift in blood."

Ice crept through the corners of my chest as the god beckoned the child closer and she was forced to move toward him. Her mother ran to catch her, but Andvari knocked her to the ground, making fear crash through my flesh.

The villagers were forced aside by the god's almighty power, allowing the young child to reach Andvari. Screams pitched through the air, the horrified wails of the child's mother puncturing my ears while the other villagers bayed for mercy.

Andvari approached the child, taking a glinting silver knife from within his robes.

"No," I snarled, stepping forward to the very edge of the shadows.

"A fine sacrifice," the god growled and the villagers cried out her name in desperation.

"Lisi! We love you, Lisi! Come back to us!"

My fangs prickled with rage and I steeled myself, storming out into the sun, its burning rays cutting a path through my body and weakening my muscles. I squinted against the blazing light, the sting of the sun's beams like acid against my skin as I moved in front of the little girl, stopping Andvari from approaching.

"No blood will be spilled here," I demanded. "These are good people. They will not be hurt for the sake of us heathens."

"But I must have a gift," Andvari chuckled, not seeming bothered by the stand I was making.

A man ran forward from the crowd, raising a bone blade to his throat. "I offer myself as sacrifice!"

"No!" I bellowed, but I was too late as the man slashed his own knife across his jugular and blood poured down his naked chest. He hit the ground and the child's mother ran to him, falling to her knees and crying out as he gargled, choking to death.

I bared my fangs, lowering down to take hold of the child's shoulders and pushing her back toward the crowd. Her mother reached for her, gathering the little girl into her arms, rocking back and forth as she wept.

"That will do, I suppose." Andvari grinned then twisted sharply away from me, vanishing into thin air.

"Forgive us!" Clarice called to the people and the leader bowed his head, signalling that he did.

"We will leave to intercept the slayers," Fabian called to them. "Bring us your weapons!"

The villagers hurried forward, laying hatchets, clubs, bows and spears at our feet, muttering prayers of luck and war. I had my own obsidian blade at my hip, but I picked up a hatchet, weighing it in my palm and mentally preparing for what was to come. I tucked Andvari's rune stone into my pocket, wishing someone hadn't had to die for it. But every gift of the god was always paid for in blood, one way or another.

"To the trees," I ordered my family as they finished arming themselves and we took off through the village, a cheer going up as we headed toward the forest.

"We will protect you!" Miles called to them, and they cheered our names, praising us like saints instead of the sinners we were.

As I slipped into the darkness between the boughs, the sun slipped from my skin and my strength fast returned. I glanced back at the village, praying we would come back. That we would finish the slayers at last and be able to continue our lives here. I made a silent promise to myself that if we won, I would try to enjoy the world once more. I would spend time with the people, attend their feasts and celebrations. I would be more than just a predator, I would attempt to be a man again.

We moved further into the dark forest, the sounds of birds and small mammals chirping around us. Soon, we arrived in a clearing not too far from the sea and spread out around it, working to conceal ourselves. If the slayers were coming, they would surely take the easiest route. And this was it.

I scaled a nearby tree, crawling onto a thick branch which hung above the clearing. Clarice slipped into the covering of the leaves on a large tree across from me. When she fell still, she was invisible, the foliage concealing her entirely.

Fabian and Miles were soon hidden too, and we fell deathly quiet, waiting. I remained as rigid as the branch I clung to, moulding myself to its shape, my gaze pinned on the ground below.

The first sign of movement was a group of monkeys swinging through the branches. I was so still that one perched on my back for several moments before heading on to join its companions.

I strained my ears, then tensed as something large shifted through the undergrowth below. A huge boar appeared, grunting as it trotted across the clearing.

"Oh hello, Magnar," Clarice whispered on the breeze and a chuckle escaped my throat.

The minutes merged into an hour, and I started to wonder if we had made a wrong assumption. Perhaps the slayers wouldn't come this way. Perhaps they had forged a path through the swamp to the south. Or they might have headed that way first before circling back. But this area was the direct route to the village from the sea. If they had sensed our presence before, they would certainly be heading in this direction.

Doubts pricked my gut as I wondered how many might be moving toward us. We'd had to run from them before, but I wasn't prepared to flee again. I was no coward. And at least this time we would have an advantage. Death would descend on them before they knew what was happening.

I stilled as Magnar's dark head appeared between the shrubs, cutting a silent path toward the clearing. Anger rose in my blood and a lust for his death consumed me.

I am tired of being hunted. You shouldn't have followed us, slayer.

He moved silently into the clearing, hovering on the edge of it as he raised one of his golden blades as if trying to sense our presence. He frowned, sweeping the sword through the air before lowering it, evidently assuming he was safe. The stones worked, and the slayers would never detect us again.

I waited with a ripple of anticipation spreading through me, letting my instincts take over. I was a predator, born to kill. And though spilling more blood didn't appeal to me, I knew we had to end the slayers or they would never stop hunting us. They were a threat to our new way of life. Our home. And I refused to allow anyone to take that from my family again.

Magnar strode further into the clearing and I rose silently onto my knees, taking the hatchet from my hip. As he stepped beneath the branch where I was hiding, I gritted my teeth and launched my attack.

Energy surged through me as I fell from the tree, raising the hatchet above my head and silently descending for the kill. Magnar looked up at the last second, his sword knocking my weapon aside and I collided with him, bringing us both to the forest floor. I raised my arm with a yell of fury, readying my weapon to kill him.

"How?" he gasped in horror.

I brought my arm down to cleave him apart, but he grabbed my wrist, turning his head at the last second so the hatchet barely grazed his ear and sliced deep into the earth.

His fist connected with my jaw and my head whipped backwards as I was thrown off of him into the dirt. Clarice dove from the trees as Magnar regained his feet, drawing his second sword with a feral growl.

Fabian sped at him from behind, throwing a kick against his back.

Magnar stumbled forward, slashing his swords through the air to keep Clarice away as she tried to grab him.

I bared my fangs, stalking around him as he swung his blades to keep us at bay.

"Devils! How have you hidden your presence from me?" he boomed.

Miles darted into view beside Fabian, aiming his bow at Magnar's head. He loosed the arrow and Magnar whipped his sword sideways to knock it from the air. I dove on him, taking the advantage of his distraction as I grabbed hold of his head and yanked sideways, ready to break his neck.

Magnar bellowed, reaching behind his head and launching me over his shoulder with force.

I gained my feet, turning back to him with a snarl, but he came at me with rage scorching in his eyes.

"Magnar!" someone shouted beyond the trees and in moments, the slayers descended on us.

Fabian, Miles and Clarice darted into the undergrowth to intercept them, leaving me alone with Magnar Elioson.

He slashed his blades at me in two heavy strikes, but I avoided the blows, dancing between their deadly edges so he never landed a hit.

With a rush of agility, I got between them, ramming my fist into his ribs. He growled as something cracked, slashing his swords at me again. I leapt over his head, turning fast and throwing my weight into his back so he stumbled forward. He swept around just as quickly, keeping upright as he brought a golden blade towards my heart. I snatched his wrist, twisting hard and he gasped in pain as the bone broke, dropping the sword to the ground. I kicked it away, but the moment cost me too much as he stabbed his other sword into my side. I cried out in horror as the searing pain ricocheted through my body. He ripped it out and I hit the ground, clutching the gaping wound above my hip.

"How did you evade our swords?" he demanded, standing over me and holding his blade above my heart.

"The gods help you as they help us," I hissed.

He considered that, lifting the sword higher, readying to finish me, and I raised my chin to face my end.

Clarice crashed into him so hard that the two of them slammed against a tree and broke the trunk in two.

I got to my feet, wincing as I moved, cursing myself for this failure.

Miles ran to my side, throwing my arm over his shoulder as he helped me move, the metal of the slayer blade causing me an agony untold. "There's too many of them. We have to run."

"No," I growled, determined to end this today.

"Don't be a fool, brother," Miles begged, and I noticed a deep gash on his arm, dripping blood.

Clarice shrieked as Magnar sliced deeply into her leg and fear found me for my sister. But she sprang away from him, running to meet us, limping as she moved.

"Go!" Fabian roared, tearing through the trees with a slayer's head swinging from his fist. He tossed it at Magnar's feet, stalling him in his tracks, a sharp grief pooling in his eyes.

"Run!" Fabian yelled and he and Miles dragged me into their arms before speeding off into the trees.

Magnar's voice followed us, his yell full of grief and rage. "Your deaths are mine! Run and hide but I will find you and cut out your monstrous hearts if it's the last thing I ever do!"

MONTANA

CHAPTER TWENTY

I wanted to talk to Erik. Though we were parted, I still felt closer to him than ever, and no amount of distance seemed to change that. The mark on my palm urged me to act on the insane ideas crawling into my mind and keeping me awake. I'd sworn to walk away. I had made that vow to myself as well as him. But Julius's phone was so close, and it would have been all too simple to indulge in this wild desire.

Checking Callie was deeply asleep beside me, I crept to the phone Julius had left on the floor, taking it in my palm. In that moment, it was more than a piece of technology, it was a direct line to Erik Belvedere. I didn't want to do this for purely selfish reasons, but shit, I knew that was part of it. The other part…well, maybe I could talk more sense into Erik than I could to the slayers. It was a long shot, but the prophecy wasn't going to solve itself, and if we could only work together, maybe we could all figure it out somehow.

This could be a completely pointless endeavour anyway. I had no idea if Erik had found Valentina's phone after I'd hidden it under the bed in his home. But maybe he was close enough to hear it right now.

I moved through the museum, putting some space between me and

Callie in case I woke her. And I soon found a rusted door left ajar, leading into a storage room. I slipped inside, using the light on the phone to illuminate the space, revealing shelves packed with boxes, dusty hats and small models of the statue.

I padded to the back of the room and slid down to the floor, pressing my back to the wall. With my heart crashing against my chest, I found my way to Valentina's number on the phone.

My throat was thick as I pressed dial and lifted the cellphone to my ear.

A ringing noise resounded in my ears, over and over until I was certain he wasn't going to answer. My heart sank as disappointment rose in my chest.

Well, that was that.

I held the phone in front of me, moving to press the button that would cut the call.

"Hello?" Erik's voice sounded through the device.

I stilled, my mouth opening but no words came out. Perhaps it was only a few seconds, but it felt like an eternity before I could make any noise at all. "Hi," I breathed, lifting the phone back to my ear.

"Rebel?" Erik hissed. "Tell me it's you."

"It is," I sighed, shutting my eyes as I drank in his rumbling tone, letting it seep through every inch of my body. It shouldn't have felt this good to hear his voice, but it did, it fucking did.

"Are you safe?" he demanded.

"Yes, I'm fine," I said. "Well, not exactly fine."

"What's wrong? Do you need help? I'll come for you-"

"No," I cut him off, my pulse skyrocketing. "I just…miss you."

The admission made my cheeks flush hot and I instantly regretted those words passing my lips. They were wrong. I should never have felt that way, but knowing I wouldn't see him again was a burden that weighed on me every second we were apart. It was the right thing to do, but it didn't make it any easier. And expressing that to Callie, the one person I could once tell every secret of my heart to, was all but impossible.

Silence fell on the end of the line, but finally, Erik answered.

"I miss you too," he sighed heavily, and I could feel the strength of this affliction hanging between us. This desire for each other that could never be fulfilled. "Fuck...you have no idea."

I clutched the phone tighter, feeling like it was the only thing present in the world right now.

"I told my sister about us," I revealed, and Erik released a dark laugh.

"I'm sure that went well."

"As well as you might expect. Although...I think she's trying to understand. Even Julius-"

"Don't," he growled as if the slayer's name pained him to hear. "Don't talk about him. Just the thought of you with him, with those slayers, it antagonises me to no end. Just tell me - did you make it out of the city? Are you somewhere away from harm?"

"Um..." I bit into my lower lip, unsure how much I should say. I hadn't really considered the fact that Erik might ask about our whereabouts.

"Forget I asked," he muttered.

"I'm safe," I said.

"Promise me, rebel."

"I promise."

He released a low noise in his throat. "I hate this."

"I hate it, too. But it was the right thing to do."

"I know why you left, Montana. I'd have been a fool to think you would stay."

My heart cleaved apart and a tear rolled smoothly down my cheek as I thumbed the wedding band on my finger.

"I'm still yours," I whispered, that truth slipping free of me before I could stop it.

Silence tracked between us and all I could hear was my thrashing pulse.

"You're killing me," he groaned. "Put the camera on, let me see you."

Heat blazed a path through my skin. "I don't know how."

"Press the camera symbol at the bottom and hold the phone in front

227

of you."

I angled the phone toward me and pressed the button he'd described. My face stared back at me on the screen, lit up in blue by the light of the phone. A beat later, it shrank to a small box and Erik filled the screen instead. My throat closed up as I absorbed the sight of him. He was sat up in bed, bare-chested with his hair tousled, his storm grey eyes glittering hungrily as he gazed at me.

"There you are." He grinned darkly and my stomach coiled into a knot.

Even though he was miles away, the video made him seem so terrifyingly close that my body reacted the way it always did around him. Remembering to breathe became a chore, and my rational thoughts became harder to hold onto.

"I thought you might be busy tonight. With Wolfe," I said.

"You know about that?"

"We watched the ceremony," I revealed, and his eyes grew a little darker.

"I didn't want to release him, you know that. But I gave him hell before we did. But we're hoping he might be of use now to catch Valentina."

I nodded, releasing a breath. I knew that was important, but my expression gave away my disappointment. I wanted Wolfe dead for what he'd done.

"He suffered well, rebel," Erik vowed, his eyes sparking with the violence he had delivered my enemy.

"Suffering isn't death," I said.

"It is worse," he said, his brows drawing low. "I assure you of that."

I nodded slowly, seeing his point, but Wolfe was still free now. That was more than my father had been gifted in life.

"We ran into Valentina," I said cautiously. "She tried to take Magnar. I don't know why, but she was determined."

"Shit," Erik growled. "There were reported sightings of her, but we didn't get there in time. Did she hurt you?"

"She tried to, but I'm fine. She wanted me dead, of course. But that's not exactly the surprise of the year. She said that you and her were together once and that you were going to marry her." I ignored the rising heat in my body as I stared at his expression, trying to assess his reaction to my knowledge of that.

Erik's face contorted. "I never promised any such thing."

"But you were together?" I asked.

His brow creased with lines. "I wouldn't put it that way. She was just a distraction."

I nodded, not liking the picture of them together in my mind, but Valentina was beautiful. She was a vampire, too. Unbreakable, immortal. A good match for him before she went full psycho, I supposed.

"I never had feelings for her, rebel. It was just sex."

"Okay whatever," I said, wrinkling my nose. "I don't want the details."

A slow smile took over his face. "You know I don't want anyone but you. I've never wanted anything like I want you. You're the first woman to ever claim my heart." He rested a hand on his chest. "It's un-beating, and likely as black as tar, but it is yours, rebel."

A breath got stuck in my chest as I nodded, accepting what he was saying even if it defied all logic.

"We weren't made to love each other," I exhaled.

He inclined his head, misery touching his eyes, and it hurt me to see this immovable creature looking so broken. Was it really because of me?

"The gods divided us," he said. "It's up to us to bridge that divide."

"It's too late for that, don't you think?"

"Perhaps," he muttered.

"So what will you do about Valentina?" I asked.

He bared his fangs at her name. "We're tracking Wolfe. He should lead us to her any day now."

My thoughts took a sharp turn toward the slayers and their father. "Erik...I know you don't want to talk about this, but I feel like such a hypocrite right now. I wished for revenge on Wolfe more than anything for what he did to my dad. But that's how Magnar and Julius feel about *you*."

His face became grave, twisted with discomfort.

"You think I'm like Wolfe," he stated.

"No," I said, my chest too tight. "Or at least, I want to hope you're not. Maybe you did something terrible once, but maybe you regret it?"

Erik scored a hand over his face. "That day is still burned into my mind so vividly, it is sometimes clearer than yesterday."

"Tell me about it," I urged, desperate to hear his side of the story.

"After I was turned, I knew I needed to do something to appease Andvari. I longed to pay his debt and was desperate not to be the bloodthirsty beast he'd made me into. So I barricaded myself in a cave. I didn't drink blood for two hundred years. I thought if I starved myself, it might break the curse."

My heart clenched at his words as I thought of the pain he must have put himself through.

He went on, "Then one day, Fabian came for me; he took me to a battle between us and the slayers. Andvari filled me with his power. I was so strong. And so fucking hungry. I couldn't feel anything but the thirst. I was an animal. A fox in a chicken coop." He gave me a tense look as if he was concerned about continuing, of what I might think of him beyond this point.

I waited, giving him an encouraging look.

"I lost every part of myself that day," he muttered. "And when the hunger withdrew and my humanity returned, I saw what I'd done. I found myself before the final slayer left alive on the battlefield. He was dying...weak. The man was the Eliosons' father. Andvari whispered the prophecy in my ear. Warrior born and monster made...I thought he was telling me that turning a slayer into one of us was the answer. That I could break the curse that way." He glanced away as if he didn't want to meet my gaze. "I was wrong, rebel. Tricked. But not without blame."

My breathing quickened as I absorbed his words. "The slayers think you did it to kill their clan by sending him back to them. They think it's even worse that he was turned. That it would have been better if he died a warrior's death."

Erik's brow furrowed. "I suppose I can see why they would think that. But it wasn't my intention. I know Magnar killed his father when he returned home, disgusted by what had happened to him. The slayers cannot see us as human. And there are times that we're not. Creating this empire was a way to counter that. We thought that if we could set up a society with laws which would prevent humans from dying at our hands, then we might regain some sense of morality. But even that has gone to hell... Every single standard I thought I was upholding was a fucking lie." He glowered and I reached out to brush my fingers across the screen, wishing I could be there beside him to soothe his pain.

It wasn't okay what he'd done, but at least he knew that. At least he was trying to be better. I could see the regret in him like a dark shadow looming over his soul. Wasn't that worth something?

"I forgive you," I said quietly. "Even if you can't forgive yourself. You are good, Erik. Even if you've done bad things. We've all done bad things..."

"What have you ever done that's so wrong?" A flicker of light returned to his eyes and I breathed a laugh.

"Hm...I once wished this kid I grew up with would be taken to the blood bank. He was always bullying me, shoving me in the mud." I shook my head. "I didn't say it out loud. But I thought it. How messed up is that?"

"What a dark soul you have," Erik taunted. "You have no idea of the terrible things I've wished upon some people. It's what we act on that counts. Which is why I am damned for all eternity and your soul is clean."

"Don't say that," I said sharply. "You're making up for things now, aren't you?"

"Well, I hear Fabian is erecting statues of your sister in the Realms, would you like me to do the same? I'll make sure they're twice the size. That might make up for some of my bullshit." His mouth twisted into a smile and laughter burst from my chest. "Rebel," He sighed heavily. "I won't deny you Wolfe's death again. When I find Valentina, I'll be sure he gets caught up in the massacre that I'm going to bring down on her and her followers."

Relief spilled through me. "Thank you."

He gave me an intense look. "Please tell me where you are, I promise I'll leave your friends alone if it means I can spend tonight with you."

Erik's eyes moved to my lips, that single look sparking flames at the base of my spine. I remembered how he had once had me beneath him, his tongue dragging across my clit, how hungrily he had devoured me.

"It didn't work out so well the last time we tried to do that," I remarked.

"Second time's the charm," he said, all hellion as his gaze raked over me, peeling me apart with his eyes.

"We have the small issue of sitting on opposing sides of an age-old war," I said, trying to keep my tone light as we slipped toward discussing the cruel reality of our situation. The most important reason I'd called him.

"How about we try to rewrite our version of Romeo and Juliet so we don't end up dead?" Erik suggested.

I laughed softly, knowing the story from my dad's best attempt at recounting it. "I think this is the version where they go their separate ways."

"That sounds like a rather boring version, rebel. Don't pursue a career as a writer."

"Well how would *you* like it to go?"

"Firstly you end my torment by coming to my bed tonight. Then tomorrow we can take a boat and sail for anywhere that isn't here."

"And leave everyone we love behind to deal with this mess?" I scoffed.

"They'll figure it out." He smirked, then his expression fell a little as he considered something. "Unfortunately, things are not so simple."

"I'm well aware of that."

"Look, I think you need to talk to the slayers. Convince them to let you and your sister come to us. We know you're a part of the prophecy. We can figure out the rest together and break the curse. Surely the slayers would be satisfied with that? Are they so determined to murder us all even with that fact staring them in the face?"

I sighed, dropping my eyes. "Callie couldn't bear to be near Fabian again. And even if I could convince the others, it's personal when it comes to you, Erik. I don't think they'd let us go without a fight."

His eyes darkened, purest deadly intension filling his gaze. "You're right."

My pulse thumped in my ears as I grew fearful of what he was thinking. "But a fight would be a terrible idea."

"I disagree. I'd fight for you with more strength than I'd ever fought them with before."

"Erik, don't even joke about that," I hissed. "You're not fighting them. You don't even know where we are."

"True," he said, but I sensed he wasn't about to drop the issue.

Oh shit, what have I done?

"Montana," Julius's voice hit me like a gut punch. I nearly dropped the phone as he pushed through the door across the room, just a dark silhouette as he stormed toward me. "Hang the fuck up," he commanded.

I didn't, so he snatched the phone and glared right at Erik. "Stay the hell away from her, bloodsucker." He ended the call and fury crashed through me.

I sprang to my feet, shoving him as hard as I could. "You asshole, you had no right!" I reached for the phone, but he tucked it swiftly in his back pocket and batted my flailing arms aside, his strength too much for me to counter.

"Magnar's right, Montana. You need to forget about him. And don't ever call him again."

"Fuck you." I stormed from the room, my blood curdling in my veins. He had no right to tell me how to feel. To treat me like a naughty kid. Who the hell did he think he was?

I strode back to the fire where Callie was sleeping and dropped down onto the floor, seething as I felt Julius following me.

"Erik is going to fall one way or another," he whispered, laying a hand on my back.

I flinched away from him, turning to glare up at his face where he stood over me.

"Then maybe I'll fall with him," I snarled.

Julius backed up, his eyebrows drawn tightly together. "You don't mean that," he hissed.

I laid down and rolled over, ending this conversation as I muttered, "If you ever hurt him, I'll never forgive you."

CALLiE

CHAPTER TWENTY ONE

I awoke to a light chill skimming across my skin and pushed myself upright. It took me a moment to realign my brain with where we were, and I frowned into the smouldering fire as I shook off the confusion that was drowning me.

I'd gone to Fabian for answers, but I felt like I'd left with more questions. I didn't really know anything about the prophecy except that it could be a way for the vampires to end their curse. Magnar hadn't mentioned much about it though, and I presumed he thought it wasn't going to be what finished them. I guessed his thirst for vengeance meant he wouldn't have wanted to accept that alternative anyway. It wouldn't be enough for him to see the vampires returned to their mortal forms. He hungered for their blood almost as much as they hungered for ours.

I stretched my arms above my head and pushed myself upright so I could lean closer to the fire. Montana and Julius were sleeping soundly beside it, so I guessed that meant Magnar was on watch at the top of the statue. The wards should have been more than enough to keep any vampires from discovering us, but the slayers didn't want to take chances this close to the city and I couldn't say I disagreed.

My thoughts kept landing on what Fabian had said about Erik trying to repay his debt by starving himself for two hundred years. I couldn't begin to imagine such a thing. Had he managed to hold out for so long without succumbing to his primal desires? Or had he chained himself and leapt into the sea so he couldn't go back on his decision?

And why would he have thought that hunger would pay a debt to right old wrongs? Hunger had never earned me anything other than misery.

I wondered what Dad would have made of the prophecy. He'd always had a mind for solving problems and if there really was some way that Montana and I were caught up in it, then I was sure he would have been able to figure it out.

I raised my hand to the chain he'd given me where it still hung around my neck and held Mom's wedding ring in my fist. It felt warm. Warmer than a piece of metal should have been simply from lying against my skin. And my heart felt glad as I clung to it.

I started fiddling with it as my mind continued to turn in circles, each answer opening up more questions until I was making myself dizzy with it all.

I pushed the ring onto my finger and suddenly everything fell silent, but not in the usual sense of the word. I could still hear the crackle of the fire and Julius's soft snores, but it was like everything else was cushioned. Like I could see things more clearly.

I frowned as I tried to figure out what the difference was and sucked in a sharp breath as I realised it was Fabian. I could see him for what he was again. My thoughts of him weren't clouded with unwanted desires. I was free to hate him with as much venom as I had before the wedding. Although I was loath to admit that that was harder than it should have been now that I knew more about him.

The ring was doing more than that too. I felt light, like a great weight had been lifted from my shoulders and I could suddenly do everything and anything...

I pulled the ring from my finger and the weight of my obligations came crashing back down on me. I gasped in shock and Montana stirred opposite me.

I quickly pulled the chain over my head and held it before my eyes so I could look at the ring more closely. I'd seen it so many times in my life that I wasn't sure if I'd ever *really* looked at it.

It was a chunky, golden thing with a green stone in its centre. Mom had always called it an emerald, but I'd been too young to understand what she'd meant by that. I knew it had been her mother's and her mother's before that. Back and back for as long as anyone in her family remembered. But I didn't really know anything else about it.

I unclasped the chain and pulled the ring free of it before slowly pushing it onto my finger again.

The silence found me once more and a smile pulled at my lips which bubbled up into laughter at the back of my throat. I didn't know how, but I was free. I could sense it. There were no rules, no commands, no deity to push her way into my body...just me. And without my tie to Fabian, everything seemed so much clearer once more.

I pushed myself to my feet and silently crossed the room before heading up the wide stairwell which led to the viewing point in the statue's crown.

My heart pounded in time with my footsteps as I moved higher and higher.

I didn't grow tired as I climbed, even though I knew I would have before I'd taken my vow. My gifts were still mine, like they were some intrinsic part of me, but the weight on my soul was completely removed.

I stepped into the viewing area and found Magnar staring out into the night at the illuminated city.

My nerves floundered as I closed in on him and he turned to look at me in surprise. It wasn't like this undid what he'd done, but at the same time it did put us back on level ground. It took away his power over me and made certain that every action I chose here and now was my own. And I was sick of this anger burning between us.

"Are you having trouble sleeping?" Magnar asked as I drew closer.

I shook my head, unsure how to say what I thought I'd discovered. If I was wrong, I would only disappoint him, but if I was right...

My gaze roamed over his face before dropping lower, taking in the breadth of his powerful shoulders, the span of his muscular chest, his entire body which was really a weapon waiting for a target at all times.

I kept moving until I was barely a foot from him and reached for the edges of the bubble of calm that surrounded me.

The magic, or shield, or whatever it was, felt like an extension of myself and by pushing my will into the ring, I was able to surround him with it too.

Magnar frowned as he felt the energy slipping over him and I took the final step, closing the distance between us.

"Tell me to stop," I said, a smile pulling at my lips as I looked up at him, my hurt and anger fading as I stood before him with a way around his hold on me.

My fury over the bond Idun had placed upon us was really about how powerless it made me – just as the bond she had given me with Fabian had stolen my control over myself too. But if I was right about this, then I didn't need to be angry about it anymore.

"Stop what?" Magnar asked me in confusion.

"Just command me to stop and you'll see," I teased, waiting for him to wield his power over me, anticipation growing in my gut, coiling like a monster ready to spring free.

Magnar looked into my eyes, a frown tugging his brow low, and I had no idea what he was thinking.

"Stop," he said firmly.

I felt his command crash into the bubble of safety and fizzle away to nothing. The rush that flooded me felt like I'd just jumped into deep water all over again, except this time I wasn't sinking, I was floating.

My smile widened as I reached for his chest and gripped his shirt in my hands. I pushed up onto my tiptoes and pulled him towards me, slowly, so achingly slowly as my need for him devoured me whole. My anger had wanted me to deny this, but the truth was that I'd been hopelessly lost when it came to this man for far too long now.

We hung in that breath of space between our lips as I slid my hands further up his chest and his heart pounded beneath my palm, his gaze questioning and cautious, like he didn't dare believe in what he was seeing.

I kept going, my progress drawn out as I half expected Idun to notice what I was doing and force me to stop at any moment. But she couldn't touch me here. I wasn't even certain she could see me anymore.

My fingertips skimmed across his collar bone and danced over his neck, the warmth of his skin making me tremble just a little. I wanted this, him, so badly and for the first time since I had sworn myself into his power, I felt like I could actually claim him if I wanted to.

Magnar's throat bobbed beneath my thumb, his stubble grazing my skin and his gaze burning through me like I was made of nothing but sawdust, waiting to be consumed by the heat in their depths.

I had no idea how the ring was doing this, but I was finally free. Finally myself again and in charge of my own choices. And I chose him. I would always choose him no matter how many obstacles stood between us, no matter how fucking infuriating I found him or how much he made me want to punch him sometimes. No matter what Idun or any of the other gods tried to throw in our way.

He was meant to be mine and I was meant to be his. It wasn't fate or divine intervention. It was just real, and it had been staring us in the face since the moment when he had first driven me up against that wall and plucked me from the grasp of the vampires. I wasn't going to let anything take it from us.

Barely a heartbeat divided us, and I wasn't sure if I was even breathing as his presence devoured every other thought. I was a moth before a flame, and I danced closer hoping he wouldn't be my end but somehow not minding if he was. Because he was power and danger and hope and safety and everything I'd never realised I'd needed so desperately.

My lips met his and I was consumed by the fire raging inside me. It burned through my blood, heating every inch of my body and catching light to everything it touched. I knew I was going to fall apart beneath the weight of this desire.

Magnar stilled for a moment as though he was unable to believe this were real, or perhaps he was afraid that if he tried to claim it for himself then it would be stolen away again. But I wasn't going to let that happen. I'd put up a shield against the outside world and here and now, there was no one and nothing else but us.

His hesitation didn't last long and his hands found my waist so he could pull me against him, his thumbs skimming over my hips as our bodies pressed to one another. His lips were soft and teasing like he wasn't sure if he should dare to offer them, but I hadn't come here for gentle, I'd come for the creature of war who had stood alone for a thousand years in the face of more torment than any man should ever endure.

Magnar pulled back for half of a moment, looking at me as though he had to be sure I was real. I met his wild gaze with my own, promising him that, and so much more.

Then he kissed me again and it was anything but gentle. It was like he *had* to have me or the world would stop turning, had to devour me because without this he'd been starving.

Oh hell.

I groaned with longing as I fell into his kisses, and he pushed me back against the wall with a sold thump that made my breath expel in one harsh burst. But his mouth never left mine, his grip on me relentless, his need for me so potent that I could taste it on every sweep of his tongue over mine.

It was like he'd lost me to the darkness for a while, but now he'd found me. We were bathing in sunlight together and he would never let me go again.

His hands shifted beneath my shirt and he lifted it higher as I arched my back, feeling his desire as keenly as my own, the solid ridge of his cock driving against my core and making me moan with need.

His fingertips drew a line up my spine as the material was hoisted free and we broke apart just long enough for him to pull it over my head.

I gazed up at him as the moonlight shone in his golden eyes, reflecting a perfect silver crescent back at me.

"I love you, Callie," he breathed, and my heart bloomed with the words he hadn't spoken before. I'd felt it in all the things he'd done for me but hearing him say it had me coming apart. "I was afraid to say it in case she took you from me. I was afraid to feel it too because I fear I'm fighting a losing war and I didn't want to drag you down with me when I fall, but you're all there is for me now. You're the reason I want to keep fighting even after seeing how much those monsters achieved in my absence. You're the reason I have any hope left at all."

I placed my hand on his cheek, feeling the rough bite of his stubble against my palm and aching to feel it on the rest of my body as well.

"I used to be afraid of so many things," I replied steadily. "But you make me brave. And if we have to be brave to love each other then that's what we'll be. I won't deny my heart any longer and you shouldn't hide yours. Let Idun try to tear us apart if she must – I'm done dancing to her tune."

Magnar held my gaze and anticipation throbbed through my body as I waited for him to take me hostage again. Because that's what I was with him; a captive to everything he was. Bound to him in ways that had nothing to do with being slayers or fulfilling vows. I was entirely at his mercy because he held my heart in his palm, and I held his in mine too.

"I have been dreaming of all the things I would do to you once I could get my hands on you again, drakaina hjarta. I've been aching to get between your thighs and make you scream my name in that breathy, blissful way of yours."

I sucked in a breath and he smirked that cocky smile which made my toes curl before he grabbed my thighs, hoisting me into his arms as I wrapped my legs around his waist obligingly. He drove me back against the wall again and his mouth slammed into my own as he drove his hips between mine, making sure I felt every solid inch of him.

I moaned as he shifted his attention from my mouth to trail a line of rough kisses down my neck, and a desperate ache began to build inside me.

More, I need more.

My hands fisted in the material at the back of his shirt and I yanked on it, pulling it over his head so I could feel the heat of his skin against mine.

His mouth made it to my collar bone, and I leaned back as he travelled lower, his movements filled with urgency like we were running out of time and forever wouldn't be long enough. His mouth moved across my skin, finding every inch of bare space and marking it with his lips. His breaths came harder, faster, matching my own as the need in our bodies grew desperate to be sated.

His hand skimmed across my throat before tugging my bra strap from my shoulder and releasing my breast so his mouth could claim that too, his tongue riding over the hardened peak of my nipple. I moaned with longing as a knot tightened in my gut and my nails dug into his broad shoulders as my body begged for more.

Shit, I was out of my depth with him, but I'd just dived in feet first and there was no way I was swimming for the surface yet.

He pinned me against the wall with his hips and his hands moved over my skin, raising goosebumps along my flesh as I ached for more and more of his touch. He was toying with me, keeping me in the moment between then and now where he knew I was falling apart with my need for him.

I pushed him back, using my gifted muscles as he tried to refuse my command and drawing a deep laugh from him as he dropped me to my feet where I kicked my boots off.

He drank in the sight of me as he backed up and the look in his eyes made me want to drown with him.

"You're so beautiful, Callie," he breathed, and my skin flamed as I took in the utterly perfect sight of him. "I'm going to enjoy every second of destroying you."

He dropped to his knees before me, making me suck in a breath in surprise as he gripped my ass and tugged me towards him. His mouth fell on my stomach, his teeth nipping at my skin as he unfastened my pants and drew them down my legs.

I steadied myself by fisting his hair as his fingertips carved lines down the backs of my thighs and he dragged the material off of me inch by inch.

I stepped out of them obligingly, needing there to be nothing at all between me and this beast of a man, needing to finally feel him inside me and claim that final piece of him for my own.

But of course, Magnar wasn't simply going to give me what I wanted and fuck me. He growled as he dropped his mouth from my stomach, closing his lips over my underwear and sucking on my clit through the thin fabric.

I cursed, my hold on his hair tightening as my knees almost buckled and he laughed against my pussy, the deep timbre of his voice sending a jolt of pleasure through me.

Magnar wove his fingers through the sides of my panties and tugged them down, a groan of longing escaping him as he bared my body for his pleasure.

His gaze rose to meet mine, his tongue wetting his lips like he was desperately hungry for me, and I just stared at him as he tugged my panties off and tossed them aside.

Magnar's hand coiled around my ankle and he tugged sharply, making me gasp in alarm. I almost lost my balance as he slung my leg over his shoulder.

I had barely begun to curse him out when his hands grasped my ass and he yanked my hips forward, his mouth landing on my core at once and his tongue sinking inside me.

"Oh, fuck," I panted, gripping his hair tightly as I fought to balance myself like that because his tongue was circling and then withdrawing, licking straight over my clit and I was in fucking heaven already.

Magnar devoured me like a starving man, my curses and moans of pleasure echoing in the cold chamber as I clung to him and tried to keep my balance even though my legs were trembling.

He gripped my ass harder, tilting my hips and lapping at my clit until I came with a cry, ecstasy exploding through my body and my spine arching so I almost toppled to the floor.

He pushed my leg from his shoulder, licking the taste of me from his lips as he got to his feet and stole a brutal kiss from my lips which was thick with the taste of my own lust.

His hands fumbled with the catch on my bra and he tugged at it sharply, almost tearing it from me before I managed to regain my head enough to unclasp it for him and free the last of my skin.

Magnar palmed my breasts, tugging on my nipples and making me whimper with the need which was consuming me as he walked me backwards to the wall again.

I reached for his belt, my fingers ripping at it in my desperation to have him, to feel every glorious inch of him buried within me.

I finally tugged it free, sinking my hand into his pants and moaning as I took his cock into my fist, sliding my palm along his shaft and rolling my thumb through the moisture which crowned his tip.

Magnar let me toy with him for a few moments, his mouth on mine the entire time before he snatched my wrist and tugged my hand away.

He spun me around, ignoring my protests as he pushed me up against the frozen wall, my breasts scraping against the cold metal and my breath catching in my throat.

"Bend over and use the wall to support yourself," he growled in my ear, and I looked over my shoulder at him in surprise.

His golden eyes blazed with a thousand sin-filled thoughts and any protests I might have been considering fell away as I found myself nodding. His hand pressed to my spine as he stepped back to give me room and I bent over before him, bracing my palms against the wall.

"So you *can* follow orders?" Magnar taunted.

"Only when the rewards are worth it," I bit back, and he chuckled.

"Oh, they're worth it, drakaina hjarta."

He ran his hand down my spine then over my ass, his fingers sliding lower until he sank two of them into my pussy at once and made me moan for him.

"Tell me that you want to come on my face again, Callie," he purred, driving his fingers in and out of me. "Tell me you want me to lick your sweet cunt until you're coming so hard you can't fucking see."

"Yes," I gasped, the rhythm of his fingers making it hard to form words. "That, all of that. But then I want you to fuck me, Magnar. I want all of you this time and no more excuses."

He chuckled as he dropped to his knees behind me and I moaned as he pumped his hand faster.

"Whatever you desire, drakaina hjarta. I am yours to command tonight."

I opened my mouth to make some snarky comment in reply to that but he had dropped his mouth to my core again, his tongue pushing between his fingers as he drove them into me and the combination made a sultry moan tumble from me instead.

He was so fucking good at…everything. In that moment I couldn't even pretend to be able to find fault in him because he was destroying me just as he'd promised he would, and the combination of his mouth and his fingers was driving me utterly wild with need.

Magnar tugged his fingers out of me, and I whimpered at the emptiness left behind.

He pushed my thighs apart, fully exposing me to him and tilting my hips so he could take my clit captive with his mouth once more.

I gasped, my body coiled so tightly that I wasn't sure I could survive the rush of pleasure that I knew was coming for me.

I panted his name, begging him to stop, begging him to never stop and then his fingers were driving into me again and his tongue was riding my clit and I was coming with a cry that exploded from my lungs and made my entire body fall apart.

But he had me. Of course he had me and I found myself in his arms before the cold, metal floor chilled my skin as he pressed me down onto my back.

The heat of his body made up for the cold, and I panted beneath him as his turned his attention to my breasts, his mouth worshipping one while his hand claimed the other.

He carved a line across my flesh with his mouth, his stubble grazing my sensitised skin as he marked every inch of my body as his own and so far as I was concerned, he could have it.

I surrendered to him as he kissed and stroked my skin, giving me a moment to recover from the cataclysm which had just taken place in my body before his hand dropped between my thighs again.

"You're so wet," he groaned, toying with me, slipping his fingers in and out, watching me writhe and whimper beneath him. He was enjoying having me at his mercy, but if all that time that being a slave to his will came with this much reward, I couldn't summon the energy to complain about it.

"And so fucking tight," he added, pushing a third finger into me and making my hips buck beneath him.

He smiled down at me and I managed to grip his waistband around the utter perfection of the movements of his fingers inside me. I shoved his pants down and he replied by driving his fingers in deeper and pressing his thumb down on my clit.

The world divided and broke apart as I came so suddenly that my fucking heart missed a beat.

I was moaning his name, melting into a puddle beneath him and unable to focus on anything at all as he withdrew for a moment.

Then the world slammed back together as I realised he wasn't close to done with me.

Magnar kneeled over me, his pants gone and cock solid in his fist as he looked down at me and stroked it in lazy, fluid motions, like he just couldn't help himself while I lay beneath him like that.

I licked my lips as I let my eyes feast on the sight of him, my throat bobbing as I took in just how big he was and wondered what it would feel like to have all of that buried within me.

"I need you," I panted. "Now Magnar. No more holding back."

"No more holding back," he agreed, and his mouth moved back up my body again, starting on the inside of my knee then travelling up my inner thigh.

He swirled his tongue over my clit once more, making me moan his name but he didn't linger there this time, his mouth trailing up my stomach then taking turns with my peaked nipples.

I gripped his shoulders, tugging to make him move faster, my fingernails biting into his skin.

I arched my back, my fingers twisting in his hair as I pulled him to me, needing to kiss him again and losing myself in the feeling of his mouth against mine. His weight pressed me down onto the cold floor, but it wasn't enough.

My hands travelled the broad slope of his shoulders and the arching curve of his back before gripping his ass and tugging him closer so I could feel every solid inch of him driving against me.

He made a noise which set my bones trembling as he gave in to my command and kissed me deeply, one hand pushing into my hair while the other ran down the side of my thigh.

Before I could catch my breath, he hooked my knee into his grip and angled me so the tip of his cock drove against my entrance.

I broke our kiss, looking into his eyes as he sank into me, inch by glorious inch, filling and stretching me until I couldn't breathe, or think, or feel anything at all apart from that sinful fullness.

I cried out as he pushed all the way to the hilt, the size of him so much to handle at once and he breathed my name like a prayer as he lost himself in me.

Magnar silenced me with more kisses as my breathing came in heavy pants and my hands fisted in his hair as he drew his hips back then sank into me again.

His body pressed to mine as I wrapped my legs around him and I realised I'd never felt anything like this. I'd never felt anything as sharply or intensely as I did when I was with him. His touch was electric, lighting me up from the inside out and binding me to him in a way that would never be undone.

I knew the world was still spinning out there, but it was hard to remember that anything existed except him. His blazing eyes, his skin moving against mine and his perfect body which had captivated me mind, flesh and soul. I was his, all his and he was mine too.

"Magnar," I gasped and his grip on me tightened at the sound of his name on my lips.

I was caught between begging for more and crying out for him to release me from this torment when he finally did. The world shattered around us, and my body dissolved into nothing and everything as he took each piece of me and gave it back renewed.

His weight pressed me down as he drove into me harder, his grip on me bruising and his thrusts punishing as he fucked me like the heathen he was, wringing his pleasure from my flesh and using me for his every desire.

I cried out with every drive of his hips, clawing at his back and rocking my hips in time with his feral movements until he was coming, roaring his release and driving himself deep inside me as he finished with a thrust that destroyed me entirely.

He collapsed over me, his weight crushing me in the most delicious way, and I drew him closer as we both tried to catch our breath, tangled in each other's arms.

His forehead pressed to mine, the tip of his nose touching my nose and our heavy beathing heating the space between us. I bit my lip on the shit-eating grin which was trying to dominate my face. I'd known it would be good between us but fuck, I never could have predicted that level of annihilation.

"How?" Magnar breathed finally when we were able to think clearly again.

He rolled off of me, propping his head on one hand and I looked up at this savage creature of mine as he brushed my hair out of my face.

"My mother's ring," I replied with a shrug.

I had no idea how it had worked; I'd only known what I wanted as soon as it had, and that nothing about this decision could be anyone's but my own.

Magnar took my hand in his, turning it so the ring caught in the moonlight. He brushed his finger against it and a surge pulsed through the bubble of energy which surrounded us.

"That's no ordinary ring," he said, withdrawing his hand as a frown gripped his features, at odds with the way I felt about it. "Where did your mother get it?"

"I just know that it's been in her family for as far back as anyone can remember. Passed down between daughters to wear as their wedding rings. After she died, Dad hung it from his neck until one of us was ready to inherit it. I'd never put it on until today."

"That ring was not made by mortals," Magnar said quietly as though he were afraid we might be overheard. "It has a presence. Like the blades. Or the stones the vampires use. It was created by a god."

"A god?" I frowned in confusion.

Why would my mother have had a ring created by a god? Where would her family have gotten it?

"Yes. And a powerful one at that. You see how it hides us? I'd wager they cannot see us at all while you wield its power. That's why their rules can't hold you." He moved his hand to my side and began painting soft circles across my skin.

"So if I keep it on, I can be free of them?" I asked hopefully.

"I doubt it is as simple as that. The gods know of your existence; you're already caught up in their games. If you were to just disappear, they'd know something powerful was being used to hide you. And I'd imagine the god who created that ring is missing it. If they figure out you've got it, they'll do everything in their power to take it back."

"But if they're looking for it then why haven't they found it?" I asked in confusion.

It wasn't like my mom had tried to hide it. And I couldn't remember her ever saying anything about it holding any kind of power either. But we knew my dad wasn't the one who had given us our slayer blood, so that meant it had to have come from her. How long had her family kept this hidden? And where had they gotten it in the first place?

"I doubt the power in it could be awakened by anyone who hadn't taken their vow. You are touched by the gods; enough so that you're able to tap into their power and wield their own creation against them."

"So we can do this any time we want?" I asked, biting my lip as my gaze travelled over his body.

Magnar hesitated before he answered, and I could see a war taking place behind his eyes. "We should be cautious with using this. If the gods were to find out-"

"But, *now* for example, we're already hidden..." I grazed my fingertips across his jaw and left the suggestion hanging between us.

His resolve shattered quickly as a wicked smile lit his features, his cock already hard again, making his desire clear enough.

"Well I suppose you're right about that," he purred.

He propelled me on top of him, taking my hands in his grasp and pinning them at the base of my spine. I cried out in surprise before falling silent at the ruinous look in his eyes.

"I want to watch you ride me, drakaina hjarta. I want to see the look in your eyes as you take my cock and I make you shatter so many times that you lose all sense of everything beyond the two of us. And when you can't take it anymore, I want you to beg me to bend you over and fuck you even harder until I'm coming inside that sweet cunt of yours again and you forget your own name."

"Okay," I agreed on a breath because honestly, I didn't even have a snarky retort to any of that, I just wanted him to make good on those demands and stop wasting time on anticipation.

Magnar gave me a dark smile as he moved his free hand to my ass and dug his fingers into my skin before pulling me down onto his cock and delivering on every single one of those promises and several more besides.

Maybe the gods would rage when they discovered the freedom we had snatched from their grasp, but I didn't really give a shit what they had to say on the subject.

MONTANA

CHAPTER TWENTY TWO

I watched from the window as the sun rose slowly on the horizon, struggling to penetrate the thick clouds. Perhaps Valentina was keeping the weather this way so that her biters could remain out in the city. Was she still hunting for us right now? I didn't understand why she wanted Magnar. Was it just out of revenge? But if that was the case, why wouldn't she have tried to kill him when we'd encountered her before?

Julius had mentioned that Callie and Magnar were upstairs but as the scent of cooking oatmeal filled the air, they appeared.

I glanced over at Callie and her cheeks flushed as she stepped away from Magnar's side. Her shirt was torn at the hem, and I was fairly sure she didn't have a bra on. She wouldn't meet my eye as she hurried to the fire and took a bowl from Julius.

Magnar took one too, sitting beside Callie and wolfing the oatmeal down.

Julius eyed them curiously. "Hungry, Magnar? I only ever see you eat that quickly when you've worked up a real appetite."

Magnar shrugged and Callie's cheeks turned scarlet.

"What's going on?" I asked, moving away from the broken window and dropping down in front of the fire.

"We'll talk later," Callie whispered to me as Julius's gaze swung between them, seeming confused and excited.

"You're both still bound by the vow, but if I didn't know any better, I'd assume you'd just fucked each other's brains out." Julius grinned and Callie half choked on her spoonful of food.

"Well you do know better so shut the fuck up and eat your breakfast," Magnar said, but his eyes danced with mirth.

Julius smiled casually, scooping a spoonful of food into his mouth.

The phone rang and I nearly jumped out of my skin at the sound.

Julius plucked it from his back pocket, scowling at the screen. "Fuck off, Belvedere." He stamped his thumb down to cut off the call and I scowled.

"How do you know it's a Belvedere?" Magnar demanded as the phone started ringing again.

I ground my teeth as Julius looked to me, fronting out whatever he was about to say. "Because *someone's* been calling her vampire husband."

"You didn't!" Callie gasped, staring at me in horror.

Heat poured through my veins and I raised my chin. "Yes, I did. And can you just answer the damn phone, Julius? Erik might have something important to say."

Julius didn't respond, but Magnar nodded. "Answer it."

"Why?" his brother balked.

"Because I said so," Magnar snarled. "He might spill some information that allows us to go find him and rip his head off."

I rose from the floor, furious at both of them as I strode toward Julius and held out my hand for the phone. He didn't pass it over but tapped a button on the screen and Erik's voice sounded out loudly through the speaker.

"I assume this is one of my enemies answering and not my beloved wife?" he asked casually, and a ripple of heat spread through my stomach at his reference to me.

"You assume right," Julius growled. "And if you're hoping to speak to her again, permission denied."

"Stop being such an asshole," I snapped at Julius and Erik's low laughter filled the room.

Magnar bristled, rising to his feet with his hands curling into fists. "What do you want, parasite?"

"I want to offer you something you can't refuse," Erik said, and my heart started beating wildly in my chest.

"Your head on a silver platter?" Julius asked.

"Better," Erik said.

"All of your family's heads on four silver platters?" Julius suggested, and my scowl grew.

"Or in a sack?" Magnar added and the temperature in my veins somehow increased.

"I am thoroughly amused," Erik said dryly. "Even decapitated, I am sure my wife would still prefer me to you, Julius Elioson, so how about you listen to someone she actually gives a shit about?"

Julius fell unnaturally quiet, glaring at the phone.

"Go on," Magnar hissed.

"I'm offering you the chance of a duel. Man to man. The two of you against me and Fabian."

"No way," Callie snapped. "If you're fighting, I'm fighting too."

"No deal," Erik said smoothly.

Magnar and Julius shared a glance, and I stared between them, fearing them agreeing to this.

"I sense there's more to this offer?" Julius asked.

"There is," Erik confirmed. "Whoever wins – as in whoever kills their opposition first – takes the twins. If I win, I get my wife back and her sister, too. If you win and we die, then your vendetta against me is done."

"What?" I gasped in disbelief. He was placing a fucking wager and we were the prize. He had no goddamn *right*. "No way-"

"Silence," Magnar commanded, and I stared at him in shock.

"You can't actually think we're going to let you agree to that?" Callie half-laughed, but she looked concerned when the brothers didn't join in.

"We're not some fucking trophy to be won," I snarled.

"I'll give you an hour to decide. If you agree, we fight at sunset," Erik said then the line went dead.

I folded my arms. "Well that's not happening."

"Exactly," Callie agreed, moving to my side in solidarity.

Magnar ignored us, staring at his brother. "We have waited a thousand years for this fight. We will win it."

"Um, hello? Are you not listening?" I demanded. "You are not fighting Erik. And we are not the reward for some insane brawl."

"I know, brother," Julius answered Magnar, ignoring me entirely. "We shall drive our blades into their hearts and finish this at last."

"Excuse me," Callie growled, planting her hands on her hips. "We aren't agreeing. We're not allowing this. The answer is *no*."

"I am glad it's Fabian joining Erik, he has wronged you deeply, Magnar. And when they're dead, we'll finish the rest of their siblings." Julius nodded firmly.

Magnar beamed. "We'll kill them all together."

I gaped at Callie and she shook her head, clearly as pissed off as I was.

"You aren't fighting," I insisted. "This duel is not happening. We're not going to stand and watch while you offer us up to be some fucking prize."

"Exactly, and if there *was* a fight, I'd damn well be a part of it," Callie snapped.

Magnar and Julius finally gave us their attention, not seeming particularly bothered by our reaction.

"We will win," Julius said with conviction. "There's nothing to worry about."

"Nothing to worry about?" I cried, taking a step towards him. "You're talking about killing Erik. And I don't care what you all think of him, I won't let you hurt him."

"Details." Magnar shrugged and rage burned a hole right through me.

I drew Nightmare from my hip, pointing it at him. "It's not happening, Magnar."

Callie took my arm, slowly lowering it to my side. "Don't worry,

Monty. They won't do it."

"Psh." Julius waved her off. "We'll do what we like."

"You can do whatever you want with your meaty ass, Julius, but you don't get to decide for me and my sister," Callie said in a steady tone. "We're not going to be a part of this fucked up game."

"We should be working *with* the vampires to break the curse," I implored. "This is madness." I couldn't believe Erik had suggested this, but then again, how could I really be surprised? His promises meant shit. He had broken them before, and now he was breaking them again. He'd let me go, but now he was reneging on that promise with some bullshit centuries-old duel that he thought he had the right to use me as a wager for.

"That's never going to happen," Magnar said icily, fixing me in his gaze.

Julius sighed. "We can't expect them to agree to this, brother."

Magnar eyed him, nodding slowly. "It seems like a wasted opportunity to refuse, but it appears we must."

I glanced between them suspiciously, unsure why they were backing down so quickly now. Were they really seeing sense?

Callie straightened her spine. "Maybe we should keep trying to figure out this prophecy. It could end all of this before anyone has to fight."

"Enjoy your endeavours. I'm going to check the wards," Magnar said, striding off toward the exit. After a beat, Julius followed him, whistling softly to himself in the most obvious, unsubtle way known to man.

"They're lying," Callie said, giving me an anxious look.

"Yeah, no shit," I breathed. "What can we do?"

"Well we're not going to be sitting ducks here. If they think we're going to be the trophy in their fight, they're going to be sorely disappointed."

"So what are we gonna do?" I hissed again, gripping her arm.

Callie chewed her lower lip. "I guess…if we figure out the prophecy before sunset, maybe we can stop this."

"How are we going to do that?" I ran a hand into my hair, anxiety

257

burrowing into my core.

Callie dropped down to the floor, patting the space beside her. I sat, folding my legs as I gazed at her, clinging to this slim hope even if it was futile.

"What do we know so far?" she asked.

I recited the prophecy slowly so Callie could absorb it.

"A warrior born but monster made, changes fates of souls enslaved. Twins of sun and moon will rise, when one has lived a thousand lives. A circle of gold shall join two souls, and a debt paid rights wrongs of old. In a holy mountain the earth will heal, then the dead shall live, and the curse will keel."

I turned over those words in my mind, knowing it was time to reveal what I knew about the first line. The truth I had ignored but had been following me into my nightmares and showing me as that creature with blood staining her lips.

Callie wasn't going to like it one bit, but we had to lay everything on the line now. It was our only chance to stop this fight to the death.

"Julius and I think a warrior born but monster made might mean me turning into a vampire," I said thickly. "And Andvari basically confirmed it." I cleared my throat and Callie glared at me in utter horror.

"What?" she gasped, grabbing my hand. "That can't happen. I won't let it."

"I know," I said through my teeth. "It's not like I want that, Callie. Shit, the thought is terrifying and I hope it's not true, but I had to say it."

Those words hung between us, Callie shaking her head in refusal of them and I ached to take them back. But there was no time for lies or half-truths anymore. We had to face the possibilities of what Andvari wanted from us.

"Let's just focus on the next part," I urged.

She looked ready to fight me but gave in at my pleading expression. "Which changes fates of souls enslaved," she murmured the next line. "So *if* you turn then that could set things in motion maybe? It changes the vampires' fates...for the better I guess." Discomfort crossed her features at the mere idea of that happening and my chest twisted with it too.

I nodded, having nothing better to offer and wanting to move swiftly on from that part of the prophecy. "Then twins of sun and moon will rise...Nightmare whispered that to me at the wedding. So I suppose that's what that means? We've risen because we married princes? That makes us royal too. Princesses."

Callie nodded, delivering the next part. "When one has lived a thousand lives - that was when I took the vow. I have access to a thousand lives, a thousand memories as if I've lived them all."

Excitement grew in me. That was over half the prophecy already. "Okay so...it's the rest we're unclear on. A circle of gold shall join two souls. And a debt paid right wrongs of old."

Callie fiddled with Mom's ring hanging from her neck, her brow heavily furrowed. "Could it be this?" she asked, glancing away awkwardly. "I put it on last night and it seemed to break my bonds for a while. My link to Fabian and the power holding Magnar and I apart just disappeared." Her cheeks flushed and I realised what she meant.

"Callie," I gasped. "Does that mean you and Magnar...?"

"Yes." She suppressed her smile, placing a hand over her mouth.

"How was it?" I whispered, grinning at her, relieved she had found some light in this godforsaken world.

"Good," she breathed. "Better than good. Monty, he's everything. I can't get enough of him and now this ring gives me a way to be with him." She took it from her neck and my heart swelled as I reached out to it.

As my fingers grazed the metal, my mind exploded with images.

I was trapped in a vision, torn from the room and propelled high into the sky above the statue. My stomach lurched and a silent scream got stuck in my throat as I flew over New York City at high speed. I felt Callie's presence right next to me and we seemed to merge into one being, watching the land sweep beneath us at a colossal pace. We sped across great forests and ruined towns until the landscape shifted into a dusty red desert. It grew wider and wider, all the way to the horizon until the only thing I could see was crimson sand.

The world whipped by in a blur and suddenly we were standing before a huge mountain, rising from the ground and dominating everything in the land. It disappeared high up into the clouds like a looming beast. Something about it was unearthly, its aura powerful and forbidding.

A ring of gold joins two souls, a whisper filled my ears. *Mount Alma awaits.*

I was yanked back into the room and the ring fell between us, tinkling as it hit the floor.

"What the hell was that?" I gasped and Callie shook her head, tentatively picking up the ring again.

"I don't know," she panted, resting a hand against her heart. "But did you hear that voice?"

I nodded, my breathing finally steadying out. "Do you think that mountain we saw was the holy mountain the prophecy mentions?"

She nodded quickly. "It has to be." She sprang to her feet, ushering me up. "Come on, we have to tell the others."

CALLIE

CHAPTER TWENTY THREE

We hurried towards the exit and Montana reached out to grasp the door handle. I caught her arm as the sound of Julius and Magnar's voices reached me from outside.

"Hang on," I whispered as I tilted my head to listen in.

Montana's eyes widened as she realised what I was doing, and she pressed her ear to the wooden door to try and hear them too.

"-shouldn't have to let this opportunity pass us by," Julius said irritably.

"I know we shouldn't," Magnar replied. "But it's not exactly our place to make that deal. The twins will feel like we are bargaining with their lives, it makes it seem as though we think we own them."

"Better to be owned by us than the Belvederes," Julius replied dismissively, and Magnar snorted a laugh.

"I'd wager being owned by a worm would be preferable to that."

"And anyway, just because we agree to such a thing, it wouldn't tie the twins to anything. Like you say, we *don't* own them, so any deal we made would be irrelevant. I could just as easily promise them the sky if they beat us. It doesn't make it mine to give."

"You have a point," Magnar said, and I could sense that he was tempted to give in.

I almost pushed the door open so that I could reiterate my opinion on being used as a bargaining chip, but if they hadn't heard me the first time then I doubted they'd listen now. And if I interrupted them, they'd only be more careful not to be overheard again. It wouldn't stop them having this conversation.

"But on the off chance they won, I'd be placing Callie in danger."

"Pfft," Julius scoffed. "Two Belvederes beating us? They spent ten years running and hiding from us because they knew our strength was superior. We're more than a match for them."

"And it's unlikely we will ever be given an opportunity like this again where we will only be asked to face two of them. Once they're dead, Miles and Clarice will be easy prey," Magnar said, a hint of excitement in his tone.

"So we're agreed?" Julius asked.

"What are they saying?" Montana hissed, and I flinched at the loudness of her voice as my heightened hearing adjusted.

"They're going to take Erik up on his offer," I said, biting my lip.

I wasn't sure what we could possibly do to convince them not to fight but before I could ask Montana if she had any ideas, she pushed the door wide and stormed out.

Julius and Magnar stood on the far side of the statue, and they looked up at us guiltily as we moved towards them.

"So our opinions just mean nothing to you then?" Montana growled as she closed in on them and I hurried to match her pace.

"We were only talking over our options," Julius replied defensively. "No need to throw a tantrum, damsel."

"Don't talk to her like that," I said angrily, glaring at him. "She's not a child so don't patronise her. This whole issue is about me and my sister, so you have no right to choose for us."

"It's not about you," Magnar replied, folding his arms. "Not for us anyway. We've spent our whole lives waiting for a chance to take these parasites down – we sacrificed the time we could have had living out our years surrounded by our clans and family, and now they're offering us the perfect opportunity."

"Maybe that's why Idun bound you to Fabian," Julius piped up before I could respond. "If those marks on your hands make them stupid enough to risk their lives for you, then why shouldn't we take advantage of it?"

"And have you really thought about that?" Montana asked. "Have you considered how difficult it will be for us to see them hurt? Callie begged you to spare Fabian's life because of what she feared would happen to her if he died. Or don't you care about that anymore?"

Magnar shifted uncomfortably, his gaze sweeping over me before he answered. "Of course I care about that. But after last night, I believe that tie isn't as strong as we'd feared. Closing yourself off from it didn't hurt you; it freed you. And I think killing him will make that freedom permanent."

"You can't know that!" Montana protested. She turned to me for backup as my mind swam over what he was saying, and I wondered if it could be true. "You said you thought you'd die if Fabian died, surely you still feel that?"

"I... I don't know," I admitted.

A deep pain sliced into my heart as I considered the idea of the world without Fabian in it, and I was struck with the urge to drop to my knees and beg Magnar not to hurt him. But as I remembered how I'd felt in the slayer's arms last night, I hesitated. I couldn't trust myself when this bond to my enemy was intact, but when I'd been free of it, I'd finally felt like myself again.

I raised a hand to the ring, wishing I could put it on now, but I'd promised Magnar I'd use it as sparingly as possible. He was certain the gods would be searching for such a powerful item and if they realised I had it, it could put us all in danger.

"You see," Julius said triumphantly to Montana. "Even *she* knows it. And I get that you're obsessed with Erik of your own free will, but you can hardly expect us to forget what he is. To forget what he's done to our family, just because you think he's dreamy."

My sister looked at me like I'd just stabbed her in the back, and I dropped my eyes guiltily.

"Of course I don't expect you to forget what happened to your father," she said to the slayers. "And you know I understand that pain too. But what if there's a better way? The prophecy-"

"The prophecy is nothing more than a riddle designed to drive us all insane," Magnar growled.

"It's not. Callie, tell them what we saw when we touched the ring." She looked at me pleadingly, and I nodded. I may have been unsure about the best way to deal with my bond to Fabian, but I knew how much it would hurt Montana if anything happened to Erik. I owed it to her to try and convince the slayers to look more closely at the prophecy.

"We had a vision," I said. "Of the holy mountain. Mount Alma-"

"Alma? That means soul," Magnar replied, and I was glad that they were listening at least.

"Callie and I were bound together as one soul when we saw it," Montana said eagerly. "And that line in the prophecy talks about a circle of gold joining two souls as well."

The brothers glanced at each other, and I could tell they were unnerved by that statement.

"Nightmare said it was time for us to rise when we were made into princesses. When Callie took the vow, she said she was given the memories of a thousand slayers. We're the twins of sun and moon. We know about the holy mountain. So if the 'monster made' part is about me becoming a vampire then we only have to figure out what the debt to be paid is and-"

"And what?" Magnar boomed, and I could see anger simmering in his gaze. "You want to become one of them? You're willing to risk your soul and undergo that unholy transformation? All because you *hope* you've figured this out?"

"No," she breathed, fear lacing her voice. "I don't. But if that was the only way…"

"You can't," I said quickly. "You can't do that Monty, promise me you'll never become one of them."

"But if it's our chance to break the curse," she whispered. "Then-"

"I don't care," I growled. "I'm not losing you just so that you can help the bloodsuckers."

"But it wouldn't just help the vampires," she protested. "It would

266

help the humans too. They could be free-"

"Only if you're right and it works," Julius said. "In which case great; you'll be human again, you can come to your senses about that parasite and dump him for me. But if you're wrong-"

"If you're wrong, your sister's vow will demand she kills you as it demands we destroy them," Magnar growled. "You will be mortal enemies, driven to destroy each other."

My mouth fell open and I stared at him in horror for even suggesting such a thing. "I'd *never* do that."

"It's a good thing you won't be faced with that choice then," he said. "Because there's no way I will let it happen. Our people spent centuries trying to solve that prophecy to no avail." He turned his gaze on Montana. "I won't allow you to damn yourself based on some guesswork which you have no way of proving is true."

Montana seemed unsure for a moment then nodded. "It's not like I want to be one of them. The thought alone horrifies me," she said. "I only want to figure this out."

"We can keep trying," I said. "So long as we have time to do it." I raised an eyebrow at Magnar and he sighed in defeat.

"Fine. Tell the parasite we won't take his deal."

Julius opened his mouth to object then closed it again slowly. He shrugged one huge shoulder and pulled the cellphone from his pocket.

He hit a few buttons and a ringing filled the air.

"Have you made up your mind?" Erik's voice came through the speaker.

"The twins say no and it's up to them. We don't own them. They don't want the two of you anywhere near them," Julius replied dismissively.

Fabian's voice sounded in reply and my heart leapt with excitement. "I want my wife back you fucking-"

"I'm dealing with this," Erik snapped. "Are you too afraid to face us?" he asked, addressing the slayers again.

Magnar released a noise which sounded like the growl of a wild beast.

"Leave the twins out of it and I'll gladly come for your head," he snarled.

"No deal," Erik replied icily. "They belong with us. The tables have turned; look who's hiding in the shadows now."

Fury lined Montana's features at Erik's words, a hint of betrayal in her eyes that was clearly cutting her deeply.

"The day I hide from a parasite like you will be a cold day in hell," Julius growled, and I could feel the tension rising around me like a physical force as the vampires continued to goad the slayers.

"So tell us where you are if you're not afraid," Fabian hissed, and I had to fight against the thrill I felt at hearing his voice. I longed to rip the phone from Julius's hand and just sit and listen to him talking for hours and hours... I shook my head aggressively to force the ridiculous idea back out of it.

"No," I bit out before the slayers could say anything stupid.

"Callie?" Fabian breathed. "Are you alright? Have you been able to find enough food? Are you keeping warm en-"

"Don't speak to her," Magnar snarled, stepping towards the phone as if he wanted to punch Fabian through it.

Julius swung it out of his reach, waving him back.

"If you've laid a hand on my wife," Fabian snarled. "I swear on all the gods that I will carve every organ from your body and-"

"He's laid more than a hand on her," Julius sniggered, and I glared at him in outrage. We hardly needed to make the vampires any angrier. What the hell was he playing at?

Fabian roared so loudly that I flinched in shock, "I'M GOING TO FUCKING KILL-"

"Calm down, brother, they're trying to antagonise you," Erik snapped, and Fabian fell silent.

Julius started laughing and Magnar joined in. I wasn't sure if I wanted to punch them or laugh too, and Montana was staring at them like they'd gone insane.

"If you won't fight us like men then why not let the twins come to us?" Erik asked icily. "We can figure out the prophecy and the curse will end. Surely that would suit you too?"

"If you think we'd just hand them over to you then you really must be deranged," Julius replied.

"I thought you said you don't own them?" Erik reminded him. "Let *them* decide if that's true."

Montana looked at me with a frown like she was considering Erik's words, but there was no way in hell I was going anywhere near Fabian again. The damn mark on my hand was tingling with excitement at the mere thought of it; if I actually got close to him, I wasn't sure if I'd be able to keep fighting it and if I ever gave in to his desires, I'd never be able to forgive myself.

"I would sooner die than spend one more minute in your company," I spat, and Magnar gave me an approving look.

Montana sighed and I looked away from her as I realised I'd let her down. I hated being so divided with her over this, but I just couldn't see the vampires as she could. Working with them wasn't an option.

"Callie, please," Fabian begged. "At least let me see that you're alright!"

"What?" I asked in confusion. "How can you see me?"

"He means to turn the camera on," Montana explained quietly.

"Please," he asked again, and I could hear the desperation in his voice.

"Oh why the hell not?" Julius said with a dark smile. He slammed his thumb down on a button at the bottom of the screen as he pointed it towards me and Montana.

Suddenly I was looking back at an image of the two of us with the statue looming in the background. There was no mistaking where we were, and I wondered what the hell Julius was playing at. He must have known the Belvederes could find us now.

I glanced at him in confusion and he shrugged innocently as the picture of us shrank and Erik and Fabian appeared.

I stared at them in surprise, but Montana gasped in horror as she realised Julius had done it intentionally.

"You asshole!" she swore as she lunged for the phone, but Julius only laughed as he swung it around to face him and Magnar.

"See you at sunset, assholes," Julius said before hitting another button and ending the call.

"You said you wouldn't fight them!" Montana shouted angrily.

"No. We said we wouldn't offer you as prizes. However, we made it clear that we have every intention of killing them." Julius shrugged.

"But what about the prophecy?" she demanded.

"Our quarrel with them wouldn't end if they stopped being immortal. They're still the reason our people were wiped out. Erik still murdered our father," Magnar replied coldly.

"So you didn't even care what we said?" I asked. "You always planned on fighting them?"

Magnar glanced at his brother and shrugged. "I don't know why that would surprise you."

I stared at him in outright hostility, wondering what the fuck I was supposed to say in response to that.

"I can convince Erik to stay away," Montana breathed. "I can go to him and keep him from coming. Or we can just leave here, get as far away as we can before they get here-"

"No chance, damsel. We aren't running from them and you can't swim so you're stuck here too," Julius said stubbornly.

Montana stared between the two slayers hopelessly, but it was obvious that their minds were made up.

"Callie?" she asked, looking to me for help.

I was torn, unsure what the best move was. I hated the idea of going anywhere near Fabian, but if we let this fight take place then one of us was going to end up with a broken heart. And despite all my misgivings about her and Erik, I couldn't willingly put her through that.

"You're sure you can trust him?" I asked, my heart beating faster as I considered doing the unthinkable.

"I swear it, Callie. You know I'd never risk you getting close to him if I wasn't certain."

I glanced at Magnar but he didn't say anything, clearly not concerned about the fact that I was considering leaving with her. His arrogance made my jaw tick and pushed me to make a decision I hoped I wouldn't regret.

"I'll take you then. So long as he doesn't let Fabian anywhere near me."

"He won't," she promised, her eyes lighting with hope.

"Callie?" Magnar called, and my heart stuttered as I looked back up at him.

"I can't let you fight them," I began, but he cut me off.

"You must not wear your mother's ring."

"Why not?" I frowned at him in confusion as his command fell over me and I knew I wouldn't be able to so much as raise a hand towards the ring.

But that was all he said to me. No pleas for me to stay with him. No begging me to reconsider. Did he even care that I was planning to leave him here while I headed towards our enemies? He hadn't even asked if I was planning to come back.

Magnar glanced at Julius and they exchanged a knowing look but made no move to stop us from going. They didn't even try and convince us to stay.

Anger and hurt prickled at me, but I refused to let him see it. I turned away from them, grabbing Montana's arm and steering her towards the water.

"You're actually agreeing?" she asked in surprise, and I let my anger fuel me as I reached for my gifts so I would be ready to swim across the river back to the city.

"Yes," I growled. "Hold onto me and I'll pull you across."

I glanced back at Magnar and Julius, but they hadn't moved. They both stood watching us with folded arms and barely concealed amusement on their faces like they thought something was hilarious.

I turned my back on them as Montana laced her arms around my neck and I crouched to dive in.

I took a deep breath and propelled myself forward but instead of diving into the water I crashed into something immovably solid and fell onto the floor with Montana on top of me.

Magnar and Julius started laughing behind us and I scowled at them as I scrambled back to my feet in confusion.

"You can't leave remember, novice?" Magnar said.

I glanced at Montana in alarm as I realised he was right. The stupid vow which bound me to him stopped me from abandoning him or my cause. So if he wanted to stay on this island and wait for the Belvederes then that meant I was stuck here too. He'd stopped me from using the ring so I couldn't block his power over me and without it, I was bound to his will all over again.

"You motherfucker!" I yelled at him, but before I could launch into a tirade about his behaviour and exactly what I thought of him, my gaze fell on my sister's devastated expression. "I'm sorry, Monty," I breathed as I realised this fight was going to happen whether we liked it or not. One of the men we loved was going to die.

Her face fell and she looked back out towards the city desperately, as though she was hoping she might see Erik standing on the distant bank so she could convince him to stay away.

I stormed back towards Magnar and Julius, half wanting to punch both of their stupid faces and half wanting to never look at either of them again.

"You know, sometimes, I really fucking hate both of you," I growled.

MONTANA

CHAPTER TWENTY FOUR

I was so angry with Julius and Magnar that I couldn't bear to look at them as I stormed back into the museum. Callie's shouts carried after me as she tried to talk them out of this fight, but their minds were clearly made up.

I wasn't going to give in though. I'd find a way to reach Erik and stop this from happening. I wasn't going to see him or the slayers die. I refused to let either of those fates come to pass. And no matter how furious I was at all of them for forcing Callie and me into the middle of all this, it didn't stop me from panicking about the outcome. The thought of Erik turned to ash kept playing in my mind and my pulse thrashed with terror.

As I moved through the dusty room, I searched for what I needed. Crossing the river with my feeble swimming skills was impossible. But maybe I didn't need to swim the whole way. I just needed something to keep me afloat.

I moved to one of the wooden shelves on the wall, sweeping the contents off of it to the floor and taking Nightmare from my hip. Jamming the blade between the wall and the bracket holding it up, I wrenched it sideways and the shelf came loose. With a thrill dancing in my chest, I yanked the other bracket free and took the wooden plank in my grip. All I had to do was lay it on the water and kick my legs. I could make it to shore. I had to. Because there was no way I was going to let Erik come here and risk his life or kill either of the slayers.

I wouldn't get far with the others watching me, so I headed to the broken window and used the plank to clear the shattered glass from the sill. Tossing the shelf first, I took hold of the window ledge and launched myself over it. I hit the ground and stumbled, managing not to fall as I picked up the plank and tucked it under my arm.

I circled the statue away from the slayers, spying the city in the distance. With a surge of adrenaline, I started jogging, then running flat out toward the river, knowing I was screwed if they realised I was missing.

I ran into the shallow waves, placing the plank down and making sure it floated. I watched as it bobbed on the surface, digging deep for my courage. The city suddenly seemed a hell of a lot further away than I'd banked on, but I could make it that far if it gave me a chance to stop tonight's bloodbath.

I lowered myself into the icy water, holding onto the wood and kicking out my legs. I started moving further into the river and a smile gripped my features as I managed to gain some speed. I was fighting against the current, but a strength was growing inside me, helping me to battle it.

I can do this. Just keep going. Don't give up.

A splash sounded behind me and I glanced back, my heart lurching as I spotted Julius powering toward me.

"No!" I shouted at him, kicking harder, willing my legs to get me away from him. But he was closing the distance fast, and it became clear I couldn't outpace him.

His arms seized me, and rage swallowed me up. I started hitting him, losing my grip on the shelf as he dragged me against his body.

"Stop," he groaned, but I couldn't. I was so angry. So hurt that he was willing to put us through this.

He cupped my cheeks, forcing me to look at him. "Stop, just stop, Montana."

I fell into a pit of despair as tears sailed down my cheeks. "Don't take him from me," I begged, clinging to his shoulders as the plank sailed away down the river and I had no choice but to hold on to him.

He started swimming us back to shore and I fell limp in his arms as he sealed my fate. I'd have to watch them fight. I'd either have to see them kill Erik or be killed by him. And neither option was bearable.

My feet met the shallows and I stood upright in the icy water, pushing away from Julius but he caught my hand. I couldn't look at him as he tried to turn me toward him. I didn't want to face whatever he was going to say. I didn't want to hear it.

"Listen to me," he said gently, and I finally found it in me to lift my eyes to meet his. Water trickled steadily down his furrowed brow, his expression torn. "This fight between the slayers and the vampires is nothing to do with you and Callie. We've clashed a hundred times; we're made to kill each other. This battle was always going to happen, whether Erik knew you or not."

I ground my teeth, struggling to accept his words.

He went on, "I don't want to hurt you, Montana, but this *is* going to happen. If it wasn't today, it would be tomorrow, or next week, or next year. It's already been put off too long. So today is as good a day as any to see it done."

I tugged my hand free of his, sensing a wall building between us. But I could see that there was no way around this, and I accepted it while despising it at once. I was stuck here and the slayers were going to fight Erik and his brother whether I liked it or not. And when the sun rose again tomorrow, my heart would be shattered one way or the other.

"I care about you," I whispered. "I don't want you to think Erik's the only one I'm trying to save here. But if he dies, there'll be no place in my heart for you anymore."

A heavy weight seemed to hang over him at my words. "I wish things could be different."

"Me too," I said stiffly, setting my eyes on the statue as I headed back onto dry land. The cold was nothing. I was too numb to feel it.

The sun was already arcing through the sky toward the horizon. Time was slipping away too fast as if the day was anxious to give way to dusk. And the moment it did, the moon's eye would rise to watch our fates be written in blood.

CALLIE

CHAPTER TWENTY FIVE

The sun fell lower in the sky and my gut clenched as I watched it dipping towards the horizon. I sat beneath the statue, my gaze straying to the sunset over the river more than once.

Magnar and Julius were sparring, but I didn't join them. I could feel Fabian drawing closer to me as if the missing part of my soul travelled with him too. I fiddled with my mother's ring, wishing I could put it on to block out the piece of me which cared about him. I didn't want to be thinking about the colour of his eyes or hoping he might arrive earlier than expected.

Magnar laughed as he knocked Julius on his ass, and I forced my attention onto them.

Julius leapt to his feet and Magnar flexed his muscles as he stood his ground and absorbed the blow when they collided. The earth trembled at the force with which they hit each other, and my lips parted in astonishment as they moved so quickly that it was hard to follow.

"What if I offered to leave with Erik when he gets here?" Montana asked as she finally stopped pacing and took a seat beside me.

The slayers had insisted we stay within their sight, and she'd been raging about it all afternoon. My own anger had begun to wane, and a heavy kind of acceptance hung over me. Magnar and Julius had been waiting for this fight for a long time. Nothing we could say would discourage them now.

"Once the slayers see him, they won't let him go without a fight," I replied softly, knowing it wasn't what she wanted to hear.

"Then what if I can convince Erik to discuss the prophecy before it gets to a fight?" she suggested hopefully, and I could tell the alternative terrified her. If they couldn't find some middle ground, no matter how tenuous, it was obvious the whole thing would end in violence.

"Honestly? I don't think the slayers care about the prophecy. They want justice for their father. I understand that feeling well enough." I started chewing on my thumbnail then stopped. The old habit irritated me, and I refused to keep doing it every time something was bothering me.

"Then we need to have a plan to stop them if it comes to it. Because there isn't a way that the fight can end without at least one of us having our heart broken," Montana said desperately.

"As much as I don't want to admit it, I think my heart will be broken either way," I muttered, thinking of Fabian despite my desperation to keep him from my mind. I let out a heavy breath as the vampire prince dominated my thoughts once more.

Magnar glanced over at me, and my gut clenched with guilt as I realised he'd heard that. Julius slammed into him and knocked him to the ground, using the distraction to his advantage. I winced slightly, though any feelings of guilt were tempered by my irritation over the bonds which held me at their mercy.

I wondered how Magnar would manage to regain the upper hand from the ground, but then he landed a boot in Julius's chest and sent him flying before I could spend too much time considering it.

"Do you think there's a way to break your link to Fabian?" Montana asked, dropping her voice to try and keep our discussion private.

I shrugged, glancing at the silver cross on my palm. "Maybe...if I killed Idun."

The wind chose that moment to pick up and swirl around us. Montana eyed it warily as if she thought the goddess might be responsible. And maybe she was, but I was beyond giving a shit anymore. If she hadn't realised I hated her yet, then she was deluded. And if there was any way to kill a goddess, I'd be more than tempted to try it.

"Or if Fabian dies?" Montana wondered, but she didn't seem to be saying she wanted that.

My heart leapt with panic at the mere thought of it and I almost snapped at her simply for suggesting it. I clenched my fist tightly, trying to wrangle my emotions so I could give her a sane response.

"That's obviously what Magnar thinks. But I still can't bear to imagine it. It's not like that's all because of the mark anyway." I took a deep breath, unsure of how much to tell her. I didn't want her getting her hopes up about how much I was able to understand what she was going through, but she deserved to know that I was trying. "I listened to what you were telling me about Erik yesterday, but it's still so hard for me to imagine that he could be..." I couldn't quite make myself say good. "Not evil."

"And?" Montana pressed.

"I wanted answers, so I visited Fabian in his dreams again last night."

"You did?" she asked, her eyes widening with surprise. "What did you ask him?"

"Lots of things, but mostly I just wanted to try and see what you can see. The men beneath the monsters."

"And did you?" she asked, desperation lacing her tone as she snatched my hand and gazed into my eyes.

"Callie!" Magnar snapped, and I looked around to find him glaring at me. Julius was standing beside him with his arms folded. "Come here."

I gritted my teeth as I tried to remain where I was. Montana's grip on my fingers tightened as though she wished to help me break his control too. It was only a little command but the fact that he was wielding his power over me so soon after our night together sent anger coursing through my bones.

The seconds dragged and sweat started to bead on my temple but eventually, I caved. My fingers slipped through Montana's and I stalked towards Magnar with a scowl on my face.

"What?" I asked angrily as I came to a halt before the two brothers.

"Did I hear that right?" Magnar demanded. "Have you been cavorting with vampires again?"

"Cavorting?" I asked, raising an eyebrow at him irritably.

"Do I need to spell out to you the laws of our people? Did you think that when you swore to destroy all vampires there was a loophole which encouraged you to try and *understand* them?" he asked, his tone dark.

"You didn't seem to mind me breaking the rules so much last night when it came to *cavorting* with *you*," I replied evenly.

Julius snorted a laugh then quickly schooled his expression.

For a moment, I could have sworn Magnar was trying not to smile too.

"That is a separate issue," he said eventually.

"Not really," I replied. "I see it all as the same issue. I don't like being bound to rules that I didn't choose for myself. I don't like being told what to think without being given the opportunity to question it. And I don't have any intention of playing along willingly. So if you feel the need to bind me to your will, then do it. But just know that I will fight it and fight it until I break it and I will remember what you did."

"Shit Magnar, you couldn't have chosen a more compliant woman?" Julius teased. "There is so much fire between the two of you that I've no idea how you don't simply burn up in it."

My lips twitched with amusement and Magnar sighed.

"I hope we will clash less once I no longer have to be your mentor," he said, his tone softer. "And I'm glad that you are so determined to break my hold over you because I would like nothing more than for this bond between us to be gone. But in the meantime, I swore to protect you. So I have to do what I think is right, even if you don't like it."

"I'm pretty sure you don't have control over my dreams," I replied, wondering what he was trying to get at.

"No, I don't. But I do have control while you're awake. Give me your mother's ring." He held his hand out and I stared at him in total confusion. Why would he take it away when he'd already commanded me not to use it?

"Once Fabian arrives, I'll be drawn to him. I assumed you'd let me use it once they got here," I protested as I pulled the chain which held the ring over my head. "Without the ring, how am I supposed to stop myself from going to him? Why would you want to risk that?"

"I'm sorry, Callie, but you can't use the ring when the Belvederes are here. I've no doubt the gods will be present, and you cannot wield its power while they are watching." He placed the chain over his own head, and I could see how much it pained him to have to allow my connection to Fabian to remain in place.

Magnar hesitated and Julius laid a hand on his arm. "Do what we discussed, brother. It's for the best," he urged.

"Do what?" I asked, looking between the two of them in confusion.

"Julius, why don't you give us some privacy?" Magnar snipped, and his brother tipped his head to me in farewell before walking away from us to join Montana.

I watched him go and waited for Magnar to answer my question.

"I'm sorry about this, Callie," Magnar breathed. "But I hope you understand why I have to do it."

"Do what?" I demanded again, my heart fluttering as I sensed a trap.

"When it comes to a fight between us and the Belvederes, you must not intervene in any way," Magnar commanded and I felt the power of his words binding me. "And if at any point it seems that we may lose, then I command you to *run.*"

I shook my head as the force of his words washed over me and I realised the other reason why he'd taken the ring from me. He wanted to maintain his control over me. He was making sure I had no choice but to bow to his commands in this.

"You think I could run from you if I thought you might die?" I breathed in horror. The idea of being forced to do such a thing making me sick to my stomach. It was a betrayal of my free will that cut so deeply, I could hardly breathe.

"No. Which is why I have compelled you to do so." His eyes burned with a ferocious intensity, and I could see how much he wanted to protect me from this fight but it shouldn't have been his decision to make.

"And how would you expect me to live with myself if I'd run from you when you needed me?" I asked, anger replacing some of the horror in my tone. "If I left you to die alone?"

"If that were to happen and you didn't run, then Fabian would claim you once more. And I could not bear to die leaving you in his hands," Magnar growled.

"But you could bear to die?" I spat. "What about trying to figure out the prophecy?"

"Do you really think you've unravelled the prophecy in the space of an afternoon when others have tried and failed for over a thousand years? Your answers are little more than guesses. This day cannot end in any other way than bloodshed." His voice was soft, and I could tell that he truly was sorry for the fact that doing this would hurt me. But I knew he had no pity in his heart for the vampires he was planning to kill.

"You didn't answer my question," I breathed. "Are you really willing to die for this? When we could be so close to finding another way?"

My words hung between us, and Magnar dropped his head as if he knew what his response would do to me. "All men must die, Callie. I do not wish to leave you, but if my time has come then so be it."

Pain spiralled through my chest in a never-ending torrent which filled me up and overflowed until all I could see were stars dancing before my eyes and a chasm of despair waiting to swallow me whole. How could he do this to me after everything?

I stepped forward and punched him as hard as I could, forcing his head to wheel aside as the blow struck his jaw and pain lanced through my hand. Then I turned and strode away from him, not looking back once. Fuck him. Fuck him for thinking that his idea of what was best for me meant more than my own free will. Fuck him for using his control over me again even after spending the night in my arms. And fuck him for the way my heart was pounding with terror over the idea of losing him now. This was why I had never let anyone get close to me before. This was why I had kept my guard up and refused any hint of what I now felt for him, because the loss of it was far worse than the prospect of never having held it at all. My worst nightmare was coming true, and there was nothing I could do to stop it.

Montana jumped up as I reached her, and she fell into step beside me as I marched away from the statue and headed to the far side of the island where I could scream or curse or rage without Magnar breathing down my neck.

How could he talk about leaving me so casually? How could he even consider that possibility after all we'd been through?

The wind picked up again and my hair whipped around me as my anger grew into its own storm within my chest.

It took me several more minutes of furious pacing before I realised there was more to the breeze than was natural. A heaviness had filled the air and my lungs began to struggle with the effort it took to breathe the tainted oxygen. It felt like trying to inhale syrup.

Montana caught my hand and we looked about wildly. The waves lapped the shore before us in a rhythmic pattern which began to sound wholly unnatural.

I turned back to see if Magnar and Julius had noticed it too, but they weren't there. The door to the room beneath the statue was closed and I was fairly certain they were inside.

"What's happening?" Montana breathed, and I gripped her hand more tightly.

A thick mist built above the waves, growing into a swirling cloud which blocked our view of the city.

"Oh no, no, no," Idun's seductive voice purred on the crest of a wave. "This won't do at all."

Montana cried out as heated raindrops began to splatter over us, scalding our skin as they struck our bodies.

My feet were glued to the ground, and I wrapped my arms around my sister as we were trapped in the maelstrom Idun had created. We clung to each other as the rain grew heavier, burning away our clothes and painting us in new ones.

I scrunched my eyes shut as the acidic rain pummelled us and fear washed through me. Not for myself, but for Montana. I tried to shield her with my own body, but the rain drenched us both regardless.

It took me several long seconds to realise it didn't hurt. Though I could feel the scalding heat of it, no pain raced over my skin. In fact, I felt weirdly...dry.

I opened my eyes and blinked a few times as the rain stopped falling, the burn of it fading to nothing.

We slowly pulled away from each other and I stared at Montana in surprise. Her clothes had been replaced with a white dress made with folds of overlapping fabric. It clung to her body, revealing her curves and dropping to her feet. Around her waist was a silver rope with a crescent moon suspended from it. Nightmare hung from her hip in a leather sheath, and I ached to have Fury by my side too.

Her dark hair was no longer lank and dirty from her dip in the river but hung in perfect, tumbling curls. Upon her head was the crown she'd been given at the wedding just days ago.

It took me another moment to realise I was dressed exactly the same as her. It reminded me of when we were tiny and our mom had liked to make us match. But the rope around my waist was golden and a sun dangled from it instead of a moon.

I reached up to touch the crown upon my head and my lips parted in wonder at the power the deity held.

"What is this..." Montana murmured as she stared at my transformed appearance too.

"Prizes must appear at their best if they are to be fought for," Idun laughed and the air around us seemed to tremble. "Prepare to greet your husbands, ladies."

I felt her presence withdraw, though I was sure she was still close enough to observe us.

A dark speedboat broke through the mist and Montana gasped as she spotted Erik standing at the wheel, guiding it towards us. Fabian was at his side, the two of them dressed in black outfits which matched the darkness in their eyes.

My heart stilled as I gazed at the man I'd been forced to marry. No, not man; *vampire.* I ground my teeth as the power of my bond with him began to whisper false feelings through my body.

The boat spun about, and a wave washed over the shore as Erik cut the engine.

Though I felt drawn to look at Fabian, my eyes snagged on his brother. Erik was staring at Montana like she was the reason the world kept turning, his relief in being reunited with her clearly plastered over his face. And though a part of me still wanted to blame the mark which bound them, in my gut I knew it was more than that.

Somehow, impossibly, she'd been right when she'd said he cared for her. I could feel his love in the air like a living thing.

I was pushed aside, Montana's hand wrenched from mine as Idun's power separated us. The mist swept towards the shore, swirling into the space which divided us and hiding my sister from view.

Fabian leapt off of the boat and reached out for me, snaring my attention. As soon as he left Erik behind, the mist swallowed him too so that we were left alone. I could feel Idun's amusement on the wind as Fabian advanced on me and she waited to see what would happen.

The warring halves of my soul disagreed on what to do, but I managed to step back before he could lay a hand on me.

"Don't," I breathed.

I felt totally unprepared for the closeness of him. I'd forgotten the pull I experienced when I looked into his eyes. Or how my blood heated when my gaze fell to his mouth and... I wanted to punch him in his stupid jaw.

I closed my hand into a fist and forced my face to cooperate so I could glare at him. I ignored the piece of me which was begging me to reconsider and throw myself into his arms.

"Even when you visit me in my dreams, you do not look so captivating as you do in the flesh," Fabian said in a low voice, filled with desire.

"I hope you don't think I got dressed up for you," I replied, trying to put some venom into my voice and failing. "You can thank Idun for this nonsense. And you can have this back too." I took the crown from my head and tossed it to him. I'd left it behind on purpose the last time I'd taken it off and I certainly didn't want it back.

Fabian's face fell as he caught it and I reached towards him as if I might try to comfort him before managing to force my arm back down again.

"I... I brought you something," he said, seeming to lose his composure for a minute. I hated how easily I could disarm him. It seemed to go against his nature entirely and whether I thought he was a monster or not, I didn't like having that power over someone else.

"I don't want anything from you," I replied. *Except to feel your mouth against mine and the touch of your-*

I clenched my fists so hard that I was sure my nails were drawing blood from my palms. But I didn't care; the pain helped me to force out the desires I refused to recognise.

Fabian hesitated again then raised a box I hadn't noticed him holding. It was heavy, made of lead and inlaid with carvings of runes. I tried to decipher them and got the feeling they were designed for containment and protection but before I could look too closely, he flipped the lid open.

I gasped in delight and a wide smile lit my face as I grabbed the golden blade from inside it.

Hello, Sun Child, Fury purred, and I could have kissed it.

I leapt at Fabian, wrapping myself around him before I could consider what I was doing. His arms closed around me and he held me tightly, inhaling deeply as he pressed his face into my hair.

"I'm so glad you like it," he whispered, nuzzling my neck.

I felt his lips brushing my skin as my pulse raced and I froze, suddenly terrified. His fangs were so near to me, it would take nothing at all for him to bite down. And there would be nothing I could do to stop him.

I was at his mercy.

A tremor rolled through my body, but I didn't dare move. He seemed to notice and his grip on me loosened ever so slightly.

"What's wrong?" he asked gently, like he was afraid he might scare me away.

I felt the movement of his lips against my neck and a whimper escaped me. He was the monster who'd haunted my dreams since I was a child. I felt so out of control with him and now I'd managed to put myself into the most dangerous position imaginable. This wasn't like a dream. I had no power here and even with Fury in my hand, I didn't think I'd be able to stop him if he gave in to the basest part of himself.

"Let me go," I breathed, hoping that his false feelings for me outweighed the call of my blood.

Fabian recoiled as if my words had been a blow to the face. He released me and I stumbled back, raising Fury between us as I regained some sense of myself.

"You thought I was going to bite you?" he asked, a frown pulling at his brow.

Yes. No. I didn't even know anymore. Being around him was the sweetest form of torture.

"Why couldn't you just leave me alone?" I asked and my hand shook as I tried to draw on my ancestors' strength but failed.

Fabian seemed so lost and confused, like he couldn't understand what I was saying. But our bond was different for him. He hadn't grown up fearing and hating me. He wasn't in love with someone else. Perhaps from his perspective, it did seem simple. And I doubted there had been many things he'd wanted during his long life which he hadn't simply been able to take. But I would never surrender to my feelings for him. I'd keep fighting no matter what it cost me.

Before he could answer me, a strong wind pushed against us, and I was forced back as Idun grew bored of watching us.

The mist surrounded me and I lost all sense of my place in the world for several long seconds.

It moved away just as quickly and I found myself beside the statue in a glimmering golden cage. I moved to grip the bars in fear, waiting for Idun to release her hold on my sister and Erik. Once she'd had her fun with them, the real challenge would begin.

MONTANA

CHAPTER TWENTY SIX

The thick mist lifted, and I was gifted a moment alone with Erik Belvedere. My husband.

Our eyes were locked, and so much rage burned through me at what he had done that I could barely stand it. But that anger was melded with something even hotter, something so fierce it could bring the sky crashing down upon the earth.

My desperate heart was yearning.

My fractured soul was re-mending.

And my frantic thoughts were tumbling, diving, free-falling-

I raced to the water's edge and waded into the river as he dropped from the speedboat, my name falling from his lips.

A wave crashed against me, forcing me back, but I didn't stop moving, thirsting for his touch almost as much as I wanted to strike at him. He pushed through the waves with more force than the tide, his jaw gritted and his iron eyes fixed on me like there was no other thing in existence. His black shirt was plastered to his skin and his pants hung low on his hips as the water lapped against him.

I jumped through the fierce pressure of the water and struck him with a slap that should have made his head wheel from the force of it.

But he was immovable as always, my strike nothing to him, leaving no imprint on his perfect exterior.

"How could you do this? You swore you'd let me go," I snarled as the waves churned around us, and he stared at me like I'd kissed him instead of hit him.

"Seeing you last night solidified my choice," he said, yanking me into his arms and hoisting me above the waves. I wrapped my legs around him, clinging to him when I knew I should have been pushing him away. "You want me as I want you, and you desire the answer to the prophecy. So let's not squander any more time. I have already lost far too many precious seconds without you. If I am to find a path to mortality, then I'll be damned if I don't seek it now so that I might join you in your lifetime."

"I won't allow this fight, this isn't the answer," I said, shaking my head in refusal of his choice.

"This battle was written by the hands of gods a thousand years ago. There are no more paths to evade it," he said darkly, then cupped my cheek in his hand, supporting me with the other, his strength so vast that I felt like I weighed no more than a feather in his hold. "Listen to me, Montana. Whatever happens here this night, know this. You returned the lustre to my world. You awoke me from a numbness I never thought I would escape. I love you for that and so much more besides. I know that my love is a noxious thing, and that the heart of a villain is worth little more than a jar of sand, but all I have to give is yours. Only yours."

I shouldn't have felt the joy I did at his words, but I was lost to it, and our lips crashed together as fiercely as the tide around us. He released a primal growl as I tasted the salt water on his mouth, savouring every delicious part of this moment, letting myself be selfish by stealing this sinful moment with him. I gripped his hair, kissing him until I was sure my soul was going to burst and the fractured pieces of our beings would collide.

Our lips finally parted and he pressed his cool forehead to mine, his expression taut as he clutched me tighter and the turbulent river raged around us. I realised it was more than the usual pull of the tide, Idun was moving the waves in a roiling storm. The water twisted around us and

I gasped as the pebbly shore became visible beneath Erik's feet. The water swirled up higher and higher, forming a sheer vortex that moved around us, cocooning us within the waves.

Fear tore at my heart as Erik dropped me to my feet and my bare toes sunk into the tiny wet stones. He clutched my hand, gazing up at the dusky sky above us, his fangs bared at the deity who had come to taunt us.

"A moment of privacy for the ill-fated lovers," Idun's velvet voice filled my ears.

I turned, trying to spot her in the murky water that circled around us like a tornado, expecting her to appear at any moment.

When she didn't, I faced Erik with one furious thought in mind, needing to speak it before it was too late. "Don't fight Magnar and Julius, we're so close to figuring out the prophecy. If we work together, we can finish it."

"Truly?" he asked with hope flaring in his iron gaze.

I nodded, hurriedly explaining what my sister and I had come up with. How the ring had shown us the way to a mountain far in the south and leaving the worst part of it until last.

"The first line," I whispered. "Andvari showed me a vision of me as a vampire. I think, perhaps…that might be the answer."

Terror caved in my chest as those words left my throat, the mere thought of it too terrible to linger on. But it had to be spoken at least. It had to be considered.

Erik snarled, his eyes darkening to pitch. "I will never turn you into a vampire. I would not place this curse on you if you begged me on your knees for it."

I coiled my fingers in his damp shirt as desperation clawed at my insides. "I don't want it. Honestly, I can't even think of it without wanting to run and run and never stop. But if it's the answer, wouldn't it be wrong of me to refuse?" Tears pinched my eyes as Erik pushed a tendril of hair away from my face. Could I really be brave enough to walk that path? Could I stand it for the greater good? My gut told me no. That it would be too horrible to endure, that I'd despise the unchanging flesh I wore and seek any way to rid myself of it.

"I've been tricked too many times by Andvari." Erik ran his thumb over my bottom lip, a fire simmering in his gaze. "I will not risk this being another lie. And even if it were the only way…" he trailed off, the glint in his grey eyes telling me he would rather remain cursed than place the crown of his bane upon my head.

"Please, just talk to the slayers," I begged, locking my fingers around the back of his neck, focusing on the most urgent one of my problems.

He hesitated, his gaze tracking over my face, then he nodded. "I will try. For you."

"Thank you." I crushed myself against him, resting my cheek to his chest, almost surprised when I heard no heart beating there. Though it shouldn't have been so easy to forget what he was.

"What doubts you have," Andvari's voice sent a tremor through to my core. "I have never tricked you, Erik." He appeared from the waves, stepping out of the tempestuous water like a phantom. He drew closer, wearing earthy robes which were somehow entirely dry. "You made your own choices."

Erik ground his teeth, holding me tighter as Andvari advanced.

"A world of possibilities is so close and yet you shy away from it." Andvari waved a hand, and I blinked heavily as the air rippled around me.

The water faded out of existence, revealing a garden of wildflowers before a stone cottage on the hill.

My thoughts cracked and were reformed anew. Memories filled me of a life in this place. I knew it well. This was my home. And right now…I was alone, but completely at peace.

I relaxed as some strange darkness lifted from my mind. I had no need to worry. This was where I lived, and it was the most tranquil place in the world.

I gazed down at the bunch of purple flowers in my hands, continuing what I must have been doing just moments ago and picking more of them. I gathered them into my fist and smiled serenely as I headed up to the house, the sun so bright today, its warmth was like a balm against my skin.

I pushed through the wooden door and the sound of a child's

laughter filled my ears. My smile stretched wider as I walked through the hallway into the kitchen which was filled with cream cabinets and wooden furniture. Erik had a little girl on his shoulders; he was wandering around the room and pretending to look for her while she giggled wildly, tossing her head back as she held onto his neck, her dark hair cascading like a waterfall down her back.

Erik stood upright as he spotted me, a slanted smile on his face. "Have you seen our daughter? I can't find her anywhere."

I tapped my lips, sweeping my eyes across the room. "Hm, no I can't see her anywhere."

The little girl laughed her delight, patting Erik on the shoulder. "I'm right here, Daddy!"

He swung her down into his arms and started tickling her. She screamed through her laughter, wriggling to try and escape. Twirling her upright, he planted her on her feet and she scampered out of the kitchen, crying, "You can't catch me!"

I turned to chase her, but Erik caught me by the waist, spinning me back to face him. "Where have you been hiding?"

"I was picking these." I waved the flowers under his nose, and he grinned, cornering me against the table. He took the bunch from my hand, placing them down and sliding a finger under my chin. "I don't need flowers to light up the house; I have you." He propped me up on the table and stepped between my thighs, capturing my mouth with his.

I clung to his neck and the warmth of his skin heated my hand, the thump of his pulse beneath my fingers like a rhythmic tune.

His mouth skated from my lips to my ear and I sighed as a fire lit inside me. Desire raced through my skin and heat burned between my thighs.

"We have a child to find," I laughed, pressing him back and his eyes sparkled with the game.

He blinked suddenly, shaking his head. "What?"

"Our little girl," I said, trying to get past him.

His expression darkened and he caught my waist again as I tried to escape, the light beyond the window dimming. "Wait, this isn't real."

"What are you talking about?" I ran my hand down the hard plane of his chest, but his body was suddenly cold, too cold.

"Rebel," Erik growled, and his face seemed to pale, his skin glimmering with the power that lay beneath it.

Reality struck me so fast, I wasn't remotely prepared as I was suddenly thrown out of the vision and into the waves. I inhaled water and spluttered, frantically trying to swim up to breach the surface. Arms surrounded me and in moments, I fell back against the rocky shore, gasping for air.

Erik knelt over me, cupping my cheek, his brows knitted as he checked me over.

"Warrior born and monster made." Andvari's shadow fell over me, sucking the light of the sunset from existence and replacing it with his dark presence. "You know what to do, Erik. I have waited many years and you have suffered deeply. It is time to fulfil the prophecy."

I felt myself traitorously turning my head, exposing my neck to Erik, Andvari controlling my movements. My pulse pounded in my ears and fear slid into my chest, my arms suddenly like lead at my sides as the god incapacitated me, laying me out as an offering for the vampire who had claimed my heart.

I don't want this.

The words wouldn't pass my lips, but I screamed them inside my head. *No, stop, please stop!*

"No," Erik growled, planting his hands either side of my head as he fought the will of the deity. His shoulders tensed from the strength it took to resist Andvari's will and terror thrashed within me as Erik bared his fangs, his gaze settling on my neck.

"Turn her," Andvari encouraged. "See if her guess is correct. Perhaps she is right. Perhaps this is your long-awaited answer, Erik Larsen."

"I will never turn her!" Erik roared, but started bowing toward me, doing the opposite of what he wished.

"Stop," I pleaded as his mouth grazed my throat and I trembled beneath him, a slave to Andvari's will.

Idun appeared, her golden light falling over us like the rays of the sun. "Enough. The fight will happen, Andvari. The slayers have waited a thousand years for this chance. They are owed it."

"It is time for the games to end," Andvari bit at her, but Idun's aura grew around Erik and as it surrounded him, he was able to move back from me, regaining his will.

"One more game," Idun demanded of Andvari, her eyes flaring with crimson fire.

Andvari tilted his head, observing her while his gaze grew cooler. "This is the last time."

"I swear it," Idun agreed.

Erik moved back onto his knees and Idun floated to his side, running her fingers into his hair. He flinched away from her, but she didn't stop, caressing his cheek as she angled him to face me. "Fight for her, monster. Prove your love holds an ounce of worth."

Andvari gripped my arm, dragging me upright and shoving me behind him, his power over me absolute. My heart lurched as I stumbled into the mist and golden bars appeared around me.

Callie caught my hand, turning me to her. "We're trapped," she said, fear and rage lighting her eyes.

Panic reared inside me as the mist lifted around the cage and I spotted Erik and Fabian standing rigidly before the towering statue of the green woman.

"Erik!" I called to him, and he turned to me with acceptance in his gaze. He lifted his left hand to his mouth, pressing his lips to the wedding band on his finger before striding toward the statue like a predator on the hunt.

"No!" I begged, grabbing hold of the bars.

I shared a look of desperation with Callie as she kicked the bars, but the metal didn't buckle. We were trapped and we were going to be forced to watch the men we loved destroy each other.

My heart beat madly for Erik. I couldn't see him die.

Realisation crept over me as I stood at Callie's side. In this golden cage of the gods, either my sister or I was going to be broken forever. And there was nothing we could do but watch.

MAGNAR

CHAPTER TWENTY SEVEN

I threw my weight against the doors for what felt like the hundredth time. Julius roared as he slammed into them beside me, having just as little luck as me in breaking them. The gods had trapped us within the confines of this forsaken room just as our enemies had been due to arrive and I could only imagine what games they were playing.

Callie was stuck out there with the Belvederes now and I had no way of getting to her. Guilt formed a lump in my chest as I imagined her falling under Fabian's spell once more. I'd taken the ring to protect her from the wrath of the gods, but in doing so, I'd left her at their mercy. And to make it worse, I couldn't even place myself between her and that monster.

"Curse you, Idun!" I bellowed as the door continued to resist our combined strength.

Tinkling laughter filled the room as she watched us.

I backed up and Julius moved to my side as we set our sights on the wooden barrier to the outside world once more.

We took off together, racing towards the doors like a pair of human battering rams.

My shoulder slammed into the wood and it finally gave way with a splintering crash. The doors were thrown from their hinges as we burst out into the hazy golden light of the setting sun and my gaze fell on the creature I'd given my life to hunting down.

Erik Belvedere bared his fangs at me, and a terrible stillness fell over the world. The wind dropped. The sound of the waves crashing against the shore seemed to pause. Even my heart stilled in my chest just long enough for a silent promise to take place between us.

This was where our feud would end.

Neither of us would turn from this fight. The moment for revenge had come and there would be no backing down. It was time for this to be over.

My father's final words echoed through my mind alongside the oath I'd made to him. The cost of his blood would be repaid. Death demanded death.

"Elder!" Callie's voice spilled through the air, and I forced my eyes away from my foes as I sought her out.

She stood with her sister in a giant, golden birdcage which stood beneath the shadow of the statue. It was positioned to our left but was at an equal distance from us and the undead monsters who faced us. Her fingers gripped the bars, and her blue eyes were pleading as she gazed at me.

The goddess had dressed her like something from a dream. Her beauty spoke to me in a way which set my blood alight, and I wished I could have heard her speak my name in case it was the last time.

"You swore you'd discuss the prophecy!" Montana shouted, her eyes on Erik.

He ground his teeth, clearly finding it as hard to resist the urge to start our fight as I did. But he turned to look at her instead of us.

"If the answer to the prophecy lies in giving you my curse, I won't do it," Erik said firmly.

"Then we agree on one thing," I growled.

"And there is nothing more to discuss," Julius added.

"Please don't do this," Callie begged, reaching for me between the bars.

My heart ached to give in to her. To give her anything she asked of me and more. But not this. This was the one thing I could never do for her.

The Belvederes' deaths were written into the essence of my soul. Erik had cost my family everything and he needed to pay the price for it.

"You know that we must," I replied, forcing my gaze away from her and fixing it on my immortal enemies once more.

I couldn't look at her again. I couldn't see what my refusal was doing to her. This fight was mine to claim, my birth right, and I would not turn from it.

I took a step forward, my muscles flooding with power as I readied myself to destroy the monsters who faced us.

But before I could continue my advance, the air shimmered and Idun appeared, stepping out behind a curtain made from the very fabric of the wind. She moved between us and the vampires, barring our path and stopping our combat from beginning.

Twisting vines covered with yellow flowers moved across her body like writhing snakes, revealing and concealing her nudity in a constantly changing pattern.

She stepped towards the cage which held the twins and placed a shimmering padlock around the bars, locking it with an ornate golden key.

All eyes followed her as she moved between us, her gaze sliding from Julius to me, then to Fabian and finally Erik as a coy smile pulled at her full lips.

She held the key aloft and it floated from her hand until it hung in the sky above us. Tantalisingly close yet impossibly far away.

"We've waited a long time for this day," the goddess murmured.

Another fissure opened in the air and Andvari spilled from it, his brown cloak ragged and his eyes brightest white.

"Let's make it a fair fight," he growled, pointing a gnarled finger at my brother and me.

Venom and Tempest were dragged from their sheaths on my back and Menace was ripped from Julius's hip. They spiralled away from us, cartwheeling end over end until they were embedded in the heart of the huge statue high above us.

"That suits me just fine," I growled. "I will happily tear their black hearts from their chests with my bare hands."

Fabian bared his teeth and hissed in response to my words while Erik only glared.

Idun pursed her lips like she wasn't pleased with Andvari changing the rules.

"But what of concealed weapons?" she asked. "I don't trust your twisted creatures to have come here unarmed."

"We don't need tricks or blades to kill your slaves," Erik snarled in response.

Idun opened her lips as if to protest, but I was done waiting for this fight.

"Enough," I snapped. "We carry no weapons and neither do they. Now move aside so that we can finish this."

Idun's eyes lit with anger for a moment and a jagged spear of lightning forked through the evening sky.

"As you wish. To the victors go the spoils," she breathed, pointing her finger at the key floating above us.

Lightning flashed in the burnt amber sky once more and Andvari moved to her side, his pale lips sliding into a mocking smile.

"Fight," the gods commanded as one, the word slamming into me like a shockwave rolling through my body.

The gods vanished and I locked eyes with Erik, my blood boiling with hatred.

A ragged growl grew in my throat and I raced towards him with Julius at my side, his gaze set on Fabian.

Callie and Montana were screaming but I drowned them out with my thirst for vengeance. There was only one way to end this.

Erik leapt at me and I jumped into the air, meeting the force of his attack with my own.

We collided and a great crash tore across the heavens as he slammed his fist into my face. I absorbed the blow and caught his throat in my grip, using his momentum to spin him away from me and launching him into the giant statue behind us.

The sound of him colliding with it was enough to split the sky in two. A huge chunk of stone fell away from the base of the statue and he hit the ground in a mountain of rubble. I bellowed a challenge as I raced after him, ready to finally finish this.

ERIK

CHAPTER TWENTY EIGHT

I hit the ground in a cascade of bricks and Magnar sped toward me with his face twisted into a furious snarl. I stooped down, grabbing a jagged stone and waiting for his attack.

He leapt at me and I swung my right arm, smashing the makeshift weapon against his temple, and he stumbled back as blood poured.

A scream tore through the air which I was sure belonged to Montana's sister, but I refused to acknowledge it. The twins had been in our lives for so little time in comparison to this age-old feud. Magnar and I had been enemies for a thousand years. No force on earth could rectify that but death.

Magnar threw a heavy punch, and I danced aside, evading a barrage of attacks as he stormed toward me. Vengeance burned in his gaze like acid, and I met it with an ire of my own. "I will have your heart in my fist by the end of this," he growled.

I dodged another punch, but his other fist impacted with my jaw, and I snarled as pain flared through the bone. I slammed my palms to his chest and launched him into the air with all my strength. As his body hit the ground a hundred feet away, a great crack tore along the centre of the cement and a tremor quaked the earth beneath my feet. Adrenaline surged through me as thunder cracked like cannon fire above, the thrill of the brawl setting my blood alight.

Fabian and Julius were fighting near the shore, moving in a surge of motion as they parried each other's fists.

My gaze whipped to the key high above us and I stalked toward Magnar as he gained his feet, rolling his shoulders back. This fight was written in the stars. Today we'd finish this madness. I'd be rid of Idun's pawns forever, and I'd take my goddamn wife back.

Magnar roared a challenge as I approached, sprinting to meet me. I moved at full speed, readying for the collision as the two of us hit with the force of a car crash. A tremor resounded in my bones as I tried to keep a hold of him, his muscles tensing and his fists swinging.

He swept out my legs and my back slammed against the ground, the blood-red sky silhouetting him for half a second before he fell on top of me, throwing a jaw-splitting punch into my face. I caught his next fist, twisting his arm so sharply that he growled in agony. His free hand locked around my throat and dark laughter bubbled from my chest.

"I don't breathe, you fool," I spat.

"I am not trying to choke you, parasite." He yanked his other arm free, and I slammed my knuckles into his gut as he locked a second hand around my throat. "I'm trying to rip your fucking head off."

I gritted my teeth and locked my own fingers around his muscular neck, squeezing until he started to turn blue. He twisted my head so sharply, I could feel my vertebrae on the verge of breaking. Pain daggered along my spine, and I tightened my fingers, snarling my ferocity. It had come down to who was going to kill the other first and I was determined to be the victor.

Julius threw Fabian toward us and he crashed into Magnar full-force, knocking him far away from me as the two hit the ground in a tangle of limbs. I gained my feet, rolling my head side to side as the damage the slayer had caused slowly healed.

I spotted Fabian on top of Magnar, grinning at the turn of events, my body alive with the clash of battle.

"I'm taking Callie home, you son of a bitch." Fabian slammed Magnar's head down on the stone, but the slayer drove a fist into his side, forcing him away.

Julius rammed into me from behind, knocking me forward several steps as he clung to my back. Something sharp collided with my head and I shouted my rage, launching myself backwards onto the ground and crushing him beneath me. A bronze door handle came free from his hand, bouncing across the stones out of reach.

I sat up, throwing an elbow back into Julius's face as he tried to hold onto me. He groaned as I got to my feet, and I turned to face him, waiting for him to rise too so he could face me man to man. If this was my last fight on earth, it wasn't going to be without honour. I'd do anything I could to increase the chance of my soul earning its place in Valhalla, even if that was a pointless endeavour.

Julius sprang upright, bending forward and sprinting to tackle me. As his shoulder slammed into my gut, I threw a solid punch into his kidney. He coughed, never faltering and I shoved him away again, batting his next attack aside with a dark smile.

"Is that all you've got?" I goaded him.

Energy poured through my veins as we circled one another. I had so much pent up anger from the past few days, it felt good to unleash it at last.

"I have plenty left to give," he snarled. "I am a man of flesh and fury. My blood is gilded with the power of the gods, and I am made to destroy you."

Julius kicked out, slamming his boot into my knee and something cracked. I growled in pain, limping back a step as it took a second too long for my body to heal. The slayer smiled ruthlessly, pressing his advantage as he smashed a palm to my chest, but I caught his elbow, twisting until a satisfying snap filled the air. He roared in pain as his left arm fell limp at his side, but he raised his other in a fist, not retreating.

"I still have one arm left to kill you with, and that will be all I need" he hissed, his eyes hooded as he advanced on me.

My leg healed, but I continued to feign my limp as I retreated, letting him think he had the upper hand. As he darted forward to seize his mistaken advantage, I brought up my healed leg and kicked him squarely in the stomach. He yelled as he flew backwards through the air, crashing into the golden cage with a deafening gong before slumping to the ground unmoving.

Satisfaction spread through me and the sound of Andvari's laughter rang in my ears.

"Erik!" Montana's eyes locked with mine as she reached for Julius's prone form through the bars. He seemed unconscious, possibly dead, but I only felt bad about that because of the look in my wife's eyes. Something akin to guilt touched the blackened husk of my heart, but I didn't have a moment to dwell on that as Fabian's agonised yells filled the air.

I turned in panic, speeding toward him as Magnar tore my brother's right arm from its socket. All I could see was red as blood poured from the gaping wound, and Fabian's screams pitched up into the sky.

An oncoming storm of rage, pain and death was approaching fast. But I would not see Fabian die.

MAGNAR

CHAPTER TWENTY NINE

Callie screamed as I hurled Fabian's severed arm away from me. I could feel the hurt in her voice as I drew closer to finishing the monster who called himself her husband, but I refused to let it stop me a second time. Killing Fabian would sever her ties to him. In the end, she would thank me for it.

Fabian howled in pain, but he managed to twist away from me, regaining his feet before leaping at me again.

His weight knocked me back as we collided and an earth-shattering groan split the air. His fangs sank into my neck and the acidic burn of his venom flooded into me. The pain was sharper than any bite from a lesser vampire and it overwhelmed my senses for a moment as I stumbled.

In the corner of my eye, I saw Erik sprinting towards us at a ferocious pace.

Adrenaline surged through me and I grabbed the back of Fabian's neck, ripping him off of me. I caught his remaining arm in my other hand and lifted him, spinning him around and launching him at his brother.

The crash that sounded as they collided set the ground rumbling, and the two of them tumbled away from me. I looked beyond them and spotted Julius slumped by the cage which contained the twins. They were both reaching through the bars, shaking him in an effort to rouse him.

My anger tripled at the sight of my brother on the ground and I roared at the Belvederes as I ran towards them both. They may have been able to heal faster than us, but we were stronger than them, and they were about to find out just how much pain I could inflict.

They scrambled upright just before I reached them but couldn't move quickly enough to avoid my attack as I tackled them, hooking an arm around each of their necks.

We slammed into the ground, gouging a crater into the concrete beneath us.

Fabian was pinned under me but Erik managed to roll free.

I slammed my fist down into Fabian's face, feeling bone shatter beneath my knuckles. I hit him again and again, pulverising his flesh before Erik grabbed my arm as I swung it back once more.

He forced me upright, catching my other arm and jamming his knee into my spine as he tried to rip my shoulders from their sockets.

I ground my teeth, straining against him, my muscles bulging with effort as I fought to free myself before he could break anything vital.

My eyes fell on Fabian as he lay still in a pool of his own blood while his face began to reform. The hand on his remaining arm twitched then snapped into a fist as his undead body began to function once more.

I ground my jaw, digging my heels into the ground and forcing my weight against Erik so that we started to move backwards.

He cursed, pressing his knee into my back more firmly and grunting with effort as he pulled harder. Pain flared inside my right shoulder as something gave way.

I managed to gain momentum, rising and slamming him back against the wall of the building beneath the statue. Bricks crumbled from it, raining down on us, and Erik's grip loosened but he didn't release me.

Fabian got to his feet and snarled as he started running towards us, the damage to his face still mending as he moved. Erik's grip tightened again as he fought to hold me in place so that his brother could finish

314

me off.

I slammed my weight back and the statue groaned as I loosened its foundations, but still the parasite clung on.

Fabian dove at me, throwing a fist into my face that made my vision falter for half a second.

Callie started screaming and I couldn't help but look her way. She clung to the cage bars, her eyes desperate as she watched the two demons take the upper hand. The pain in her gaze ripped a hole in my chest which was far more painful than any injury I was forced to endure at their hands.

Fabian drove his fist into my gut again and again as I struggled to rip free of Erik's hold.

His knuckles collided with my ribs and I felt them crack one by one.

"Fabian please!" Callie screamed desperately. "Stop! Please!"

He hesitated for a moment, her pain clearly affecting him because of their bond. His eyes remained on her, the monster seeming unsure of what to do, and I gritted my teeth against the agony of my wounds.

"For fuck's sake, *focus* Fabian," Erik growled.

"What if she can't forgive me for doing this?" Fabian breathed, his eyes still on Callie and my anger grew as I ached to force his gaze away from her.

"She would never choose you either way, parasite," I spat.

Fabian's head snapped around and he glared at me again, his lip curling back in a feral snarl.

"She belongs with me," he said. "The gods picked us for each other."

"Well I don't give a fuck what the gods want." I shoved my weight back into Erik and used his hold on me to lift my feet from the ground. Before he could release me, I slammed both of my boots straight into Fabian's chest and kicked him as hard as I could, launching him away from us.

He was thrown all the way to the river, crashing into the water and disappearing beneath the waves.

Erik snarled angrily and released his grip on my right arm before grabbing a fistful of my hair and yanking my head back so he could lock his arm around my throat. He threw his weight onto my back as he caught his wrist in his other hand and tried to choke me.

I reached over my shoulder, clawing at him as I attempted to rip him off of me, but his grip only firmed.

I spun around, trying to shake him loose as he clung to my back like a damn bloodsucking monkey.

A bellow of rage announced Julius's return to the fight and a fierce smile lit my face as my brother finally recovered from his injuries.

Erik grunted with effort and reared back, trying to rip my head from my shoulders, my muscles bunching in refusal.

I caught his arm and tore him from me, throwing him to the ground with an almighty crash.

He rolled over and sprung to his feet before I could close in on him again, baring his fangs as he glowered at me.

Fabian had made it back out of the water, but Julius was ready to intercept him. He held the vampire's severed arm and swung it at him like a club.

Julius laughed obnoxiously and a dark smile grew on my face as I stalked forward, rotating my injured shoulder as my gifts worked to heal the damage done by my enemy.

Erik snarled at me before turning his back and racing to his brother's aid instead of engaging with me again.

Fabian cursed as Julius continued to beat him with his own arm while laughing like a madman, keeping the vampire back with the vicious blows.

A series of sharp snapping noises echoed through my chest as my ribs healed with the aid of my gifts and I grinned at I dove back into the fight.

I chased after Erik but couldn't match the monster's speed and I bellowed a warning a moment before he reached Julius. My brother looked up, spotting Erik as he raced at him, dropping the arm as he moved to defend himself from the collision.

Erik crashed into him with enough force to knock him from his feet, the two of them falling into the river with a tremendous splash which sent water flooding over the land, drenching me.

"Julius!" I bellowed as I sprinted to dive in after them, but Fabian leapt into my path before I could get there, his arm knitting itself back onto his body as he held it in place.

He bared his fangs at me and raced to cut me off.

We collided with the force of a hurricane and fell to the ground once more. He managed to get on top of me, throwing his forehead into the bridge of my nose, breaking it and sending pain racing through my skull.

His hands closed on my throat and he slammed my head back onto the ground again, dazing me momentarily.

I smashed my fist into his face, cursing him as he fought to keep me from helping my brother.

My heart pounded as the seconds ticked by and still there was no sound of Julius returning to land. Fabian smiled through the blood pouring from his shattered cheek as I punched him repeatedly and he clung on through sheer determination, pinning me in place.

He knew Julius's time was running out, and my heart pounded with fear for the last remaining member of my family.

ERIK

CHAPTER THIRTY

I sank toward the riverbed, dragging Julius down with me as he tried to prise my hands from him. He pounded a fist into my cheek, but I didn't stop. I had the advantage under water. I didn't need to breathe. And Julius was already growing frantic as we dropped into the murky depths of the Hudson.

His nails clawed at my back as I locked my arm around his neck, forcing him to the muddy floor. As our feet hit the bottom, sediment rose around us in a growing cloud. Bubbles streamed from Julius's nose, sailing above us toward the faraway surface. He landed a kick to my gut, managing to throw me off. Before I could catch him, he started swimming upwards, powering toward safety.

My eyes locked on an old anchor on the seabed and I snatched up the rusted chain attached to it, swimming after him with all my might. When I gained on him, I wrapped the chain around his ankle, and he jerked violently as the weight stopped him advancing.

I swam back a foot as he tried to swing a punch at me, missing me by inches.

Silence stretched around me, but a frenzied thump reached my ears as I watched the slayer flounder in the dark water. Julius's heartbeat rioted with panic, his life hanging in the balance.

His eyes widened in fear as he fought to untie the chain, his movements growing jerky, keeping his fingers from following his commands. His heartbeat grew louder and louder. Faster and faster. And I watched, waiting for his end to come, seeing it growing closer with each passing second.

Montana's pained expression filled my head, reminding me of how she'd looked when she'd seen this slayer in pain. And a realisation filled me which I wanted to ignore but I found it impossible. This man *mattered* to her. And doing this was going to hurt her too.

Julius's body jerked as he took in a lungful of water, his eyes wide and haunted as he gazed up toward the sky that was too far away for him to reach.

Remorse found me in the darkness, ripping at my heart, begging me to be better than this.

I ground my teeth, willing myself to let this man die. He had hunted us all these years. He had put my family through hell.

"You caused his father's death," Idun whispered in my ear, and I shuddered as warm fingers stroked my spine.

I clenched my fists, willing away the doubts trickling into my body.

Julius fell deathly still and his heartbeat slowed to a dull thud, barely perceptible even to my heightened hearing.

"Let this happen. Let him die," Andvari encouraged, and I glimpsed the whites of his eyes in the muddy water before he drifted away again.

Anger burned through my veins. The gods were playing with us all. We were just pawns in their twisted games. What were we fighting over that hadn't been caused by *them*?

I stared at Julius as he floated like driftwood, moving with the pull of the tide. He was done for. And together, Fabian and I would be able to end Magnar.

I glanced toward the surface and a decision formed in my mind, not one that belonged to the gods, but one of my own.

Fuck.

I yanked the chain from Julius's ankle, dragging him up to the surface as fast as I could, cursing my own insanity with every powerful kick of my legs. The waves were choppy above us and Julius was a dead weight in my arms. It might already have been too late. His face was ghostly pale and his lips were turning blue. We'd floated far out into the river and I didn't think the others could see us here.

Good, because this never fucking happened.

I spied Magnar battling with Fabian before the statue. The twins were crying out to them but I couldn't tell what they were saying as thunder boomed like a gunshot overhead, swallowing all other sounds.

I swam for shore, circling out of sight into the thick shadow of the statue which was leaning over the water precariously. One more hit and the whole structure could go over.

I threw Julius from the river and his back impacted with the rocky shore. He nearly coughed his lungs up as he woke, and relief swept into me.

I dove under the water before he saw me, swimming in the direction of the others.

You're a fool. You had him and you let him go.

I shook off the thoughts, determined I'd made the right choice as clarity continued to consume me. It was what I had known all along, yet ignored until this very moment.

My fight wasn't with him. Or with Magnar. It was with the fucking gods.

MAGNAR

CHAPTER THIRTY ONE

"Y ou're alone now, slayer," Fabian hissed between gritted teeth as I fought to buck him off of me.

Julius had been beneath the waves for an eternity. Rage and grief flooded me in equal measures as I began to lose hope.

"I'm going to tear your guts from your body and force them down your foul throat," I snarled.

Fabian's fist slammed into my side and pain flared through me as a harsh crack sounded and my ribs broke for a second time. I coughed, bringing up blood and he laughed.

He punched me in the same spot again, sending stars swimming across my vision.

I caught his fist as he aimed for the same place a third time, squeezing as hard as I could until I felt his fingers shattering.

Fabian tried to rip his arm from my grip, but I gritted my teeth, clinging on as I twisted my hand sharply, feeling his wrist snap.

He jerked back, rolling off of me and I released him as I moved to follow. The pain in my side flared angrily and I coughed up more blood as I made it to my hands and knees. The bastard must have punctured my lung and I cursed him as I struggled to draw a breath. The injury would heal but not quickly and I didn't have time to spare. Julius needed me.

I tried to push myself to my feet and Fabian's boot landed on my side, sending me tumbling through the air.

I crashed into something and a metallic gong rang out before I struck the ground.

Someone was screaming, but I was still struggling to breathe and for a moment I couldn't open my eyes. Darkness loomed as I started to lose consciousness and more blood pooled from my mouth. I couldn't shake it off. I couldn't rouse my muscles into action. I needed oxygen but each breath was a torrent of pain and I couldn't draw enough in.

Soft hands touched my arm, shaking me with a desperate urgency as I struggled to remember where I was.

"Get up. You have to get up!" her voice was pleading, and her pain set something stirring in my chest but I couldn't quite remember what.

"Magnar," she begged, forcing her tongue to bend to her own will instead of Idun's.

The sound of my name on her lips drew me back to her. She was fighting for me as I should have been fighting for her.

I groaned as I forced a breath into my lungs and agony blossomed in my chest. But it paled into insignificance as I opened my eyes and found her looking down at me through the bars of the cage. She was beautiful. This perfect thing which had been so damaged by the world. I wanted to take her pain from her and make it my own. If I could make her truly happy for even a single moment, then I knew my life would have been well spent.

I managed to reach between the bars and my fingers brushed along her cheek for a fleeting second, the moisture from her tears coating my skin.

Callie's eyes turned from me and she looked up fearfully as footsteps approached. She reached out as far as she could, spreading her arms across me as if she could protect me from what we both knew was coming. My body was failing me. It wouldn't heal fast enough and I could hardly breathe.

"Please," she begged as tears streamed down her face. "Please- I'll do anything you want. I'll leave with you. I'll be yours; you can have me and I'll stay with you for as long as you want me. But just let him live."

Fabian stepped over me, nudging my injured side with the toe of his boot, drawing a hiss of pain from my lips. I could feel my gifts flowing through my body, fighting to repair the damage to my ribs but it was too slow and I still couldn't draw enough air into my lungs.

"You would leave with me?" Fabian asked her and I could hear how desperately he wanted her to do just that. But I would rather die than seal her to that fate. I knew she wasn't bluffing, she would give herself to him to save me. But I wouldn't let her do it. I would die first. If I was dead she wouldn't have to go with him and I knew she'd fight to escape, she would have a chance to be free.

"No," I growled, ignoring the pain it caused me to speak. "If you take her, I'll never stop coming for you."

Fabian snarled, placing his boot on my chest and pressing down so that agony raced through my body. Callie screamed but I blacked out for a moment and when I came back to myself he'd released me.

Callie's touch had left me too and she was standing within the cage, holding Fabian's arm so tightly that her knuckles had turned white.

"You swear you'll be mine?" Fabian demanded, staring into her eyes like he was searching for a lie.

"Callie," Montana breathed in horror, looking from me to her in fear.

Callie's eyes fell to me too and a desperate sob broke from her chest. "I swear," she breathed to Fabian. "Just let him live."

Fabian's eyes narrowed as he followed her gaze and I could see jealousy flaring in his expression. No matter where he took her, he could tell she'd always be with me in her heart.

I wouldn't let her condemn herself to a fate at his side just to protect my miserable existence.

"She'll never stop loving me while I live," I growled and I could see the truth of my words hitting him like a physical blow.

He knew I was right. And he knew what he had to do.

My eyes slid to Callie as he pulled his arm out of her grasp and a desperate sob broke from her lips. She was all I'd ever dreamed of. If I had to give my life to protect her then I'd do it willingly. I only wished it wouldn't hurt her like I could see it would.

Fabian grabbed my arm and hurled me away from the cage. I hit the ground hard, rolling over several times and coughing up more blood. I tried to force my body to do something, *anything,* but I could barely push myself up onto my knees.

My enemy reached me in a blur of motion and kicked me back down so hard that the concrete split beneath me. He leapt on top of me with a snarl of anger.

Fabian wrapped his fingers around my throat and started to squeeze as he leaned closer to me.

"When you're dead, I'll take my wife back to my bed and show her what it's like to be with a real man," he growled as I fought to prise his hands from me. "I'll make sure she forgets all about *you* and then I'll give her the gift of immortality. She will stand by my side for the rest of time while you fade from memory as you should have done a thousand years ago."

His words lit real fear in my soul, and I desperately tried to fight him off but my strength was leaving me.

Darkness started to curtain my vision as my damaged lung burned with pain from the ribs which pierced it. Fabian's fingers gripped me tightly, cutting off what little oxygen I could find.

My arms grew slack and her screams began to fade away. I didn't want to leave her. But if I had to die to keep her safe then my death would mean more than I'd ever hoped it could.

With me gone she wouldn't have to go with him. She could fight. She could have a chance at the freedom this life had denied her.

My only regret was that I wouldn't be there to share that freedom with her.

The life we could have had slipped away like the sun setting into an eternal night. Any chance of happiness, of having our own family and living out our days together were suddenly, unalterably over.

My cause had always been the driving force of my existence. I'd let my thirst for revenge guide every move I'd ever made. But now I realised that there had been so much more to life. And it was too late to grasp it. I'd chosen vengeance over my human desires. That path had stolen everything from me: my family, my soulmate and ultimately, the final, desperate beat of my heart.

ERIK

CHAPTER THIRTY TWO

I strode from the river and water poured from my body in a stream. My gaze landed on Fabian on the ground holding Magnar down, his fangs buried in his throat. The slayer looked weak, close to death. He was trying to fight, but it was clear something serious was wrong with him.

"Stop - please stop!" Callie screamed and Montana held onto her with silent tears coursing down her cheeks.

My newfound resolve had taken root inside me and with my gazed fixed on my girl, this change became all the more easy to secure. I had to end this. I had to convince them all of who our true enemies were.

Montana called my name as I sprinted toward Fabian, her tone laced with a mixture of relief and agony. I couldn't spare her another glance, though my heart burned in my chest, tempting me her way, to break her free of that gilded cage and take her from this blood-stained island.

I came to a standstill behind my brother and grabbed his shoulder, pulling him off of Magnar with a fierce strength.

Fabian turned, throwing a violent punch toward me, evidently expecting to find Julius there. I avoided it at the last second, clasping his shoulder as his eyes filled with confusion.

"What are you doing?" Fabian snarled through a mouthful of blood, shaking me off and turning back to face Magnar's shattered form on the ground. His face was ashen and blood poured from his wounds in a never-ending torrent.

"Fuck. We can't do this," I exhaled, wondering how the hell I was going to explain my change of heart. Even I didn't truly understand it.

I pointed up at the key high above our heads. "This is another of the gods' games, brother."

I caught Fabian's arm as he stepped toward Magnar once more.

"Did you hit your head or something?" Fabian barked at me. "Let me finish him."

"No," I snarled, moving between the two of them, but Fabian wasn't backing down. "Our fight is with the gods, can't you see that?" I demanded. "All these years we've been tormented by them. We don't need to fight the slayers, we need their help."

"What have you done?!" Julius's booming voice filled my ears.

I spotted him beyond the statue, speeding toward us, and I grabbed hold of Fabian, wrestling him back as he tried to intercept him.

"Traitor," Fabian spat at me, but I didn't let go.

Julius fell to his knees beside his brother, trembling from head to foot as he placed a hand to his neck.

"He's dead," he gasped, and Callie's anguished cry sliced the air apart.

"No," I snarled, shoving Fabian away from me as I moved to check Magnar myself.

I couldn't hear the beating of his heart and the reality of the situation descended on me.

Julius's dark gaze wheeled to me. "You did this."

"I didn't," I said evenly, and his eyes swung to Fabian who was moving toward him like a predator.

Julius rose his feet, baring his teeth as he waited for either me or Fabian to attack, lowering into a fighting stance.

"Listen to me," I commanded, stepping between the two of them to keep them apart.

Fabian growled, pushing up behind me but I didn't let him pass.

Julius's pained gaze turned to me, grief written into his features.

"The day your father died, I was under Andvari's spell," I explained.

"*Liar*," Julius hissed, lurching toward me.

I shoved his chest and he staggered back before coming at me again. I took a punch to the gut before throwing him away from me once more.

"Listen to him!" Montana called to us. "Erik's right. It's the gods who are to blame for this."

"Someone let me out!" Callie yelled. "Let me help him, someone fucking help him!"

Fabian pushed me aside. "Fuck the gods. And fuck the slayers too. They're all out to get us and I want to finish this now." He launched himself at Julius and my heart turned to ice as I ran after him.

Julius caught Fabian by the waist, launching him into the air above us with colossal strength.

"Stop!" I roared, but the slayer swung toward me and his knuckles connected with my jaw.

Fabian crashed to the ground beside us, groaning as he regained his senses.

I stumbled away in fury as Julius lunged at me again. He couldn't hear me in his agonised state. His brother was dead so how the fuck was I going to make him listen to me now?

I knew I couldn't fight back. I wouldn't kill him. We had to figure this shit out together. It didn't matter what we thought of each other. The only way we could take on the gods was if we united.

Julius threw more punches, left, right, centre. Fear grabbed me in an iron hold as Julius's rage took over his movements. He broke my jaw and I stumbled back, trying to counter his blows as they became more ferocious.

I parried as many as I could, backing up and guiding him toward the cage. If I couldn't talk sense into him, maybe Montana could. He smashed another crushing hit to my chest and bones shattered under the impact, but I let it happen, refusing to fight him now that my mind was made up.

Pain burrowed through me and my wife's screams raked my eardrums. My body was healing, but not fast enough as Julius landed a kick to my shin and an ear-splitting crack sounded. Agony scorched through my body like a wildfire, and the slayer didn't slow his advance, his gaze murderous.

Over Julius's shoulder, I spied Fabian rising to his feet with something glinting in his hand and a gasp escaped me as I realised what it was. My brother sped toward the cage, but Julius threw his weight at me and I was launched away from the twins.

"No!" I bellowed as he fell on top of me, pressing his thumbs into my eyes.

"Your life for his, parasite," Julius snarled and I roared in pain as my skull cracked beneath his hands.

The world was falling apart.

I tried to force Julius off of me, knocking his hands away from my face, but I knew I was racing toward my end. His combined strength and anger were overwhelming. He tore at my chest as if he wanted to dig my heart from my flesh.

Andvari's presence grew around me, tormented and furious. As his power slid into my body, my thoughts slipped away into darkness. He consumed me, took control of my limbs and forced my hand up to meet Julius's jaw with such power that it sent a tremor through my bones. The slayer crashed to the ground with such force that the collision ripped the cement apart.

I rose on sturdy legs, my body taken hostage, filled with the power of the god.

My mind angled towards one thing as hunger shredded my throat and my soul was soaked in darkness.

Blood.

CALLIE

CHAPTER THIRTY THREE

Grief split me in two and carved a hole right through my chest as I stared across the broken concrete at Magnar's body. He was so still, so pale, like everything that had made him, *him* was just...gone. I felt like I was standing on the precipice of an unending abyss. If I moved so much as an inch, I'd plunge in and fall forevermore into darkness.

Montana's arms were around me and she was whispering something, but I couldn't focus enough to hear it. I was torn between wanting the comfort of her embrace and hating her for loving one of the creatures responsible for my pain. She held me tightly and her tears fell on my bare shoulder.

My heart had stopped beating. Where it had pulsed with life just moments ago, now it was a cold, hard thing. A lifeless, joyless chasm within the centre of everything I'd thought I was.

Erik and Julius battled on and I was struck with the burning sense of how pointless all of it was. Death leading to death, on and on until none would be left standing in the end. And why? Julius would kill Erik and Fabian if he could, but it wouldn't bring Magnar back.

I'd never stand captured in his golden gaze again or feel the warmth of his touch on my skin.

Montana gasped in alarm, her hand clutching my wrist as she dragged me away from the bars. I resisted for a moment, not wanting to look away from Magnar, not wanting to abandon him when he needed me most. Except he didn't need me anymore. There was nothing left inside the shell which used to house his soul.

My sister pulled my arm more urgently, and I forced myself to turn and see what was wrong. Fabian was racing towards us, the golden key clutched in his hand as his gaze stayed fixed on me.

I stared at him for a moment and suddenly realised why Julius was still fighting. Killing them wouldn't bring Magnar back. But it would feel really fucking good.

Fabian jammed the key into the padlock and I grabbed my sister's arm, pushing her behind me despite the fact that she'd been trying to shield me first. He wasn't interested in her but I refused to let him near the only person I still loved in this wretched world.

Fabian ripped the gate open and stared at me like I was the only thing that existed in the entire universe.

"I'm sorry," he breathed, hesitating on the threshold of our cage. "But he was poisoning you against me. You couldn't accept the goddess's gift while he still lived. But now you're free of him. Free to give your heart to me completely."

"How could you think I could love you now?" I hissed. "Have you been dead for so long that you've forgotten what it is to be alive? Killing him doesn't just erase how I feel about him."

"I know it hurts," Fabian replied, feigning some sense of understanding while stepping towards me purposefully.

I started to back up, pushing Montana aside so she didn't end up penned in by him too. She resisted for a moment, clinging to my hand then suddenly released me and stepped away. I didn't have a moment to wonder what had changed her mind as Fabian stalked closer.

"You have no idea how this feels," I replied, my voice low with warning as he continued to close the distance between us.

My palm ached for the feeling of Fury in my grasp but I'd left the blade on the floor when I'd been holding Magnar in my arms. My gaze

336

dropped to the golden blade as Fabian stepped over it but there was no way for me to reach it.

Montana slipped out of the cage and I hoped she had the good sense to get out of danger.

Fear spiked through me and the power of my ancestors drew closer as I opened myself to my gifts. I wouldn't let this monster take me. I refused to bow to the pressure of the goddess as she tried to make my pulse race for him.

My gaze dropped to Fabian's muscular chest, but I didn't let Idun stoke any flames of desire in me. The only thing I saw was the blood which stained his skin. The blood of the man I loved.

My back collided with the bars behind me and Fabian stopped.

"Can't you feel it?" he whispered, leaning in as if he wanted to kiss me.

I could sense Idun drawing closer to us, lending more of her power to the bond as heat flamed along the mark on my palm. I ached to lace my arms around this demon's neck, to give in to the desire which fuelled his abhorrent actions. I fought against it, keeping my arms at my side and praying she didn't take me hostage as she had at the wedding.

Fabian reached out to touch my cheek, brushing my hair aside in a gentle caress.

I recoiled, staring at him in horror. How could he think I'd want him now? He was coated in Magnar's blood, looking at me like I was some prize he'd won. But I would never be his. I swore it on everything I was. If I couldn't break this bond with him then I'd end my life before I'd spend it with him.

He leaned closer and I ached to hurt him as he'd hurt me, but the fucking bond wouldn't let me raise a hand against him.

He took my inaction as an invitation and dipped his mouth towards mine.

I gritted my teeth and pressed my hand to his chest, holding him back.

My eyes fell on the mark on the back of my hand. The one I'd received when I'd taken my vow and my life had been bound to Magnar's. The one that Julius had told me would disappear if Magnar was dead.

I inhaled sharply as my eyes flicked away from Fabian to Magnar's body which still lay on the concrete. Relief flooded me, rocking the foundations of my soul as my broken pieces knitted themselves back together.

My heart swelled and my shattered soul was reborn in this dazzling ray of hope.

The mark was still intact, so he wasn't dead. And if he wasn't dead then he was healing. And if he was going to have the chance to recover before Fabian figured it out too, then I had to hold his attention.

I looked back up at the immortal monster who had me pinned beneath his gaze.

I could still feel the desperate ache of the partnership rune drawing me towards him and for once, I gave myself to its desires.

I slid my hand further up his chest, holding his gaze as his muscles tensed beneath my touch. His eyes filled with lust and he pressed me back, his hands gripping my waist.

I raised my other hand too, holding his face between my palms as I stared up at him and the space dividing us grew smaller and smaller.

"I knew you'd give in to it now," Fabian groaned longingly.

He lifted me into his arms, pressing me against the bars and I wrapped my legs around his waist.

My heart thundered with the promise of what I was about to do. Fabian's mouth lifted into a triumphant smile just before he pressed his cold lips to mine.

I ignored the tremors which rocked through me as he kissed me hungrily. I could taste the iron tang of Magnar's blood on his mouth and with it, I found myself again. Found enough of myself to push off the power of the rune and work against its hold on me.

My grip on Fabian's face tightened. Strength flooded into my muscles as I called on my gifts and with an almighty wrench, I twisted his head as hard as I could.

Fabian tried to push me back, but it was already too late. I gathered my rage, releasing a feral noise as I dug my fingers into his flesh, feeling his neck break. I growled with effort and threw every ounce of my gifted strength into forcing his neck to turn even further until with a shuddering yank, I tore his head from his shoulders. His blood flooded over me, soaking through my white dress as I bellowed my satisfaction at the watching stars.

Fabian's body fell to the ground beneath me, and I dropped his head as I fell on top of him.

Pain clawed at my fractured soul as the bond balked against what I'd done and I was seized with the desire to place his head back upon his shoulders.

I gritted my teeth and crawled towards Fury instead, pulling the blade into my hand with a sigh of relief.

Keep faith, Sun Child.

My hand trembled violently as I touched Fury to Fabian's heart and the blade urged me to force my arm down. But another part of me was screaming, wailing and begging me not to do it.

I loved him. I hated him and I loved him and wanted him dead but his death would kill me too.

Tremors racked my body as the two desires warred inside me and I was frozen between acting on either.

A groan of pain drew my attention, and I looked up as my whole world snapped back into alignment.

Magnar was beginning to move, his hand curling into a fist as he prepared to re-join the battle taking place between Erik and his brother.

With a desperate cry, I turned from Fabian's body and ran from the cage, racing to the slayer who owned my heart.

We would finish this fight together.

MONTANA

CHAPTER THIRTY FOUR

Power bled into my body, taking me prisoner and squeezing my heart, luring me away from the cage, my sister, and calming all fears that had just held me in their grip.

Andvari waited there by the base of the statue, beckoning me toward him and regarding me with intrigue. I wasn't sure if anyone else could see him and I couldn't turn my head to check. My limbs moved of their own accord, guided by him as I walked across the rubble straight into his outstretched arms.

He caressed my back and a prickling quiet fell over me.

No, Callie. I have to help Callie!

I couldn't do anything but stand there in the god's icy embrace, his will dictating mine, silencing my terror once more.

"How long I have waited for this," Andvari whispered, his breath a gust of hot air against my skin. "Come now, Moon Child, it is time your fate was decided."

I nodded, following in a daze as he led me toward the base of the statue, the sky above now thick with dusk and the sun lost to the night. Andvari's aura filled me, possessing my body and saturating me with the strength I needed to do what he willed.

I rested my hands on the stone wall, sliding my fingers into a deep fissure caused by the battle. Erik sparked into my mind and desperation filled me as I tried to force away Andvari's urges, trying to turn and look for him.

I have to get to him. I have to stop this.

"Enough," Andvari hissed. "Do not fight me."

His strength inched deeper into my body and I dragged myself up the stone wall with impossible ease. My hands and feet were guided by the god, helping me climb higher and higher. Soon I was scaling the statue itself, finding handholds that shouldn't have existed as I managed to move up the copper structure. It was leaning precariously toward the river and I was sure one more hit would send it careering into its depths.

Fear sped through me as I once again attempted to battle away the god's hold over me, but it was like trying to force an organ from my body. He was a part of me, pushing me to my limits, and I bowed to his power, unable to break free. I clawed my way up the chest of the giant woman and my hand landed on something warm, something that was cloaked in magic.

Venom, the sword purred its name as I gripped the hilt. It was embedded in the metal, but with Andvari's strength in my veins, it came easily away. The blade tumbled to the ground and I gasped, grabbing onto the hole it had gouged in the statue to steady myself.

Two more swords penetrated the statue above me, glittering as lightning spilled through the sky. A moment of clarity found me and my gut swooped at the dizzying drop below me.

"Please, let me down!" I screamed to Andvari, the icy wind drilling into my veins.

"Keep going," he snarled and my legs moved under his influence, forcing me higher.

I reached for the next blade and Menace whispered its name to me, its hunger evident for the vampires below. I hoisted myself onto it and reached for the final blade further up, resting my feet precariously on Menace. As my fingers brushed the next sword, its heavy aura grated against me.

Tempest, it revealed reluctantly.

Menace came loose beneath my feet and I cried out as it fell, promising me my death with it. But Andvari guided me and I caught hold of Tempest by the hilt, swinging wildly in the frantic breeze while panic swallowed me up.

I dug my heels against the statue to brace myself, a murmur of fear escaping me.

"Up," the god whispered, and I had no choice as I dragged myself onto Tempest, my bare feet balancing on the blade. I should have been cut to ribbons but Andvari's gifts were making my body impossibly strong. I just wished I could have used this power against him.

I ground my teeth as I rested my hands against the statue and Tempest slid free. The moment it dropped, I leapt upwards, catching a small ledge of metal and scrambling ever higher.

The wind whipped past me, fluttering my white dress around my ankles. My bare feet were frozen as they pressed against the copper, guiding me upwards while I fought to regain control of my limbs.

I didn't dare look down as I continued to scale the giant statue that reached toward the endlessly black sky.

When I made it to the shoulder of the woman, I gripped on for dear life. The structure was leaning forward, making her shoulder into a deadly slope beneath me, one slip promising my end.

"Why are you doing this?" I begged, unable to avoid looking at the nauseating view ahead. The dark river coiled toward the sea like spilled ink, and the drop below me was staggering. If the god released me from his power, I'd be stuck here, clinging on at the mercy of the wind.

"Because I have been wronged deeply and I am tired of waiting for penance," Andvari said in a gruff tone. "So I am going to start by taking it from you, Montana Ford."

MAGNAR

CHAPTER THIRTY FIVE

I lay in darkness expecting the horns of Valhalla to call me to the great hall. But in place of music and cheering, I was met with a kiss.

"Not yet, my warrior," Idun sighed, her breath washing over my lips.

A hand pressed against my chest and power flooded into me beneath her palm. It tingled between the layers of my flesh, soaking down into my bones.

Heat built in my injuries and my lungs expanded, filling with the air I so desperately needed. The shard of broken rib was forced out of my lung and the pain was swept away on a tide of power so sweet that I ached for its return.

A harsh snap sounded as my ribs realigned, the bones fusing back together.

The outside world found me as I rose towards consciousness, and I could hear people fighting, screaming, crying while I tried to remember why.

My eyes snapped open and the stars shone above me between a swirl of storm clouds, watching over the game we were being forced to play.

Idun's power continued to infuse me and my muscles swelled with the strength of the gods.

I pushed myself to my feet, feeling as fresh as if I'd woken from a deep and untroubled sleep. My eyes fell towards the cage as everything came flooding back to me and my fear for Callie returned.

I found her then. The reason I'd come back from the brink of beyond. The one pure thing I had in this foul world. She ran towards me with a relieved smile on her face and bright red blood coating her white dress. She was the most beautiful sight I'd ever seen. A vision of the truest, most desperate desires of my heart.

I noticed Fabian's decapitated body beyond her with a surge of pride. I took a step in her direction, intending to take her in my arms and hold her close for the rest of my years.

A huge crash sounded and Julius cried out in pain behind me. I turned sharply to seek him out, forgetting all else in my need to help him.

Erik had him pinned to the wall beneath the statue, his teeth lodged in my brother's throat as he drank deeply from his veins. Julius fought to free himself but his efforts went unnoticed as the demon continued feasting.

I bellowed a challenge as I raced to Julius's aid, leaving Callie behind as my commands from earlier that afternoon stopped her from following. She couldn't intervene in our battle. My will bound her and I knew it would keep her safe.

I turned my mind from her as I charged forward at an incredible speed, the goddess lending me more power than I'd ever known.

Erik's head snapped around as he heard me coming and he released his hold on Julius. My brother slumped to the ground, pressing a hand to the wound on his neck as the blood loss stole his strength from him.

I slammed into Erik with the force of Thor's hammer and the sound of our collision shook the foundations of the island we stood upon.

He absorbed the blow with a snarl of rage and I locked eyes with him, peering straight into the black depths of his soul. His pupils were two dark, round disks and I could feel the foul tang of Andvari's power flowing through his body.

The gods had picked their sides. It was time to find out which one of them had bet correctly.

Erik's fist slammed into my face and I whipped my head back as I absorbed the impact.

He lunged, his fangs aimed at my neck as his thirst drove him to act upon his basest desires.

His teeth met with my knuckles instead and I growled in defiance as his venom burned through my skin before he was thrown away from me.

I leapt at him but he spun aside with impossible speed. Landing on my feet, I skidded on the broken rubble which had been a solid footpath before our battle had begun.

Erik snarled as he grabbed my arm, his vice-like grip almost breaking the bone as he swung me away from him. He was stronger than he'd been before; Andvari's dark magic fuelled him just as Idun powered me. I flew through the air, slamming into the tilting statue with an echoing bang which vibrated the whole structure.

A scream from above met my ears as I tumbled to the ground, but I had no time to investigate it as Erik crashed into me again.

His teeth found my flesh before we hit the dirt; fire burning through my shoulder as his fingernails gouged into my chest.

We smashed onto the ground, carving another crater into existence beneath us as soil and rubble exploded around our bodies.

I threw all of my strength into my next punch, hitting the side of his skull so hard that I heard his neck snap as he was thrown off of me.

Erik rolled away, quickly regaining his feet as he glared at me with his head hanging at an unnatural angle.

He bared his teeth as he realigned his spine and his bones fused back together.

I roared in defiance as I charged towards him again.

He was the most unnatural of creatures. And before this night was done, I would rid the earth of his existence at long last.

ERiK

CHAPTER THIRTY SIX

Andvari's cold essence leaked through my veins. I was a monster in full form. A beast without thought or reason. The slayer was my target. And I had a singular desire driving my movements: to drink all of his blood until this need was sated.

I sensed Idun's power behind his blows, making him a savage opponent, one that I needed to end.

I was an animal; a starved wolf desperate for this meal, nothing but a husk to be filled. But I was done throwing punches and cracking bones, it was time to rip open flesh and sinew, find the sweet nectar my body craved.

The only way to end this agonising thirst was to give in to my most primal need.

As Magnar came at me once more, I raked my nails down his chest, tearing his skin apart. He roared his rage, throwing another punch but I dodged it, guided by Andvari's gifts as I darted between his arms. My fangs sank deep into the thick muscle of his neck and the ache in me grew more desperate, demanding I drink every last drop of his life-force.

Magnar fisted his hand in my hair, ripping my teeth free and pushing me back. His face was contorted and caked in filth. Blood marred our flesh and was reflected in our eyes. Red...everything was red.

My true self flickered on the edges of my mind, desperate to take back control. Shock momentarily seeped through me as I managed to reclaim some small part of myself. For a brief moment, I governed my own actions, just enough to stay my hand. Trembling with exertion, I wrestled to shake Andvari's hold on me. But Magnar came at me like a freight train.

As his fist impacted with my head, I caught a glimpse of who I was again. Rebel entered my mind and love spilled into all the dark shadows Andvari had cast inside me, stitching them there once and for all. But I could break the threads if only I could hold onto the thought of *her*.

I searched left and right, finding the golden cage empty and panic started a fire in the pit of my chest.

Where are you?

Another punch from Magnar brought the god's power flooding back into me like a tsunami. I fell into another desperate, endless fight with my enemy. My body was battered, torn, breaking and re-mending.

It couldn't go on forever. One of us would fall. It was all I wanted. And yet, on the verges of my being, I sensed I desired something beyond that. A yearning only my heart knew. A girl with dark hair and eyes that captivated me in every sense of the word.

I didn't know who she was, but somehow, impossibly, I needed her more than blood. More than anything.

The darkness of Andvari's magic sank deeper, burrowing into my body and driving out everything but hate. And I was a demon once more.

CALLIE

CHAPTER THIRTY SEVEN

I trembled with unspent energy as I stood in the statue's shadow, watching Magnar and Erik fighting. I ached to run to the slayer's aid, to join him as he fought and do whatever I could to protect him.

I couldn't see Montana anywhere and I just hoped she'd found some place to hide from the danger of the battle. I wasn't overly concerned for her though; she was the only one of us here who didn't have an enemy present. If she had managed to get out of the way then I knew she'd be safe.

I was trapped on the side-lines by the power of the commands Magnar had laid on me before this battle began. They flowed alongside my blood, powering my muscles as they fought for his will, working against me. I'd been betrayed by my own body yet again.

You will not intervene in any way.

But he needed me. I'd already watched him die once and there was no way I could endure it again. I had to find a way around his commands but his words had been cleverly selected. I couldn't so much as call out to him or try to cause some kind of distraction.

I swore in frustration and ran to Julius instead. He was sitting against the wall, his eyes hooded as he pressed a hand to his throat where Erik's bite continued to bleed slowly.

"Are you alright?" I breathed desperately as I crouched before him, reaching out to touch him then dropping my hand uncertainly.

"Pfft, this little thing?" he replied but his voice was weak despite his mocking tone. "Though if you really think it looks fatal maybe you should take the opportunity to kiss me?"

"Kiss you?" I snorted half a laugh at the fact that he could crack jokes while he stood on death's door.

"It could be your last chance. You don't want to spend the rest of your life wondering what if."

I rolled my eyes and ripped a length of material from my dress. I dipped it in a dirty puddle beside us before peeling his fingers from his throat so I could wipe the venom out of the wound. It wasn't particularly hygienic but he was capable of healing an infection and once the venom was gone, he'd feel a lot better.

A great crash sounded as Erik threw Magnar away from him and I ducked my head, using my body to shield Julius from the spray of debris that followed.

The ferocity of their battle had reached a new high; I could feel the power of the gods billowing around them as they fought with all the strength of the deities themselves. It wasn't right. It wasn't natural. Watching them felt like watching a show performed on behalf of the beings which guided them. They weren't fighting their own war anymore. This was between Idun and Andvari. Magnar and Erik were just the puppets they'd chosen to use, and I knew I had to find a way to stop them before they tore apart the men my sister and I loved.

"Magnar needs my help," I said desperately as Julius's wound stopped bleeding.

He followed my gaze to the battle which blazed between his brother and Erik.

"He can take that parasite," he replied, though he didn't sound sure.

"Tell me how to break his hold on me," I growled.

Julius shook his head feebly and his eyelids drooped as he nearly lost consciousness. I slapped him just hard enough to force him back to wakefulness and his gaze met mine as he scowled.

"*Ow,*" he objected, but I didn't have time for his nonsense. I needed to break Magnar's hold on me and help all of us.

"Tell me how to break it, Julius!" I demanded.

He frowned at me, clearly unsure if he should go against his brother's decision. Magnar cried out in pain behind us, and Julius gritted his teeth.

"You just have to want it enough," he replied. "You have to *know* that you know better than him. That you can take the consequences of your actions upon yourself without needing his guidance anymore. But it won't work. It takes months...years-"

I stood and turned my back on him, clenching my fists as I glared at the battle which raged on between the two men the gods had chosen for their servants.

A cold wind blew around me and my golden hair spun over my shoulders, fluttering out behind me as though the elements wished to stop my advance.

But I refused to bow to their demands. If all it took was knowing better than Magnar then that was easy. I knew that the goddess was using him. Just as Andvari was using Erik. Their quarrel had been fuelled by the deities beyond all natural solutions. Their bodies had been taken captive, their souls enslaved.

So I needed to know better than Magnar? Well I sure as hell did. I'd been bucking against Idun's rules from the moment I'd first heard her name. There was a reason I hadn't grown up fearing her. There was a reason she'd been forgotten in the years that had passed since the Vikings' reign. I needed no deity to guide my future. I accepted no greater power to steer my fate.

My life was my own. And I was done following rules that I knew to be wrong.

My chest constricted as I took a step forward, the pressure of a mountain falling upon my shoulders as the goddess fought to keep me chained.

The second step was weighed with lead, my bare foot sliding across the broken concrete as though it were fused to the ground.

The wind grew stronger as I took the third step, my golden hair flying around me in a maelstrom designed to hold me back.

But I pushed on. Because I *did* know better. And I knew exactly what we needed to stop this madness.

As I raised my foot again, the shackles fell from my soul. I felt light, dizzy, euphoric with the sudden freedom as everything Magnar had forced me to do simply fell away.

My left hand tingled and I looked down at it as the mark which bound me to my Elder faded from my skin. I was a slayer in my own right. Free of his commands.

With a vicious smile, I started running.

My bare feet pounded the concrete and my bloodstained dress streamed behind me as I tore after Magnar and Erik. Their battle had taken them to the water's edge and they moved so quickly that I couldn't tell if either of them had gained the upper hand.

I set my eyes on Magnar, his bare chest heaving with effort as he kicked Erik squarely in the centre of his torso. The vampire flew towards me and I leapt aside just before he slammed into the pathway, gouging a line through the brickwork and deep into the ground below it.

Erik noticed me as he regained his feet and he raced towards me, his face alight with a feral hunger.

I cried out, whirling to face him, raising Fury and throwing it at him as he shot closer. The blade landed in his shoulder a moment before he reached me and the stench of burning flesh sizzled through the air.

He swore at me, swinging the back of his hand into my face with all the force of a charging bull.

I was tossed away from him like a rag doll and I hit the ground, rolling over and over before I managed to push myself up onto my hands and knees.

Erik sprinted after me with his fangs bared, but Magnar collided with him before he could reach me. The sound of their impact set my ears ringing and I rose on shaky legs as the pain in my face throbbed.

I chased after them again, knowing that this insanity would only end with bloodshed unless I could get to Magnar first.

I could feel the gods watching me with amusement, wondering what I was trying to achieve. I knew I was no match for Erik while Andvari aided him, but I had no intention of trying to involve myself in their fight.

"Callie, get out of here!" Magnar shouted, trying to wield his power over me again. But I felt no urge to do as he said. No insatiable impulse to follow his every command as though my body were his instead of my own. I was free. And I was going to stay that way.

I sprinted towards them and managed to catch up as they paused to survey each other. Magnar's eyes fell on me and confusion flickered in his gaze for a moment quickly followed by a dawning comprehension.

Erik snarled as he eyed me too, both of them waiting for the other to make the first move.

I bit my lip as I noted the thirst which burned in Erik's eyes. Fury still protruded from his shoulder as though he couldn't even feel the blade cooking his flesh. He was ravenous. Greed given life. I wondered if the man Montana loved was even in there anymore.

I saw the moment his restraint snapped and he leapt at me with the promise of death in his gaze. I recoiled, knowing I was unable to move fast enough to escape him, but Magnar got to me first.

He slammed me to the ground, protecting me with his body as Erik jumped onto his back. Magnar bellowed in pain as the vampire bit him and my heart leapt in panic.

I reached out quickly, yanking the chain from Magnar's neck and ripping my mother's ring free of it. I slid it onto my trembling finger and the bubble of peace surrounded me as the gods were forced to retreat. I couldn't feel them anymore. I couldn't sense anything from the mark on my palm or its connection to Fabian.

Within this net I'd cast, no god could see me.

I smiled triumphantly as I pushed the bubble over Magnar and Erik too and the gods were forced to retreat from their bodies as well.

Magnar blinked down at me in surprise and Erik reared back, his eyes wide with horror as he wiped Magnar's blood from his mouth. He wrenched Fury from his shoulder as if he'd suddenly realised it was there and it clattered to the ground between us.

"How?" he gasped, staring at us as Magnar pushed himself upright, dragging me with him.

He guided me behind him, placing himself between me and the vampire.

Erik backed up, holding out a hand as Magnar began to advance again. The bloodlust was gone from the vampire's gaze and he suddenly seemed much more human than should have been possible.

I caught Magnar's elbow and he let me stop him as he seemed to notice the difference in our enemy too. Magnar held onto me as he glared at Erik, both of them unsure if their fight was over or not.

"Stay close," I commanded. "This protection doesn't stretch far."

"How?" Erik breathed again, staring at me as though I'd just saved him from something far worse than death.

"The gods can't see us," I said. "Were you under their spell? Controlled by Andvari?"

I desperately hoped that that was true. Montana believed there was so much good in this monster that he was deserving of her love. If I could locate even an inch of what she'd discovered in him, then perhaps we could find a way out of this that wouldn't end in death.

Magnar shifted slightly so he was between me and Erik once more. This moment of peace between them felt immeasurably fragile and I was sure that if I couldn't maintain it there would be no way to stop them again.

"Yes. I was lost to him. You pulled me out of the dark," Erik breathed, gratitude lacing his tone.

I glanced up at Magnar, unsure what to make of this exchange. He was still tense, as though he expected to fall back into battle at any moment, but he made no move to attack. I wondered if he was seeing the glimmer of humanity in his enemy that I was beginning to notice.

I reached towards Magnar, certain that he was the one I had to convince if I was truly going to stop this.

I cupped his cheek in my hand, the mess of blood which lined his skin wet beneath my fingertips. The ring throbbed with heat as it brushed against his flesh, like it could sense the writhing power that filled him.

"Magnar?" I whispered, drawing his eyes to me as he finally looked away from Erik. That act alone felt like crossing some immense barrier, like he'd overcome the first hurdle in containing his hatred. "This fight has gone far enough. We can't keep allowing the gods to drive our fates."

His jaw was tense beneath my touch but deep within the golden depths of his eyes, something softened.

"They've taken too much from us already," he growled in acceptance, and I knew his animosity had found a new target in the warring deities.

I looked back at Erik, hoping he felt the same. Though a thousand years of hatred burned between them, the gods had been the ones to invoke it. They were responsible for every foul thing that had befallen each of us.

Erik's eyes slipped to the ring on my finger and his mouth fell open as if he'd realised something critical.

"They were searching for a ring," he whispered.

I glanced down at the golden piece of jewellery, wondering who he was talking about just as a faint scream reached my ears.

Ice slipped through my body as I turned to search for its source.

My heart throbbed with a terrible surge of dread as if my other half were screaming out for help. I knew with no uncertainty that my sister needed me. She was in desperate trouble somewhere and I had to get to her.

MONTANA

CHAPTER THIRTY EIGHT

"Higher," Andvari urged, and I gazed up at the head of the statue, a shudder sliding down my spine.

A fan of sharp points shot out from the crown she wore, and I pulled myself up the side of her head, a murmur of terror escaping me as Andvari encouraged me toward the huge spikes protruding from the headpiece. I reached out for one of them and my fingers grazed the freezing metal.

"Andvari, stop!" I screamed, my stomach spinning as the drop below gazed back at me, tempting me toward death.

"Up," he purred and I reached out again, catching hold of the crown and dragging myself onto the flat space atop the spike.

The god didn't bother to quiet my fears anymore, taking control of my body and leaving me trapped inside it.

Andvari moved me like a puppet, making me stand and I raised my arms to balance myself, terrified of falling.

The wind was battering and I tried to crouch down again to hold on, but Andvari wouldn't allow it.

He appeared at the very tip of the platform the crown created as it reached out over the endless drop below. The god flexed his index finger to draw me closer and the action was a command, impossible to ignore.

"No, please," I gasped, shaking my head.

My hands curled up and I managed to clutch them to my chest, trembling all over as I resisted the force of the wind.

"Come, Moon Child," he whispered and my feet moved at his words, carrying me toward him, right to the edge of the sharp point of the crown's spire.

Andvari took hold of my arm and I snatched his robes, desperate for something to keep me from falling, my teeth gritting in determination.

"You see them?" Andvari pointed down to the ground below and I spotted the others.

They'd fallen still, their fight seemingly paused. My heart soared with the possibility. They were all alive, even Magnar was on his feet.

I screamed in fright as the whole structure suddenly buckled forward several feet, the world tipping and urging me to fall.

I flailed, gripping onto Andvari but he disappeared into thin air, abandoning me to the pull of gravity.

My stomach soared and my heart turned to ash as I plummeted forward, my hands flying out as I regained control of my body at last.

Impossibly, I caught the edge of the spike, hanging on by the tips of my fingers, my nails biting into the metal in desperation. Fear snaked through me as my legs kicked wildly and I fought to hold on with every ounce of strength I possessed. But it simply wasn't enough.

Andvari laughed, lending me his power to right myself at the last second. With shaking arms, I hauled myself up onto the tip of the platform, my heart quaking in my chest.

I gasped my relief but then Andvari made me stand once again, my toes feeling welded to the platform as I found my balance.

The god reappeared, standing on nothing but air several feet ahead of me.

Terror clawed at my insides. "Stop this," I demanded.

"Only you can stop this," he said with an ominous look that made a crack of thunder split the sky apart. "You would do anything to save your beloved monster, would you not?"

I gazed down at Erik below with Magnar and Callie and fear fractured my heart. He was outnumbered. They'd kill him together.

"Of course," I stuttered as icy tears slid down my cheeks. "Anything to stop this fight."

"Then jump," he breathed and his command dripped through me, encouraging me to obey.

My breath stalled in my lungs.

"You want me to die?" Terror took root in my chest like a tangle of thorns, choking the breaths from my lungs.

Andvari chuckled and the wind blew against my back, forcing me toward the fate he'd decided for me. My heart slammed into my throat as I teetered on the edge, lifting my arms as I managed to stay upright.

"Would you die for him?" Andvari asked, his expression suddenly soft.

I took a breath as more tears rolled down my cheeks, falling to the dark ground below. "If it would save him. If it would end this curse."

"A debt paid perhaps?" Andvari growled and fear blossomed in my chest.

"This is your debt?" I murmured.

He didn't answer, but his smile broadened.

"Jump," he growled, and I felt the ghost of his hand press into my spine.

My stomach rolled. My heart stopped beating.

Fear held me in place, but the god was pushing me, forcing me.

I shut my eyes, stealing a moment of silence and the urge to jump released me.

Death was staring me in the face and it was the cruellest thing. But if this could end the curse, wasn't this the only path I could take? For Erik. For my sister. For all of them.

I only wished I could have had a second longer in Erik's arms. We'd been offered so little time. But each moment was precious and wrapped in my heart, unable to be touched by anyone. Not even the gods could steal that from me.

I stole a look up at the stars. The fight had raged on so long that night had fully claimed the sky and the moon was rising to see my downfall. My tears turned to ice against my cheeks and a strange calm fell over me. My dad had told us about the constellations. The stories that clung to them, recounted by humans through all the years they'd watched the heavens. Generation after generation had lived and died under these stars. Were my parents up there somewhere, laying in the sky's arms and waiting to welcome me home?

A breath of resolution rolled past my lips as I turned my gaze to the dizzying drop beneath me. I spotted Magnar moving toward Erik and panic gripped me.

My heart beat with every second that passed. Every moment of hesitation could lead to his death.

"I love you," I whispered, wishing he could hear the words. But even if he couldn't, I needed to say them. I needed the world to lay witness to how deeply, fiercely and immovably I loved him.

I shifted my gaze to Andvari and my upper lip curled back as a hatred coursed through me like nothing I'd ever known. This was his doing. His divine ruling.

"Even in death I'll love him and my family more profoundly than you could ever love anything. You'll never know what that's like and you don't deserve to know. The people down there will mourn my death, but no one would ever mourn yours."

Andvari bared his sharpened teeth. He clutched his nails together before me and my heart squeezed hard in response. "I have your heart if I want it."

"No," I breathed, a strange sense of peace flooding over me. "You can't have that. It's the one thing you can't control."

He swung an arm back as if to knock me from the statue, but I refused to let him force this upon me. The choice would be my own. The last choice I ever made.

With a ragged breath, I jumped, throwing myself forward with my arms outstretched, the wind sailing through my hair, pulling my dress out like a white flag.

The momentum caused me to roll and I lost sight of the world below, finding the night sky stretching above me in a million pricks of light.

I have lived a life as a prisoner.

I have escaped that life as I promised my father I would.

I have been one half of a whole to my beloved twin.

I have loved Erik as a monster. And I have loved him as a man.

So I have been free, I have had a place in this world and I have known the deepest kind of love my heart ever had to offer.

What have you done with your eternal existence, Andvari?

CALLIE

CHAPTER THIRTY NINE

We raced back towards the statue and panic clutched at my soul. I looked about desperately, trying to seek Montana among the ruins of the island. As I glanced towards the statue, a flutter of white caught my eye and my breath stilled in my throat as I spotted her falling from the crown high above us.

My mouth parted in a desperate scream as Montana plunged from the top of the statue. She tumbled over and over, plummeting towards the ground at a tremendous pace.

My heart seized in my chest, my lungs collapsed and I was caught in this endless, eternal moment of pain as her life sped to an unavoidable end.

I couldn't believe what I was seeing. I couldn't understand what was happening. How had she gotten up there? Why would she have put herself in that position?

She hit the ground and I felt the impact deep within my bones, a scream tearing from my lungs.

I tried to run to her but Magnar caught my arm, holding me back with a fearful look in his eyes. I wrenched my arm out of his grasp and sprinted towards my twin. My other half. The one love I had in this world which was as constant as the turning of the Earth. She couldn't be gone. There was no me without her. Like there was no day without night. We were one and the same. We weren't always together but we were never apart.

I closed the distance between us but Erik got there first.

He reached for her hand but I shoved him aside, my enhanced muscles knocking him away from her.

"Don't you touch her," I snarled as I dropped down beside my twin.

She looked so peaceful. Like she was sleeping. Except that there was blood pooling beneath her, soaking through my dress as I pressed my forehead to hers.

Tears spilled down my cheeks as I begged her to come back to me, panic seizing me at the reality I was faced with.

I dragged her into my arms, her body limp but still so warm. She couldn't be gone. She just couldn't.

I could feel the gods drawing closer to us, their immense power brushing up against the bubble of safety the ring hid us in. They'd lost sight of all of us and I could tell it confused and enraged them in equal measures. Was this the gods' punishment for wearing my mother's ring? Did they throw my sister from that statue? I could feel their realisation and fury brimming around us as they desperately tried to find a way around the ring's power, but they were thwarted.

I released a scream filled with all the horror of my grief and forced my will into the ring, throwing them away from us and casting them aside. The deities disappeared back into whatever realm of pain and torment they called home and we were left alone at last. Safe from them and their twisted games, at least for now.

Erik crawled closer and I glared at him. This was more than the gods' doing, it was his fault. Whatever had driven her up there, it had started with him. When he stole her from me, or even before that when his family created the Realms. None of it would have happened without him.

"Please," he said, his voice cracking with emotion as he stared at her body. "I have to...I need to-."

I glared at him, clutching her closer to me. My heart pounded as I refused to release her and the most wonderful sensation brushed over my cheek.

I gasped, shifting my grip on her as I pressed my ear to her chest and hope blossomed deep within the pit of my stomach.

"She's alive," I whispered, so faintly that I wasn't sure anyone heard me.

I wanted to believe it so badly that I wasn't sure I could trust my own senses, but I was almost convinced I could hear her heart still beating softly, the faintest flutter of breath dancing between her lips. Or could I? I wanted it so desperately that I didn't even know. Maybe it was the aching pounding of my own heart that I could hear. She was so pale, so empty of all the things that had filled her with life. How could she have survived that fall? Tears prickled my eyes as a sob caught in my throat.

Erik met my gaze as he tilted his head to listen too, and his eyes widened with hope.

"I can save her," he said firmly, reaching for her again.

My heart leapt at the prospect and I almost smiled before I realised what he meant.

I shook my head, unable to accept that option. "She'll still be dead. She needs to live."

But I could feel the blood pooling beneath me, I could see the twisted positions of her limbs. She couldn't survive this. At least not as she was. But how could I agree to her becoming one of *them*? We'd hated them our entire lives. They were everything we feared and despised. Would she even still be herself if she was one of them? Would she want to live on if she was caged in their form?

I expected the slayers to object but they stayed silent, leaving this impossible decision to me.

"We don't have long," Erik pleaded and all of the protests I wanted to voice fell away.

I couldn't live in a world without her. If this was the only way, I had to take it, even if she ended up hating me for it.

I pressed a kiss to my sister's cheek, whispering a final goodbye to the human girl who I loved more than life itself as the vampire pulled her from my arms.

I didn't know if I was doing the right thing. But in that moment, it was the only choice I could make. Because a life without her wasn't one I could accept.

"I love you, Monty. I'm so sorry."

ERIK

CHAPTER FORTY

In the past few hours, my body had been battered, broken, bruised, but no physical pain would ever come close to this.

A thousand gods couldn't have held me back from Montana right now. Callie may have been allowing this, but I would never have let her sister die when I had the ability to save her. It had come down to an agreement or a fight and thankfully this time, it was the former.

I pulled Montana from her sister's arms, laying her gently on the ground, knowing that just hours ago I had sworn never to turn her. But I hadn't realised what it would do to me to see her on the cusp of death, I hadn't known the dangers lurking in her future. I'd thought I could protect her from this, fragile as she was. I'd thought myself strong enough to keep her alive no matter what. Yet here I was with her broken body in my arms, and as furious as I was at the gods for forcing me to make this choice, I found there was no other I could claim. Montana had to live, even if her heart no longer beat, even if it meant laying this curse on her. Because losing her was not an option, no matter how selfish that made me, or how much she would despise me for making this choice for her.

But if I couldn't bring her back, my life was already over. I was a ghost about to depart this world. I wouldn't cling to it a fraction longer than I needed to. Wherever she went, I was going too.

Fuck, why had she jumped? Or had she been forced? Had Andvari done this to her as another cruel punishment for me?

I knelt at her side, her body twisted by her shattered bones as blood spread out beneath her. Pain scorched through me at the sight of her and guilt formed a solid lump in my throat. She was here because of me. Because of a fight she should never have been caught up in. It all seemed so pointless now. What was hate when compared to love?

Montana's lips were rose red, flecked with blood, her face too still and eyes shuttered. My heart became charred and blackened, consumed in the fire I'd known our love would cause. This was the reason we never should have been together. Because mortals die when they keep the company of beasts.

I slit my arm open with my fangs, resting the wound against her soft mouth.

"Drink, rebel." She needed enough life to remain in her body for this to work. If she could swallow my blood, it would start the process. But if she was already gone...

I took hold of her wrist, running my thumb across the place a pulse should have thrummed.

Nothing.

Panic threatened to overwhelm me but I held it at bay, forcing myself to focus. I had to finish this. I couldn't give up.

I dipped my head, squeezing my eyes shut as the scent of her blood called to me from her veins.

"Forgive me," I breathed as I shattered all of my promises to her, knowing I was betraying all she had ever asked of me. Then I slid my fangs into her velvet skin as gently as I could manage, releasing the venom into her bloodstream, desperate for it to be enough. I let the curse pour into her more and more, despising myself for it but knowing it was the only way to keep her. And I'd be damned if I let the gods steal her from me.

When it was done, I pulled back, searching her face for any signs of immortal life. Her skin was near-translucent in death, so pale she resembled my kind already.

I rested my ear to her heart and a dull thump reached my ears. Once. Twice. Silence.

The quiet stretched on. She needed to die to turn, but it was agony to know in these few seconds she was no longer here, reaching toward the afterlife. But I couldn't let her go. She wasn't done living. She had so much more to give. I thought of all the things I'd show her, all that I'd give her, all that I'd be for her. I'd build a new world she'd be proud of. One she'd long to live in. If only she'd come back.

"Don't leave me," I commanded, taking her hand in mine. "You must stay. I hate to place this curse on you but I swear by all the stars in the sky, I will break it. I have never wanted that as much as I do now. I won't stop until it's done. I'll tear the gods from the heavens and kill them one by one until they rid the curse from your body. Just come back to me, Montana."

I cupped her icy cheek, despair drilling into my chest.

I cannot lose you.

I shook her softly and her sister's sobs filled the air, but I couldn't turn to face Callie's grief. If I accepted it, it would be true. Montana would be gone. My saviour. My life. And I refused to let go.

"Your heart is stronger than iron," I growled, suddenly furious with my wife. She was my *rebel*. She fought harder than anyone I'd ever known. And she was giving up. Leaving me. She wasn't fucking fighting.

My voice boomed as I continued, praying my words would guide her back to me. "Your heart is fortified, eternal, invincible. You *will not* die here, do you hear me? That's my final order to you, rebel. Don't you dare disobey me this time."

It was the longest wait of my life. An eternity on earth would have felt like a blink in comparison to these few seconds, our future balanced on each of their razor-sharp edges.

I pressed my forehead to hers, determined not to give up. Her body was so badly damaged, and I'd never turned someone with so many injuries. But maybe...just maybe...

Her hand twitched in mine, so slightly, I half thought I'd imagined it, but then her fingers flexed again and I released a raspy laugh, squeezing her hand in response.

I glanced over at her sister in Magnar's arms, her eyes brightening as I nodded. She dove from his lap, crawling to Montana's side and reaching out with a shaky hand to touch her twin's face.

"Callie..." Magnar seemed pained as he stared at Montana and anger rolled freely through me.

"What happens now?" Callie asked me, ignoring him. "When is she going to wake up?"

"She has a lot of injuries, it may take a while for her to heal," I muttered, giving her an intense look. "And she will be ravenous when she wakes. It's best I take her from here, somewhere away from the smell of your blood."

Callie met my eyes as she realised what I meant. Montana was going to try and kill them the second she woke. She wouldn't be able to help herself.

"You have to let him," Julius said in a low tone, his expression grave as if Montana really had died. The sight set my blood boiling. This was better than death, how could he not see that?

His brother shifted uneasily. "It isn't right," Magnar snarled but he didn't approach to halt this.

Callie glanced back at him, seeming broken. "It's better than losing her forever."

Magnar glowered at her, evidently not agreeing but he didn't voice any more of his thoughts.

A silent tear slid down Callie's cheek as she pressed her lips to Montana's forehead. "We'll figure out the prophecy. You won't be one of them for long, Monty. I promise."

I scooped Montana into my arms. Her skin seemed more porcelain already, the stillness of her body making her resemble a doll. But she'd be anything but fragile when she woke.

Hope clawed its way out of the depths of my soul, spreading relief through to my bones.

I glanced over at Fabian's decapitated body in the golden cage with a heavy frown, certain I couldn't leave him here.

Magnar lifted his head, seeming to sense something as he jogged through the rubble and scooped up three large swords. My gut tightened uneasily, but he sheathed two of them quickly and passed the other to his brother. Julius winced as he took it, blood still pouring from the bite marks on his neck.

Our fight was done. It was clear they'd accepted that, but I didn't trust either of them not to plunge one of those blades into my brother's heart.

Callie moved to my side and the slayers followed us over the broken concrete, keeping within the safety of the ring's power.

"You're going to let me take my brother home," I snarled, rounding on the slayers.

"I'll fetch the fucker then," Julius announced as we arrived beside the cage, apparently not up for the fight I'd expected to meet on this matter.

"Be careful with him," I warned, glaring at the slayer as he flung Fabian's body over his shoulder and snatched his head by the hair.

"I'm always careful." Julius smirked as he headed out of the cage, a dong sounding as Fabian's head collided with the bars. "Whoops. That was an unfortunate accident."

Magnar chuckled as Julius approached, and he stumbled with the weight of Fabian, his injuries clearly still affecting him. I was surprised he was on his feet at all after what I'd done to him, but I supposed his slayer gifts were working to heal him now. Magnar took Fabian's body from his arms and threw him unceremoniously over his shoulder.

I glowered, clutching Montana to my chest protectively as I led the way to the speedboat. Callie fell into step beside me, a slayer blade in her hand as she eyed her sister with concern. The golden knife was still tainted with my blood and the wound on my shoulder ached from the deep cut she'd given me. I hoped we could keep our differences aside long enough for me to get Montana away from here.

"I need to take her to shore then you can have the boat," I said gruffly and she gazed at me with suspicion.

"Fine," she said tersely.

I waded out into the water toward the speedboat and gently placed

Montana aboard. Climbing inside, I laid her on one of the leather seats, brushing a lock of hair from her cheek. She showed no signs of stirring, but I was sure it wouldn't be long before she woke, then all hell would likely break loose. Callie sprang into the boat, seating herself beside her, resting a hand on Montana's, wincing when she found it cold.

A loud thump sounded as Magnar tossed Fabian's body onto the deck, then the slayer helped Julius up and I spied my brother's head tucked under his arm.

"Put him down," I commanded, irritated by the slayers' lack of propriety.

Julius held out the head with raised brows. "As you wish."

He let go of it and it thumped against the floor and Magnar released a rumbling laugh. I scowled, grabbing a blanket from beneath a seat and throwing it over Fabian and his severed head. I didn't think it was a good idea to let my brother rise again now; it would cause way more trouble than it was worth.

Julius dropped onto a seat, clasping the wounds on his neck. "Still hungry?" he goaded me.

"I wasn't in my right mind when I bit you," I muttered. "Besides, you taste like filthy dishwater."

"Liar," Julius muttered. "I taste like a rainbow." His joke was somewhat diminished as his laughter caused him to wince, and a ripple of guilt found me that left me confused.

I turned the key in the ignition, driving us out into the harbour and pushing the boat to its limit as it carved a path through the waves. I glanced over at Montana to make sure she was alright and found Callie holding her head in her lap. I frowned, concerned that if she woke, she might try to feed from her sister. Magnar eyed her like he expected her to attack Callie at any moment, and I sensed the strange agreement we were making was as fragile as glass.

I set my eyes on the shoreline, closing the distance and finally making it to land. Moving quickly, I took Montana into my arms again, pulling her away from Callie with a frown.

She blinked away tears, squeezing Montana's hand before turning her gaze on me. "Swear you'll look after her."

"I'll protect her with my life," I vowed, and Callie nodded firmly, seeming to believe that at last.

"Get her to call me on Julius's phone the second she wakes up," she said, briefly touching my hand before realising what she'd done and retracting her arm.

"I will," I said stiffly, moving to the ladder that led up to the pier above us. I carried Montana onto it before returning to get Fabian, but he was deposited at my feet as Magnar threw him from the boat. Julius tossed his head at me and I grumbled my irritation as I caught it. I wrapped the blanket around my brother before lifting him and my wife into my arms.

"You're not keeping her," Callie called to me, her eyes holding a tempestuous sea inside them. "This is temporary, bloodsucker. Don't forget that."

I didn't reply as I gazed down at the boat of slayers. After all that had happened, there wasn't really anything I could say so I just dipped my head and walked away. And as quickly as I could, I ran to the car I'd parked just hours ago.

With a flash of guilt, I put Fabian in the trunk, slightly concerned about someone seeing him in his current state. I couldn't deal with his mood right now; he was going to be severely pissed off when he woke up.

I laid Montana on the back seat, pressing a kiss to her lips as I leaned over her.

She murmured something incoherent and my heart lifted. I didn't have much time left. I needed to get her somewhere safe. Somewhere I could look after her. And somewhere I could give her the one thing she was about to crave more than anything she had ever known.

CALLiE

CHAPTER FORTY ONE

I stared up at the dock as Julius slipped behind the wheel and the boat's engine flared with energy. He staggered a little before finding his balance again and I frowned at him in concern.

"It's fine," he said dismissively as he noticed my attention on him. "Besides, neither of you can drive, can you?"

I glanced up at Magnar but he didn't seem too worried about Julius's condition, so I left it at that and turned my eyes back to the shore.

Magnar's arm was tight around my shoulders and he held me close as the boat pulled away from the wall, leaving the land behind and my sister in the care of a Belvedere. The next time I saw her, she'd be a vampire.

My chest was heavy with doubts. Would she thank me for this choice or hate me for it?

I had thought that I'd rather die than become one of those creatures but now I'd let that very fate befall the person I loved most in this broken world.

I hoped that her guesses might have been right. That she'd been destined to take on this horrifying transformation and it might help us to solve the prophecy and end the curse. But I couldn't claim that for my reason.

In the end, the idea of never seeing her again, never hearing her laugh or holding her when she cried was too much. I couldn't bear to say goodbye. And my selfishness had allowed her to be cursed. I'd given her fate over to our enemy.

I felt like I'd left my heart behind on the land and the further we travelled, the deeper the pain burrowed. Our destinies had always been in line with one another. I'd never counted on any kind of existence without her by my side. But now she was gone. Dead. Any creature who would rise in her place might not be her at all.

Who would she be when her deepest desire was the call of blood? How could she love me when her nature would demand she kill me? And my vow would demand the same of me.

But I'd never bow to that pressure. I knew beyond all doubt that no vow, deity or any force on this Earth would ever make me raise my blade against her. I had to hold faith in the knowledge that the Monty I knew would still feel the same about me.

Julius turned the boat sharply and I lost sight of the coast. I leaned into Magnar, burying my face against his chest as he wrapped his arms around me.

Whether I'd made the right choice or not, it was done now.

I was a slayer and she was a vampire. Each destined to destroy the other. I just had to hope that our love would be stronger than the pull of the paths we'd taken.

Everything had changed, but the world was still the same. The sun would set and the moon would rise. Over and over again. You never found one without the other close by. The two of them ruling the sky in perfect harmony despite their many differences.

And perhaps that would be our fate too. Endlessly different but eternally bound. The sun would set. And the moon would rise. The point at which the day met the night was always the most beautiful. So perhaps there was a chance for us yet.

AUTHOR NOTE

Well, that took a bit of a turn there, didn't it? Hopefully you're not too mad at us and can at least console yourself with the knowledge that our sweet Monty is back in the arms of her malevolent monster.

This series continues to hold a special place in our hearts because it was the very first series which Caroline and I ever wrote together. Revisiting it feels like stepping back in time and makes it so easy to remember the learning curve which led us to the place we're at now. So please don't hate us for hurting these babies – we were learning the ways of co-writing chaos and there were bound to be at least a few casualties.

Besides, I blame the gods in all honesty. We can't be held accountable for everything.

Thank you for reading our words and falling for our characters, thank you for embracing the chaos and bracing for the pain – you're past the halfway point with this series now, so buckle up and hold on because beyond this place, monsters lie in wait.

Get your grabby hands on book five, Forsaken Relic now.

Love, Susanne and Caroline XX

WANT MORE?

To find out more, grab yourself some freebies and to join our reader group, scan the QR code below.

386

Made in the USA
Monee, IL
11 July 2024

61681461R00224